THE

Kate Collison be
miniaturists, but
talented as any of her ancestors, the fact that she was a woman in the mid-nineteenth century made it difficult for her to be recognized.

Her chance came through the tragic affliction of her father and a summons to the Normandy château of the powerful Baron de Centeville. There Kate met the chivalrous Bertrand de Mortemer, Nicole, the Baron's wordly mistress, and the Baron himself, dynamic, overbearing and arrogant, who had ordered a miniature to be painted. It was this portrait of 'The Demon Lover' which gave Kate the opportunity she had longed for; but there was a big price to pay for it. The Baron had a score to settle and he was a man accustomed to making use of people when they could serve his ends.

The story moves from an English country house to the Norman château with its feudal atmosphere, and then to Paris of the Second Empire and the fearful months when the city was under siege. But when later Kate went back to the château the dangers there seemed even more menacing than they had in besieged Paris.

Available in Fontana by the same author

Mistress of Mellyn
Kirkland Revels
Bride of Pendorric
The Legend of the Seventh Virgin
Menfreya
King of the Castle
My Enemy the Queen
The Shivering Sands
The Secret Woman
The Shadow of the Lynx
On the Night of the Seventh Moon
The House of a Thousand Lanterns
The Curse of the Kings
The Devil on Horseback
The Spring of the Tiger
The Judas Kiss
Lord of the Far Island
The Mask of the Enchantress
The Pride of the Peacock
The Landower Legacy
The Queen's Confession
The Time of the Hunter's Moon
The Road to Paradise Island
Secret for a Nightingale
The Silk Vendetta
The India Fan

VICTORIA HOLT

The Demon Lover

Grafton

This Grafton edition published 1997
by Diamond Books
An imprint of HarperCollins Publishers
77-85 Fulham Palace Rd
Hammersmith, London W6 8JB

First Published in Great Britain by
William Collins Sons & Co. Ltd 1982

ISBN 0 261 66993 1

Printed and bound in Great Britain
by Caledonian

For

PATRICIA MYRER,

to whom I want to express my deepest gratitude
for her care and wise guidance over more than twenty years,
during which she has inspired me
and never ceased to amaze me with her flair,
intuition, judgement and many talents.

Contents

Summons to the Château

It was a hot June day when I discovered my father's secret which was to change the whole course of my life, as well as his. I shall never forget the horror that gripped me. The sun was brilliant, merciless, it seemed. It had been the hottest June for years. I sat there watching him. He seemed to have grown ten years older in the space of a few minutes, and as he turned his eyes to me I saw the despair in them, the sudden releasing of pretence. He knew that he could no longer hide this tragedy from me.

It was inevitable that I should be the one to discover it. I had always been closer to him than anyone else – even my mother when she had been alive. I understood him in all his moods. I knew the exultation of the creative artist, the striving, the frustrations. The man I knew in this studio was different from the gentle, rather uncomplicated human being he became outside it. Of course it was the studio which claimed the greater part of him. It was his life. He had been brought up to it. From the age of five, in this very house – which had been the home of the Collisons for a hundred years – he had come to the studio to watch his own father work. There was a story in the family that when he was four years old they had thought he was lost and his nurse had found him here painting on a piece of vellum with one of his father's finest sable brushes.

Collison was a name in the art world. It was always associated with the painting of miniatures, and there could not be a collection of any note in Europe which did not contain at least one Collison.

The painting of miniatures was a tradition in our family. My father had said that it was a talent which was passed down through the generations and to become a great painter one must begin in one's cradle. So it had been with the Collisons. They had been painting miniatures since the seventeenth century. Our ancestor had been a pupil of Isaac Oliver, who in his turn had been a pupil of none other than the famous Elizabethan miniaturist Nicolas Hilliard.

Until this generation there had always been a son to follow his father and carry on not only the tradition but the name. My father had failed in this; and all he had been able to produce was a daughter – myself.

It must have been a great disappointment to him, although he never mentioned it. He was a very gentle man outside the studio, as I have said, and was always conscious of other people's feelings; he was rather slow of speech because he weighed his words before uttering them and considered the effect they would have on others. It was different when he worked. Then he was completely possessed; he forgot meal times, appointments, commitments of any sort. Sometimes I thought he worked feverishly because he believed he was going to be the last of the Collisons. Now he was beginning to realize that this might not be so, for I too had discovered the fascination of the brush, the vellum and the ivory. I was teaching myself to carry on the family tradition. I was going to show my father that a daughter was not to be despised and could do as well as any son. That was one of the reasons why I gave myself up to the joy of painting. The other – far more important – was because, irrespective of my sex, I had inherited the desire to produce that intricate limning. I had the urge – and I ventured to think the talent – to compete with any of my ancestors.

My father, at this time, was in his late forties. He looked younger because of his very clear blue eyes and untidy hair. He was tall – I had heard him called lanky – and very thin, which made him seem a trifle ungainly. It surprised people, I think, that from this rather clumsy man could come those delicate miniatures.

His name was Kendal. There had been Kendals in the family for generations. Years ago a girl from the Lake District had married into the family and the name came from her birthplace. It was a tradition that all the men should have names beginning with K and the letters K.C. – etched in a corner so small that they were barely perceptible – were the hallmark of those famous miniatures. It had caused a certain amount of confusion as to which Collison had executed the painting, and it had often been necessary to work out the date from the period and the subject.

My father had remained unmarried until he was thirty. He was the sort of man who was inclined to thrust aside anything that might distract him from his work. Thus, with marriage, too, although he was well aware of his duty – rather like that of a monarch – to produce the heir to carry on the family tradition.

It was only when he went to the seat of the Earl of Langston in Gloucestershire that the desire to marry became something other than a duty to the family. He had been engaged by the Earl to paint miniatures of the Countess and her two daughters, Lady Jane and Lady Katherine – known as Lady Kitty. He always said that the miniature of Lady Kitty was the best work he had ever done. 'There was love in it,' he commented. He was very sentimental.

Well, the outcome was romantic but of course the Earl had other ideas for his daughter. He had no appreciation of art; he merely wanted a Collison miniature because he had heard that 'This Collison is a good man'.

'A Philistine,' my father had called him. He thought artists were servants to be patronized by men of wealth. Moreover, he had hopes of a duke for his daughter.

But it turned out that Lady Kitty was a girl who liked to

have her own way and she had fallen as deeply in love with the artist as he had with her. So they eloped and Lady Kitty was informed by her irate father that the gates of Langston Castle were closed to her forever more. Since she had had the folly to become Kitty Collison, she would have no further connection with the family of Langston.

Lady Kitty thereupon snapped her fingers and prepared for what, to her, must have been the humble life at Collison House.

A year after the marriage I made my dramatic entrance into the world, causing a great deal of trouble and costing Lady Kitty her never very robust health. When she became a semi-invalid and unable to bear more children, the disastrous truth had to be faced: the only one was a girl and it seemed as though that was the end of the Collison line.

Not that I was ever allowed to feel that I was a disappointment. I discovered it for myself when I learned of the family traditions and became familiar with the big studio and its enormous windows placed so as to catch the strong and searching north light.

I learned a great deal from servants' gossip, for I was an avid listener and I quickly realized that I could learn more of what I wanted to know through them than I ever could by asking my parents.

'The Langstons always had a job getting sons. My niece is up there in service with some cousins of theirs. She says it's a grand place. Fifty servants . . . no less . . . and that just for the country. Her ladyship wasn't meant for this sort of life.'

'Do you think she has regrets?'

'Oh, I reckon. Must do. All them balls and titles and things . . . Why, she could have married a duke.'

'Yet, he's a true gentleman . . . I will say that for him.'

'Oh yes, I'll grant you that. But he's just a sort of tradesman . . . selling things. Oh, I know they're pictures and that's somehow supposed to be different . . . but they're still *things* . . . and he's selling them. It never works . . . stepping outside. Class and all that. And there's no son, is there? All they've got is that Miss Kate.'

'She's got her wits about her, no mistake. A bit of a madam, that one.'

'Don't really take after either of them.'

'Do you know what I reckon? He ought to have married a strong young woman . . . his own class . . . A lady, of course . . . squire's daughter or something . . . He went too high, he did. Then she could have had a baby every year till she got this son what could learn all about painting. That's how it ought to have been. It's what you get for marrying out of your class.'

'Do you think he minds.'

''Course he minds. He wanted a son. And between you and me her ladyship don't think all that much of this painting. Well, if it hadn't been for the painting he'd never have met her, would he? And who's to say that mightn't have been for the best?'

So I learned.

At the time I discovered the secret a year had passed since my mother had died. That was a great blow to our household. She had been very beautiful and both my father and I had been content to sit and look at her. She had worn blues which matched her eyes and her tea gowns were draperies most becomingly trimmed with lace and ribbons. Because she had been a semi-invalid since my birth, I felt a certain responsibility for that; but I consoled myself that she enjoyed lying on her sofa and receiving people, like a queen at her *coucher*. She had what she called her 'good days'; then she would play the piano or arrange flowers and sometimes entertain people – from the neighbourhood mostly.

There were the Farringdons who lived in the Manor and owned most of the land round about, the vicar and the doctor with their families. Everyone was honoured by an invitation from Lady Kitty, even Lady Farringdon, for social status was a great concern of hers and although the Farringdons were rich, Sir Frederick was only a second-generation baronet and Lady Farringdon was somewhat impressed by the daughter of an Earl.

My mother made no attempt to manage the household. That was all achieved by Evie, without whom our lives would have been a great deal less comfortable. Evie had been only seventeen when she came to us. That was at the time when I was about a year old and my mother had by that time slipped gracefully into invalidism. Evie was a distant cousin of my mother's – one of that army of poor relations which so often exists on the fringe of wealthy families. Some distant female member of that family had married beneath her, which meant against the family's wishes, and so took a leap into obscurity. Evie was a bud from one of those branches, but she had for some reason kept in touch and, during family emergencies, had been called upon for help.

She and my mother had been fond of each other and when the beautiful Lady Kitty found that she would spend a certain time of her life reclining on sofas it occurred to her that Evie was just the person needed to come and take charge.

So Evie came and never regretted it. Nor did we. We depended on Evie. She managed the household and the servants, was a companion and lady's maid to my mother, an efficient housekeeper, a mother to me – and all this while she made sure that my father was able to work without distraction.

So we had Evie. She arranged little parties for my mother and made sure that everything went smoothly when visitors called at the house about commissions for my father's work. When he had to go away – which he did fairly frequently – he could go, knowing that we were well looked after.

My mother loved to hear of my father's adventures when he returned home. She liked to think of him as a famous painter in great demand, although she was not really interested in what he was doing. I had seen her eyes glaze over when he was talking enthusiastically – but *I* knew what he was talking about, for I had the Collison blood in my veins and I was never happier than when I had a fine sable brush in my hands and was making those faint sure strokes on a piece of ivory or vellum.

I was Katherine too, but called Kate to distinguish me from Kitty. I did not look in the least like my mother or father. I was considerably darker than either of them.

'A throw-back to the sixteenth century,' said my father, who was naturally an authority on faces. 'Some long-ago Collison must have looked exactly like you, Kate. Those high cheekbones and that touch of red in your hair. Your eyes are tawny too. That colour would be very difficult to capture. You'd have to mix paints very carefully to get it. I never like that for delicate work . . . The result can be messy.'

I often laughed at the way his work always seemed to creep into his conversation.

I must have been about six years old when I made a vow. It was after I had heard the servants talking about my being a girl and a disappointment to my father.

I went into the studio and standing in the glare of the light which came through the high window, I said: 'I am going to be a great painter. My miniatures are going to be the best that have ever been known.'

And being a very serious child and having a passionate devotion to my father as well as an inborn knowledge that this was what I had been born for, I set about carrying out my intention. At first my father had been amused, but he had shown me how to stretch vellum over a stiff white card and press it between sheets of paper, leaving it under a weight to be pressed.

'The skin is greasy,' he told me, 'so we have to do a little pouncing. Do you know what pouncing is?'

I soon did, and learned how to rub the surface with a mixture of French chalk and powdered pumice.

Then he taught me how to use oil, tempera and gouache. 'But water-colours are the most satisfactory for the smallest work,' he said.

When I had my first brush I was delighted; and I was filled with joy when I saw my father's face after I had painted my first miniature.

He had put his arms round me and held me close to him so that I should not see the tears in his eyes. My father was a very emotional man.

He cried: 'You've got it, Kate. You're one of us.'

My mother was shown my first effort.

'It's very good,' she said. 'Oh, Kate, are you going to be a genius too? And here am I . . . so surely not one!'

'You don't have to be,' I told her. 'You just have to be beautiful.'

It was a happy home. My father and I grew closer through our work, and I spent hours in the studio. I had a governess until I was seventeen. My father did not want me to go away to school because that would interrupt the time I spent in the studio.

'To be a great painter, you work every day,' he said. 'You do not wait until you feel in the mood. You do not wait until *you* feel ready to entertain inspiration. You are there waiting when she deigns to call.'

I understood completely. How could I have borne to be away from the studio? My resolve to be as great – no greater – than any of my ancestors had stayed with me. I knew that I was good.

My father often went abroad and would sometimes be away for a month or two at a time. He had even visited several of the European courts and painted miniatures for royalty.

'I should like to take you with me, Kate,' he often said. 'You're as capable as I am. But I don't know what they would think of a woman. They wouldn't believe the work was good . . . if it had been done by a member of the female sex.'

'But surely they could see for themselves.'

'People don't always see what their eyes tell them is there. They see what they have made up their minds to see, and I'm afraid they might make up their minds that something done by a woman could not possibly be as good as that done by a man.'

'That's nonsense and it makes me angry,' I cried. 'They must be fools.'

'Many people are,' sighed my father.

We painted miniatures for jewellers to sell all over the country. I had done many of those. They were signed with the initials K.C. Everyone said, 'That's a Collison.' They didn't know, of course, that it was the work of Kate not Kendal Collison.

When I was a child it had sometimes seemed that my mother and father inhabited different worlds. There was my father, the absent-minded artist whose work was his life, and my mother the beautiful and interestingly delicate hostess, who liked to have people around her. One of her greatest pleasures was holding court while admirers revolved about her, so delighted to be entertained by the daughter of an Earl even though she was merely the wife of an artist.

When tea was dispensed I would often be there to help her entertain her guests. In the evenings she sometimes gave small dinner-parties and played whist afterwards, or there was music. She herself played the piano exquisitely for her guests.

Sometimes she would be talkative and tell me about her early life in Langston Castle. Did she mind leaving it for what must be a very small house compared with the castle? I asked her once.

'No, Kate,' she answered. 'Here I am the Queen. There I was just one of the princesses – of no real importance. I was just there to make the right marriage . . . which would be one my family wanted and which I most likely did not.'

'You must be very happy,' I said, 'for you have the best husband anyone could have.'

She looked at me quizzically and said: 'You are very fond of your father, aren't you?'

'I love you both,' I told her truthfully.

I went to kiss her and she said: 'Don't ruffle my hair, darling.' Then she took my hand and pressed it. 'I'm glad you love him so much. He is more deserving than I am.'

She puzzled me. But she was always kind and tender and really pleased that I spent so much time with my father. Oh yes, it had been an extremely happy home until that day when Evie, taking my mother's morning chocolate to her bedroom, found her dead.

She had had a cold which had developed into something worse. All my life I had heard that we had to take care of my mother's health. She had rarely gone out and when she did it would be in the carriage only as far as Farringdon Hall. Then she would be helped out of the carriage and almost carried in by the Farringdon footman.

But because she had always been delicate and Death was supposed to be hovering, because it had been like that for so many years that it had almost become like a member of the family . . . we had thought it would continue to hover. Instead of which it had swooped down and carried her away.

We missed her very much and it was then that I realized how much painting meant to both my father and myself, for although we were desolate in our grief, when we were in the studio we could forget for a while, for at such times there was nothing for either of us but our painting.

Evie was very sad. My mother had been in her special care

for so long. She was at that time thirty-three years of age and she had given up seventeen of those years to us.

Two years earlier Evie had become engaged to be married. The news had sent us into a flutter of dismay. We wavered between our pleasure in Evie's happiness and our consternation in contemplating what life would be like without her.

There had been no imminent danger as Evie's fiancé was James Callum, the curate at our vicarage. He was the same age as Evie and they were to be married as soon as he acquired a living of his own.

My mother used to say: 'Pray God he never will.' And then quickly: 'What a selfish creature I am, Kate. I hope you won't grow up to be like me. Never fear. You won't. you're one of the sturdy ones. But really what should we . . . what should *I* do without Evie.'

She did not have to face that problem. When she died the curate was still without a living, so her prayers were answered in a way.

Evie tried to console me. 'You're growing up now, Kate,' she said. 'You'd soon find someone else.'

'There'd be no one like you, Evie. You're irreplaceable.'

She smiled at me and was torn between her fears for us and her longing to be married.

I knew in my heart that one day Evie would have to leave us. Change was in the air – and I did not want change.

The months passed and still James Callum did not find a living. Evie declared that she had little to do since my mother's death and spent hours preserving fruit and making herbal concoctions as though she were stocking up the household for the time when she was no longer with us.

We settled down into our daily routine. My father refused to consider Evie's possible departure. He was the sort of man who lived from day to day and reminded me of someone crossing a tightrope who gets along because he never looks down at possible disasters in the valley below. He goes on and on, unaware of them, and for this reason travels safely across. But there can come a time when some impassable object forces a halt and as he is unable to go on he must pause and consider where he is.

We worked constantly together in perfect harmony in the studio on those days when the light was right. We depended on that for we did a great deal of restoration of old manuscripts. I now regarded myself as a fully fledged painter. I had even accompanied my father to one or two houses where restoration work was needed. He always explained my presence: 'My daughter helps me in my work.' I know they imagined that I prepared the tools of the trade, washed his brushes and looked after his creature comforts. That rankled. I was proud of my work and more and more he was allowing me to take over.

We were in the studio one day when I saw that he was holding a magnifying glass in one hand and his brush in the other.

I was astonished because he had always said: 'It is never good to use a magnifying glass. If you train your eyes they will do the work for you. A limner has special eyes. He would not be a limner if he had not.'

He saw that I was regarding him with surprise and putting down the glass, said: 'A very delicate piece of work. I wanted to make sure I hadn't miscalculated.'

It was some weeks later. We had had a manuscript sent to us from a religious order in the north of England. Some of the fine drawings on the pages had become faint and slightly damaged, and one of the branches of our work was to restore such manuscripts. If they were very valuable, which a number of them were, dating from as far back as the eleventh century, my father would have to go to the monastery to do the work on the spot, but there were occasions when the less valuable ones could be brought to us. I had done a great deal of work on these recently, which was my father's way of telling me that I was now a painter of skill. If my work was not good enough it was easy to discard a piece of vellum or ivory, but only a sure hand could be allowed to touch these priceless manuscripts.

On that June day my father had the manuscript before him and was trying to get the necessary shade of red. It was never easy, for this had to match the red pigment called minium which had been used long ago and was in fact the very word from which the name miniature had been derived.

I watched him, his brush hovering over the small palette. Then he put it down with a helplessness which astonished me.

I went over to him and said: 'Is anything wrong?'

He did not answer me but leaned forward and covered his face with his hands.

That was a frightening moment – with the blazing sun outside and the strong light falling on the ancient manuscript and the sudden knowledge that something terrible was about to happen.

I bent over him and laid my hand on his shoulder.

'What is it, Father?' I asked.

He dropped his hands and looked at me with those blue eyes which were full of tragedy.

'It's no use, Kate,' he said. 'I've got to tell someone. I'm going blind.'

I stared at him. It couldn't be true. His precious eyes . . . they were the gateway to his art, to his contentment. How could he exist without his work for which above all he needed his eyes? It was the whole meaning of existence to him.

'No,' I whispered. 'That . . . can't be.'

'It is so,' he said.

'But . . .' I stammered. 'You are all right. You can see.'

He shook his head. 'Not as I once could. Not as I used to. It's going to get worse. Not suddenly . . . gradually. I know.

I've been to a specialist. It was when I was on my last trip. I went to London. He told me.'

'How long ago?'

'Three weeks.'

'And you kept it to yourself for so long?'

'I tried not to believe it. At first I thought . . . Well, I didn't know what to think. I just could not see as clearly . . . not clearly enough . . . Have you noticed I've been leaving little things to you?'

'I thought you did that to encourage me . . . to give me confidence.'

'Dear Kate, you don't need confidence. You have all you need. You're an artist. You're as good as your ancestors.'

'Tell me about the doctor . . . what he said. Tell me everything.'

'I've got what they call a cataract in each eye. The doctor says it's small white spots on the lens-capsule in the centre of the pupils. They are slight at the moment, but they will grow bigger. It might be some time before I lose the sight of my eyes . . . but it could be rapid.'

'There must be something they could do?'

'Yes, an operation. But it is a risk, and my eyes would never be good enough for my sort of work, even if it were successful. You know what sight we need . . . how we seem to develop extra power. You know, Kate. You have it. But this . . . blindness . . . Oh, don't you see. It's everything . . .'

I was overwhelmed by the tragedy of it. His life was his work and it was to be denied him. It was the most tragic thing that could have happened to him.

I did not know how to comfort him, but somehow I did.

At least he had told me. I chided him gently for not telling me before.

'I don't want anyone to know yet, Kate,' he insisted. 'It's our secret, eh?'

'Yes,' I said, 'if that is what you wish. It is our secret.'

Then I put my arm round him and held him against me. I heard him whisper: 'You comfort me, Kate.'

One cannot remain in a state of shock indefinitely. At first I had been overwhelmed by the news and it seemed as though disaster stared us in the face; but after some reflection my natural optimism came to my aid and I began to see that this was not yet the end. For one thing the process was gradual. At the moment my father simply could not see as well as he once had. He would not be able to do his finest work. But he could still paint. He would just have to change his style. It seemed impossible that a Collison should not be able to paint miniatures, but why shouldn't he work on a bigger scale? Why shouldn't a canvas take the place of painting on ivory and metals?

On consideration his burden seemed to have lightened. We talked a great deal up there in the studio.

'You must be my eyes, Kate,' he said. 'You must watch me. Sometimes I think I can see well enough . . . but I am not sure. You know how one false stroke can be disastrous.'

I said: 'You have told me now. You should never have kept it to yourself. It isn't as though you are suddenly smitten with blindness. You have had a long warning . . . and time to prepare yourself.'

He listened to me almost like a child, hanging on my words. I felt very tender towards him.

'Don't forget,' he reminded me. 'For the time being . . . not a word to anyone.'

I agreed with that. I had a ridiculous hope, which I know to be groundless, that he might recover and the obstruction go away.

'Bless you, Kate' he said. 'I thank God for you. Your work is as good as anything I ever did . . . and it's getting better. It would not surprise me if you surpassed every Collison. That would be my consolation if you did.'

So we talked and worked together and I made sure that I did the finest work on those manuscripts so that he should not have to put his eyes to the test. There was no doubt that all this had given me an added spur and I really believed that my touch was more sure than it had been previously.

A few days passed. It was wonderful what time did, and I believed that his nature was such that in time he would become reconciled. He would always see everything through an artist's eyes and he would always paint. The work he had particularly loved would be denied him . . . but he was not going to lose everything . . . not yet, at least. That was what I told him.

It was a week or so after when I heard the news.

We had returned from a dinner-party at the doctor's house. Evie was always included in these invitations for she was regarded, throughout the neighbourhood, as a member of the family. Even the socially minded Lady Farringdon invited her, for after all Evie was a connection of that family which contained an Earl!

It had been an evening like any other. The vicarage family had been at the doctor's house. There was the Reverend John Meadows with his two grown-up children, Dick and Frances. Dick was studying for the Church and Frances, since her mother had died, had kept house for her father. I knew the family well. Before I had a governess I had been to the vicarage every day to be taught by the curate – not Evie's but his predecessor, a middle-aged serious old gentleman who bore witness to the fact that curates could sometimes remain in that lowly state during their entire careers.

We had been warmly greeted by Dr and Mrs Camborne and their twin daughters. The twins looked so much alike that I could only on rare occasions tell the difference. They interested me. When I was with them I always wondered what one would feel to have another person who looked almost exactly the same and was so close. They had been named with a certain irony, I thought, Faith and Hope. My father said: 'What a pity they were not triplets, then Charity could have been included.'

Hope was the bolder of the two; she was the one who spoke up when they were addressed. Faith relied on her completely. She always looked to her sister for support before she spoke, even. She was of a nervous temperament but there was a degree of boldness about Hope. It often seemed to me as though the human virtues and failings had been neatly divided and distributed between those two.

Hope was clever at her lessons and always helped Faith, who was much slower and found great difficulty in learning. Faith was neat and tidy and always cleared up after Hope, so their mother told me. Faith was good working with her hands; Hope was clumsy in that respect. 'I am so glad they are fond of each other,' their mother told my father.

There was no doubt that there was some mystic bond between them, which is often found in identical twins. They looked alike and yet were so different. I thought it would be interesting to paint them and see what came out, for often when one was engaged on a miniature facets of a sitter's character would be revealed as if by some miracle.

Dick Meadows talked a great deal about himself. He had nearly finished his training and would be looking for a living soon. A bright young man, I thought, he would surely be chosen before Evie's James.

Frances Meadows was her usual sensible self – content, it seemed, to devote her life to church matters and the careful running of the vicarage household.

It was just one of those evenings of which there had been so many. As we walked home I was thinking how conventional my life was . . and the life of all of us. I could imagine Frances keeping house at the vicarage until she was a middle-aged woman. That was her life – already mapped out for her. And myself? Was I going to spend mine in a little village – my social life more or less confined to dinners such as this one tonight? Pleasant enough, of course, and shared with people of whom I was fond – but would it go on and on until I was middle-aged?

I was very pensive considering it. Sometimes, looking back, I wonder whether even then I was subconsciously aware of the events which were about to break over me – disrupting my peaceful life forever.

I was certainly already becoming restive. When my father came home from his visits abroad, I questioned him avidly about what he had seen. He had been to the Courts of Prussia and Denmark – and most grand of all, that of Napoleon the Third and his fascinating wife the Empress Eugénie. He described the grandeurs of those Courts and the manners and customs of the people who inhabited them. He talked in colours and made me see the rich purple and gold of royal vestments, the soft pastel shades of the French houses and the less subtle ones of the German Courts.

I had always felt a longing to see these things for myself, and one of my secret dreams was that I should be recognized as a great painter as my father was and that these invitations would come to me. If only I had been born a man I could look forward to that. But here I was shut in – imprisoned in my sex, really – in a world which men had created for themselves. Women had their uses in that world. They were necessary for the reproduction of the race and they could do this most important of all tasks while providing a very agreeable diversion; they could grace a man's household and table; they could even help him on his way, stand beside him – but always a little in the background, always being careful to make sure that the limelight fell on him.

It was for Art that I cared, but when I realized that my miniatures could bring as great a reward as those of my father – but only because they were believed to be his – I was maddened by the unfairness and stupidity of the world; and I could understand why some women were refusing to toe the line and accept the assumption of masculine superiority.

When we arrived back at the house on that night it was to find James Callum there.

'You must forgive me for calling at such an hour, Mr Collison,' he said. 'But I had to see Evie.'

He was so excited that he could scarcely speak. Evie went to him and laid a calming hand on his arm.

'What is it, James. Not . . . a living!'

'Well, hardly that. It's a . . . a proposition. It depends on what Evie says . . .'

'It might be a good idea to ask me and find out,' Evie pointed out in that practical way of hers.

'It's this, Evie. I've been asked to go to Africa . . . as a missionary.'

'James!'

'Yes, and they think I should have a wife to take with me.'

I saw the joy in Evie's face but I did not look at my father. I knew he would be battling with his emotions.

I heard him say: 'Evie . . . That's wonderful. You'll be superb . . . and keep them all in order.'

'Evie,' faltered James. 'You haven't said.'

Evie was smiling. 'When do we leave?' she asked.

'There's not much time, I'm afraid. They've suggested in a month if that's possible.'

'You'll have to get the banns up right away,' put in my father. 'I think that takes three weeks.'

I went to Evie and embraced her. 'It's going to be awful for us without you, but you'll be wonderfully happy. It's just right for you. Oh Evie, you deserve everything of the best.'

We clung together. It was one of those rare moments when Evie allowed herself to show the depth of her feelings.

Being Evie, she made our problem hers, and in the midst of all her happiness and the bustle of getting ready at such short notice she did not forget us.

I had never seen her as excited as she was at this time. She read a great deal about Africa and was determined to make a success of this job for James and herself.

'You see, he's taking someone else's place. The previous one came home on holiday and developed chest trouble. He can't go back. That has given James his chance.'

'He deserves it – and so do you.'

'It's all worked out very well in many ways. Jack Meadows can give his father a hand until something is settled. Isn't it miraculous? The only thing that worries me is you . . . but I've been thinking and Clare came into my mind.'

'Who's Clare?'

'Clare Massie. Would you like me to write to her? Do you know, I believe she is the answer. I haven't seen her for some years but she has kept in touch. We write to each other every Christmas.'

'Do tell me about her.'

'Well, I thought she might come here. Last Christmas she wrote that her mother had died. She'd been looking after her for years. You know the sort of thing . . . the younger daughter . . . it's expected of her. The others all have their own lives to lead and there's nothing for her but to look after ageing parents. There was a sister. She married and went abroad. Clare rarely hears from her. But she was saying last Christmas that she might have to find some post . . .'

'If she's a friend of yours . . .'

'She's a distant connection . . . cousin so many times removed that we've lost count. She must have been about fourteen when I last saw her. It was at the funeral of a great-aunt. She seemed to be such a good-natured girl and already she was looking after her mother. Shall I write?'

'Oh yes, please do.'

'If I could get her to come before I left I could show her a few things.'

'Evie, you're a wonder. In the midst of all this excitement you can think of others. Please write. If she is related to you I am sure we shall love her.'

'I will . . . immediately. Of course, it may be that she has found something by now . . .'

'We'll hope,' I said.

It was only two weeks after that conversation that Clare Massie arrived. She had accepted the offer with alacrity and Evie was delighted.

'It is just right for you and just right for Clare,' she said; and she was in a state of bliss. Not only was she marrying her dear James but she had settled us and her distant relative Clare at the same time.

I went with Evie in the dog-cart to the station to meet Clare and my first glimpse of her was on the platform with her bags around her. She had looked quite forlorn and I felt an immediate sympathy for her. What should *I* feel, facing a new life among people I had never met before with only a distant cousin to help me over the first days – and that prop soon to be removed?

Evie swept down on Clare. They embraced.

'Kate, this is Clare Massie. Clare, Kate Collison.'

We shook hands and I looked into a pair of large brown eyes in a rather pale, heart-shaped face. The light brown hair was smoothed down on either side of her head to end in a neat knob. Her straw hat was brown with one yellow daisy in it and her coat was brown too. She looked nervous . . . fearful of giving offence. She must have been about twenty-eight or thirty.

I tried to reassure her and told her how glad we were that she had come. Evie had told us so much about her.

'Oh yes,' she said. 'Evie has been very good.'

'We could have the luggage sent on,' said Evie, practical as ever. 'Then we could all go in the dog-cart quite comfortably. Bring a small bag. Have you got one? Oh yes, just the things you'll need immediately.'

'I hope you are going to be happy here,' I said.

'Of course she will,' said Evie.

'I only hope I shall be able to . . .'

Evie silenced her. 'Everything will be just right,' she said firmly.

We talked about Evie's marriage and imminent departure.

'I'm glad you'll be here for it,' I said.

Thus we brought Clare home, and soon after that Evie was married. My father gave her away, the vicar performed the ceremony and afterwards we had a reception for her at Collison House with just a few friends and neighbours. Later that day the bride and bridegroom left on the first lap of their journey to Africa.

Clare quickly fitted into the household. She devoted herself to us with such assiduous care and determination to please that if she were not quite Evie – and we had convinced ourselves that nobody could be that – she was undoubtedly the next best thing.

She was extremely gentle and easy to get along with, which made us realize that, wonderful as Evie had been, she could at times imply a little criticism to those who did not conform to her own high standards . . . which of course none of us did.

Perhaps the house was not quite so well cared for. Perhaps the servants were not quite so prompt to answer our calls, and there was certainly an easing of discipline; but we were soon all very fond of Clare and delighted that she had come.

My father commented: 'I think perhaps that although we like the effect of highly powered efficiency we feel ourselves unable to compete with it and a little slackness gives us a self-congratulatory glow of comfort.'

And I agreed with him.

Clare made friends quickly and seemed to get on particularly well with the Camborne twins. My father was quite amused. He said that Faith was beginning to look to Clare almost as much as she did to Hope.

'Two rocks to cling to now,' he commented.

Clare began to show a great respect for our work and asked my father if she might see his collection of miniatures, which delighted him. It was a considerable collection. It was mainly Collisons, but he did have a Hilliard and two Isaac Olivers, which I thought were even better than the Hilliard – though possibly of not the same market value. One of his greatest treasures was a small miniature by the French artist, Jean Pucelle, who had been a leading member of a group of miniaturists at the Court of Burgundy in Paris during the fourteenth century. My father used to say that this collection was our fortune. Not that he would ever think of selling one piece. They had been in the family for generations and there they must stay.

Clare's brown eyes shone with pleasure as she surveyed these treasures and my father explained to her the differences in tempera and gouache. Even Evie had not understood about the paintings and secretly I believe had had a faint contempt for such work. But for the fact that my father earned a living by doing it I am sure she would have dismissed it as a rather frivolous occupation.

But Clare really did have a feeling for paint and admitted that she had tried her hand at a little oil painting.

It was clear that Clare was going to be a very successful addition to our household. The servants liked her; she was less definite than Evie but that could mean that she was not didactic and domineering.

There was about Clare a certain femininity which made

people feel the need to be gentle with her. The servants sensed this and whereas they might have been resentful of a housekeeper – which I suppose in a way she was – they all helped Clare to step into Evie's shoes.

And that was what she did. She was different; she was gentler; and if she lacked that complete efficiency which we had found in Evie, we were prepared to accept something less from one who was so eager to please.

After a while she began to confide in me and when she talked about her mother she would be overcome with emotion.

'I loved her dearly,' she said. 'She was my life because I had looked after her through her illness. Oh, Kate, I hope you never have to see one you love suffer. It is heart-rending. There were years of it . . .'

I knew she had an elder sister who had married and gone abroad and that her father had died when Clare was quite a child. It seemed that her mother had dominated her life, and that it had been a hard life I had no doubt. She had done a little painting herself, so she was excited to be in a household like ours.

'My mother thought my painting was a waste of time,' she said.

I guessed that her mother had not been easy to live with, although Clare never said so and always spoke of her with the utmost affection.

There was about her an air of one who has escaped to freedom; and my father and I were particularly pleased to have her in our home.

And then the commission came.

It threw my father into a state bordering on panic, exultation, apprehension, excitement and uncertainty.

It was the moment of decision for him. Here was one of the

most important commissions of his life. Could he, in his present state, take it?

As soon as we were alone in the studio he explained to me. He was holding a heavily embossed piece of paper.

'This is from the steward of the Baron de Centeville. It's in Normandy . . . not so far from Paris. It's a commission from the Baron although naturally it comes through his steward. Apparently he is to marry and he wants a miniature painted of himself for his fiancée, the Princesse de Créspigny. And when that is done, if the results are pleasing, I am to visit the lady and paint one of her, so that in accordance with the custom, miniatures can be exchanged between the happy pair. Kate, it's the opportunity of a lifetime. If he is pleased . . . if my miniatures are seen in such quarters . . . I could be painting the Empress Eugénie herself before long.' His eyes were glowing. For the moment he had forgotten his affliction. I watched him with a terrible pity and desolation in my heart as he remembered and the joy faded from his face. I had never seen him look so despairing.

Then suddenly his expression changed. 'We could do it, Kate,' he said. '*You* could do it.'

I thought my heartbeats would suffocate me. It was what I had longed for: to be commissioned by some glittering personage . . . to travel beyond our little world . . . across a continent, to visit foreign Courts, to live among people who made history.

Of all the Courts of Europe, the most glittering was that of France. The Court of our own Queen was sombre in comparison. She was still mourning the death of her Consort who had died of typhoid a few years previously. Since then the Queen had shut herself away and scarcely shown herself. The Prince of Wales seemed to live a very merry life but that was not the same thing. Charles Louis Napoleon Bonaparte, son of Louis Bonaparte who had been brother of the great Napoleon who had almost succeeded in conquering the world, had married the beautiful Eugénie Marie de Montijo, and between them they had made their Court the centre of Europe.

How I longed to see it! But of course these invitations did not come for me. They were for my father. And when he said: 'We could do it . . .' he had given me a glimmer of what was forming in his mind.

I said quietly: 'You will have to refuse.'

'Yes,' he replied, but I could see that that was not the end of the matter.

I went on: 'You will have to let it be known now. This must decide you.'

'You could do it, Kate.'

'They would never accept a woman.'

'No,' he agreed, 'of course not.'

He was looking at me intently. Then he said slowly: 'I could accept this commission . . .'

'Your eyes might fail you. That would be quite disastrous.'

'You would be my eyes, Kate.'

'Do you mean that I would go with you?'

He nodded slowly.

'I should be allowed to take you with me. I need a travelling companion. I am not as young as I was. You would be of use to me. They would think . . . perhaps to mix the paints . . . clean my brushes, my palettes . . . So they would think. And you would watch over me, Kate.'

'Yes,' I said. 'I could do that.'

'I wish I could say to them: "My daughter is a great painter. She will do your miniatures." But they would never accept it.'

'The world is unfair to women,' I said angrily.

'The world is unfair to all at times. No, Kate, we cannot go unless we go together. I, because I need you to be my eyes; you, because you are a woman. When the miniatures are done, if they are successful, I will say to this Baron: "This is the work of my daughter. You have admired it . . . accepted it . . . Now accept her for the painter she is." Kate, this might be your chance. It might be fate working in a mysterious way.'

My eyes were shining. I could scarcely bear to look at him.

'Yes,' I said. 'We are going.'

A mood of wild excitement and exultation took possession of me. I had never felt so jubilant before in all my life. I knew I could paint a miniature to compare with the greatest artists. My senses tingled and my whole being yearned to begin.

Then I was ashamed of my happiness because it came to me through my father's misfortune.

He understood. I heard him laugh softly, tenderly.

'Don't deny your art, Kate,' he said. 'You are an artist first of all. If you weren't you would not be a great artist. This could be your chance. Strike a blow for Art and Womanhood at the same time. Listen to me. I am going to accept this commission. We are going together to this château in Normandy. You are going to paint as you never did before. I can see it all so clearly.'

'There will have to be sittings . . . and the sitter will know.'

'That is not insurmountable. You will be there during the sittings. You will watch. I will paint and you will do your miniature when the sitter is absent. You will have seen him and have mine to work from. It is only the fine strokes which are beyond me. We'll work it, Kate. Oh, this is going to be the most exciting adventure.'

'Show me the letter.'

I held it in my hands. It was like a talisman, a passport to glory. I often wondered afterwards why we do not have premonitions in life . . . to warn us . . . to guide us . . . But no, the important moments in our life slip by with no special seeming significance. If only I had known then that this letter was going to change the whole course of my life, what should I have done?

'Shall you write?' I asked.

'Today,' replied my father.

'Shouldn't you wait awhile . . . consider . . .'

'I have considered. Have you?'

'Yes, I have.'

'It's going to work, Kate. We're going to make it work.'

It was a long time since I had seen my father so happy. We were like two children preparing for the treat of our lives. We refused to see the difficulties. We preferred to live in our euphoric dream convincing ourselves that everything would work out as we had planned.

'If I saw you accepted as you should be,' said my father, 'I think I could become reconciled.'

We talked to Clare. Did she feel capable of taking on the responsibilities of the household after such a short time?

She replied earnestly that she would do everything within her power to justify our trust in her.

'I feel I have good friends here,' she said. 'They are so kind at the Manor and the vicarage, and I have the Camborne twins. Oh yes, I certainly do feel that I am among friends. I am sure that if there are any difficulties while you are away – which I don't really anticipate – I shall have plenty of friends to help me out of them.'

'We are not quite sure how long this commission will take to carry out. It depends so much on the subject. Then, when we have finished in Normandy we may have to go on to Paris.'

'You can rest happy that all will be taken care of here,' Clare assured us.

So in less than two weeks after my father had received the invitation he and I were setting out for the Château de Centeville in Normandy.

Within the Château

The journey would have been tiring but for the fact that I was so excited by everything I saw. I had never been out of the country before and I was eager to miss nothing. The crossing was smooth and after what seemed like an interminable train journey we arrived at Rouen. There we took another train which would carry us to Centeville.

It was late afternoon when we arrived. We had been travelling since the early morning of the previous day and in spite of the interest of the journey I was immensely relieved to have come to the end of it.

As we left the train a man in livery approached us. I detected a look of disbelief in his eyes and I guessed that this was surprise at seeing a man and woman when he had been expecting a man only.

My father was the first to speak. His French was quite good and mine was adequate, so we had few qualms about language difficulties.

'I am Kendal Collison,' he said. 'Might you be looking for me? We were told that we would be met at the station.'

The man bowed. Yes, he said, he had come to meet Monsieur Collison on behalf of Monsieur de Marnier, Steward of the Château de Centeville.

'Then I am your man,' said my father. 'And this is my daughter, without whom I do not travel nowadays.'

I received the same courteous bow, which I acknowledged by inclining my head, and the man then proceeded to lead us towards a carriage. It was magnificent – dark blue in colour and emblazoned on it was a coat of arms, presumably that of our illustrious patron.

We were helped in and told that our baggage would be brought to the château. I was relieved because it was certainly not worthy to grace such a vehicle. I looked at my father and almost giggled. It was sheer nervousness, of course. The ceremonial nature of our reception had had this effect, reminding me that we were about to face the consequences of our very rash act.

The horses were whipped up and we bowled along through the most enchanting countryside. It was wooded and hilly and suddenly we saw the castle perched above the town – a Norman, grey stone and impregnable fortress with its massive cylindrical columns, its long narrow slits of windows, its rounded arches and machicolated towers.

It looked forbidding – a fortress indeed rather than a dwelling place, and I felt a shiver of apprehension run through me.

We were climbing the gradual slope and as we grew nearer to the castle, the more menacing it seemed to be. We should have explained, I told myself. We have come here under false pretences. What will they do if they discover? Well, they can only send us back.

I looked at my father. I could not tell from his expression whether he felt the brooding power of the place as I did.

We passed over a moat and under a portcullis and were in a courtyard. The carriage stopped and our splendid driver jumped down from his seat and opened the door for us to alight.

I felt suddenly small standing beside those immense walls of stone. I turned to look up at the Keep, with the tower on it which must give a view of miles surrounding the castle.

'This way,' said our driver.

We were facing a studded door. He rapped on it sharply

and it was opened immediately by a man in livery similar to that worn by the driver.

'Monsieur and Mademoiselle Collison,' said the driver as though announcing us at some function. He then bowed to us and prepared to leave, having delivered us into the hands of our next guide.

The servant bowed in the same ceremonious fashion and signed for us to follow him.

We were taken into a large hall with an arched roof supported by thick round stone columns. There were several windows but they were so narrow that they did not let in a great deal of light; stone benches were cut out of the wall; there was a long, beautifully carved table in the centre of the hall – a concession to a later period, for I presumed the hall itself was pure Norman, and another concession was that there was glass in the windows.

'Excuse me for one moment,' said the servant. 'I will acquaint Monsieur de Marnier of your arrival.'

My father and I looked at each other in suppressed awe when we were alone.

'So far, so good,' he whispered.

I agreed, with the proviso that we had not yet come very far.

In a very short time we were making the acquaintance of Monsieur de Marnier who quickly let us know that he held the very responsible post of Majordomo, house steward of the Château de Centeville. He was a very impressive personage in a blue coat with splashes of gold braid on it and large buttons which depicted something. As far as I could see at the time it seemed to be some sort of ship. Monsieur de Marnier was both gracious and disturbed. He had been misled. He had been told one gentleman.

'This is my daughter,' explained my father. 'I thought it was understood. I don't travel without her. She is necessary to my work.'

'Of course, Monsieur Collison. Of course. An oversight. I will discover . . . It will be necessary to have a room prepared. I will see to that. It is a bagatelle . . . of no importance. If you will come to the room which has been prepared for Monsieur, I will arrange for one to be made ready for Mademoiselle. We dine at eight of the clock. Would you care for some refreshment to be sent to your room meanwhile?'

I said some coffee would be excellent.

He bowed. 'Coffee and a little *goûter.* It shall be done. Please to follow me. Monsieur de Mortemer will see you at dinner. He will then acquaint you with what is expected.'

He led the way up a wide staircase and along a gallery. Then we came to a stone spiral staircase – typically Norman, which was a further indication of the age of the castle, each step being built into the wall at one end leaving a round piece at the other as the shaft. I was a little concerned for my father as his eyes might fail him in the sudden change of light on this rather dangerous staircase. I insisted that he go ahead and I walked close behind him in case he should stumble.

At length we came to another hall. We were very high and I could see that up here the light would be good and strong. We turned off the hall to a corridor. The servant opened the door to that room which had been allotted to my father. It was large and contained a bed and several pieces of heavy furniture of an early period. The windows were long and narrow, excluding the light; and the walls were decorated with weapons and tapestry.

I could feel the past all around me but here again there were a few concessions to modern comfort. I saw that behind the bed a *ruelle* had been made. It was an alcove in which one could wash and dress – a kind of dressing-room which would have no place in a Norman fortress.

'You will be informed, Mademoiselle, when your room is ready for you,' I was told.

Then we were alone.

My father seemed to have cast off a good many years. He was like a mischievous boy.

'The antiquity of everything!' he cried. 'I could fancy I was back eight hundred years and that Duke William is going to appear suddenly to tell us that he plans to conquer England.'

'Yes, I feel that too. It is decidedly feudal. I wonder who this Monsieur de Mortemer is?'

'The name was spoken with such respect that he might be the son of the house.'

'Surely the Baron who is about to be married wouldn't have a son . . . one who is old enough to receive us at any rate.'

'Could be a second marriage. I hope not. I want him to be young, unlined . . . Then he will look handsome.'

'Older faces can be more interesting,' I pointed out.

'If people realized it, yes. But they all long for the contours of youth, the unshadowed eyes, the matt complexions. For an interesting miniature give me the not so young. But so much depends on this. If we can make our subject look handsome . . . then we shall get many commissions. That is what we need, daughter.'

'You talk as though they are going to accept me. I have my doubts. At the Court of François Premier they might have done. *He* loved women in every way and respected their equal right to intelligence and achievement. I doubt we shall find the same in feudal Normandy.'

'You're judging our host by his castle.'

'I sense that he clings to the past. I feel it in the air.'

'We shall see, Kate. In the meantime let us think up a good plan of action. I wonder where we shall be working. It'll have to be lighter than these rooms.'

'I am beginning to wonder where this will end.'

'Let us concern ourselves first with the beginning. We're here, Kate. We're going to meet this Monsieur de Mortemer tonight. Let's see what he has to say to your presence here.'

While we were talking there was a knock and a maidservant came in carrying coffee and a kind of brioche with a fruit preserve. When we had eaten, she said she would return and take me to my room, which was next to my father's. Then water would be brought for us to wash. We had plenty of time before dinner.

The coffee and brioche were delicious and my spirits rose. I began to catch my father's optimism.

My room was very like his. There were thick carpets on the floor and the draperies at the window were of dull purple velvet. There was an armoire, some chairs and a table on which stood a heavy mirror. I knew I could be comfortable here.

My luggage was brought in and I prepared to change for dinner.

What did one wear in a place like this? I had imagined that there would be a certain amount of ceremony, and I was thankful for Lady Farringdon's parties for which I had had several dresses made.

I chose a fairly sober one of dark green velvet with a full skirt and fitted bodice. It was by no means a ball gown but it had been suitable for the musical evenings which Lady Farringdon had given and I thought it would fit the present occasion. Moreover I always felt my most confident in that colour green – jewel colour, my father called it. 'The old masters were able to produce it,' he said. 'No one else was very successful with it after the seventeenth century. In those days colour was important and great artists had their secrets which they kept to themselves. It's different now. You have to buy it in a tube and it is not the same.'

When I was ready I went to my father's room. He was waiting for me and I had not been there more than a few minutes when there was a discreet tap on the door. It was the steward himself who had come to conduct us down to dinner.

We seemed to walk some distance and were in another part of the castle. The architecture had changed a little. The castle was evidently vast and must have been added to considerably over the centuries. It seemed to have changed from early Norman to late Gothic.

We were in a small room panelled with a painted ceiling which caught my eye immediately. I should enjoy examining that at some later time. In fact there were so many features of this place about which I had promised myself the same thing. We had been hurried through a picture gallery and I was sure my father found the same difficulty as I did in not begging the steward to call a halt so that we might study the pictures.

This was like an anteroom – the sort of place, I thought, where one might wait to receive an audience with a king. This Baron de Centeville seemed to live like a king. I wondered what sort of face he had. I had a strong feeling that it was not going to suit a miniature.

Someone had entered the room. I caught my breath. He was the most handsome man I had ever seen. He was of medium height with light brown hair and eyes; he was elegantly dressed and his dinner jacket was of a rather more elaborate cut than I was accustomed to seeing at home. His very white shirt was daintily tucked and his cravat was of sapphire blue. A single stone sparkled in it as only a diamond could.

He bowed low and taking my hand kissed it.

'Welcome,' he said in English, 'I am delighted to receive you on behalf of my cousin, the Baron de Centeville. He regrets he is unable to see you tonight. He will be here tomorrow. You must be hungry. Would you care to come to dinner immediately? It is a small affair this evening. We dine . . . *à trois* . . . very *intime* . . . I thought that best on the night of your arrival. Tomorrow we can make arrangements.'

My father thanked him for his gracious welcome. 'I fear,'

he said, 'that there may have been some misunderstanding and only I was expected. My daughter is also a painter. I find it difficult nowadays to travel without her.'

'It is our great pleasure to have Mademoiselle Collison with us,' said our host.

He then informed us that he was Bertrand de Mortemer, a distant cousin of the Baron. The Baron was the head of the family . . . He was a member of a smaller branch. We understood?

We said we understood perfectly and it was very good of Monsieur de Mortemer to show such solicitude for our comfort.

'The Baron has heard of your fame,' he explained. 'As you may have been told, he is about to marry and the miniature is to be a gift for his bride elect. The Baron may ask you to paint a miniature of his bride if . . .'

'If,' I finished bluntly, 'he likes the work.'

Monsieur de Mortemer bowed his head in acknowledgement of the truth of this.

'He will most certainly like it,' he added. 'Your miniatures are well known throughout the Continent, Monsieur Collison.'

I was always deeply moved to see my father's gratification at praise and it was particularly poignant now that his powers were fading. I felt a great surge of tenderness towards him.

He was growing more and more confident every minute – and so was I. One could not imagine Monsieur de Mortemer being anything but pleasant and if the great and mighty Baron were like him, then we were indeed safe.

'The Baron is a connoisseur of art,' said Monsieur de Mortemer. 'He enjoys beauty in any form. He has seen a great deal of your work and has a very high opinion of it. It was for this reason that he selected you to do the miniature rather than one of our own countrymen.'

'The art of miniature painting is the one I think in which the English can be said to excel above others,' said my father, off on to one of his favourite subjects. 'It is strange because it was developed in other countries before it came to England. Your own Jean Pucelle had his own group in the fourteenth century while our Nicolas Hilliard, who might be said to be our founder, came along two centuries later.'

'It requires much patience, this art of the miniature,' said Monsieur de Mortemer. 'That is it, eh?'

'A great deal,' I corroborated. 'Do you actually live here with your cousin, Monsieur de Mortemer?'

'No . . . no. I live with my parents . . . south of Paris. When I was a boy I lived here for a while. I learned how to manage an estate and live er . . . *comme il faut* . . . you understand? My cousin in my patron. Is that how you say it?'

'A sort of guiding influence, the patriarch of the family?'

'Perhaps,' he answered with a smile. 'My family estate is small in comparison. My cousin is . . . er . . . very helpful to us.'

'I understand perfectly. I hope I am not asking impertinent questions.'

'I am sure, Mademoiselle Collison, that you could never be impertinent. I am honoured that you should feel such an interest in my affairs.'

'When we . . . when my father is going to paint a miniature he likes to know as much as he can about the subject. The Baron seems to be a very important man . . . not only in Centeville but in the whole of France.'

'He *is* Centeville, Mademoiselle. I could tell you a great deal about him, but it is best that you discover for yourself. People do not always see through the same eyes, and perhaps a painter should only look through his own.'

I thought: I *have* asked too many questions, and I can see that Monsieur de Mortemer is the soul of discretion. But *toujours la politesse*. A good old French saying. He is right. We must discover this all-important Baron for ourselves.

My father turned the conversation to the castle. He obviously felt that would be a safe subject.

We had been right in thinking that the original structure dated back to some time before 1066. Then it had been a fortress with little more than sleeping quarters for the defenders and the rest equipped for fighting off invaders. Over the intervening centuries it had been added to. The sixteenth century had been the era of building. François Premier had set the fashion and had built Chambord and restored and embellished wherever he went. A great deal had been added to Centeville in his day, but this was apparent only in the interior. Wisely, the Norman aspect had been preserved outwardly, which was probably the reason why the place was so impressive.

Monsieur de Mortemer talked enthusiastically about the castle and the treasures it contained.

'The Baron is a collector,' he explained. 'He inherited many beautiful things and he has added to them. It will be my pleasure to show you some of the rare pieces here.'

'Do you think the Baron will permit that?'

'I am sure he will. He will be gratified by your interest.'

'I am a little concerned as to where I shall paint the miniature,' said my father.

'Ah yes, indeed. The Baron has employed artists here before. He understands about the light which will be needed. Previously the work has been executed in what we call the Sunshine Room. That is a room we have here in that part of the castle which is the most modern, by which I mean it is seventeenth-century. It was built to let in the sun on all sides. It is high and there are windows in the roof. You will see it tomorrow. I think it will please.'

'It sounds ideal,' I said.

We talked desultorily on one or two other topics. The journey we had had, the countryside compared with that at home and so on, until finally he said: 'You must be absolutely exhausted. Let me have you conducted to your rooms. I hope you will then have a good night and in the morning you will feel refreshed.'

'Ready to meet the Baron,' I added.

He smiled and his smile was very warn and friendly. I felt a glow of pleasure. I liked him. I liked him very much. I found his perfect grooming not in the least effeminate, only very pleasant. I thought he had a charming smile and although his implication that we bestowed a privilege on Centeville by being here might not be entirely sincere, it had certainly put us at our ease, and I liked him still more for that.

It was a relief to get into bed that night. I was very tired, for the journey and the apprehension as to what we should find at the end of it had exhausted me so completely that I was asleep almost as soon as my head touched the pillow.

I was awakened by a gentle tapping at the door. It was one of the maids bringing *petit déjeuner* which consisted of coffee, rolls of crusty bread with butter and confiture.

'I will bring you hot water in ten minutes, Mademoiselle,' she told me.

I sat up in bed and drank the coffee, which was delicious. I was hungry enough to enjoy the rolls.

The sun was shining through the long narrow window and I felt a pleasurable sense of excitement. The real adventure was about to begin.

When I was washed and dressed I went to my father's room. He had been awakened when I had, and had enjoyed his coffee and rolls and was now ready.

Monsieur de Marnier appeared. He had instructions to take us to Monsieur de Mortemer when we were ready.

We followed him to that part of the castle where we had taken dinner on the previous evening. Bertrand de Mortemer was awaiting us in what I called the anteroom with the painted ceiling.

'Good morning,' he said, smiling most agreeably. 'I trust you have slept comfortably.'

We assured him that we had and were most grateful for all the concern of our well-being which was shown to us.

He spread his hands. It was nothing, he told us. Centeville was privileged.

'Now you will wish to see the Sunshine Room. Would you follow me.'

We were delighted when we saw it.

It had been built by one of the Barons who had had an artist working in the castle on a permanent basis. 'Do you think it will suit you?' asked Bertrand.

'It's perfect,' I told him and my father agreed with me.

'So often one is expected to paint in rooms which are quite inadequate,' he said. 'This will be just what we need.'

'Perhaps you would like to arrange . . . what has to be arranged. Bring up the tools of your trade, as they say.'

I looked at my father.

'Let us do that,' I said. 'Then we shall be all in readiness.'

'Shall you start the portrait as soon as the Baron arrives?'

My father hesitated. 'I like to talk awhile with my subject first . . . to get to know him, you see.'

'I am sure the Baron will understand that.'

'Well, let us prepare,' I said to my father.

'Do you think you can find your way back to your rooms?' asked Monsieur de Mortemer.

'We have to learn,' I replied.

'Well, now that you have seen the Sunshine Room let me take you back. After that you can find your own way, perhaps.'

'I shall note the landmarks as we pass through,' I said with a smile.

So my father and I spent an hour or so taking our materials

to that room. It was what we would call in England a solarium and was of course ideal for our purpose. My father commented that everything was working out splendidly.

I thought he looked a little tired and I did notice once or twice that he blinked in the strong light of the room. I could see all sorts of obstacles about to rise before us. I could not quite picture how we were going to pretend he was painting the miniature when actually I was going to do it. It would certainly be a new and interesting way of working. I wondered how it would end.

It would be dreadful to produce something below Collison standards on such an important occasion.

When we had returned to our rooms I suggested that my father rest for a while. There was an hour or so before *déjeuner* and the journey and excitement of coming here had been a little too much for him.

I persuaded him to lie down and then thought I would like to look at the château from outside. I put on a hat and found my way down to the hall. There was the door through which we had entered on the previous night. I went through into the courtyard.

I did not want to leave the precincts of the castle so I did not cross the moat. I looked round and saw a door. I went through this and was in a garden. I gathered I was at the back of the castle. Before me stretched out the undulating countryside with the woods in the distance. It was very beautiful. The gardens, which ran down to the water of the moat, had been carefully cultivated. Flowers grew in profusion with colours perfectly blended. Our Baron had a feeling for colour – unless of course he employed people to select them for him, which was most likely.

I went down to the moat's edge and sat down. What peace! I thought of Clare at home running the house and Evie far away in Africa. I was uneasy and kept assuring myself that there was nothing to be uneasy about. If the Baron discovered that my father could no longer paint, and if he wanted a Collison, his only alternative was to take mine. And if he refused? Well, then we should just return home.

I heard footsteps and turning sharply saw Bertrand de Mortemer coming towards me.

'Ah,' he said as though surprised. 'Have you finished your preparations?'

'There is not much to do until the . . . er . . . subject arrives.'

'Of course not.' He sat down beside me. 'Well, now you have seen the castle by the light of morning what do you think of it?'

'Grand. Massive. Impressive. Overpowering. I can't think of any more adjectives.'

'Those already supplied are sufficient.'

He was looking at me steadily and I noticed that his handsome appearance had not diminished with daylight. Rather, I thought, was it accentuated.

'To think of one man owning all this . . . it's rather staggering,' I said.

'Not for the Baron. He was brought up to it. He's a scion of his forefathers. Wait until you meet him, then you'll understand.'

'Is he . . . like you?'

Bertrand seemed very amused. 'I think you would have to look very hard to find a resemblance.'

'Oh.'

'You sound disappointed.'

'I am. If he were like you I should feel very relieved.'

He put his hand over mine suddenly. 'That is a very nice compliment,' he said.

'It's not a compliment. It's a statement of fact.'

He smiled at me . . . a little sadly, I thought. He said: 'No, you will find him very different.'

'Please prepare me.'

He shook his head. 'It is better for you to find out for yourself. People see others differently. You see him for yourself.'

'That is what you said last night and yet you do give me certain hints. I have the impression that the Baron is not easy to please.'

'He knows what is best and he will want the best.'

'And his fiancée?'

'Is the Princesse de Créspigny.'

'A princess!'

'Oh yes. The Baron is not only one of the wealthiest men in the country, he is also one of the most influential.'

'And the Princesse?'

'She comes from an old French family with royal connections. The family managed to survive the revolution.'

'The Baron also?'

'The Baron would always survive.'

'So this is the marriage of two noble families. One very rich, the other not so rich but royal.'

'The Princesse is connected with the royal families of France and Austria. She will be most suitable for the Baron. The Créspigny estates could be restored. If anyone can do that it is the Baron.'

'With his immense wealth,' I murmured.

'It is a useful asset.'

'And the Baron is happy with his coming marriage?'

'Believe me, if he were not, there would be no marriage.'

'Be careful,' I said. 'You are beginning to give me your picture of the Baron before I have met him.'

'You are good to remind me. My lips are . . . what you say . . . sealed?'

I nodded.

'Now we will talk of other things,' he said.

'Yourself?'

'And yourself?'

Then I found myself telling about life at Collison House – the gatherings at Farringdon Manor, the vicarage family and the Camborne twins, of my mother's romantic marriage and the happiness she and my father had shared, of her death, of our luck in having Evie who had now married her missionary and left the cosy predictability of our English village for the perils of darkest Africa.

'But she left us Clare,' I added. 'She saw to that before she went. Evie was one of the natural managers of those around her. She looked after us all . . . every one.'

He looked at me steadily. 'I think you are one of these . . . managers.'

I laughed. 'Me? Oh no. I am deeply involved in my own affairs.'

'I know. Painting! For I gather that you paint too. It means much to you. Are you going to paint miniatures like your ancestors?'

'That is what I should like to do more than anything.'

'More than anything. Do you not want a lover . . . marriage . . . little children?'

'I don't know. Perhaps. But I want to paint.'

He was smiling at me, and I thought: I am talking too much. I hardly know this man. What was it about him that won my confidence? That infinite kindness which I had sensed in him from the moment we met; that air of worldliness which probably was nothing more than a mode of dress and behaviour.

He invited confidences and I seemed to have given him far too many. I thought: I will be telling him about my father's encroaching blindness next.

'It is your turn to tell me something about yourself,' I said.

'It has been the life of so many in my position.'

'I gather you spent some part of your childhood here.'

'Yes, I did. The Baron said he would have me here to learn something of life.'

'What of life?'

'Oh, how it is to be lived here in the country . . . at Court. That has become formal now with the Empress Eugénie setting the standards. The Baron regrets the disintegration of the monarchy but he is reconciled to the Second Empire and supports Napoleon the Third . . . not with real enthusiasm but as the only possible alternative to republicanism.'

'Is the Baron often at Court?'

'Quite often. But I think he is happiest here in Normandy.'

'Is he a very complicated man . . . difficult to understand?'

He smiled at me. 'And therefore a good subject for a painter. We will see if your father probes those hidden depths of character.'

'He would probably need a large canvas to do that. The miniature is to go to his lady-love. It should therefore be romantic.'

'You mean . . . flattering.'

'It is possible to be romantic without flattery.'

'I fancy the Baron might not be flattered to be called romantic. He prides himself on his astute approach to life.'

'Romance is not necessarily a stranger to astuteness.'

'Is it not? I thought in romance one saw everything through a rosy glow.'

'That is how my father must make the Princesse see the Baron . . . through a rosy glow. I think it is time I returned to the house.'

He sprang up and held out his hands. I gave him mine and he helped me up.

He stood for a while holding my hands. It was only for a few seconds but it seemed longer. I thought how still everything was; the quiet water of the moat, the tall massive walls about us, and I felt myself tingling with excitement.

I flushed a little and withdrew my hands.

He said: 'Perhaps this afternoon . . . if you are not busy . . .'

'We shall not be busy until the Baron returns,' I said.

'Do you ride?'

'A great deal. I helped to exercise the Farringdon horses. The local big house I told you about . . . They pretended I was doing them a service when they were so obviously doing me one.'

'That's the way to do a service,' he said. 'If it is given with a request for gratitude it is no service.'

'You are right, of course. But why do you ask if I ride?'

'Because if you say yes, you do, I suggest we ride this afternoon. I could show you the countryside which might interest you. Does that appeal?'

'Very much.'

'Have you a habit?'

'I brought one with me . . . hoping . . . and not really believing in my hopes . . . that they might be realized so soon.'

He touched my arm lightly. 'I am glad you came,' he said earnestly. 'It is very interesting . . . getting to know you.'

Little quivers of excitement continued to come to me. I thought what a lovely morning it was here in the sunshine, close to the strong walls of the castle, the silver sparkle of the water and this interesting and most handsome young man looking at me with very thinly veiled admiration.

Riding out through the beautiful country with Bertrand de Mortemer was an exciting experience. I loved to ride and was very interested to explore new terrain. I was about to embark on an adventure and I was adventurous by nature. I felt I was on the verge of discovering that life was exciting; it might be dangerous but perhaps I was of a nature to enjoy a spice of danger and therefore went to meet it instead of taking the cautious line and avoiding it.

I could not really explain this exultation which I felt now. I could only say that I was enjoying this ride as I had never enjoyed a ride before.

Of course it had its beginnings in this young man's company. I was more drawn to him than I had ever been to anyone else on such short acquaintance. It was fascinating to talk to him and the little pitfalls of language into which now and then we fell amused us both. We talked and we laughed and the time flew by most pleasantly.

I said to him: 'We seem to have become friendly in a very short time.'

'Time is always too short when good things happen,' he answered. 'Life is too short. I tell myself that you have come here with your father who is to paint a picture and you will soon be gone. How am I to get to know you if I do not do so quickly? How long will it take to paint the miniature?'

'I cannot say. So much depends on how the work progresses.'

'Not long, I am sure.'

'I imagine the Baron will want it done with the greatest speed.'

The mention of the Baron brought a chill into the afternoon. I must have been enjoying it so much that I had forgotten him.

I didn't realize what was happening to me that afternoon, but it was an enchanted one. I began to believe afterwards that this was what people meant by falling in love – something which had never happened to me before. I had met very few young men; I supposed I had lived a fairly sheltered life. I had certainly never met anyone in the least like Bertrand de Mortemer. His outstanding good looks, his elegant clothes, his determination to do everything he could to help, his gentleness which mingled with a certain worldliness enchanted me. And yet on the other hand I felt protective towards him, which was a strange way to feel. I didn't know why – but then my emotions were so mixed and so strange to me. I was in the first place overcome with astonishment that I could feel so strongly about a man who was almost a stranger.

So naturally I was excited as we galloped across the meadow and the castle came into sight. The wind caught at my hair under my hard bowler hat and I loved the feel of it. I loved the sound of thudding hoofs; and he was beside me, laughing, enjoying it as much as I did.

Excitement. Adventure. Daring. And Danger . . . oh, definitely danger. To come here under false pretences, to work out a devious plan for painting a picture which would be mistaken for my father's work . . . that was surely courting danger.

Oh, but it was exciting.

Even as we rode into the stables I was aware of the change. One of the grooms came running to us.

The Baron had returned.

I felt my excitement immediately tempered by apprehension. I looked at Bertrand de Mortemer. He seemed to have shrunk.

The testing time had come.

I had not expected it quite so soon, for as we came into the great hall the Baron himself was there.

There was a second or so of silence while he looked at us. I felt then that my greatest fears had some foundation.

He was an overpowering man – but I had expected that. He was very tall and broad, which gave an impression of bulk rather than height. He was dressed in dark riding clothes which accentuated the blondeness of his hair, which was thick and glistened in the light which came through the narrow windows. His eyes were steely grey, his nose was rather prominent but straight, and he had a fresh colour which gave the impression that he was full of health and vigour. There was something about him which set the alarm bells ringing in my head. I suppose I was wondering how we were going to deceive such a man.

He came towards us, his eyes on me. His brows were raised slightly ironically.

'Bertrand,' he said, 'why do you not present me to your friend?'

'Oh,' replied Bertrand with a little laugh which could only indicate embarrassment, 'this is Mademoiselle Collison.'

'Mademoiselle Collison?' He paused and looked at me quizzically.

I had always believed that when one was on the defensive one must go into the attack, so I answered quickly: 'I came with my father. He is Kendal Collison who is to paint the miniature of the Baron de Centeville.'

He bowed.

I hurried on: 'I travel with my father. I can be of some use to him.'

'I trust they have looked after you,' he said. 'I mean within the household. I can see that Monsieur de Mortemer has performed his duty as host in my absence.'

'So,' I replied, 'you are the Baron de Centeville. I am glad to meet you.'

'You have been riding, I see.'

'While we were waiting for your arrival I thought I would show Mademoiselle Collison the countryside,' Bertrand explained.

'What do you think of our countryside, Mademoiselle Collison?' His English was good but his accent slightly more foreign than that of Bertrand.

'Very beautiful.'

'And the castle?'

'What was your description,' Bertrand asked, turning to me. 'Impressive. Impregnable. Majestic . . .'

'I am delighted, Mademoiselle Collison. I confess I am

gratified when people admire my castle. I wish to meet your father.'

'I will bring him to you. He is resting at the moment.'

He shook his head. 'No matter. I shall meet him for dinner. Will you tell him that I wish to start on the portrait tomorrow morning.'

'Tomorrow morning. That's rather early. My father likes to get to know his subject a little before he embarks.'

'He will quickly sum me up, I am sure. Arrogant, overbearing, impatient and self-willed.'

I laughed. 'You have a poor opinion of yourself, Baron.'

'On the contrary, it is very high. Those are the qualities necessary I believe to enjoy life fully. Tell your father to be ready to start tomorrow morning. I do not wish to waste too much time sitting.'

I lifted my shoulders and glanced at Bertrand. I said: 'That is not really the way in which to approach the matter. It is not simply a process of putting paint on ivory or vellum or whatever the support is to be.'

'Oh? Then what else is involved?'

'Getting to know the sitter. Finding out what he or she is really like.'

'Ah, Mademoiselle Collison, I should not wish anyone to know what I was really like, particularly the lady to whom I am affianced. There are some things in life which are better hidden.'

He was studying me intently and I was aware of my untidy hair which was escaping from under my bowler hat. I felt the colour rise to my cheeks and I thought: He is laughing at me, while all the time he is putting me in my place, reminding me that we are employed here to carry out his wishes. I disliked him immediately and I thought: Is this the sort of treatment we are to expect from the wealthy? Do they regard artists as tradesmen?

I felt defiant and did not care if I offended him. We could

go home and he could find another miniaturist to paint the sort of picture he wanted for his fiancée. I was not going to let him treat me in this way.

I said to him: 'If you want a pretty, conventional picture, Baron de Centeville, it is not necessary to call in a great artist. If you will excuse me, I will go to my room and tell my father that you are here. He will see you at dinner and then plans can be made for tomorrow's sitting.'

I felt his eyes watching me as I turned away and went upstairs.

Then he said something to Bertrand which I did not hear.

I dressed myself in the green velvet for dinner and attended carefully to my hair, piling it high on my head. I looked slightly older than my years and the green velvet always gave me confidence. I knew I was going to need it.

I had warned my father that the Baron might well prove difficult. 'Of course, I only saw him briefly in the hall. He has a great opinion of himself and is inclined to patronize. A rather obnoxious character, I'm afraid . . . quite different from Monsieur de Mortemer.'

'Ah,' said my father, 'there is the perfect gentleman.'

I agreed.

I said: 'Father, I don't know how we are going to deceive this Baron. It is going to be difficult. And if he discovers what we are doing, he will be most unpleasant I am sure.'

'Well, let's look at it this way,' said my father. 'He can only send us back to England and refuse to have the miniature. If he does that it will be because he knows nothing about art. Your miniature will be every bit as expert as anything I can do. He'll get a Collison, so he'll have nothing to complain about. Don't worry. If he sends us back . . . then we shall have to think what we are going to do in the future.'

When we were ready, Bertrand arrived. He said he had come to take us down.

That was very thoughtful of him. He must have guessed that my first encounter with the Baron had been disturbing.

'The Baron is so used to everyone agreeing with him immediately,' he said by way of explaining the Baron's manner.

'And he clearly does not like it when they do not.'

'I think it is more astonishment than anything else. In any case, you can stand up to him. After all, your father is the well-known Kendal Collison. I think the Baron will have a great respect for him. He really does admire artists.'

'And clearly does not admire their daughters.'

'Oh . . . he was quite amused.'

'He has a strange way of showing amusement. In any case I am not sure that I like being a figure of fun.'

'You will do very well. Do not let him see . . . how do you say it? . . . that he rattles you? If he realizes that he does he will try it all the more to discountenance you.'

'A most unpleasant character.'

'He would agree with you on that.'

'He's a throw-back to a different century from this,' I said. 'Fortunately we have moved forward into civilization.'

Bertrand laughed. 'How vehement you are. He was not so bad, was he? I think you take too much interest in this Baron.'

'I have to . . .' I paused. I was going to say 'if I am going to paint a picture of him'. I finished lamely . . . 'to help my father.'

My father had come out of his room. He looked frail and I was filled with the urgent need to protect him. If the Baron slighted him in the smallest way, I should definitely tell the man what I thought of him.

The Baron was already in the room with the painted ceiling and with him was a woman. I was struck immediately by her appearance. At first I thought she was a great beauty, but I realized as the evening progressed that she owed that impression to her gestures, her clothes and the manner in which she wore them, to her poise and sophisticated manners. She was the sort of woman who could put on beauty as one might a piece of jewellery. It was an illusion but a clever one. Her mouth was too large, her eyes too small and her nose too short for beauty . . . and yet she exuded that soignée, chic and really beautiful impression.

The Baron turned to greet us. He wore a dark blue velvet dinner-jacket and very white linen. He looked very elegant. I felt my green velvet was somewhat outmoded, and it no longer did for me the things it did at Farringdon Manor.

'Ah,' said the Baron, 'here is the artist. You are indeed welcome, sir, and we are honoured to have you with us. Nicole, this is Monsieur Kendal Collison and his daughter, Mademoiselle Collison. They have honoured us . . . you know for what purpose. Mademoiselle Collison and I have met already. Oh briefly . . . too briefly. My dear Monsieur and Mademoiselle Collison, allow me to present Madame St Giles.'

I was looking into that beautiful face. The small dark eyes were friendly, I thought, and if she made me feel gauche and unattractive, that was not her fault. I did not dislike her as I did the Baron.

'Bertrand, I think we should go in to dinner,' said the Baron.

'Yes,' said Bertrand and gave Madame St Giles his arm. The Baron took mine.

I was startled. I had not expected this formality, and I found close proximity to the Baron something which repelled me.

Oddly enough, I think he knew that I was shrinking from him and disliked laying my hand even on his coat sleeve.

He looked over his shoulder at my father. 'Alas, Monsieur Collison,' he said, 'we have no lady for you. Well, you are the guest of honour so that is your compensation.'

My father said it was a great pleasure to be here and the Baron was too kind.

I thought grimly: We will wait and see if that is so.

Dinner was an elaborate meal – more so than it had been on the previous night, but not nearly so enjoyable. This was due to the Baron's presence.

The conversation, out of deference to my father, generally concerned art.

'My father was a collector,' the Baron told us, 'and he taught me to follow in his footsteps. I have always had a strong appreciation of the creative arts . . . whether it be in literature, sculpture, music, or painting . . . I have always believed in absolute honesty regarding them. I know you will agree with me, Monsieur Collison. All great artists must. I do not like because I am told I must like. A work of art must please *me*. I think it is a disservice to art to abandon honesty for the sake of being in the fashion. I like a work of art for what it means to me . . . not for the signature in the corner if it is a picture, or on the cover of a book if it is literature.'

I couldn't help applauding this sentiment. I would remind him of it if he were to discover I, a woman, had painted his portrait – that would be after he had expressed approval of it, of course.

'You are quite right, Baron,' said Madame St Giles. 'I could not agree more.'

He looked at her mischievously. 'In your case, Nicole, it might be wiser to take note of the name of the artist . . . because, my dear, I'm afraid you lack the judgement to decide for yourself.'

Nicole laughed. 'The Baron is right, you know,' she said, looking at me and my father. 'You will find me a complete ignoramus. One virtue I have, though. I am aware of my ignorance. So many people are completely oblivious of theirs. Now this is a virtue, is it not?'

'A very great one,' said the Baron. 'Ah, if only everyone had your good sense.'

'But who is to say whose judgement is to be respected?' I asked. 'There is a saying in my country that "Good taste is what I have. Bad taste is what everyone else has who does not agree with me."'

'I see we have a philosopher here,' said the Baron, fixing me with his cold grey eyes. 'Answer that if you can, Nicole, for I cannot attack such logic.'

Then he talked to my father. We would start the portrait the following morning. He was anxious to get it completed quickly and could not stay long at the castle. He had business in Paris.

'A work of art cannot be hurried,' I said.

'I see now why you have brought your daughter with you,' retorted the Baron. 'She is going to keep us all in good order.'

'Oh, Kate is very useful to me,' said my father. 'I have come to rely on her.'

'Everyone should have someone on whom he – or she – can rely. Don't you agree, Nicole? Mademoiselle Collison? Bertrand?'

Bertrand said that it was comforting.

Madame St Giles said it was necessary.

I said I thought that one should be selfreliant if that were possible.

'As you are, Mademoiselle Collison, I see. How do you work, Monsieur Collison? I did so admire the miniature you did of the Graf von Engheim. I saw it when I was in Bavaria. In fact it was what decided me that I would ask you to execute this commission for me.'

'The Graf is a charming man,' said my father. 'It was a very pleasant stay in the Black Forest. What an enchanting place that is. I shall never forget it.'

'I liked, too, the one you did of the Gräfin. You made her look like a princess of romance.'

'A beautiful woman . . .'

'I thought her features very irregular.'

'An inner beauty,' mused my father. 'Difficult to define in words.'

'But you captured it in paint. An etheral quality . . . yes. It gave a suggestion of goodness. A lovely piece of work. I can tell you the Graf was delighted. He showed it to me with great pride.'

My father beamed with pleasure. 'I hope that you will be equally pleased, Baron,' he said.

'I must be. I want the best you have ever done. My Collison must be supreme. I already have one Collison in my collection. You must see my miniatures. This one dates back . . . according to the costume . . . to the mid-seventeenth century. I fancy it was painted just after that time when the Roundheads were making such havoc in your country . . . as the mob did for us not so long ago. That miniature is one of my most highly prized.'

'Do you know who the subject is?'

'No. It is just called An Unknown Woman. But there is the distinctive K.C. in the corner. We had difficulty in finding it but I knew it was a Collison by the style. Having seen your daughter, I have come to the conclusion that it is a picture of a member of the family. There is a resemblance. Colouring and a certain' he paused and I could not read the expression in his eyes '*je ne sais quoi* . . . But I have always been aware of it.'

'I very much look forward to seeing that,' said my father.

'You shall. You most certainly shall.'

I was excited by the talk of art and his obvious knowledge. I was most eager to learn as much as I could about him and I felt I was not doing too badly. I knew that he was arrogant, rich, powerful, that he had always had his own way and planned to go on doing just that. He was knowledgeable about art and had a real feeling for it. It would be almost impossible to deceive him, I was sure. I was eager to talk with my father as to how we should deal with this difficult situation and the thought that it would begin the next morning filled me with apprehension.

When we rose from the dining table we went back to the room with the painted ceiling. Liqueurs were served there; I found the drink sweet and pleasant.

After a while the Baron said: 'Monsieur Collison is tired, I see. Bertrand, you will conduct him to his room. Mademoiselle Collison, I see that you are not tired. You would, I am sure, prefer to remain and chat a while.'

I said that was so, and Bertrand took my father to his room, leaving me alone with the Baron and Madame St Giles.

'Tomorrow,' he said, looking at me, 'I shall show you my treasures. Have you explored the castle yet?'

'Monsieur de Mortemer has been very good. He has shown me a little.'

The Baron snapped his fingers. 'Bertrand has not the feeling for the castle . . . wouldn't you say so, Nicole?'

'Well, it is yours, isn't it? He, like the rest of us, is but a guest here.'

The Baron patted Nicole's knee rather affectionately. I thought he must be on very familiar terms with her.

'Well, Mademoiselle Collison,' he said, 'you know how it is. This is my home. It is built by my ancestor and is one of the first the Normans built in France. There were Centevilles living here from the early days when Great Rollo came harrying the coast of France with such success that the French King said that the only way to stop this perpetual harassment is to give these invaders a corner of France, which he did. And there was Normandy. Never make the mistake of thinking we are French. We are not. We are the Norsemen come to France from the magnificent fjords.'

'The French were a very cultivated people when the

savage Norsemen came in their long ships looking for conquest,' I reminded him.

'But the Normans were fighters, Mademoiselle Collison. They were the unvanquished. And Centeville Castle was here at the time our great William the Duke conquered you English and forced you to submit to Norman rule.'

'The Normans won on that occasion,' I said, 'because King Harold had just come down to the south after winning a victory in the north. If he had been fresh for the fight, the victory might have gone the other way. Moreover, you say you defeated the English. The English of today are a mixed race. Angles, Saxons, Jutes, Romans . . . and yes, even glorious Normans. So it seems to me a little misplaced to crow over the victory of William all those years ago.'

'You see how Mademoiselle Collison corrects me, Nicole.'

'I am delighted that she puts forward such a good case against you, Rollo.'

Rollo! I thought. So that is his name. I must have shown my surprise for he went on: 'Yes, I am Rollo. Named after the first Norman to turn this corner of France into Normandy. His battle cry was "Ha! Rollo!" And it continued to be the Norman battle cry for centuries.'

'It is no longer in use, I trust.'

I could not understand this impulse in me to attack him at every turn. It was most unwise since we had to try to please him; and here I was antagonizing him before we began.

But he did not look displeased. He was actually smiling, and it occurred to me that he was enjoying the conversation. I was being as unpleasant as I could without being rude. How strange that he – who was used to sycophants – should not object. It must be because it was so rarely that anyone stood out against him.

But Nicole was by no means a sycophant. Perhaps that was why he liked her – as he obviously did.

Bertrand had returned.

He said to me: 'Perhaps you would like to take a walk in the grounds before retiring for the night?'

I rose with alacrity. 'That would be delightful,' I said.

'You need a wrap. Shall I go and get one?'

'Take mine,' said Nicole. 'It will save a journey up to your room. I don't need it.'

She handed me a scrap of chiffon which seemed to take its colour from whatever it covered. It was decorated with a border of sequinned stars.

'Oh . . . thank you,' I said. 'It looks too . . . pretty. I should be afraid to harm it.'

'Nonsense,' said Nicole coming to me, and herself put it round my shoulders. I thought she was very charming.

Bertrand and I went out through the courtyard to the moat.

'Well, what did you think of the Baron?' he asked.

'It's rather too big a question to answer briefly,' I said. 'It's like confronting someone with the Niagara Falls and asking for an immediate opinion.'

'He would be amused to hear himself compared with them.'

'I would say he is very conscious of his power and wants everyone else to be too.'

'Yes,' agreed Bertrand. 'He likes us to recognize that and to do exactly as he wants us to.'

'Which is all right as long as it coincides with what one wants oneself.'

'You are perceptive, Mademoiselle. That is exactly how it has been for me so far.'

'Then,' I said, 'you must be prepared for the day when it is not. I thought Madame St Giles charming.'

'She is considered to be one of the most attractive women in society. Her association with Rollo has lasted for several years.'

'Her . . . association!'

'Oh! Did you not guess? She is his mistress.'

'But,' I began faintly, 'I thought he was going to be married to this Princesse.'

'He is. I suppose it will have to end with Nicole then . . . or perhaps there will be just a lull. She's prepared for that. She's a woman of the world.'

I was silent.

He laid his hand on my arm. 'I'm afraid you are rather shocked. Did you not know that there was this relationship?'

'I'm afraid I'm rather unworldly. Nicole . . . she doesn't seem to be upset.'

'Oh no. She always understood that there would come a time when he would marry. He has several mistresses, but Nicole was always the chief.'

I shivered beneath Nicole's wrap. His hands would have been on that chiffon, I thought. I pictured him with Nicole . . . sensuous . . . cynical . . .

It was a horrible picture. I did not want to paint that miniature. I realized that one could learn too much about a subject.

The next morning our ordeal began. I arranged a chair for the Baron where the strong light fell on his face. My father sat opposite him. We had decided that the support should be ivory which had proved to be ideal since the beginning of the eighteenth century. I sat in a corner watching. I was memorizing every line of his face: the sensuous lips which could be cruel, the rather magnificent high brow and the strong blonde hair springing from his head.

He had told us that the completed miniature would be set in gold and the frame should be studded with diamonds and sapphires. For that reason he wore a blue coat and it certainly accentuated his colouring; it even put a hint of blue into the grey eyes.

My fingers itched to hold the brush. I was deeply aware of

my father. He worked quietly and without apparent tension. I wondered whether he was aware of how much he could not see.

This morning would tell us a great deal – whether it was possible to carry out this plan or not. I was not sure what sort of miniature I could do from memory or from my father's work. I was sure I could have made a superb portrait if I could have gone about it in the normal way. I would bring out his arrogance. I would capture that look which suggested that the whole world was his. I would paint in a little of the animosity I felt towards him. I would make a portrait which was absolutely him . . . and he might not like it.

He talked while my father worked and mainly to me.

Had I been to the Bavarian Court with my father? I told him I had not. He raised his eyebrows as though asking: Why not, since you came to Normandy?

'Then you did not see the picture of the Gräfin and her inner beauty?'

'I very much regret not having seen it.'

'I feel I have met you before. It must be in the miniature of the Unknown Woman. I suddenly feel she is unknown no longer.'

'I look forward to seeing it.'

'And I to showing it to you. How is it going, Monsieur Collison? Am I a good sitter? I look forward to seeing the work as it progresses.'

'It is going well,' said my father.

'And,' I added, 'we make a rule that no one sees a miniature before it is finished.'

'I don't know if I shall agree to that rule.'

'I am afraid it is necessary. You must give a painter a free hand to do what he wishes. To have your criticism now would be disastrous.'

'What if it were praise?'

'That, too, would be unwise.'

'Do you always allow your daughter to lay down the rules, Monsieur Collison?'

'It is my rule,' said my father.

He told me then about certain paintings he possessed – not all miniatures by any means.

'How I shall enjoy gloating over my treasures to you, Mademoiselle Collison,' he added.

After an hour my father laid down his brush. He had done enough for the morning, he said. Moreover, he guessed the Baron must be tired of sitting.

The Baron rose and stretched himself, confessing that it was unusual for him to sit so long at one time.

'How many sittings shall you need?' he asked.

'I cannot say as yet,' replied my father.

'Well, I must insist that Mademoiselle Collison remains with us so that she may divert me,' he said.

'Very well,' I replied, perhaps too eagerly. 'I shall be there.'

He bowed and left us.

I looked at my father. I thought he seemed very tired. He said: 'The light is so strong.'

'It is what we must have.'

I studied the work he had done. It was not bad but I could detect an unsure stroke here and there.

I said: 'I have been studying him closely. I know his face well. I am sure I can work from what you have done and what I know of him. I think I had better start immediately and perhaps work always as soon as he has gone so that I have the details clearly in my mind. We'll have to see how it goes. It will not be easy to work without a living model.'

I started my picture. I could see his face clearly and it was almost as though he were sitting there. I was revelling in my work. I must get that faint hint of blue reflected from the coat into those cold steely eyes. I could see those eyes . . . alight with feeling . . . love of power, of course . . . lust . . . yes, there was sensuality about the mouth in abundance. Buccaneer, I thought. Norseman pirate. It was there in his face. 'Ha! Rollo!' . . . sailing up the Seine, pillaging, burning, taking the women . . . oh yes, certainly taking the women . . . and taking the land . . . building strong castles and holding them against all who came against him.

I don't think I ever enjoyed painting anyone as much as I enjoyed painting him. It was because of the unusual method, I suspected; and because I had a strong feeling of dislike for him. It was a great help to feel strongly about the subject. It seemed to breathe life into the paint.

My father watched me while I worked.

I laid down my brush at length. 'Oh, Father,' I said. 'I do want this to be a great success. I want to delude him. I want him to have the Collison of all Collisons.'

'If only we can work this together . . .' said my father, his face breaking up in a helpless sort of way which made me want to rock him in my arms.

What a tragedy! To be a great artist and unable to paint!

It was a good morning's work and I was very pleased with it.

After *déjeuner* which my father and I took alone as Bertrand had been summoned to go off somewhere with the Baron and Nicole, I suggested that my father take a rest. He looked tired and I knew that the morning's work had been more than a strain on his eyes.

I conducted him to his room, settled him on his bed and then, taking a sketch-pad with me as I often did, I went out.

I went down to the moat and sat there. I thought of how Bertrand and I had come here and how we had talked and what a pleasant day it had been. I hoped we should see more of each other. He was so different from the Baron – so kind and gentle. I could not understand why women like Nicole could demean themselves as she had done for the sake of men like the Baron. I found him far from attractive. Of course he had great power and power was said to be irresistible to some women. Personally I hated all that arrogance. The more I saw of the Baron the better I liked Bertrand. It seemed to me that he had all the graces. He was elegant, charming and above all kindly and thoughtful for others – qualities entirely lacking in the mighty Baron. Bertrand's task had been to put us at our ease on our arrival and this he had done with such perfection that we had become good friends in a very short time, and instinct told me that our friendship had every chance of deepening.

While I had been thinking I had been idly sketching, and my page was full of pictures of the Baron. It was understandable that he should occupy my thoughts as I had to paint a miniature of him in a manner I reckoned no miniature had ever been painted before.

There he was in the centre of my page – a bloodthirsty Viking in a winged helmet, nostrils flaring, the light of lust in his eyes, his mouth curved in a cruel and triumphant smile. I could almost hear his voice shouting. I wrote below the sketch 'Ha! Rollo.'

Round the page were other sketches of him . . . in profile and in full face. I wanted to know that face from every angle and in several moods. I had to imagine those I had not seen.

Then suddenly I heard a laugh and turning sharply, I saw him. He was leaning over my shoulder. His hand shot out and he took the paper from me.

I stammered: 'I didn't hear you.'

'My grass is thick and luxuriant here by the moat. I confess . . . seeing you there so absorbed . . . sketching away . . . I crept up to see what could be of such interest to you.'

He was studying the paper.

'Give it to me,' I commanded.

'Oh no. It's mine. *Mon Dieu*, you are a very fine artist, Mademoiselle. Ha! Rollo. Why, that is magnificent.'

I held out my hand pleadingly.

'I feel as though I have been stripped bare,' he said accusingly, but his eyes had lost their steely grey. He was amused and pleased. 'I did not realize that you knew me so well,' he went on. 'And to draw this without a model! Why, you are a draughtsman, Mademoiselle. I often say that the reason so many artists today are mediocre is because they never learned how to draw. How did you come to know me so well?'

'I don't know you. I know a little of your face. But I was with you this morning during the sitting.'

'I noticed how you kept your gimlet eye on me. Mademoiselle Collison, *you* should be painting a miniature of me.'

'That is for my father,' I said. 'You can destroy that paper.'

'Destroy it! Never! It's too good for that. I shall keep it. It will always remind me of you, Mademoiselle Collison. I have something else to remind me too. The miniature of which I was telling you. You must see it. I can't wait any longer to show it to you.'

He held out a hand to help me to my feet.

I said: 'My father is resting. I thought he should do so.'

'Well, after a trying morning . . .' he said almost mischievously. 'Now you and I will go and see the miniatures, shall we? I refuse to wait a moment longer before showing you your double.'

I went with him into the castle. He was carrying my sketch-pad. Fortunately there was nothing else on it but a few sketches of trees and the moat.

He took me to a part of the castle where I had not been before.

'This section was restored in the mid-eighteenth century,' he told me. 'It's rather elegant, don't you think?'

I agreed it was. 'Entirely French,' I commented, and I could not help adding: 'Rather different from the comparatively crude aspect of Norman architecture.'

'Precisely,' he replied, 'but lacking the antiquity. Why, it is not a hundred years old yet. So modern! But a fine piece of architecture all the same. What do you think of the furniture? It was made by Gourdin and Blanchard Garnier.'

'Delightful,' I said.

'Come with me.' He opened a door and we were in a small chamber, the ceiling of which was painted with a celestial scene. Angels floated across a heaven of exquisite blue dotted with golden stars.

The walls were panelled and on these hung the miniatures. There must have been about fifty of them and they were all exquisite and of great value. They were of all periods dating back to the early fourteenth century and many of them were on supports of vellum and parchment, metal, slate and wood which was largely used at that time.

'They are beautiful,' I cried.

'I think so too. It's a delightful expression of art. More difficult to execute, I imagine, than a large canvas. The artist must be restricted. You must have very keen eyes for such work.' He hesitated and my heart started to beat very fast. For a moment I thought: He knows! Then he went on: 'I should have liked to be a painter myself, Mademoiselle Collison. I love art. I understand it. I can criticize it . . . see what is wrong . . . even feel I know how it should have been done . . . but I can't paint. That's rather a tragedy, don't you think?'

'You are an artist manqué,' I said. 'Yes, I do think that is rather sad. It's better I think to be born without the urge to paint than to have it and not be able to use it.'

'I knew you would understand. I lack the divine spark. Is that what it is? I could mix the paints. I have an eye for colour . . . but alas, the spirit which makes painting great is lacking. But let me show you my Unknown Woman.'

He took me to it, and I was startled. It could have been a painting of me. The reddish tint in the fine abundant hair escaping from the jewelled snood which held it . . . the tawny eyes . . . the firm chin . . . they might well have been mine. The Unknown Woman was dressed in green velvet and the colour of the dress brought out this striking tint in her hair.

He laid a hand on my shoulder. 'There! Now you see what I mean.'

'It's extraordinary,' I agreed. 'And it really is a Collison?'

He nodded.

'Nobody knows which one. You tiresome people always call yourselves K. If only you had had a variety of initials what a lot of trouble you would have saved.'

I couldn't stop looking at the picture.

'It's always been a favourite of mine,' he said. 'Now I need no longer call it the Unknown Woman. It now has a name for me: Mademoiselle Kate Collison.'

'Have you had it long?'

'It has always been in the family collection for as long as I can remember. I think in the past one of my ancestors must have been on very friendly terms with one of yours. Why otherwise should he have wanted a miniature of the lady? It's a very interesting thought, don't you agree?'

'It could have come into his possession in some other way. You don't know the identity of several of the people portrayed, I am sure. It is certainly a collection you can be proud of.'

'I shall hope to add two more to it shortly.'

'I thought the one . . . my father was painting was for your bride elect.'

'It is. But she will live here, and our two miniatures will be hung side by side on this wall.'

I nodded.

'I hope,' he went on, 'that I shall have the pleasure of showing you other treasures of mine. I have some fine pictures as well as furniture. You are an artist, Mademoiselle

Collison. Oh fortunate Mademoiselle Collison . . . a real artist . . . not an artist manqué such as I am.'

'I am sure you are the last person to feel sorry for yourself. Therefore you cannot expect other people to be.'

'Why so?'

'Well, you happen to think you are the most important person not only in Normandy but throughout the entire country, I imagine.'

'Is that how you see me?'

'Oh no,' I said. 'It is how you see yourself. Thank you for showing me the miniatures. They are most interesting . . . Now I think I should return to my room. It is time to dress for dinner.'

The days which followed were the most exciting of my life – up to that time. I had made two discoveries which could not be denied – one sad, the other exhilarating beyond my expectations. My father would not be able to paint miniatures again. I could see clearly that the necessary deftness of touch had deserted him. He could not see well enough, and to be the smallest fraction of an inch out of place in such a small area could change a feature entirely. He might go to larger canvases for a while but in time even that would be over for him. The other discovery was that I was a painter worthy of the name of Collison. I could put those initials on my miniatures and none would be able to question the fact that they had not been done by a great artist.

I could not wait to get to work every morning. I don't know how I sat through those sessions while my father worked and the Baron sat there smiling a rather enigmatic smile, making lively conversation with me or sometimes lapsing into what seemed like a brooding silence.

I would dash to the drawer in which I kept my work and take out that picture. It was growing under my hands; it laughed at me; it mocked me; it was cruel; it was amused; it suggested power and an immense ruthlessness. I had captured this man and shut him up in my miniature. To have brought all this into such a small space was an achievement, I knew.

My father gasped when he saw it and said he had never seen anything of mine – or his, for that matter – to equal it.

I began to think that this way of working was perhaps more rewarding than conventional sittings. I felt I knew the man. I could almost follow his thoughts. My excitement was so intense that I would find myself gazing at him during meals or whenever I was in his company. Several times he caught me at it; then he gave me one of those enigmatical smiles.

What strange days they were! I felt as though I had stepped outside the life I had known into a different world. The Farringdons, the Meadows, the Cambornes seemed miles away . . . on another planet almost.

This could not last, of course. I think perhaps it owed its fascination to the fact that it was inevitably transient.

I should go away from here. Forget the Baron who had obsessed me all these days; but the time I had spent here would in a way be caught up and imprisoned in the miniature.

Then there was Bertrand de Mortemer. Our friendship was progressing at unusual speed. It was a great joy to be with him. We rode together often. He described the family estate which was situated south of Paris. 'Not a big one,' he said. 'Nothing like Centeville . . . but it is pleasant . . . with the Loire close by and all those beautiful castles to make one feel proud every time one catches a glimpse of them.'

'I should love to see them.'

'They are far more beautiful than this stark old Norman fortress. They are built for living in, for celebrations, banquets, river pageants, *fêtes champêtres* . . . yes, for enjoying life, not fighting for it as they did in this grey stone castle. I feel so different when I'm at Centeville.'

'Are you here often?'

'Whenever I am sent for.'

'You mean by the Baron?'

'Who else? His father set himself up as head of the family and Rollo has inherited the crown.'

'Still, I suppose you could escape from the yoke.'

'Rollo would frown on that.'

'Who cares for Rollo . . . outside the precincts of the Castle of Centeville?'

'He has a way of showing his displeasure which can be uncomfortable.'

'Does that matter very much?'

'It's usually a practical displeasure.'

I shivered.

'Let's talk about more pleasant things. How is the miniature going?'

'Very well, I think.'

'Is your father pleased with it?'

'Very.'

'I dare say we shall be seeing it soon. What does Rollo think?'

'He hasn't seen it yet.'

'I should have thought he would have demanded to.'

'He doesn't exert the same power over visiting artists as he does in his family circle, you see.'

He laughed and then was serious. 'Kate,' he said – for some time he had called me by my Christian name. 'When it is over, you will go away from here . . .'

'If our work is approved we shall go to Paris to paint the Princesse.'

'But you will go from here . . .'

'And you?'

'I shall hear what I am expected to do. There is always

something. When Rollo asks me here it is for a reason. He has not yet explained that to me.'

'Can't you ask him?'

'He has not precisely said there is something. I am merely surmising there is because when I am invited here it is usually because I am going to be asked . . . no, *told* . . . to do something.'

'The more I hear of the mighty Rollo, the more I dislike him.' My lips curled. I was thinking of that gleam of acquisitiveness I was going to get into his eyes – cold grey with a hint of blue reflection from the coat he was wearing.

'He doesn't care about being liked. He wants to be feared.'

'Thank heaven I am beyond his sphere of influence. If he doesn't like my . . . my father's work . . . we shall shrug our shoulders and depart, taking the miniature with us . . . without the magnificent diamond and sapphire frame, of course . . . and perhaps it will be for sale in some London jeweller's. It would be rather fun to call it Portrait of an Unknown Man.'

'Yes, I can see that you are not in the least overawed by him. He sees it too. Everyone else is . . . except Nicole. Maybe that is why he is fond of her.'

'How can he be fond of her when he is going to marry someone else? I wonder Nicole stays here. Why doesn't she tell him to get on with his marriage and simply go away.'

'It is how things are in some circles. No one thinks any the worse of Nicole for being Rollo's mistress.'

'I suppose if she were the coachman's mistress it would be a different matter.'

'But of course.'

I burst out laughing. We both did. The incongruity of the situation struck us simultaneously.

We walked arm in arm through the gardens.

'Things are run differently in France from in England,'

explained Bertrand. 'We are more formal perhaps, but more realistic.'

'More formal certainly. I suppose Nicole's staying here in these circumstances is realistic because it is actually happening. But I do think it is . . . what shall I say . . . cynical.'

'Cynical perhaps,' he agreed.

'The Baron,' I went on, 'is certainly cynical. He thinks this is a perfectly normal situation . . . for a Baron. 'I want this woman,' he says. 'I no longer want this woman. It is time I married. Here is a suitable match. Goodbye, Nicole. Welcome, Princesse, to Centeville.' I suppose it is because she is a princesse that she is so welcome.'

'Undoubtedly.'

'And you calmly accept that?'

'I accept it because I can do nothing else. Moreover it is not my affair.'

'*You* are not like that, Bertrand, are you?'

He looked at me steadily. 'No,' he said. 'I am romantic and I think you and I are alike in some ways, Kate.'

He drew me to him then and kissed me; and I was very happy.

People came to stay at the castle – sophisticated people from Paris. In the evenings we dined in the great hall. There were no longer the intimate dinners. There was music, dancing and a great deal of gambling. Bertrand always sought me out at these gatherings and we would talk a great deal together. Our friendship was ripening. I would look for him as soon as I joined the assembly. He was so kind and always helpful. My father retired early on these occasions. He could see even less now than he could when we arrived in France.

The Baron took little notice of me when he was entertaining his guests, but I continued to observe him. My mind seemed divided between him and Bertrand. The contrast between them grew more and more marked. I thought of them as Beauty and the Beast.

Nicole acted as hostess, which surprised me yet once more. Everyone accepted her as the mistress of the place.

'It's rather like the King's mistress,' Bertrand explained to me. 'She was the most important person in France.'

People often talked to me about my father. These friends of the Baron were like himself, very cultivated and greatly interested in art and, as my father's daughter, I was accorded some respect.

Bertrand said: 'We live differently at home. Much more simply. I want you to meet my mother and sister. I am sure you will like each other.'

I thought that was almost a proposal.

On another occasion he said: 'In our little château there is a room which would be good to paint in. It's very light and another window could be put in.'

I was growing more and more fond of him and was happy and relaxed in his company. I was in a way in love with him, but I was not completely sure of the intensity of my feelings because it was difficult to direct them away from the Baron and the miniature. When that was finished, I promised myself, I would be able to sort out my true feelings. At the moment – and this was natural enough – I was obsessed by my work, even to the exclusion of Bertrand.

The time was approaching now. The miniature was nearly finished.

I gloated over it. I was almost sorry that it was nearing completion. I felt it would leave a great gap in my life.

One afternoon when the castle was quiet, my father was resting and everyone else seemed to be out. I went to the room to look once more at the miniature and perhaps put one or two finishing touches if I considered they were needed.

I opened the door. Someone was at my drawer. It was the Baron and he was holding the miniature in his hands.

I gasped: 'What are you doing here?'

He turned and faced me. His eyes were shining. 'It's superb,' he cried.

'You should have waited . . .'

He was looking at me slyly. 'It's not the first time I've seen it,' he said. 'I've watched its progress. There is no part of my castle that can be closed to me, Mademoiselle Collison.'

He looked down at the miniature. 'I can't stop looking at it,' he said. 'I see something fresh every time . . . It's sheer genius.'

'I'm glad you appreciate it.'

He laid the miniature down in a manner which I can only call reverent. Then he turned to me and greatly to my dismay put his hands on my shoulders.

'The man in the painting is ruthless . . . power-seeking . . . lecherous . . . cynical . . . It's all there. But there is one thing he is not, Mademoiselle, and that is a fool. Would you agree?'

'Of course.'

'Then do not go on believing that you deceived me for one moment. I knew what was happening from the first morning. What is it? Your father's eyes? Or have his hands become unsteady? He was a great artist once. It is becoming clear to me why you came with him. "I always go with my father,"' he said, imitating me. '"But I was not at the Bavarian Court. I was not in Italy with him. No. It is only to Centeville that I always come.' Dear Mademoiselle, I do not like to be deceived, but I will forgive a good artist a great deal.'

'You are right,' I said. 'That is my work. And now you are going to find fault with it and say that a woman cannot paint like a man and that although this miniature is tolerably good, it is not worth the price you agreed to pay . . .'

'Are you a little hysterical, Mademoiselle Collison?'

'I am never hysterical.'

'My confidence in the English is restored. I have always heard they are so calm in any crisis. Now . . . you are deceiving yourself as you attempted to deceive me. I admire your sex. There are many things you do . . . divinely. Where should we be without your sex? And I see no reason why a woman should not be given credit for her painting as well as all the other gifts she bestows on us for our joy and our comfort.'

'Then you accept the miniature?'

'Mademoiselle Collison, I would not part with this miniature for anything.'

'I thought it was to be presented to your fiancée.'

'To be brought back here and placed in my castle. I shall put it next to my lady with the hazel eyes and tawny hair, she who was an unknown lady to me and is now so no more. Mademoiselle, I am as you pointed out an artist manqué, but I know what is good art and let me tell you, you are a great artist.'

I felt tears in my eyes and was ashamed of them. The last thing I wanted to do before this man was show emotion.

I stammered: 'I am so pleased . . . that you care for the miniature.'

'Sit down,' he commanded, 'and tell me what is wrong with your father.'

'It is his eyes. He has a cataract forming.'

'That's a tragedy,' he said with genuine feeling. 'And so you came here to do his work for him.'

'I knew I could do it and that you would get value for your money.'

'Indeed. I have that. But why did you not explain? Why set up this ridiculous charade?'

'Because you would never have accepted a woman. You would have thought, because of my sex, I could not be as good as a man.'

'Yet I knew all the time and I think I am going to be as proud of this miniature as of any in my collection.'

'You . . . are more enlightened than most people.'

'Hurrah! I have found favour in your sight at last! All those sketches you did of me . . . they are excellent. Perhaps some day you will paint a full-length portrait, eh? I very much liked the winged helmet. Done with a little irony, eh? How many sketches have you of me, Mademoiselle Collison?'

'I wanted to get as many aspects of your face as possible and weld them into one. I did not want to miss anything.'

'There speaks my great artist.' He picked up the miniature again. 'It's not exactly a handsome face, is it? Not exactly a kindly face. There's cruelty in it . . . and all those unpleasant characteristics which alas you have discovered.'

'It is a portrait of you, Baron, not of Prince Charming.'

'Ah, you would have to get Bertrand to pose for that. As this is to go to my fiancée I think I shall call it 'The Demon Lover'. Do you think that appropriate?'

'Perhaps,' I said as coolly as I could. 'But you would know best about that.'

I was flushing a little. I felt he knew too much about me, and while I had been observing him I had not gone unnoticed in his eyes.

'Now,' he went on, 'what are you going to do?'

'I shall go to your Princesse if you wish me to.'

'I mean after that.'

'We shall go home.'

'And then? Your father cannot continue with his work, can he?'

'He is capable still of some work. It is only the very small and detailed work which he cannot manage.'

'I have a plan. I am going to show the miniature. Everyone wants to see it, you know. They talk of little else. I shall have a ball and the miniature will be on show. The Jeweller is already working on the setting. It will look magnificent nestling in that gold frame with sparkling gems surrounding it. Then . . . I am going to tell the truth. I am going to introduce you as the artist. I will tell the pathetic story of your father's encroaching blindness . . . and say that in his daughter we have an artist worthy to take her place with her ancestors.'

'Why?'

'Why? Oh come, Mademoiselle Collison. Don't you see? These are rich people. Many of them will be wanting a Kate Collison. I agree that there might have been prejudice against your sex. But your little deception . . . although it did not deceive me . . . has worked satisfactorily.'

I said: 'You will do this . . . for us . . .'

He smiled at me quizzically. 'I will do it for a great artist,' he said.

I did not want to stand there any longer with that strong light on my face. I did not want him to know how anxious I had been and how happy I was suddenly. And that it was due to him was ironical and hard to accept.

I murmured: 'Thank you.'

And turning I went slowly out of the room. He did not attempt to detain me. He stood still and I felt he was watching me.

When I saw the completed miniature in its jewelled frame I felt it was the greatest moment of achievement in my life. My father had been delighted that the deception was at an end, and that the Baron, far from being annoyed, was highly delighted, and was going to proclaim me as the artist at one of his lavish gatherings in the great hall of the castle.

He had talked to my father, commiserated with him on his affliction and congratulated him on having passed on his genius.

My father was happier than he had been since the discovery that he was going blind, and it occurred to me that all this euphoria had come about through the Baron whom I disliked so heartily.

He seemed to take a delight now in arranging our affairs. I was to go to Paris and my father should go home when he left Centeville. There was no longer any need for the deception. From now on – woman that I was – I should be accepted as a great painter and respected in the same way that my father and his ancestors had been. He, the Baron, would arrange that.

'Somewhere at the back of my mind I hoped it would turn out like this,' said my father when we were alone. 'I don't mind losing my sight so much now. You will carry on and the fact that you are a girl is not going to stand in your way. I feel I have done my duty. It is wonderful of him to give this . . . celebration or whatever it is . . . to launch you . . . to introduce you. He is such a powerful man that his word will count for a good deal.'

Bertrand regarded me with some awe.

'Why,' he said, 'you are more wonderful than ever. I suppose I must be more respectful to you when I speak to you.'

'You must be exactly as you were. I can honestly say it was you who made me feel so comfortable and at ease when I first came to work here. That feeling is necessary, you know, if good work is going to be achieved.'

'Then nothing has changed between us?'

'How could it be?' I asked, and he pressed my hand warmly.

Nicole came to congratulate me. 'The miniature is quite beautiful,' she said. 'A wonderful piece of work. The Baron is delighted.'

'He has told me so.'

'And he does want to . . . what he calls launch you. He hates to think you may be handicapped by your sex.'

'I was really surprised that he is prepared to take so much trouble,' I said. 'I suppose one shouldn't . . .'

She smiled at me. 'Judge one's fellow beings?' she asked.

'No. One certainly should not . . . until one knows all the circumstances – and it is rare for one person to know all about another. Now for the grand occasion. Rollo has put me in charge of it. He is going to make an announcement about you and tell them that you are leaving for Paris. You will probably find one or two people will want to make definite appointments with you to paint miniatures for them.'

'It is a great opportunity, of course. My father . . .'

'You need not worry about your father. If you are anxious about him the Baron will send someone back to England with him to look after him during the journey.'

'Would he do that?'

'But of course.'

'I am overwhelmed by all this kindness.'

'When the Baron takes action he is a rather overwhelming man. What do you propose to wear for the occasion?'

'I don't know. I haven't many clothes with me . . . and nothing in any case which would match up to these smart French society women. I suppose my green velvet will have to do.'

'Your green velvet is very becoming. Would you let my maid come along and do your hair.'

'That is kind. I know mine is invariably untidy.'

'You have beautiful hair and it is worth a little attention.'

She smiled at me serenely. I could not help liking Nicole. I should have loved to talk to her and ask her how she felt about this extraordinary situation. Here she was, like the mistress of the house, and accepted as such, when all the time her lover was making no secret of the fact that he was soon to be married to someone else.

The great day came. I was very excited and so was my father. Nicole's maid came to dress my hair and it was amazing what she did to me. She brought me a comb with green stones in it, the colour of my dress, and when it was fixed in my hair, I thought I looked like a different person –

not unworthy to mix with the soignée guests below. But perhaps that feeling would change when I moved among them as it used to even at the Farringdon Manor gatherings; one's appearance seemed to be able to undergo a great change between the bedroom mirror and the eyes of the other guests.

However, I had little time to think of my appearance. Everyone was admiring the miniature and calling attention to its excellence as they discovered something fresh which appealed to them.

The Baron took my hand and led me up to a dais. We mounted the few steps and I stood there with him on one side of me, my father on the other.

He then explained briefly my father's affliction and the fact that I had painted the miniature. They seemed to have no doubt that I was a great artist. There I was . . . so young and talented. He was certain that before the end of my life I was going to be the greatest Collison of them all.

People came up to congratulate me. I had to promise on the spot that as soon as I was free I would go to the house of Madame Dupont to paint her two daughters. It was a definite commission. A Monsieur Villefranche made me promise to come and paint his wife.

It was triumph such as my father and I had never dreamed of.

The Baron was smiling with a faintly proprietorial air. He was obviously delighted with the reaction of his guests.

When the musicians began to play a waltz he seized me and swept me off my feet.

'Do you dance as well as you paint, Mademoiselle Collison?' he asked. He was smiling. Here was a new aspect of him. He was really quite pleased by my success. I had not thought him capable of feeling pleasure for other people, but I supposed that as a lover of art he was so delighted with the miniature and there was also a good deal of gratification because he had been aware of the deception from the beginning.

I tried to keep up with him but his dancing was a trifle erratic. He had a trick of lifting me off my feet so that I felt as though I were flying through the air.

'A successful evening, eh?' he said. 'The start of a great career. My blessings on you.'

'I have to thank you,' I said.

'We are friends at last. Is that not charming?'

I said it was.

The dance came to an end. He released me and a short time after I saw him dancing with Nicole.

Many people sought my company that night. It was my time of triumph, and I was young and inexperienced enough to enjoy every moment of it. For me it was over all too soon.

The following day could not be anything else but an anticlimax. My father and I were to leave Centeville on the day after. My father would go home. The Baron had insisted that one of his men should accompany him. I was to be taken to the home of the Princesse where I should begin on my miniature. After that I could decide when I wished to execute the several commissions which had been offered to me, and I could plan my life from there.

I spent the morning packing and then took a walk round the grounds. I was joined by Bertrand who said that the Baron was out riding with Nicole and he thought he would be away until evening. On his return he wished to have an interview with Bertrand.

'It is coming now,' he said. 'I am to be given my orders. I think he probably waited until the miniature was completed before giving them to me.'

'Perhaps he merely wants to say goodbye. You will be leaving soon, won't you?'

'I plan to travel to Paris with you and your father.'

'That will be very pleasant for us.'

'I understand someone will be accompanying your father to England.'

'That is that I have been told.'

'Then you will have nothing to worry about. How do you feel about going to the Princesse?'

'Do you mean, do I feel nervous? The answer is no . . . not after what happened. The Baron has really done a great deal for me.'

Bertrand nodded. 'We will meet when you are in Paris.'

'That will be very nice.'

'You didn't think I would let you slip away, did you?' He looked at me earnestly. 'Kate, when you have finished this commission you must come and stay with my mother. She wants to meet you.'

'I should like that very much. I'll look forward to it.'

'Kate . . .' He hesitated.

'Yes?'

'There is something I have to say to you.'

'Well, I'm listening.'

'I . . . er . . .' He paused. 'I think I hear sounds of arrival. It may be Rollo is coming back already. He'll probably be wanting to see me. He must have changed his plans . . . I wonder what my orders will be. Perhaps we can talk it over later.'

'All right then . . . later.'

'Au revoir, Kate.'

He was smiling at me in a rather bemused way. I guessed what he had intended asking me. It must surely be that he wanted to marry me. I felt a certain pleasure at the prospect. I was not really sure. I had been living in circumstances alien to everything I had known before. It was understandable that I should be affected by them – and to such an extent as not to be able to make a sound judgement, I had known Bertrand such a short time, yet I should feel desolate if I should have to say goodbye to him and never see him again.

And yet . . . I was so uncertain. I was rather glad that the Baron had decided to return early and so had put off the moment of decision even for a little while.

It must have been an hour later when Bertrand came to my room. He seemed like a different man from the one I had known. His face was blotched and his eyes slightly bloodshot. His mouth twitched with uncontrollable rage.

'Bertrand,' I cried. 'What on earth has happened?'

He stepped into the room and shut the door. 'I am leaving the castle . . . at once.'

'When? Why?'

'Now. Immediately. I just came to tell you. I will not stay here a minute longer than I need.'

'You have quarrelled with the Baron?'

'Quarrelled?' he cried. 'I will never speak to him again. He's a devil . . . He's worse than I believed him to be . . . and God knows that was bad enough. He's a demon. I hate him. And he hates me too. Can you guess what he wants me to do?'

'No!' I cried, bewildered.

He spat out: 'Marry! Marry Nicole.'

'What?'

'He wants her settled comfortably . . . and he has ordered me to make an honest woman of her.'

'No!'

'But yes. That is what he has just told me.'

'How could he suggest such a thing!'

'He just did.'

'And Nicole?'

'I doubt she knows anything about the transaction. That's how it is with him. He makes the laws and other people carry them out.'

'But how could he suggest such a thing. What did he say?'

'He said that now he was marrying he wanted to find a husband for Nicole and he thought that I would fit the book very well. He would make her an allowance and one for me and I should be considerably richer than I am now. I just let him run on and then I shouted at him. I told him I would never marry his cast-off mistress.'

'He must accept that.'

'He didn't. He said I was a young fool. I was turning down a good offer. He wanted me to marry Nicole and that was the best reason in the world for my doing so. He was going to put all sorts of opportunities in my way. He would be my generous patron . . . I kept shouting at him that I would not marry a mistress he no longer wanted. I said I had my own plans for marriage.'

'You . . . said that?'

'I did. He didn't believe me. Then I said: "I'm fond of Kate, and I think she is of me."'

'What did he say to that?'

'He was stunned for a few seconds. Then he laughed at me. He said: "Nonsense. She'd never have you. In any case I should consider such a match most unsuitable." I lost my temper. I remembered all those times when we . . . my family . . . had had to do what he wanted. This was the last straw. I went on shouting about his throwing his cast-off mistresses at me and that I would never marry any of them. Then I went to my room and started getting my things together . . .'

'Oughtn't you to wait until tomorrow?'

'Stay under this roof! Never! There is an inn not far from here. I will go there for the night and then tomorrow morning I'll be waiting for you and we'll travel to Paris together.'

'Oh Bertrand,' I said. 'I am so sorry.'

'I had to make a stand some time. There comes a time when it is simply not possible to take any more. You gave me courage. He can do me no harm. He might endeavour to make us poorer . . . never mind that now. I can get by without him. Oh Kate, in a way I feel wonderfully relieved. I feel free. Do you think I was right to act as I did?'

'Absolutely right.'

'And don't you think it was a horrible thing to suggest?'

'Despicable.'

He took my hands and kissed them.

'Kate,' he said, 'will you marry me . . . when we've had time to work things out?'

'Yes,' I replied. 'I will.'

Finally he released me. 'I shall be out of this castle in a quarter of an hour,' he said. 'I will see you on the train to Paris.'

Then he had gone.

I was appalled by what Bertrand had told me, and I reproached myself for having felt I liked the Baron a little because of what he had done for me. He was ruthless, cynical and a man of no principles.

At dinner one or two people asked where Bertrand was and the Baron said that he had been called unexpectedly to Paris.

The next day my father and I left Centeville in the company of one of the Baron's upper servants.

I felt completely bewildered by everything that had happened. In a short time I had not only been accepted as an artist of repute but had become engaged to be married. I wished that I did not feel so uneasy. Had I perhaps been hurried into accepting Bertrand's proposal because of the Baron's despicable conduct? Poor Bertrand had been so distressed. I had felt I had to comfort him as best I could. It seemed to me that the Baron was changing the course of my life even if unwittingly, merely by being there – a malignant presence.

I was fond of Bertrand. Of course I was. I liked what I knew of him, but how well did I know him?

I wished I had not been so impulsive. I was of course

pleased that our relationship had not ended, but was I rushing ahead too fast.

I wished I could stop thinking about the Baron. It seemed so strange that a man who had done so much for me could have behaved as he had towards Bertrand.

It was fortunate that I was leaving the castle. When I had driven the Baron from my mind I would begin to see that life was offering me a wonderful future.

I must take it with both hands and be grateful for it.

The Streets of Paris

I loved Paris from the moment I entered the city, and I promised myself that I would see as much of it as I possibly could during my stay there.

First we saw my father off at the Gare du Nord and then Bertrand, who had accompanied us on the train to Paris, said he would take me to the house in the Rue du Faubourg Saint-Honoré which was the Paris home of the Princesse de Créspigny and where I was to paint the miniature.

I was received by a dignified manservant who begged me to come in, so I said goodbye to Bertrand, who promised to see me within a few days, while the manservant summoned a maid and told her to take me to the room which had been prepared for me.

It was a magnificent house, and I was impressed by the wonderful staircase which wound upwards from the reception area. It was indeed a small palace and from the moment I entered it I was struck by the rather subdued but what, in my opinion, seemed the faultless taste of the decor. There was a great deal of white – the faintest touch of red and a certain amount of gold. It gave an impression of unobtrusive richness.

We went quite a long way up and I had an opportunity of examining the intricate ironwork of the staircase.

'Madame la Princesse will see you tomorrow,' I was told. 'We have instructions to make you comfortable and supply what you need. Madame la Gouvernante will see you later. She thought you would wish to settle in after the journey.'

It was as well that I had improved my French lately for she spoke in an accent of the south which was not easy to follow.

We came to a landing and a door was opened. I was in a rather large, pleasant room. The double bed had white lacy curtains about it held back by gold-coloured bands. The oriental carpets were subdued in colour – pinks, blues and pastel shades; there were several pieces of furniture in the Louis Quatorze or Quinze period – highly polished and extremely elegant.

The maid asked if I would like hot water with which to wash and I said gratefully that I would.

While I was waiting I went round the room examining its contents. How different from the castle at Centeville! I wondered if this elegant house reflected the personality of the Princesse as the castle certainly did that of its owner. Even at this moment my thoughts went back to him. What impudence to attempt to pass off his discarded mistress to Bertrand. I was glad Bertrand had stood up to him so fiercely. It had just taken that to turn me impulsively towards him. When he became so angry he seemed to become a man I could admire – strong, determined. Previously perhaps I had wondered whether he were not too much in awe of the Baron, which had indicated to me a certain weakness and made me wonder whether the protective kind of love he inspired in me was the right sort one should have for a husband.

It was too bad to let that odious Baron intrude into this charming house. But of course he must intrude. He was the reason I was here. It was good of him to have acknowledged the quality of my work. No, I thought fiercely, it was not. It was just plain honesty. The biggest rogue on earth could be honest about art and dispense with the ridiculous prejudices which prevailed against women.

I wondered if the miniature of the Princesse would excite me as much as painting the Baron had done. It was hardly likely. There would not be the same intrigue and subterfuge, which although it had been frightening at times had in fact been very stimulating.

I washed and changed into a black skirt and white blouse and unpacked the rest of my things while I awaited the arrival of Madame la Gouvernante.

She came at length – a middle-aged woman wearing a black dress, very simply but elegantly cut. At her throat was a small diamond brooch, her only jewellery.

'Welcome,' she said. 'I trust you had a good journey. The Baron sent word that you would be arriving today but was unsure of the time.'

'It was good of him,' I said. 'We saw my father off and came straight here. My father is returning to England.'

'I am glad you speak French. Language can provide such difficulties. If there is anything you lack, you must ring.' She indicated the white rope hanging near the bed. 'I thought you would like your dinner sent up this evening. You must be weary after your journey. That will be in an hour's time.'

'That will be splendid,' I told her. 'The Princesse . . . er . . . is she eager to be painted?'

She smiled. 'The Princesse has been painted many times. She thinks little of it. You might find her an impatient sitter and I would advise you not to keep her too long at a time.'

'Thank you. I gather she is very young.'

'She is seventeen years old.'

'She should make a good subject.'

'I am sure, Mademoiselle Collison, you will see to that. Madame la Comtesse tells me that the Baron de Centeville has highly praised your talents.'

'It is kind of him.'

'He would not do so unless he meant it, Mademoiselle.' She was smiling at me. 'I suppose you are accustomed to going into people's houses.'

'Well, I have just come from the Château de Centeville, where I have been for nearly three weeks.'

'This is a change from the château, is it not? Those old castles are so draughty. But perhaps you do not mind.'

'This seems very comfortable certainly.'

'Madame la Comtesse likes her comforts.'

'Forgive me, but I am unaware of the household arrangements. Who is Madame la Comtesse?'

'She is a distant connection of the Princesse and is her guardian, as it were. The Comtesse is launching the Princesse into society and making the arrangements for her marriage. The Princesse is an orphan. Her family suffered greatly in the past troubles.'

'And you are her governess?'

'Oh no, Mademoiselle. I am the *gouvernante*, which means the *femme de charge* . . . of the household, you see.'

'Oh, I understand. In English we should say housekeeper.'

She repeated the word slowly, smiling as she did so.

'Now I know,' I said. 'It is good of you to take such care for my comfort.'

'I shall have food sent up to you . . . for tonight. Then we shall see. No doubt the Comtesse will say how things are to be done. You can see the Princesse in the morning. I will have *petit déjeuner* brought to you with hot water at eight o'clock. Would that be convenient?'

I said it would be very convenient and she went out, leaving me alone.

A feeling of intense loneliness swept over me. I missed my father. I wondered where he was now. Possibly preparing to cross the sea. I wondered where Bertrand was. On the way home, probably, to tell his family that he was planning to marry me and that he had had a quarrel with the all-powerful Baron whom he had vowed never to see again.

How different this was from arriving at the castle. I tried to recapture the feeling of excitement and apprehension, that determination to succeed in the most difficult project I had ever undertaken, and then the mingled feelings of exhilaration and revulsion which had resulted in attempting to know the face of that wicked man who was capable of such outrageous conduct.

But what a subject he had been! I was beginning to think that in painting him I had achieved my masterpiece. He had aroused such strong feelings; he had had such an interesting face. When should I ever find such a complicated person – wicked, ruthless . . . in fact one only had to think of the worst qualities in human nature and they seemed to apply to him. And yet he loved beautiful things and he had made an honest assessment of my work, and because he found it good he had defied the conventional belief of his sex that women should play an inferior role because it was all they were capable of. He had had the courage to stand up and say what he meant. Courage! It was no courage. He needed no courage to do and say whatever he pleased. He was all-powerful in his little world. He made the rules.

Ah, I thought, but there are times, Baron, when you find people who are not ready to obey you. Dear Bertrand! He was a fine young man, not to be dictated to by the worldly cynical Baron. I laughed aloud and said: 'Now, Baron, you will have to find another husband for the mistress you no longer want.'

Stop thinking of him, I commanded myself. This is a new assignment. You will never see the Baron again. Why let him intrude into this elegant atmosphere where everything is going to be so different from what it was in the Norman castle?

I had come here in a blaze of glory – acknowledged as a painter of merit. I was going to paint a seventeen-year-old girl – innocent, unmarked by life. A lovely subject for a portrait which did not demand too deep an assessment of character. The skin would be smooth and unmarked by time; no secrets in the eyes; no lines on the brow. A pretty picture –

that was what I was going to do now. An innocent virgin, I thought, who was going to be handed over for that monster legally to deflower. Poor child. I was sorry for her.

Then I said aloud: 'Stop thinking of the Baron. You have done your work for him superbly and he has rewarded you adequately. Be suitably grateful and forget him.'

My tray was brought in. It contained cold chicken with a little salad covered in an unfamiliar dressing, but very pleasant. There was a fruit tart and a carafe of white wine. It was all very palatable.

In due course a maid appeared to take away the tray and I thought I might as well retire for the night. It had not been exactly an exuberant welcome, but I must remember that I was really employed here. This was the real French aristocracy who, I understood, were more formal than any in the world. I should see more tomorrow, and in any case, within a short time I should be on my way home. I had decided that I would go back before coming out again for the two definite commissions I had – one with Madame Dupont and the other with Monsieur Villefranche – accepted on that night when the Baron had shown my miniature of himself.

My father had been all in favour of this arrangement. He had said I must definitely accept these commissions for they would help to establish me in France where, with the backing of someone as influential as the Baron, I was likely to get more standing than I should in Victorian England.

'Once you have a name,' he said, 'you can dictate what you will do. But get the name first. The name is everything.'

If I married Bertrand . . . when I married Bertrand . . . I should insist that I carried on with my painting. He would readily understand. He had made that clear already. Bertrand would be a very understanding man.

I was very fortunate to be loved by him. How different I was from the girl who had come out to France such a short while ago!

I took off my dress and put on a dressing-gown. Then I let down my hair and sat at the mirror on the dressing-table, brushing it. My thoughts went back to the night when Nicole had sent her maid to dress my hair. Poor Nicole! To be bandied about. I suppose people would say she should never have become his mistress in the first place. Her fate now was the wages of sin.

There was a gentle tap on my door.

'Come in,' I said.

A young girl entered. She wore a black dress with a white apron over it.

'I have come to see if you have everything you want.'

'Yes, thank you. Did Madame la Gouvernante send you?'

'No . . . I came because I wanted to.'

She had a small face with a pointed chin, a rather long nose and darting mischievous eyes.

She shut the door. 'Are you settling in?'

'I have only just arrived.'

'You're going to paint a picture of the Princesse, aren't you?'

'That's what I'm here for.'

'You've got to do something very nice.'

'I hope to.'

'You'll have to. She's not very pretty.'

'Beauty is often a matter of opinion. Are you a housemaid?'

She sat on my bed. I thought she was rather impertinent and was on the point of telling her to leave me. On the other hand I did not want to turn away any possibility of learning something about the Princesse who was to be my subject.

'What do you mean, a matter of opinion?' she asked.

'Exactly what I say.'

'You mean that she could look pretty to you though no one else thought so. So you're going to paint her pretty.'

'I shall paint what I see.'

'You have just painted the Baron de Centeville. How did you paint him?'

'The Princesse has the miniature now. Perhaps she will show it to you. Do you work near her?'

She nodded.

'Then perhaps you'll see it.'

'I have.'

'Then you know.'

'I think he looks rather . . . frightening.'

'Really. Now . . . I was just going to bed.'

'But I'd like to talk.'

'But I – as I said – am about to go to bed.'

'Don't you want to know about the people here?'

'I shall find out in due course.'

'Do you have to know a lot about the people you paint?'

'It helps.'

'You're a sort of sorceress.'

'I hadn't thought of myself as that.'

'I don't think the Princesse will like it if you pry.'

'Really, I must ask you to leave now.'

She sat up. 'Tell me about the Baron,' she said. 'He has twenty mistresses, they say . . . like Solomon or something like that.'

'I believe Solomon had more than twenty.'

'You don't tell anything, do you? That's because I'm just a housemaid . . . of no importance.'

'You go off to bed,' I said.

'Are you going to ring and have me removed?'

'Not if you go quietly.'

'All right,' she said. 'I could have told you a lot,' she added ominously . . . 'a lot you ought to know.'

'I am sure you could. But another time, eh?'

I pushed her out and shut the door.

What an extraordinary maid! I wondered what she could have told me about the Princesse.

I locked the door and got into bed, but it was a long time before I slept.

My tray came promptly in the morning and by nine o'clock I was ready. I did not have to wait long before Madame la Gouvernante was knocking at my door. She said 'Good morning' very civilly and expressed the wish that I had passed a good night.

Madame la Comtesse was ready to receive me and if I would follow her she would take me to her . . .

We descended the beautiful staircase to a lower floor and I was conducted to a salon furnished in white and gold with those rare touches of red. The furniture was exquisite and of the sixteenth and seventeenth century I guessed. But my attention was immediately focused on the Comtesse.

She was rather short and a little plump but carefully dressed to minimize this. Her hair was worn piled high to give her height; she was soignée and fitted the surroundings perfectly.

I must admit to feeling a little gauche, for clearly I did not pay the same attention to my appearance as she did to hers.

'Mademoiselle Collison!' she cried, advancing and holding out her hand.

She took mine in a limp handshake.

'I am pleased to welcome you here. Monsieur le Baron is so eager for you to do this miniature of the Princesse de Créspigny. He has such a high opinion of your work. I know the name, of course. It is well known here . . . but he says you are the first lady in that great line of painters.'

'I am eager to meet the Princesse and to start the work,' I said. 'I was wondering if there is a room where we can get the maximum light.'

'Yes, yes. All that has been considered. The Baron has told us what will be needed. But the Princesse has made it clear that she will not want to sit too long at a time.'

'Sittings are necessary,' I said. 'I think I must be allowed to decide the length of them. A painter may have discovered something exciting . . . and then if the sitter goes away before the discovery can be made use of . . . You understand?'

'Oh, you will have to work that out with the Princesse. She is very young.'

'Seventeen, I believe.'

The Comtesse nodded. 'She has been brought up quietly until a few months ago when I took her into my care and brought her to Court. It is necessary for me to keep . . .'

She paused and I said: 'A firm hand?'

'Exactly. It is something of a responsibility. However, I have sent someone to tell her we are waiting for her. She should be along at any moment.'

'Thank you.'

'Pray be seated, Mademoiselle Collison.'

I sat, looking uneasily at the door.

'You have come straight from the Château de Centeville?'

She was making conversation for she knew that I had.

'Yes, Madame.'

'You must have . . . er . . . spent a long time with the Baron . . . at your sittings, I mean.'

'Yes. He was a good sitter. He is a man who is greatly interested in art.'

'Let us hope that the Princesse will be equally good.'

She went to the bellrope and pulled it. There was silence until a maid appeared. She wore a black dress and white apron similar to that of last night's visitor, but it was not the same girl.

'Will you please go at once to the Princesse and tell her that Mademoiselle Collison and I are waiting for her in the salon.'

'Yes, Madame.' The girl bobbed a curtsey and was off.

The Comtesse sat down and made uneasy desultory and

rather disjointed conversation.

'She knew that you had arrived last night,' she said. 'I cannot imagine . . .' She bit her lip as though trying to curb her annoyance.

'I suppose she wants this miniature done?' I asked.

'The Baron wants it. Oh I have great responsibilities, Mademoiselle, great difficulties.'

At that moment we heard the sound of horses' hoofs and the Comtesse went quickly to the window.

She turned back to me.

'It's the Princesse,' she said. 'She is going riding.'

I went to the window. I saw the back of a trim, slight figure surrounded by a party of horsemen and women.

The Comtesse looked at me helplessly.

I lifted my shoulders. 'It's a pity. I wanted to get a start. If you will show me the room where I am to do the portrait I will prepare my materials, and then I thought I might take a walk.'

'Do you know Paris?'

'This is my first visit.'

'I should perhaps get someone to accompany you.'

'I prefer to be on my own.'

She hesitated. 'You wish to explore, I see. Do you find your way about well?'

'I think so.'

'Don't stray too far from this area. You could wander down the Champs-Elysée to the Tuileries. That should be very pleasant. I would not cross the river if I were you. There are many bridges across the Seine. Stay on this side and if you get lost then . . . take a fiacre . . . a cab . . . and you will be brought back to the Rue du Faubourg Saint-Honoré.'

'Thank you so much. I shall do that.'

'I apologize for the Princesse's behaviour.' She shrugged her shoulders. 'She has been used to having her own way. You know how it can be.'

'I understand,' I said, 'and I shall look forward to meeting her later.'

I went to my room and collected what I should need. Then I was shown the room where I should work. It was a kind of attic. Ideal, I thought, for there was plenty of light. I set out my paints, brushes and little palette. I prepared my supports and went back to my room.

I thought: Our little Princesse has high spirits and bad manners – but perhaps she thinks such behaviour is acceptable from a Princesse. I am already learning something about her without seeing her.

Now there was the excitement of Paris – and how that enchanted me! I loved the wide boulevards, the beautiful bridges and the old Palace of the Louvre. Best of all I loved the noise of the streets, the incessant chatter, the cafés outside which tables were set up under coloured sunshades, and gay music floated out. I did not need that vehicle to take me back. I found my own way. I was rather good at it.

I had enjoyed my morning and was grateful to my ill-mannered little Princesse who had made it possible.

Déjeuner was served in my room, again on a tray, and I wondered whether this was how I should take all my meals. It was clear that these people did not know how they should treat me. I expect they must have regarded me as a kind of servant. How different it had been at the château, where artists were considered to be of some account.

It was not important. I should complete my portrait and then go home before returning to France to carry out the other commissions.

Madame la Gouvernante came to my room after I had finished my food and told me that the Princesse and her party had not yet returned. She had learned that they were visiting a house on the way to St Cloud. They would probably be back soon and I should remain in so that I should be available if the Princesse needed me.

I accepted this, but it was not until past four o'clock when a summons came to me to tell me that the Princesse was in the attic waiting to receive me.

I went straight up. She was standing by the window looking out and did not turn as I entered. She was dressed in a very bright red ball gown; her shoulders were bare and her long dark hair loose. From the back she looked like a child.

I said: 'Princesse . . .'

'Come in, Mademoiselle Collison,' she said. 'You may start now.'

'That is quite impossible,' I replied. 'The light is not good enough.'

'What do you mean?' She swung round. Her face was vaguely familiar. Then it downed on me. I should have recognized her at once but for the red ball dress and loose hair which made her look rather different from the girl who had worn the black dress and apron on the previous night.

So, I thought, she plays tricks. And I knew then that she was going to make my stay difficult.

I went towards her and inclined my head. I was not going to curtsey to such a child; after all, royalty did not mean the same in France as it had before the Revolution.

'You see, Princesse,' I explained, 'I need the best possible light for such fine work. The morning is the only time I care to work . . . unless it is a very bright afternoon . . . certainly not on an overcast one like this.'

'Perhaps we should get an artist who can work at any time,' she said haughtily.

'That is for you to decide. I will merely say this: There will be no sitting this afternoon. If you are not riding tomorrow morning, I should like to start then . . . at, say, ten o'clock.'

'I am not sure,' she replied.

'I cannot stay here indefinitely,' I told her.

'Well perhaps . . .' she said grudgingly.

'Perhaps you would allow me to stay now and chat for a while. I must know something of my subjects before I attempt to paint them. May I sit down?'

She nodded.

I regarded her steadily. She had the thick Valois nose which, while it might proclaim her ancestry, did not fit in with modern notions of beauty. Her eyes were small but they were bright; her mouth was rather petulant but perhaps that changed with her moods. It should not be impossible to make a charming picture. She had the glow of youth; her skin was good, so were her teeth . . . if she could be prevailed upon to smile. The colour of the dress was quite wrong for her.

She said: 'You will have to give me a better nose.'

I laughed. 'I want to paint *you*,' I said.

'That means you're going to make me ugly.'

'Indeed it does not. I see possibilities.'

'What do you mean . . . possibilities?'

'Do you ever smile?'

'Certainly I do . . . when I'm pleased.'

'Well, we'll have you pleased. You have very beautiful teeth. What is the point of hiding them? A lovely smile would take off the length of the nose; and if you opened your eyes wide and looked interested they would brighten and look bigger. Also the dress is wrong.'

'I like the dress.'

'Well, that is good enough. We must paint the red dress because *you* like it.'

'But you say you don't.'

'No. Red is not your colour . . . nor is the black you wore last night.'

She flushed pink and started to laugh. She looked almost pretty.

'That's better,' I said. 'If I could catch that . . .'

'You pretended you didn't recognize me.'

'I recognized you immediately.'

'Not last night.'

'How could I? I had never met the Princesse . . .'

'And when you saw me here . . .'

'I knew at once.'

'And what did you think last night? Was I a good maid?'

'No. An impertinent one.'

She laughed again and I laughed too.

'I don't want this picture done, you know,' she said.

'I do realize that.'

'I *hate* having it done.' Her face crumpled suddenly and she looked like a frightened child. 'I hate it all . . .'

I understood. Moreover my attitude towards her had changed completely. I was sorry for her. Poor innocent child to go to that man!

'Was that why you were so ill-mannered this morning?'

'Ill-mannered?'

'In going riding when it was arranged that there was to be a sitting.'

'I don't think of it as being ill-mannered. We don't have to worry about . . .'

'Servants?' I said. 'Or artists . . . but perhaps artists are servants.'

'They come here to work for us . . . and are paid for it.'

'Do you know what one of your greatest kings once said?'

'Oh . . . history!'

'It is pertinent to the occasion. "Men make kings but only God can make an artist."'

'What does that mean? I thought God was supposed to have made us all.'

'It means that God gives the art of creation to a few chosen people and great ones are more important than kings.'

'That's the sort of thing they said during the revolution.'

'On the contrary, it was said by one of your most autocratic kings – François Premier.'

'I suppose you are very clever.'

'I'm good at my job.'

'The Baron said you were good, didn't he?'

'He appreciated my work.'

'You did a picture of him. He sat for you.'

'He did and I am glad to say that he was a very good sitter.'

'I suppose I shall have to sit for you.'

'It is the reason why I'm here. I should like to see you in blue. I think that would suit you. It would bring out the glow of your skin.'

She touched her face. I thought how young she was and I forgave her everything – her silly little masquerade of the night before and her rudeness in breaking her appointment. I saw her as a frightened child.

'Would you like me to see what you have to wear?' I asked. 'We could perhaps find a favourite dress of yours. I myself prefer blue, but it may be that you have something else which would be equally good.'

'I have a great many dresses,' she said. 'I have been presented to the Empress. I thought I should have some fun perhaps, but when the Baron decided to marry me that put an end to that.'

'When are you to marry?'

'Very soon. Next month . . . on my eighteenth birthday.'

She looked at me suddenly and stopped and it occurred to me that she would very easily share confidences. Poor child! I had discovered a good deal about her in a short time and I knew that she was lonely and frightened.

'How would it be if we decided on the dress now,' I said, 'and we could start the miniature tomorrow morning. I should like to be early . . . soon after nine o'clock. The light should be good then. The miniature, I understand, is to be mounted in the same way as the one I did of the Baron. It is in gold with diamonds and sapphires. It is absolutely magnificent, as you know. That is one of the reasons why I thought blue for the dress.'

'All right. Come on . . . now.'

She led the way down from the attic. Her bedroom was very grand – white and gold with rich carpets and beautiful tapestries on the walls.

'This house was damaged during the Revolution,' she told me, 'but the Emperor was very insistent that Paris should be beautiful again. They say Paris was like a phoenix rising out of the ruins.'

'It is very beautiful,' I replied. 'How fortunate you are to live in such a place.'

'Some people are happy without beautiful houses. I saw a girl in a modiste's shop when I was riding past the other day. A young man was with her and she was trying on a hat. He looked at her and kissed her. She looked so happy and I thought: She's happier than I am. And I wondered if she was going to marry the young man who kissed her. He would be someone she had chosen for herself.'

I said: 'You never know what is going on in other people's lives. I was once envious of a girl in a pastrycook's shop. She was serving the cakes and she looked so beautiful among all the loaves of freshly baked bread and fancy cakes. I had a governess then and I could not get my sums right. I hated arithmetic and when I saw that girl serving the cakes I said to myself: *She* never has to do horrid sums. How I wish I could change places with her. A few weeks later that shop was burned down and I heard that the beautiful girl had been burned to death.'

The Princesse was staring at me incredulously.

'So,' I went on, 'you should never envy anyone. You should never really want to change places for something you really don't know very much about. If you don't like what's happening to you, find a way out of it or accept it . . . whichever you think best.'

'Why . . . was the girl burned to death? Why did the shop catch fire?'

'Something went wrong with her father's ovens, I suppose. But it taught me a lesson which I'm passing on to you. Now, shall we look at the dresses?'

There were rows of them. I found a peacock blue silk which I thought would tone in well with the sapphires. I asked if she would try it on so that I could see her in it.

She was only too ready to, and when she had done so I decided it was just right.

'That's settled then. Tomorrow morning. Is nine too early?'

'Nine-thirty,' she said; and I knew that she would be there.

So began my acquaintance with the Princesse Marie-Claude de Créspigny. It flourished quickly. She apparently liked my attitude to her moods. I neither complained nor was I subservient; I just maintained a cool indifference. I was there to paint a picture and I wanted to do it as well as I could. Over the first sitting we became quite friendly. She talked a great deal, which was what I wanted. There was something very appealing and feminine about her. I would bring that out in the portrait . . . a complement to the overpowering bully of a man who was to be her husband. I would make the miniatures a study in contrasts – the overwhelmingly masculine man and the decidedly feminine woman. They would be an exquisite pair in their diamond and sapphire settings – both in blue – that lovely shade of blue. No wonder people called it heavenly.

I was enjoying this now. To sit in that room and paint – and not to have to do it surreptitiously as I had at Centeville. Ah, Centeville, there could never be another experience such as that! I laughed to think of all the precautions we had taken when all the time the Baron knew.

'You're smiling, Mademoiselle Collison. I know why. You are thinking of Bertrand de Mortemer.'

'Bertrand de Mortemer,' I murmured, flushing. She was delighted to see me momentarily embarrassed.

'Oh yes. I heard that he brought you here. And he said he would call on you. He is very good-looking. I suppose you like him a great deal.'

'I like him.'

'Shall you marry him, Mademoiselle Collison?'

I hesitated and she cried: 'Oh, you will. That will be so nice too. You'll become French. People do change their nationality when they marry, don't they? They take that of their husbands. Why shouldn't men take the nationality of their wives?'

'This is a weighty subject,' I said. 'Women are reckoned not to be as good at anything as men. But that is changing. See, here am I . . . an artist in my own right, though a woman.'

'I heard at first that you just helped your father and that he was the great artist.'

'The Baron changed that. He recognized fine art when he saw it – and rightly, he doesn't care who painted it.'

'Tell me what you think about the Baron?' Her mood had changed. It was sullen almost. I did not want that expression to creep in.

'He is a very artistic man.'

'I don't mean that.' She looked at me steadily and then she said: 'I don't want to marry him. I don't want to go to his castle. Sometimes I think I'd do anything . . . just anything to stop it.'

'Why do you feel thus about him? Do you know him well?'

'I have seen him three times. The first was at Court when I was presented to him. He didn't take much notice of me then. But my cousin the Comtesse said that he wanted to marry me. It was a good match and we were in difficulties over the estates. Money . . . it is always money. People never worried about it – so they say – before the Revolution. Now most people have to . . . people like us, that is. The Baron is rich. It would be a good thing if we got some money into the family. I am a princess and he likes that. My grandmother managed to escape the guillotine. She went to England for a while and had a baby there. That was my father. He was a prince, so when I was born I became a princess . . . without fortune, of course, but our family was a very noble one. You see, the Baron boasts about being Norman, but that does not stop his wanting to marry into the royal blood. It's something to do with children. I shall have to have a lot of children. The Baron thinks it is time he married and produced them, and because I'm a princess, I am the one chosen to bear them.'

'It's a familiar story,' I said. 'This sort of thing has been happening to people for generations. Very often it turns out well. Some of these marriages of convenience are very happy.'

'How would *you* like to marry the Baron?'

I was not in time to hide the look of revulsion which spread across my face.

'There. You have spoken . . . although you have said no word. You have seen him, you have spent some time painting his picture, you know what he is like. I dream of him sometimes. I am lying in the middle of a big bed and he is coming towards me. Then he's there . . . smothering me . . . and I hate it . . . hate it . . .'

I said: 'It would not be like that at all. Whatever his faults, the Baron would have good manners . . . er . . . in the bedchamber.'

'What do you know about his manners in the bedchamber?'

I quickly admitted that I knew nothing.

'Then how can you talk of them? I am so frightened of this marriage. Even if I got used to him, it would be terrible having all those children . . . all that discomfort and pain as well as the way of getting them.'

'My dear Princesse, I believe you have been listening to lurid gossip.'

'I know how babies are conceived. I know how they are born. Perhaps it is all right with someone you love. But when you hate . . . and you know he doesn't really like you . . . and you have to go on doing that for years and years . . .'

'This is an extraordinary conversation.'

'I thought you wanted to get to know me.'

'I do, and I understand how you feel. I wish there were something I could do to help you.'

She was smiling at me, sweetly, pathetically, and I thought: If I could capture that smile it would be beautiful.

'You might,' she was saying. 'Who knows? At least I can talk to you.'

That was the nature of our conversation. It meant that our friendship was growing, and I thought she was beginning to like me.

She certainly came punctually to her sittings and wanted to go on talking after I had laid down my brushes.

I now had meals with the Princesse and the Comtesse. I had heard the Princesse telling the Comtesse that artists must be treated with respect. God made them and men made kings.

She was a serious girl. I think she had probably had a sad upbringing and as an orphan had been passed from one member of the family to another – her great asset being her title.

After each sitting she would look at the portrait. I was pleased that she liked it.

'My nose looks inches shorter,' she commented.

'If that were true it would not be there at all. On a tiny picture like that a fraction of an inch can decide whether your nose is hooked or retroussé.'

'How clever you are! You have made me look much prettier than I am.'

'That is how I see you. You are prettier when you smile.'

'That's why you want to make me smile all the time, is it?'

'I like a smile for the portrait, but I like it anyway, and if I were not painting your portrait I should still want to make you smile.'

She did not say that she enjoyed the sittings, but it was obvious that she did. There were no more broken appointments and once she said: 'Don't finish it too soon, will you, Mademoiselle Collison?'

She wanted to know what I was going to do when I finished here. I told her that first I should go home. I described Collison House to her and the neighbourhood as well. She listened avidly. 'But you will come back to France,' she said.

'I have several commissions.'

'And you will marry Bertrand de Mortemer.'

'That's for the future.'

'You are lucky. I wish I were going to marry Bertrand de Mortemer.'

'You don't know him.'

'I do. I've met him at several houses. He is handsome and charming . . . and kind. I suppose you're in love with each other.'

'That would seem a very good reason for marrying.'

'Not a marriage of convenience for you.'

'I have no grand titles and I don't think he has vast wealth.'

'Lucky people!' She sighed and was sad again.

The next day she came to her sitting in a mood of excitement.

'I'll tell you right away. We are invited to a *fête champêtre*. Do you know what that is?'

'My knowledge of the French language makes it perfectly clear to me.'

'What do you call it in English?'

'Oh . . . an al fresco party . . . a picnic.'

'A picnic. I like that. Picnic.' She repeated the word laughing. 'But a *fête champêtre* sounds far more beautiful.'

'It does indeed. But tell me about this party to which you and the Comtesse are invited.'

'It is at the house and gardens of the family L'Estrange. Evette L'Estrange invites us. The house near St Cloud is very charming. The *fête* is an annual event with them. We have . . . what is it . . . a picnic? . . . in the gardens and fields. And there is the river and little boats and swans. It is very charming. Evette L'Estrange engages the best musicians to play for us.'

'You will enjoy it.'

'And so will you.'

'I?'

'When I said *we*, I did not mean the Comtesse. I meant you and me. They are anxious to meet the famous artist. They have heard of your fame.'

'I don't believe it.'

'Do you tell me I lie, Mademoiselle? Let me tell you that the Baron is so pleased with the picture you did of him that he is telling everyone about it. It seems as though a great many people want to meet you.'

I was overwhelmed. I did not know whether I was pleased or not. I did not want too much to be expected of me until I had proved myself. I had had my success with the Baron's picture, but first I wanted to make sure that I could repeat it. I wanted to build up gradually. At the same time all this appreciation was very sweet.

'What shall you wear?' demanded the Princesse. 'You haven't any *fête champêtre* clothes have you?'

I agreed that that was very likely, and she said that she

thought her seamstress could make a dress for me in an afternoon. It had to be rather simple . . . it was that sort of occasion.

'Rather like Marie Antoinette playing at being a country girl at the Hameau.'

'You seem to know a great deal about our history. More than I do.'

'You would find it interesting to know more perhaps.'

'What I do know is the sort of dress you must have. Muslin with sprigs of flowers on it . . . green for you . . . and a white straw hat trimmed with green ribbons.'

She was as good as her word and the next day the dress was made. The material was not muslin but fine cotton and the decoration little green bells not sprigs of flowers. It didn't matter. It was charming to see the Princesse so pleased and determined to make me look right for the *fête champêtre*.

She and I went off together in the carriage. There was a certain air of recklessness about her which puzzled me. I thought how childish she was since the prospect of an entertainment like this could drive all thoughts of her marriage from her mind; she certainly knew how to live in the moment, which was perhaps just as well.

It was a very pleasant afternoon. I was warmly received by Evette L'Estrange – a young woman with a much older husband. There was a stepson, Armand, who must have been about twenty years old.

Several people came up to tell me that they had heard of the wonderful portrait I had done of the Baron de Centeville, and they hoped they might be allowed to see the one I was painting now.

It was all very enjoyable.

And then I had my surprise. The food was about to be served and tables had been set up in the large field. Flunkeys were running about in all directions and the white tablecloths looked very pretty fluttering in the light breeze. They were undoing the hampers and taking out cutlets, cold venison, chicken and pies with a variety of sweetmeats. Wine was sparkling in the glasses.

Someone from behind me said: 'Shall we find a place and sit together.'

I swung round. Bertrand was smiling at me.

He took my hands and held them tightly; then he kissed me on either cheek.

'Kate,' he said, 'it's wonderful to see you.'

'Did you . . .'

'Did I know you would be here?' He nodded. 'Evette L'Estrange is a great friend of my mother. My mother is here. She is with my father and sister. They wish to meet you. They are delighted and are wondering what such a famous lady can possibly see in me.'

I gasped. 'Famous!' I cried. 'But it is only since the . . .'

I stopped, not wanting to mention his name on such a day. This was a day for happiness.

The weather was perfect. The sun warm but not too hot. Elegant men and women . . . they all seemed beautiful and they were all charming and kind to me. It was indeed a wonderful day.

I was warmly accepted by the Mortemer family. I knew then that I wanted this marriage. It was the first time I had felt so sure. Previously I had thought that I had been carried along too fast and too many new impressions had come too quickly. Bertrand had seemed delightful because he was such a contrast to the Baron. Everything had been so different from what I had known before. I had been bemused, bedazzled by different customs and people who seemed so far apart from the mundane life at Farringdon. But now I felt at home here, and it was Bertrand's people who had made me feel that.

I had a long talk with his mother, who said she quite understood that I should want to wait a little time before marrying. She had explained this to the impatient Bertrand. She said: 'It has all been so quick, my dear. You have been rushed off your feet. Go home and tell them all about it . . . and then you will see that it is right for you.'

I thought she was charming and I liked his father and sister. Elegant as they were, there was a homely charm about them – and by that I meant a naturalness. And I was happy with them.

'You must bring your father out to visit us,' they said. 'The families must get to know each other.'

That seemed an excellent idea, I replied. I had some commissions to do and should have to come back to France very soon. I wanted to go home first, though, because I was a little anxious about my father.

She understood perfectly.

That was a cloudless afternoon and one which filled me with delight – almost – because I felt I knew which way I was going. But two things did happen in the late afternoon which caused me a prick or two of anxiety.

Bertrand and I had left the rest of his family and taken one of the boats to row down the river.

I sat back under my sunshade while Bertrand rowed. He sat there smiling contentedly, talking of our marriage.

'We shall not be rich,' he said, and added smiling: 'But you will have to earn a lot of money for us with your painting.'

'I should like to do that.'

'Not for the money . . . for the love of art, eh? I want you to be happy, Kate, and you never would be without your painting. We will turn one of the rooms at Mortemer into a studio for you.'

'That would be lovely.'

Oh, it was a perfect day.

'You will plan how you would like it when you come to stay with us. My mother said you have promised to come . . .

you and your father. Perhaps then we can make all the necessary arrangements.'

'For the room?'

'For our marriage. For both.'

'I should like a room similar to the one at Centeville.'

It was tactless. I had brought a shadow into the perfect day. I should never have mentioned Centeville.

He was silent and I saw the anger in his face. He clenched his fist and said: 'I could murder him.'

'Don't think of him . . . on a day like this.'

But Bertrand could not stop thinking of him. 'If you could have seen him . . .' he went on. 'He sat there . . . smiling. "I want her settled," he said. "I'm fond of Nicole. You like her, too. You won't suffer for it . . ." I could not believe my ears.'

'Never mind,' I said soothingly. 'It's over. You told him clearly what you thought of such a suggestion.'

'He looked at me as though he could have killed me when I shouted at him. It's not often people shout at him. I said: "Keep your cast-off mistress. I wouldn't touch any woman of yours. It would make me sick every time I went near her. I'd think of you with her . . . all the time."'

'Forget it,' I pleaded. 'It's over.'

But Bertrand could not stop. He went on: 'He said: "You're going to marry my mistress and not be a fool. It'll be the making of you." I went mad then. I shouted at him. I told him: "Never, never, never . . ." And then I came away. I don't suppose anyone has ever spoken to him like that before.'

'You made your feelings very clear to him. Now, do let's forget him. You need never see him again. He might try to harm you. But how could he? Financially? Never mind. We don't want money that comes through him. I'll paint. It will be a wonderful life.'

He smiled at me and went back to his rowing in silence. But the magic had gone from the day.

The other incident concerned the Princesse.

I saw her come out from the woods along the river bank, hand in hand with Armand L'Estrange. She looked flushed and very happy and there was about her an air of . . . what I can only describe as proud defiance. For a moment I was startled; and then I thought: She is only a child.

We were silent as we rode back to Paris. I thought how beautiful the city looked in the fading light as we came through the Bois de Boulogne past the Arc de Triomphe and into the Rue du Faubourg Saint-Honoré.

At length the Princesse spoke. 'What an exciting day! For both of us, I think. So it is now definite. You are going to be Madame de Mortemer. As for me . . . who knows?'

She was so happy. I was not going to make the mistake of mentioning the Baron's name for the second time that day.

The day after the *fête champêtre* the Princesse was not well. She was pale, listless and depressed. Poor child, I thought. Her coming marriage alarms her so much and she can't forget that it is coming nearer and nearer every day. She did not look in the least like the pretty young girl who was beginning to emerge in the miniature. Marie-Claude was no beauty; her features were irregular and the lower part of her face too heavy; she had to be happy to be attractive. She was effervescent by nature, and when I thought of the happy girl at the *fête champêtre* she seemed to bear little relationship to this pale-faced girl in the bed.

She did not leave her room and sittings were cancelled.

She did ask me to sit with her, which I was glad to do. At times I thought she was on the point of confiding in me but I did not encourage this because I knew it was going to be about her fears for her coming marriage, and there was little I could say to comfort her about that. To tell her that marriages of convenience often turned out happily was banal really. I tried to put myself in her place. I was sure I should have done something about it. But how could I preach rebellion to my poor helpless little Princesse?

I tried to talk of other things – of my home and the life we led in Farringdon; and sometimes I made her smile a little.

I took a walk every afternoon. Each day the spell of Paris wove itself more tightly about me. I was enchanted by this beautiful city and I thoroughly enjoyed exploring it. Marie-Claude thought I was very adventurous, for she was naturally not allowed to go out without a chaperone. I felt free – independent of everyone. After all, here I was executing a commission for a nobleman of France. When I came to think of it, the Baron had done a good deal for me. Not only had he given me acknowledgement of my art but he had made a person of me in my own right. I suppose I should be grateful for that.

I must stop thinking of the man. He had even intruded into the wonderful afternoon of the *fête champêtre* and brought an ugly cloud. Because of him poor Marie-Claude was suffering at this moment – for I was sure her illness was nothing more than an attack of nervous apprehension. Meanwhile her indisposition gave me free time to explore during an extended stay in Paris. I was not sorry, because I was a little troubled by the miniature. I did want to get something as good as the one I had done of the Baron but at the same time I was eager to make the Princesse appear at her most attractive. Oddly enough, the Baron had been an easier subject.

I would go out every afternoon at two o'clock precisely and I covered a great deal of ground, for I was a good walker. I wandered through the streets – down the Avenue du Bois de Boulogne to the Louvre and found my way to the Gardens of the Luxembourg. Most impressive of all was the great Cathedral of Notre Dame. From the moment I entered it I felt a tremendous excitement. It was gloomy inside and a scent of incense hung in the air. I explored a little, but I knew this was not the way to see the cathedral and that I should come back and back again for as long as that were possible. All that I had ever heard about the place came flooding back to me. I remembered that our own Henry the Sixth had been crowned King of France here more than four hundred years ago. Later Henri of Navarre had married Marguerite de Valois – in the porch because as a Huguenot he was not allowed inside – and that marriage had been followed by the terrible massacre of St Bartholomew; and twenty years later when he had taken possession of the city, the same Henri, having agreed to become a Catholic, had said it was worth a mass.

I was fascinated by the hideous gargoyles, and I stood for a long time gazing from one to another wondering why it had been thought necessary to adorn – but perhaps that was hardly the word – such a holy place with such demoniacal figures. The expressions in the faces were something one would see in nightmares. Indeed I wondered whether I should ever forget them. What did they mean to convey? Cunning . . . yes, that was there . . . cruelty, lust, greed . . . all the seven deadly sins. And above all, I think, a certain cynicism.

As I stood there looking at them, one of these – the most saturnine of them all – seemed to move and the features slide into a different shape. For a moment I thought it was the Baron who was looking at me. He looked like a demon. What had he called himself? The Demon Lover? Lover! It was hardly likely that he would ever love anyone but himself. I stared. The stone had set back into that cruel face and it could have been laughing at me.

I must get that man out of my mind.

I had stayed longer than I realized and decided I would take a cab. There was one waiting by the cathedral and I hailed it, gave the *cocher* instructions. He touched his white hat and we set off.

After that I made a habit of using cabs. I found that I could wander where I liked, stay longer and then simply hail a cab and be back at the house at the time I set myself.

The Princesse was always interested to hear where I had been and I liked to talk about my little trips. I think she was beginning to see Paris through new eyes.

I told her that I had been to the cathedral and how enthralling I had found it. I intended to go back the following day.

'It's quite a long way.'

'I'm a good walker and I can take a cab back.'

'You are lucky, Mademoiselle Kate. How wonderful it must be to be free.'

I looked at her sadly. I knew that this illness of hers was just a desire to hold back time. She did not want the miniature to be finished; here in her bed she found a small refuge against the encroaching future.

The following morning when I was preparing to go out after *déjeuner* at the usual hour of two o'clock she asked if I was going to Notre Dame and if so would I call in at the little modiste's shop close by. She wanted me to take a note there. It was about a hat she wanted made.

I went to the cathedral. I had taken a sketch-book this time and I sat inside and made a few sketches, but all the time what I really wanted to sketch was the gargoyles. I did some from memory, but I thought I invented expressions and in all of them there was something which reminded me of the Baron.

I came out of the cathedral and found my way to the modiste's shop. I delivered the message and took a cab back to the house.

When I went in to tell Marie-Claude that I had given in the note she seemed better.

'I want you to go again tomorrow,' she said, 'and make sure the modiste can carry out the order.'

The next day I did the same. They were still waiting for delivery of the material, they told me.

I went back in a cab. I really enjoyed these trips across the City, and I was beginning to know the streets through which we passed. I had a good sense of location and when I returned to the house and talked to Marie-Claude I felt a great desire for this to go on. Like her, I did not want time to pass too quickly; like her, perhaps I was apprehensive about the future and that was what made the present so desirable. I was still unsure about my marriage. Wasn't I marrying into a foreign country and to a man whom I had known for a very short time? Had Marie-Claude made me realize the pitfalls one could find in marriage? Had I plunged into this relationship too impulsively? Was I caught up in the excitement of so much that was new? Would I do better to go home and think about it all for a while?

Each day I said: 'Do you feel ready to resume the sitting?'

'Another day,' she would insist.

But the next day it would be 'Not just yet . . . perhaps tomorrow.'

I had paid several visits to the modiste's shop. 'I am so eager to hear that she has what I want,' said Marie-Claude. 'It is so important that it should be exactly right. So you still go to Notre Dame?'

'I am interested in the surrounding district. But . . . I can always go wherever you want me to.'

'Thank you. Don't wander into any of those narrow winding streets which I believe are somewhere near the cathedral. There is a district where they used to make the dyes . . . and there are streets where women live . . . the Street of Prostitutes. Oh dear. Mademoiselle Kate, take care and do not go there. There are thieves who have all sorts of ways of robbing you. You can't imagine how wicked they can be.'

I assured her that I could.

'So avoid the narrow streets. The Emperor has widened a great many of the roads, but there are still some of those wicked ones remaining.'

'Never fear. When in doubt I take a cab.'

'Are the *cochers* polite?'

'Moderately. Some of them pretend they cannot understand me. It's my accent, I suppose. They make me repeat Faubourg Saint-Honoré sometimes, and for the life of me I cannot see the difference in the way in which I say it and the way they do.'

'It's because they know you're a foreigner and they probably guess that you're English at that.'

'A double fault,' I said lightly. 'Oh, I have no fear of the *cochers*. I like them. In fact they all look alike in their blue coats and white hats.'

'Don't forget to call at the modiste's.'

I did call there and it was after that when the strange thing happened and I was plunged into terror.

I went to the shop. Yes, there was good news. The materials had arrived and Madame would give me a note to take to the Princesse describing in detail what they had. They would go ahead with the work as soon as she gave them permission.

I came out of the shop. It was a rather hazy afternoon – hot but not sunny. I looked for a cab. Sometimes I had to walk a little way before I found one, but on this afternoon one was just cruising past as I emerged. The *cocher* slowed down. I stepped towards him and told him where I wanted to go. There was no pretence this time of not understanding.

I settled down, delighted that my mission to the modiste had at last proved successful. I wondered vaguely why the Princesse did not send for the modiste. Why did she send those messages back and forth? She must be buying lots of hats and gloves for her wedding. I would ask her. I had been so immersed in my own daily adventures, and because of my love of exploration and complete fascination with the Cathedral I had not given much thought to the matter until now. Marie-Claude was a strange girl and was capable of making an adventure out of buying hats.

I looked up. I did not know the street we were in. Perhaps in a moment we would break into one of the familiar boulevards.

We did not. I thought the driver was driving rather fast.

I called out: 'Did you hear me correctly? I want to go to the Rue du Faubourg Saint-Honoré.'

He turned his head slightly and shouted: 'A short cut.'

I sat back. A short cut! But where were we?

Five minutes later I started to get seriously alarmed. I called out: 'You are not taking me to the Saint-Honoré.'

He did not look round but merely nodded.

Then I thought of Marie-Claude's warnings. They did like to play tricks on foreigners. He was going to pretend he had not understood my accent and taking me out of my way would demand a large fare.

'Stop!' I cried. 'I want to talk to you.'

But he did not stop. He whipped up the horses and we were now travelling at a great speed and I was getting really frightened. Where was he taking me . . . and for what purpose?

I looked out of the window. I had never seen this district of Paris before. I believed he was taking me away from the centre of the City.

The palms of my hands were clammy. What did it mean? What could his motive be? Was he going to attack me? I imagined him driving his cab into some dark coach-house. Perhaps he would kill me. What for? I had little jewellery. I did not look exactly rich.

I must do something. We were still in a built-up area and were passing through streets with shops on either side. I must try to attract someone's attention. I must not allow myself to be driven out of the built-up area.

I knocked on the window. No one looked my way. I supposed I could not be heard above the noise of the street.

We had rounded a bend in the road. Ahead of us cabs and carriages were close together. My mysterious *cocher* had slackened speed. He had to. There was no help for it.

Now, I said to myself. Now. It could be my only chance.

I opened the door and jumped down into the road. Someone shouted at me. It must have been the driver of an oncoming cab. I was quick. I dashed almost under the horse's nose and I was on the pavement. I started to run and I did not stop running for fully five minutes.

Then I paused and looked about me. I was in a street I did not know, but it was comfortingly crowded with shoppers. Outside a café people were sipping coffee or apéritifs. Men and women strolled by and young girls with bandboxes on their arms hurried past me. I looked about for a cab. I should be terrified to get into one again; but I had to. It was absurd to be afraid. They had always been all right before.

People looked at me curiously and looked away, dismissing me no doubt as a tourist, gazing about as she explored the town.

I started to walk and it seemed that I walked for miles, but my sense of direction was good and I knew I was going the right way. I must have walked for nearly an hour when the familiar towers of Notre Dame loomed up in the distance.

I knew where I was then.

I had to take a cab. I could not possibly walk all the way back. There were plenty about now. Would I know my *cocher* again? What if he had followed me and was waiting to pick me up?

I had to take a chance.

I hailed a cab. My relief was intense. The *cocher* was a middle-aged man with a big moustache. I asked if he would take me to the Rue du Faubourg Saint-Honoré.

'But certainly, Mademoiselle,' he said with a smile, and soon we were rattling along the familiar streets.

With great relief I entered the house. I had emerged from a terrifying adventure . . . unharmed.

As soon as I was in the house I remembered the note which I had carried for the Princesse. I took off my cloak and went immediately to her room.

'Have you got . . .' she began. She stopped. Then she went on: 'Mademoiselle Collison . . . Kate . . . what has happened? You look as if you have seen a ghost.'

I said: 'I have just had a terrifying adventure.'

She clutched the letter in her hand and was already opening it. 'What?' she cried.

She glanced at the letter and her lips curled up at the corners. Then she looked at me waiting.

I said: 'I went into the modiste's shop and when I came out I got into a cab. There seemed nothing unusual about it. The *cocher* looked like all other *cochers* in his blue coat and white hat. Then I noticed we weren't going the right way. I spoke to him. He said it was a short cut. But soon . . . I knew he was taking me somewhere else . . .'

'Kate! What for?'

'I've no idea. He drove me across the City, and when he knew that I'd realized something was wrong, he started to drive very fast. I knew then that he had been waiting for me . . . with his cab . . . It was just outside the modiste's. He wasn't going to stop. Thank God we got into a huddle of traffic and I was able to jump out. Otherwise . . .'

'Otherwise? Oh . . . what can it mean?'

'I can only think that he was going to rob me . . . perhaps murder me.'

'Oh no!'

'But surely if it was robbery, he would have chosen

someone else. There was nothing I had that was worth taking all that trouble for.'

She was looking at the letter in her hand. Then she said slowly: 'You had this. That was what it was. It was the Baron. He knows. It is one of his men. He has spies everywhere. He knew. He wanted the letter.'

'Tell me what you mean,' I commanded.

'This letter is nothing about hats. I use the modiste as a sort of *poste restante*.'

'Who was the letter from?'

She hesitated and then said: 'Armand L'Estrange.'

'So you have been carrying on a correspondence with him and I have been your courier?'

She nodded. 'I knew the modiste would help so I arranged with her to take letters from me to him and for him to leave his there to be collected.'

'I see,' I said slowly.

'You don't see half of it. I'm in love with Armand. That's what makes everything so much worse. We're lovers, Kate. Real lovers. I mean we have been with each other as married people.'

'Oh!'

'You're shocked. You pretend to be so advanced, but you're shocked. I love Armand and he loves me.'

'Perhaps a marriage can be arranged. It is not too late.'

'The Baron has decided to marry me!'

'It takes two to make a decision.'

'No one would ever let it happen. Armand wouldn't either. The Baron could ruin him. But that doesn't prevent our . . . being together . . . when we can arrange it.'

'But you are so young.'

'I'm old enough. I am seventeen. It started before my seventeenth birthday. Don't think the first time was at the *fête champêtre*.'

I was trying hard to take in what this meant. It was

following too closely on that other shock for me to think clearly. I was so sorry for the poor girl lying in the bed. She was truly terrified.

She said, her voice shrill with fear: 'He knows. He has discovered. He knew you went to the modiste's shop to collect the notes and deliver them, so he had you waylaid. You would have been driven somewhere and the note taken from you.'

'It is too wild a scheme.'

'Not for him. Nothing is too wild for him. He would have a watch on me. Perhaps he had heard rumours about me and Armand. People talk and he would have ways of making them talk. He has heard rumours and tracked me down to the modiste's. That was why you were waylaid. Thank God you escaped. If this letter had fallen into his hands . . .'

For a while I believed her because I was so shaken by my own experience. I thought of her experimenting with love, for I was sure that was what it was. She was so young; she had lived in such a sheltered fashion; it was cruel to force her into marriage with such a man.

I tried to comfort her, and as I did so I began to see how absurd her conjectures were.

'My dear Princesse,' I said, 'if he had known there was a note at the modiste's shop all he had to do was go in and demand it. She wouldn't have dared hold out against him.'

'No, this is like him. He would abduct you and get the note from you and pretend it was normal robbery. He wouldn't want me to know he knew. He would be thinking of some terrible revenge for me. He is determined to marry me for my royal blood. That's what he wants me for . . . the continual childbearing.'

She looked down at the note and kissed it romantically.

'If he knew we had been lovers, think of how furious he would be.'

'That might be said to be a natural emotion.'

'I'm no virgin.'

'He is hardly that himself. Why don't you tell him everything that has happened? Tell him you love Armand. Ask him to release you.'

'Are you mad? What would happen to us all? There'd be ruin. The L'Estranges would go crazy. He knows how to take his revenge.'

'Can any man be as bad as we all seem to think he is?'

'One man could. And they want me to marry him!'

'I don't think you are right about the cab,' I said. 'I think it was probably intended robbery. On the other hand, it might just have been an attempt to get a big fare out of me. The fact that I'm a foreigner would make it so easy for him to say he misunderstood.'

'It was the Baron,' said the Princesse. 'I know.'

I went back to my room. I was horribly shaken – not only by my experience but by what the Princesse had told me.

Before the next week was out I had finished the portrait. It had been a busy week for me. I took short walks, never going so far that I was not prepared to walk back. I had taken a deep aversion to cabs.

The Princesse brightened up considerably on the days after her confession. She seemed rather pleased with herself, and there was an air of defiance about her. I could detect the loss of innocence which I had come to realize is sometimes apparent in very young girls who have had sexual experience.

I wondered what her future life would be like if she were actually going through with the marriage; and what his reaction would be if he discovered she had taken a lover before marriage.

I did not like to contemplate too deeply. I saw a far from felicitous union. But that was no concern of mine. I was merely the artist who had painted the miniatures of the betrothed pair.

I was recovering from my experience, which seemed less terrifying on contemplation. I certainly did not believe the story of the Baron's spy and was growing more and more certain that it had been a plan of robbery or mischief. Had I gone on in the cab, I might have been robbed of my possessions and left to find my way back – or else paid an excessive fare. Unpleasant, but not so very sinister.

The finished portrait was exquisite. Not such a clever piece of work as that of the Baron, but very charming in appearance. The miniature was to be taken back to Centeville so that the Baron's jeweller would fit it into its frame.

A letter arrived from the Baron to me. It was written in perfect English, and I wondered if he had written it himself or whether it was the work of his secretary.

My dear Mademoiselle Collison,

I am very eager to see the miniature. Madame la Comtesse tells me that it is beautiful . . . the sort of work I should expect from you. I could send someone down to collect it. I would, however, be so pleased if you would bring it yourself. First I should like to give you my opinion of it, and there is the matter of the account to be settled. Moreover, I do not like the idea of this precious picture being in any hands that do not understand its value.

You have been so good in the execution of this commission and your work has given me a great deal of pleasure. May I encroach on your goodness to oblige me with this other small service?

Your servant,

Rollo de Centeville.

I let the letter fall from my hands. I had planned to leave for the coast within a few days and then cross the Channel for home.

I had heard from my father that he had arrived home safely and that he was delighted with my success. The enterprise could not have turned out more satisfactorily, he pointed out. He believed that soon mine would be a name to be reckoned with in the Paris *salons* . . . and acclaim in England would naturally follow.

If I went to Centeville my return home would be delayed and I told myself that I was annoyed by this request, but that was not exactly the truth. I should really like to go to Centeville once more; I should even like to see the Baron, for I did want to watch his face as he saw the miniature for the first time. That he would give a frank opinion, I knew; and if he were indeed pleased with it, I should feel very happy indeed because whatever else he was there was no doubt that he was a practised connoisseur.

There would be a delay of a week, but I decided I must go. He had done so much for me. I had to do this small service.

I wrote to my father and told him that my return would be delayed. I mentioned that I had finished the picture of the Princesse and was pleased with it. I now hoped the Baron would be. I explained that he wanted me to take it to him and that this was what I was doing.

'He has promised to pay me,' I wrote, 'and that is important. Some people think it is a little bourgeois to pay their bills promptly and sometimes never do, as you know well. It will be nice to have the money and if he likes the portrait I shall feel I really am on my way.'

The Princesse had been delighted with the picture. 'It flatters me,' she said.

'No,' I told her. 'I just painted you at your best.'

She silently kissed me then.

'I'm sorry we have to say goodbye to each other,' she said

sincerely. 'I have liked your being here. And now you know my secrets.'

'They will be safe with me.'

'Pray for me, Kate. Pray for me on my wedding night.'

I laid my hands on her shoulders and said: 'Don't be afraid. If you have done something which is not right, remember that he has too . . . much worse, I imagine.'

'You are a comfort. I hope we meet again.'

Then I left the Rue du Faubourg Saint-Honoré and Paris, which I had grown to love.

It was late afternoon when I took the train to Rouen.

The Demon

I arrived in Rouen in good time and there had to change to a branch line which would take me to Centeville.

As I stepped off the train I was greeted by a man in the Centeville livery. He said: 'It is Mademoiselle Collison, I believe.'

'That is so.'

'There has been some trouble on the branch line and there will be no more trains through tonight. I have been sent from the château to drive you there. Have you the portrait?'

I told him I had.

'That is good. If you will follow me I will take you to the carriage.'

I did so, and as I stepped into the carriage I wondered when I was going to stop feeling that quiver of alarm every time I got into a vehicle of any sort.

It was foolish to feel this now. I was on my way to Centeville and since there were no trains that night it was very thoughtful of them to have sent the carriage.

We drove quickly through the streets of the town and came out into the open country. It was just beginning to get dark.

'Is it far to the château?' I asked.

'It's a fair drive, Mademoiselle. We could be there in just over an hour. The roads aren't very good though. It's all that rain we've been having.'

'Do they often have mishaps on the railway line?'

'On the branch one now and then. They're not like the main lines from Paris.'

'No, I suppose not.'

We had been driving for about half an hour when the carriage stopped with a jerk. The driver got down and surveyed it. I peered through the glass but could not see very much. There would be a half moon later but it had not yet put in an appearance, and it was not dark enough to see the stars.

The driver came round to the window looking dismayed.

'We're stuck in a rut,' he said. 'I don't like the look of the wheel.'

'Where are we?'

'Oh. I know the place well. We're about five miles from the château.'

'Five miles. That's not so very far.'

'There's a bit of forest over there . . . hunting place. There's a lodge too. You'll be comfortable enough. I reckon you could wait there while I get the wheelwright.'

'We are near a village then?'

'Not far. I know this place like the back of my hand. Nothing to fret about.'

I thought: Another mishap! And in another carriage! It seems that carriages and I do not get along very well together.

'If you would like to get out, Mademoiselle, I'll take you into the lodge. Then I can get a message down to the castle. I reckon the best thing is for them to send up another carriage. Yes, that would be best. Shall I give you a hand, Mademoiselle?'

He helped me down. I took the miniature with me. I had no intention of losing sight of that. We walked across the road and I could see the forest he had mentioned; and yes, there was a house among the trees. I saw a light in one of the windows.

The driver knocked on the door, which was opened immediately by a plump woman holding a candle.

'*Mon Dieu!*' she cried. 'Is it you then, Jacques Petit?'

'Yes, Marthe, it's only old Jacques. I've got the young lady artist here. There's been a mishap with the carriage. I don't trust that wheel and don't fancy going on with it. I thought at first of getting the wheelwright but perhaps I'd better leave it till morning. If you look after the young lady, I'll take one of the horses and get down to the château. Then they can send for her.'

'Well, bring the lady in. Don't leave her out there. What will she be thinking of us.'

She was a cosy-looking woman, large-hipped and large-busted, dressed in black with pieces of jet shining on her bodice. Her greying hair was drawn off her face and ended in a sizeable knot at the nape of her neck.

'Come along in,' she cried. 'My goodness, you would have thought Jacques Petit would have looked to his wheels before he set out. It's not the first time that sort of thing has happened, I can tell you. Are you cold?'

'No, not at all thank you.'

'I keep a bit of a fire in the evenings. It's cosy.'

There was a pot on the fire and something savoury simmering in it.

'You'd better make yourself cosy. It'll take him the better part of an hour to get there. Then he's got to see about a carriage.'

'It was fortunate that it happened here,' I said.

'It was indeed. I was just about to have a bite to eat. Will you join me? I'm Marthe Bouret. We've kept this lodge for years. It's not used much now, but they used to do a bit of hunting in the old days. I remember the old Baron when he came here. But now . . . well, it's very near the castle and they wouldn't want to stay the night here, being only five miles or so away. The Baron used it when he was a boy, though. He liked to do that. Used to have his young friends here. I remember them days. Not much to offer you, I'm afraid. Just the *pot au feu*.' She nodded towards the pot on the fire. 'Not as if I had been expecting visitors . . . but there's some bread and some good cheese and a drop of wine. It's castle wine and I can recommend that.'

'Thank you,' I said. 'You're very kind.'

'Well, by the look of it it will be some time before you get anything to eat at the castle. I'll just set a cloth on the table.'

'Do you live here all by yourself?'

'Just now I'm here by myself. It's my job to keep the place in order. This is my little cottage part. It joins on the lodge really. I have girls in to help me. We manage.'

'I see.'

'Is that the picture?'

'Yes.'

'Shall I put it out of harm's way. I heard the Baron is very eager to see it.'

'Yes. That is why I have brought it myself. I am anxious to know what he thinks of it.'

'I'll put it here on this table. Wouldn't do to get the stew on it, would it? Then you'd have to do your work all over again.'

'It's well wrapped up,' I told her.

'Shall I take your cloak or do you want to keep it on?'

'Thanks. I'll take it off. It's very warm in here.'

She took my cloak and hung it in a cupboard. Then she opened a drawer and took out a white cloth, which she put on the table. I was rather hungry and the stew smelt appetizing. She took plates to the fire and ladled it out.

There was a small cupboard in one corner of the room. It was about waist high and had a flat top which could be used as a shelf. She took out a bottle of wine and poured out a glass for me which she brought to the table.

'You'll find it good. It was a good year. We had plenty of sun. A vintage year. You'll enjoy it.'

She looked at the bottle. 'Oh, I've given you the last. Never mind. There's another in the cupboard. She opened another bottle, poured out a glass for herself and returned to the table.

She lifted hers to me. 'The very best of good fortune, Mademoiselle. I hope your stay at the château will be a happy one.'

'Thank you,' I replied, 'and the best of good fortune to you.'

'My,' she said, 'I feel honoured, I do, having a famous artist sitting at my table.'

'I can't tell you how grateful I am to you. I should have hated to sit in the carriage waiting for someone to come and rescue me.'

'Good fortune for us both,' she said. She tilted her glass and drank deeply. I did the same.

'Let me fill your glass.'

'Thank you,' I said.

She took it to the cupboard and refilled it.

'Your *pot au feu* is delicious,' I told her.

'It's a family secret.'

'I wasn't going to ask you to divulge it.'

'You speak good French Mademoiselle. That's a mercy or this would be a bit of a dumb show.'

I laughed. I was beginning to feel a little sleepy. It was the warmth of the fire . . . the food . . . the wine, I supposed. My eyelids seemed as though they would press down. It was getting harder to stay awake.

'Feeling a bit drowsy are you?' I heard her voice, which seemed to come from some distance. I saw her face near my own. She was peering at me, smiling.

'It's the wine,' she was saying. 'Makes you sleepy. I reckon you was tired after that journey. Never mind . . . a little nap never harmed anybody.'

It was unnatural. I had not been tired when I arrived and it was not very late. I felt I was being rather impolite after she had taken such pains to entertain me.

Something was happening. There were voices . . . I struggled with the overpowering drowsiness. Somewhere at the back of my mind I thought: It's Jacques, back with the carriage. He hasn't been long . . . or am I dreaming?

Sleeping . . . sleeping . . . the room was fading away. Someone was close, looking at me. Someone had taken my hands. I felt myself lifted up. Then I was completely lost in darkness.

I awoke suddenly. I did not know where I was. I was in a strange room. I was lying . . . naked . . . on a bed and my hair was loose.

I tried to lift myself, but my head was swimming and I felt dizzy. I was dreaming and this was some sort of nightmare. Where was I? I could not remember what could have brought me here.

I tried again. Something stirred beside me . . . someone.

I gave a little scream. My eyes had grown accustomed now to the darkness. I saw a window with bars across and my eyes could make out the outline of pieces of furniture.

I fought off the dizziness and sat up.

Immediately hands were pulling me down, strong hands. A voice said: 'Kate, my beautiful Kate . . .' It was a voice I knew. A voice I had often thought of. It convinced me that I was in some sort of nightmare.

I caught my breath and as I did so he pulled me down; he forced himself down on me. I cried out in disbelieving horror. This could not be happening to me. It was indeed a nightmare. I must wake up quickly.

But I did not wake up. I heard his triumphant laugh, and it was in truth the Baron who was misusing me . . . and something told me that he had always intended to do this and that at the back of my mind I had known it . . . feared it . . . dreaded it . . . and – the shame of it – half wanted it. I tried to shout out, but his mouth was over mine pressing down on me. I was aware of the strength of him and was powerless. I tried to struggle but my limbs were leaden. There was nothing I could do to resist him.

It was a shattering experience. I felt as though I were floating above the Earth into a world which was quite unknown to me. Strange, hitherto undreamed – of sensations took possession of me. I was not resisting any more. I felt myself to be part of him . . . and I was fighting against a sense of exhilaration which threatened to overwhelm me.

It was over almost as soon as it had begun. He drew away from me, but his lips were still on my face and he was kissing me almost tenderly.

'Dear Kate,' he murmured.

I was struggling back to reality. I put out my hands and felt his body. I was trying to collect my thoughts as they eluded me. The heavy drowsiness was still with me and I felt a great urge to close my eyes and lie there trying to recapture that strange sensation which I had just experienced.

His arms were about me. They felt like iron bands. I heard his voice whispering words which seemed strange coming from him. 'Kate . . . sweet Kate . . . Oh Kate, how happy you have made me.'

I heard myself say: 'This is a nightmare.'

'It's a heavenly dream,' he corrected me.

'Dreams . . . dreams . . .'

'Kate.' His mouth was close to my ear. He nibbled it gently. 'Don't try to think now. You can't. You're still in a state of blissful pleasure. Don't try to wake yourself out of it . . . yet.'

Now was the time for me to wake up, to find myself in bed at the castle, perhaps, since that had been where I was remembering I had been going. No doubt I had arrived late and so tired that I had slept heavily . . . and being in the castle had had this strange dream.

But the bars at the windows . . . They suggested a prison. A prison!

I felt consciousness coming back. This was not a dream. I was still here. I was lying in a bed with the Baron . . . and we were . . . lovers. Lovers! What a travesty of the word!

I tried to sit up, but he held me down. I could not but be aware of how strong he was and how puny I was in comparison.

'This can't be true,' I said.

His voice was low and triumphant. 'But it is. Too late for regrets now, Kate. It has happened. You and I . . . as I knew as soon as I set eyes on you it must be . . . and it was going to be.'

I continued to struggle.

'Be still, Kate,' he said. 'You're bewildered. You are just realizing what has happened. Last night you became my beloved mistress.'

'This is . . . madness.'

'The effect of the wine is still with you. It will last some time yet. It had to be, Kate. It was the only way. Now if I had appeared suddenly and said – "I want you, Kate. My desire for you is so overwhelming that it must be satisfied" – what would you have said? You would have laughed me to scorn even though somewhere at the back of your mind was the thought: How I should like to give myself up to the pleasure he can provide. He is the only one. I want to be taken by him as his ancestors took women when they raided the coast.'

My mind was clearing with every passing moment. I murmured: 'I was with that woman . . .'

'My good servant.'

'The carriage had broken down . . .'

'It was all arranged, darling. I'm sorry it had to be like that. If you had come willingly . . . but you never would. Your stern upbringing would have suppressed your natural instincts and you would have convinced yourself that they did not exist.'

'I can't . . .'

'Don't try. Lie still. Oh Kate, it was wonderful. You are magnificent. You're a woman as well as an artist. I admire you so much, Kate.'

Through my befugged sensations came the appalling realization of what had happened. He had planned it and I had been the victim of . . . *rape*. I, Kate Collison, had been raped by the man I most detested . . . this arrogant Baron who thought he had only to beckon to a woman to make her come running. He followed the customs of his marauding ancestors who had lived by rape and pillage. And I . . . *I* had been his victim. I could not believe it . . . even now.'

I said: 'Let me get out of here.'

'My dearest Kate, you will go at *my* pleasure.'

'At your pleasure! You are a monster.'

'I know,' he agreed. 'But in your heart you rather like this monster, Kate. I will have you recognized as a great artist. Just think what I have done for you already.'

'I can think of nothing but what you have just done to me.'

'Proud Kate, taken in a drunken stupor.'

'That wine was drugged. That woman . . .'

'Don't blame her. She was obeying orders.'

'A sort of pander . . .'

'Hardly an apt description. What is done is done, Kate. You are a woman now. You and I have explored the realms of delight together . . .'

'Of degradation!' I said. 'You are cynical. You are laughing at me. That is what I would expect of you.'

'Do you hate me still?'

'A thousand times more than I ever did.'

'Perhaps while you are here I can make you change your mind.'

'The more time I spent with you, the more I should hate

you. What do you mean . . . while I am here?'

'You are detained . . . on my baronial pleasure.'

'You can't mean you would *keep* me here.'

He nodded. 'I could,' he said.

'For what purpose?'

'I thought I had demonstrated that.'

'You've gone mad.'

'Mad with desire for you.'

I tried to rise but he was still holding me down, and when I lifted my head I felt dizzy.

'What is your purpose?' I demanded.

'First to turn a rather haughty self-possessed young lady into a warm and passionate woman.'

'I will never feel anything but hatred and contempt for you. And you say . . . first . . .'

'There is something else.'

'Well?'

'I think we will discuss it later when you are feeling a little refreshed.'

'I want to know now.'

'My dear Kate, it is I who make the rules here. Haven't you learned that yet?'

'What am I supposed to be . . . a sort of slave?'

'A very favoured slave.'

I was silent, still trying to convince myself that I was not dreaming.

His voice was gentle in my ear. 'Try to be calm, Kate. Accept this. You and I have been lovers all through this night.'

'Lovers! You are not a lover of mine and never will be.'

'Well, just say that last night you became my mistress. That's rather important.'

I felt weak suddenly and very frightened. It seemed that my life had taken an abrupt turn into an entirely different world.

'Sleep, dear Kate,' he said soothingly and he gathered me up in his arms as though I were a baby.

I must have slept, for when I awoke it was morning. My head had cleared and I sat up in bed and looked about me. I was alone. I realized that I was naked and when I saw the bars across the windows, the monstrous happenings of the previous night came flooding back to me.

I looked about the room. It was like a part of the castle – large, with a high vaulted roof supported by strong stone pillars. There was a great fireplace and the embers there showed that there had been a fire last night. The bed was large and had velvet curtains about it and there were carpets on the floor. In spite of this it was like a medieval stronghold.

I had undergone a change. I felt bruised and unclean. I had to face the truth. He had brought me up here; he had taken off my clothes, put me into this bed and committed rape.

I put my hands over my face as the hot flush spread there. Nothing would ever be the same again. Since I had come to France everything had changed. The cosy world of Farringdon was slipping away from me and I had been plunged into intrigue . . . and rape . . . the sort of thing that had happened centuries ago.

And there was one man who was responsible for this. I could not get his face out of my mind. I realized I had been seeing it ever since I had left the castle. I had seen it in the gargoyles of Notre Dame. I had seen it in my dreams. I wondered briefly if he had some supernatural power – a gift passed on from those pirate forebears.

I had to be calm. I had to consider the position in which I found myself. I think I had always known that he had desired me. There was something in the way he had looked at me right from the beginning. I should have been warned, for when he desired a woman he thought he had the right to take her, whether she was willing or not. That was what the marauding Normans had done, and he lived up to the old traditions.

I should never feel the same again. I should never feel clean. He had defiled me and gloried in it. He thought that because he had humiliated me, he had made me his slave.

I had to get out of here quickly. Then I would think about revenge. Nowadays no man should be allowed to act as he had done. It was all very well to make love to a woman if she consented. But to snare a virtuous woman and drug her and then take advantage of the situation, that was the way cowards and demons worked.

My hatred was so intense that I was shaking. I must get out of here. That was the first thing. I would go down to the woman who had given me the wine. I would tell her that I was going to the police.

Could I? How? I imagined he controlled most things round here. He would say: 'She spent the night with me willingly . . .' For he was capable of anything. Lies would be second nature to him.

I would dress immediately.

I stepped out of bed. I looked at the pillow still indented where his head had been. I punched it in sudden fury and was then ashamed of my childish gesture. It was an act of petulant folly and in spite of what happened I prided myself on being a sensible woman.

I had been betrayed. I had been raped. My attacker had been the one man in the world whom I hated most. But it was done. I had been violated. My body . . . my mind . . . my freedom to act had been taken into his control. I had been forced.

But now . . . the first thing was to get out of this place.

I looked for my clothes. I could not find them. They were all gone . . . my shoes . . . everything.

There was a counterpane on the bed and I wrapped this

round me. Then I set out to explore. To my momentary delight the door was not locked. I was on a kind of landing and before me was a small flight of stone stairs – the usual spiral kind cut out of the wall, wide at one end and narrowing by the post. I saw that there was one room in which there were toilet facilities. I caught sight of a mirror on a table and a wash basin and ewer. There were cupboards. I thought my clothes might be in one of them, so I opened them all. There were towels and such things, but no clothes.

I saw that there was another room. In this were a table and chairs. It might have been a dining-room. But there were no clothes.

Cautiously I descended the stairs. A big door was facing me. It had iron studs in it and looked very strong. I tried to open it. It was locked.

I looked about me. Barred windows everywhere, a heavy locked door, and no clothes. I was indeed the prisoner of the Baron's pleasure.

I was suddenly frantic. My resolutions to be calm slipped away from me.

How long would he keep me here? Would he come again? I would refuse to drink more wine. Perhaps he would not care. He could easily overpower me. I had been aware of his immense strength last night.

Locked up here . . . within these stone walls with barred windows I should not have a chance.

I started to hammer on the door. Then I sat down on the stone step and gave way to my despair.

I heard a voice. 'All right. All right. I'm coming!'

I was alert and kept my eyes on the door. If it was the woman I had seen last night, I might be able to get past her. I might find my clothes. My baggage might be somewhere here. The man – Jacques Petit – he had brought it in from the carriage lastnight. If I could get dressed I could escape. This place was on the road – five miles or so from Centeville. I had an idea of the direction. I could only think of escape.

I heard a key turning in the lock. The door creaked open. I was waiting, tense.

The woman was carrying a copper jug of hot water. She came in and set it down. It was my chance and I took it. I dashed to the door. A man was standing there. He was tall and his arms were folded across his chest. He shook his head at me. I tried to elude him, but he caught me and lifting me up, as though I were a child, he put me back behind the door. Then he shut it.

'No use,' said the woman, looking as cosy as she had on the previous night. 'There are guards.'

I cried out: 'What is this? Some medieval game?'

'Baron's orders,' she answered.

She lifted the jug and went up the stairs to the room where I had seen the basin and ewer.

'Now,' she said briskly, 'I brought the water first because I thought you'd be one of them ladies as like to wash first. Now I'll bring your *petit déjeuner*. You'll find everything you want. I'll bring you something to put on. That bed coverlet is not ideal, is it? And your poor feet? These stone floors can be that cold – don't I know it.'

I followed her up and when she had put down the jug I caught her arm.

'You gave me drugged wine last night,' I said.

She lifted her shoulders.

'You deceived me . . . wickedly.'

'It was orders,' she said.

'Baron's orders,' I repeated.

She was silent.

I went on: 'Does he make a habit of this sort of thing?'

'You never know what he's going to do. He's had ladies here before . . . Most of them have come willingly, if you know what I mean.'

'And the unwilling ones have to be drugged?'

'Well, we've not had any of those before . . . only them that had to be persuaded, like.'

'It's like finding oneself back five hundred years. Bring my clothes . . . my own clothes.'

She shrugged her shoulders again.

I let her go and went into the toilet room. At least I should feel a little better if I washed. I felt emotional as I saw myself in the mirror. There were bruises on my body and I was glad of my long hair which covered me like a cloak. I felt better when I had thoroughly washed and by that time the woman came back with hot coffee and rolls with butter and preserves.

I resisted the impulse to run to the stairs because I knew that was futile.

She took the tray into the room which I had thought was a dining-room and set it on the table. Then she was gone but in a few moments she was back carrying a long fur-trimmed robe. It was greenish with a thread of gold in it and the fur edged the hem as well as the long wide sleeves. She carried three pairs of satin sandals.

'I wasn't sure of the size,' she said comfortably.

'Oh my God, does he have victims of various sizes?'

'It's for you to choose, Mademoiselle.'

Clothes were necessary for me if I was to plan some action so I selected a pair of the sandals and took the robe from her.

When she had gone I put it on. It was soft and silken and very comfortable. It was amazing what a difference washing and putting on clothes made to me.

I was surprised that I could eat anything, but I did and the coffee was good. As soon as I had drunk it I thought I had been a fool to touch it. How could I know whether anything was drugged or not.

But why should he want to drug me now; he had done his evil work.

That reminded me afresh and I felt the bitter humiliation creeping over me. I wished that I could have remembered, and then I was glad that I had not. There had been moments of consciousness and later when I had been coming out of my drowsiness he had taken me . . . almost casually.

I hated him. How I hated him! My father used to say, 'Envy is a negative emotion. It hurts the one who feels it more than the one against whom it is directed.' So with hatred.

Think constructively, I told myself. How am I going to get out of this place? I must make a plan.

I went into the toilet room to look at myself in my robe and sandals. I had been transformed. I had never worn anything like this before. I looked almost beautiful with my hair hanging loose and the green and gold of the furred robe did something to my eyes. They looked bigger and brighter. I am different, I thought. He has made me different.

There was a little table in the room I called the dining-room. It was by the window and on it were several pencils with a sketching-pad.

He had put that there for me, I thought.

I went to it and savagely drew his face. I sketched in that part of Notre Dame where I had seen the most grotesque of all the gargoyles – the one which leans on the parapet by the door at the top of the steps and seems to be gazing malevolently towards the Invalides.

I went on sketching. It was wonderful how it soothed me.

The woman came back and cleaned the place; she made the bed and removed the ashes from the fireplace, laying another.

I wanted to scream out because it all seemed so normal. It was as though I were a visitor in some friend's house.

She said: 'I'll bring up your *déjeuner* at half past twelve if that suits.'

I said: 'How am I to know it has not been treated with

something which would not be good for me?'

'I've had no orders,' she said seriously.

I wanted to laugh – in a rather hysterical way, I knew, so I suppressed it.

She brought in the food. It was a delicious soup with meat and salad and fruit.

Oddly enough, I could eat it, and in due course she came to collect the tray.

'I should have a little rest,' she said. 'You need it . . . to sleep off what we had to give you. You'll be tired still.'

It's mad, I thought. Am I really in this incongruous position?'

I obeyed her though and lay on the bed. I did sleep long and deep; and when I awoke my first thought was: He will come again. Of course he will come again. Otherwise, why should they hold me here.

At dusk it was the woman who came. She brought more water for me to wash. I did so. I heard her in the dining-room and when I went to see what she was doing – for she seemed a long time – I found her setting the table for two. There was a silver candelabrum in the centre.

I thought: Then I am expected to sup with him as though all was well between us.

I would never do that. I would refuse to sit down with him.

I went back to the bedroom and stood by the barred window. I tried to shake the bars, but they were firmly embedded in the stone. I wondered then how many had stood at that window in desperation. I wondered what tortures had been inflicted on them in this place.

Who would have believed this could happen in these days? How easily people slipped back into savagery. That man did not have to slip back. He had never been anything else but a savage.

There was a movement behind me and he was there, smiling at me.

He was dressed in a robe not unlike my own. It was deep blue and, like mine, the sleeves were edged with fur, as was the hem.

'You could never break those,' he said. 'They were made to withstand any onslaught.' He came towards me. I turned sharply away, but he caught me firmly and tried to kiss me. For a second or so I eluded him, then he released me but caught me again, taking my face in his two hands, finding my mouth and holding me in a hideous embrace.

Oh God, help me, I thought, it's beginning again.

He released me, smiling. 'I trust the day has not been too monotonous without me,' he said.

'Any day would be better for not having you in it,' I retorted.

'Ungracious still! I had hoped that you, being a reasonable woman, would come to terms with the inescapable.'

'If you ever think I would come to terms with you, you are mistaken.'

'We came to terms once . . . about the picture, I mean. By the way, I like the one you brought. A worthy Collison.'

I turned back to the window. I wanted to look anywhere but into his face.

'I also like the sketch.'

'What sketch?'

'The one you did of me, of course. It is so gratifying to know that even when I am not here I am in your thoughts. Am I really as terrible as that? I recognize the thing. I've often seen it. It's at the top of the steps, isn't it? It's recognized as being the most grotesque and evil gargoyle in the whole of Paris.'

'Yes, I know.'

'And you have made it my face. *Mon Dieu*, Kate, you are a clever artist. It's undoubtedly that particular gargoyle and yet I'm there too. We are combined.'

'It represents the forces of evil,' I said. 'I know what those gargoyles mean now. They were modelled on evil men . . . demons . . . such as ordinary people do not know exist. But they existed when Notre Dame was built and they exist today. At least one of them does.'

'True. But there is a little good in the worst of us. Did you know that?'

'I would find it hard to believe of you.'

'You are ungrateful. Who launched you into the Paris world of art?'

'You liked the picture I had painted and said so. I don't think such an act will assure you of a place in Heaven.'

'I'm thinking of this life rather than the life to come. I intend to enjoy this one to the full.'

'Which I believe you do . . . at the expense of others.'

'Some have the good sense to want what I want.'

'Some may have the greater good sense to fight you.'

'Which would be mere folly if the odds were against them.'

'You mean . . . as they are with me at this time?'

'I fear so, Kate. Will you be gentle tonight? I know how you can be. Will you forget that you have to pretend you do not like me?'

'It is impossible to forget something which is so blatantly true.'

'You hate me as a person? Is that so? You despise everything I do. I have a certain power which allows me to get what I want now and then. That you hate. I understand it. But forget it, Kate. Think of me only as your lover.'

'You talk nonsense.'

'No. I talk from a superior knowledge of the emotions.'

'Please do not attempt to tell me what I feel.'

'I have had great experience of women.'

'You speak the truth there for once.'

'I know how you feel towards me. You hate me . . . but hate and love can be very close, Kate, in certain moments.

Passion is blind to the differences of the mind. This is a mating of bodies. You and I were made for each other and that fierce reluctance of yours . . . too fierce to be entirely natural . . . just adds to the perfection. Do you understand what I mean?'

'No.'

'Then I shall teach you.'

'I would rather be taught how to escape from the place, to leave you and never see you again.'

'Much as I would like to indulge you in all things, you ask too much.'

'How long do you intend to keep me here?'

'That depends. Would you like a little wine before we sup?'

'Drugged wine?'

'Oh no. That was only for convenience in the first instance. Just while we got over the er – preliminaries. It won't be necessary now.'

'Just ordinary common rape?'

'How outspoken you are! You astonish me. I should not have thought a well-brought-up lady would talk in such a way.'

'Who would believe that a well-brought-up lady would be in such a position.'

'Such things happen a great deal more frequently than you would think. One doesn't hear of them. I will tell them to bring in the wine.'

I watched him go to the door, the blue robe swinging round him.

He was in the dining-room. If I could get down the stairs, surprise the guards . . .

He was beside me, smiling at me. 'You would never do it,' he said. 'And suppose you got out? Imagine being on the road dressed like that. No money . . . People would think you were mad.'

'What have I ever done to you that you should treat me like this?'

'Bewitched me, for one thing. Come. They are bringing the wine.'

The woman came in and set it on the table. He went over to it and poured two glasses. One he handed to me.

'Drink it,' he said.

I took the glass, but did not drink. He went to the table and took his, sipping it, looking at me.

'I assure you . . . no drugs,' he said. 'Here. Give me your glass. You take mine.'

He took mine and thrust his into my hand. He drank quickly. 'There, you see.'

My throat felt dry and parched. I felt I needed some stimulation if I were to face what lay before me. I sipped a little of the wine.

'That's better,' he said.

'When my father hears what has happened,' I began, and I hesitated, wondering what my father would do.

'Yes,' he prompted.

I was silent.

'Suppose I said, "She came of her own free will. She was so insistent that gallantry demanded that I comply."'

'Would even you be capable of such lies?'

'You know that I would. Can you think of anything evil of which I should not be capable? No, Kate. You can do nothing, and wise woman that you are, you know this. Therefore you will, metaphorically, shrug your shoulders and make the best of your fate.'

'I do not give in so easily.'

'I'm glad in a way. I wouldn't want you to be other than the strong woman you are.'

He drained off the wine. 'Come,' he said, taking my arm. 'I will conduct you in to supper.'

I refused to take his arm and he seized me and put

mine through his. It was a gesture which implied that even on the slightest matter he was going to have absolute obedience.

The servants had gone. The table looked beautiful with the eight lighted candles of the candelabrum. He took me to a chair at the table and pressed me down into it. Then he took his place opposite me. The table was not large, as it had obviously been made for two, so he was close to me.

'There is soup,' he said, lifting the lid of the tureen, 'and I shall serve you. The old woman is an excellent cook and I am sure you will enjoy this.'

He handed me the plate but I turned away, so he sighed and brought it round to me.

'Please don't be tiresome,' he said.

I stood up but he ignored me and started on the soup. 'Pheasant, I think,' he commented. 'Excellent. Where are you going? Are you so eager for bed?'

I sat down helplessly. The soup did smell delicious. He brought me a glass of wine. 'Undrugged, I promise you,' he said again.

I looked at him defiantly and started on the soup.

'That's better,' he said, lifting his glass. 'To us. Suspicious still? I'll drink some of mine and pass it to you. A sort of loving cup.'

I am going to fight him, I thought. I am going to use all my strength to resist him. I'll eat . . . sparingly . . . but I must eat.

He drank and offered his glass to me. I did not want to drink much wine, which would make me sleepy. Yet on the other hand, might it not be more bearable if I felt drowsy? Would I be more resigned to accepting what I knew had to come?

'Such deep thoughts,' he said. 'I can only guess at them. Now a little of this venison. I told them to serve something cold as I did not want them intruding on us while we ate. I thought you would prefer it that way. You see, Kate, how I consider you.'

'I have noticed that,' I said with heavy sarcasm.

'Of course, as an artist you are observant. You shall do another miniature of me. I so much enjoyed our sittings. Your little deceit was so amusing.'

I was silent. He ate a great deal and I went on thinking of the possibilities of escape. Would that woman come in to remove the dishes? If she left the door open . . . It was just hopeless and I knew it. I felt furiously angry and yet I could not suppress a certain indefinable excitement.

'The venison is good, is it not?' he said. 'She has done well, our old woman. You must not blame her . . . or the coachman. They were merely obeying orders.'

'I know that.'

'So you see they could do no other than what they did.'

'All must do the will of the mighty Baron.'

'That is so. They are not to be blamed. You must blame me, but guileless virgins who cease to live in that debatably happy state cannot be entirely blameless either.'

'Save your crude jests for those who enjoy them.'

'I will,' he replied. 'But you are here, Kate, and how easily you walked into the trap. You should have enquired about the trains . . . not just walked into the web. You were very quick in Paris.'

I stared at him.

'Ah. I see I have caught your attention at last.'

'Are you talking about that cab?'

'It was rather clumsy, wasn't it? Too involved, too tricky. We had to get you across Paris and you were too sharp for us. You were beginning to know the city too well and you realized you were going in the wrong direction. You jumped out. That was a very dangerous thing to do. Knowing the Paris drivers, I wonder you were not run over. A foolish plan, really. Not worthy of me. It just came to me on the spur of the moment and it appealed to the sense of adventure in me. I realized almost at once that it was not very clever and it owed a lot to chance too. He'd been several days trying to pick you up.'

'Why did you do it?'

'I should have thought that was obvious.'

'So you were determined on . . . rape.'

'Well, I was hoping to achieve my ends to our mutual satisfaction.'

'You are a monster.'

'Worthy to deface the façade of Notre Dame.'

'I would not have believed that any man of today could behave as you have done.'

'Your knowledge of the world is not very great.'

'Perhaps I have lived my life among civilized people until –'

'Until now. I am sure that is true. But alas, my dear Kate, you have become the victim of the most depraved.'

'Can I appeal to your sense of honour . . . your sense of decency . . . to let me go?'

'There is no sense in appealing to something which does not exist. If I let you go now you cannot change yourself back into the woman you were before last night.'

'I want only to get away from you, to try to forget I ever saw you . . . never to see you again.'

'But I want just the opposite. I want you to stay here and remember me forever. The best lover you ever had, for I shall be that, Kate.'

I felt bewildered. I was living again that nightmare ride in the cab. The Princesse said it had been arranged by the Baron and she had been right about that, though not for the reason she had suggested. I was thinking of that moment when I had opened the door and stepped out almost under the horse's nose. And all so that he might satisfy his lust.

I stood up suddenly. 'Let me go,' I cried.

He was beside me. 'Now, Kate,' he said, 'you know very well that I am not going to let you go. That will come in good time. Be patient. Our little adventure is not yet over.'

He was about to seize me and I picked up a knife which was lying on the table. I turned the blade towards him.

He laughed.

'What!' he cried. 'Would you kill me then? Oh, Kate! I never would have thought that of you.'

'Do not goad me too far,' I cried. 'If I killed you it would be no great calamity for the world.'

He opened the robe he was wearing and bared his chest. 'Come along, Kate,' he said. 'Right through the heart. It's about there, I think.'

'You would be surprised if I did.'

'I should be in a condition where it would not be possible to show my surprise. What are you waiting for?'

'I said don't goad me too far.'

'That's exactly what I meant to do.'

I lunged at him. He caught my wrist and the knife dropped to the floor.

'You see, Kate,' he said, 'you couldn't do it.'

'I could. You prevented me. If you were so sure, why did you make me drop the knife.'

'To save your feelings. I'll tell you this: Well-brought-up English ladies do not stab their lovers. They try to shatter them with words . . . with tears perhaps . . . but not knives.'

'You have a great deal to learn about well-brought-up English ladies.'

'I have . . . and I am rejoicing in the education.'

He had taken me now and was holding me against him. 'Kate,' he said softly, 'sweet Kate, it is no use fighting. Submit. I should like to see you submissive. I should like you to put your arms about me and tell me that you are so happy that I brought you here . . .'

I drew myself away from him and because he held me at

arms' length, I began beating that bare chest. He was laughing at me. He knew as well as I did, that I should never have used that knife against him. He was right. People who had been brought up as I had did not do such things – no matter what was done to them.

He swept me up in his arms. I wriggled and tried to break away, but he revelled in making me aware of his strength.

'You make me impatient,' he said.

It was a long time afterwards before I could bring myself to think of that night. It had been different from the previous one. Then I had been in a drugged state and only half aware. I fought him . . . with all my strength I fought him . . . knowing from the first moment that I could not win. But I hoped I showed him my resentment, my loathing, my anger, my fury. At least that offered some balm to my humiliated senses.

But he did not care. He liked that. After all, his very nature was that of a fighter.

Perhaps I realized that I was playing into his hands. I was giving him what he wanted, because, for a man of his nature, the greater the resistance, the greater the triumph when victory was won.

And victory was inevitable. I might score occasionally in our verbal battles but physically I was no match for him.

But I fought . . . how I fought! I whipped up my hatred for him and somewhere at the back of my mind I realized that I was fighting not only him but something in myself . . . some erotic curiosity, some desire for this conflict . . . some craving for the ultimate satisfaction. I was vanquished but I felt a certain wild exhilaration in defeat and the stronger my hatred, the greater my excitement.

The bed was like a battlefield that night.

The next day passed as the previous one. I was beginning to feel I had spent a lifetime in my prison. I wondered whether his object was to keep me here until he had subdued my spirit to such an extent that I meekly submitted to him. If he ever did that, I felt, he would probably be tired of the adventure and let me go.

Sometimes still I thought I was dreaming. There was such an atmosphere of unreality about the whole matter, and yet, knowing him, I supposed it was natural enough.

He saw a woman; he thought he would like to seduce her and he set about his purpose. But he had known that there would never have been an easy submission with me. It had to be force, and so it had been.

The evening supper was served as before. I thought he was a little different. Was there a shade of regret . . . tenderness. Oh no. That was too strong a word. He could never be tender. However, there was a change in him and I wondered what it meant.

He said rather soberly as he poured the wine: 'Kate, it has been a wonderful experience . . . our being together.'

I was silent.

'Would you believe me if I told you I had never enjoyed an association so much?'

'No,' I said.

'It's true. Why should I lie to you? There is no reason, is there?'

'I have not found you reasonable, so why should I expect you to be so now?'

'You will learn that my actions have been well within the bounds of reason. I really acted with a very good reason for doing so.'

'Which was the satisfaction of your lust, your desire to exert your malevolent powers.'

'Absolutely right. Dear Kate, what an observant woman you are.'

'It does not need a great deal of observation to assess a man's character when his actions are those of a barbarian.'

'Not all.'

'You are going to remind me that you launched me on my career. I wish I had never heard of you. I wish I had never come to your castle and learned that there are people in the world who are nothing more than savages.'

'Such tirades are not very interesting and the theme of this one is becoming somewhat repetitious.'

'It must be when everything I say to you has to tell you how much I loathe and despise you.'

'Do you know, I got a different impression last night.'

'You have degraded me. You have treated me as no honourable man would ever treat a woman. What you have done is a criminal offence. In those old days of which you are so fond, you would have been hanged or sent to the galleys for what you have done.'

'Not a man in my position. I believe that one of my ancestors used to waylay travellers, bring them here and hold them to ransom. Yet he was never asked to account for his misdeeds.'

'A little game which might appeal to you.'

'It doesn't appeal in the least. I have money in plenty.'

'How fortunate for the travellers!'

'If one has sufficient power and – er expertise, shall I say, one can do a great deal which other people cannot. I am going to tell you a true story of one of my ancestors. Would you like to hear it?'

'I would prefer to walk out of this place and never see you again.'

'You would continue to see me in your mind's eye and my voice would haunt your dreams.'

'I shall do everything in my power to wipe them from my memory.'

'Oh, Kate, has it been so hateful for you?'

'Words cannot describe how hateful. When I leave here I shall be able to see it in all its horror and I will never forget or forgive you for what you have done to me.'

'Those are harsh words.'

'Deservedly so.'

'Let me tell you this story of my ancestor. I think it will interest you.'

I did not answer and he went on: 'It happened a long time ago, in the thirteenth century to be exact, in the reign of Philippe who was known as Le Bel because he was so handsome. This ancestor of mine was Florence, Earl of Holland. A strange name for a man, you think. But some names are used for men and women here. Florence was a man who had had many love-affairs.'

'I can understand your affinity, though *love*-affairs seems an odd way to describe them.'

He ignored the interruption. 'Florence had a mistress to whom he was rather grateful. He had many mistresses, of course, but this one had become more important to him than any of the others had been. There came a time when he had finished with her and he wanted to see her settled into respectable marriage.'

'With someone else, I presume, since he no longer had any use for her?'

'Oh, you are listening then. I'm glad of that for I am sure you will find this very interesting. He asked one of his ministers to marry her. This minister indignantly refused, saying that he would never marry one of Florence's cast-off mistresses.'

'I am not surprised that he refused.'

'Florence didn't like it. He was very powerful. Can you guess what he did?'

I was looking at him intently now and slow horror was beginning to dawn on me. I said: 'You want to tell me, don't you?'

'That minister was at the time enamoured of a woman whom he wished to marry. He married her and snapped his fingers at his master. There was no question then of his being forced to marry Florence's mistress.'

'So poor Florence did not get his way for once?'

'Oh, he did. He never allowed anyone to get the better of him. Can you guess what he did. He waylaid the new wife one day and had her brought to his castle. Can you guess what happened?'

I stared at him in mounting horror.

'He kept her there for three days,' he said, watching me intently. 'The records say that he violated her against her will. Then he sent her back to his minister with a note saying: 'You were wrong. You see you did marry one of my mistresses."'

'What a terrible story.'

He was silent for a few moments, regarding me over the candelabrum.

'I tell you this,' he said, 'to let you know what my ancestors were like. So what can you expect of me?'

'I knew already that they were barbarians. What happened to the noble Florence?'

'He was murdered later on.'

'Oh!' I'm glad. The story has the right ending after all. The wronged husband murdered him, I suppose.'

'It was generally believed to be so.'

'It should be a lesson to all barbarians.'

'Barbarians never learn that sort of lesson.'

'No, I suppose not.'

He was smiling at me. I felt sick with apprehension. This was beginning to take on a new meaning. Before I had felt I would fight every inch of the way even though the battle was lost. But now . . . I could not bear to think of what this meant. He was more cynical than I had believed even him to be.

I stood up. He said: 'Are you ready? Where are you going?'

'I would go anywhere to get away from you.'

'Poor Kate!' he said and caught me in his arms.

For the first time I felt as though I want to burst into tears. I could see what he was doing. This was nothing to do with his desire for me. I was a symbol. He had discovered that Bertrand and I were betrothed and he had demanded that Bertrand marry Nicole. Bertrand had refused. So the Baron had taken me so that he could say as his ancestor had before him: 'You will marry a mistress of mine after all, even though she is not the one I planned for you.'

I believe I could have killed him if I had been capable of the physical strength. He deserved the same fate as his ancestor.

'Kate,' he said. 'I'm in love with you.'

'I know you are capable of every evil, but you are not capable of loving anyone, so there is no need to tell blatant lies.'

'There is no need, is there, for me to say what I do not mean?'

'You love yourself . . . your pride . . . your lust . . . your greed . . . that is what you love.'

'I love myself, yes . . . but next to myself it's you . . . for tonight.'

I laid a hand on his arm. 'Let me go . . . please?' I begged.

'So appealing. So beautiful,' he said and he picked me up in his arms.

I lay on the bed . . . supine . . . indifferent almost. Violation had become commonplace. My body was no longer my own. I was weary, tired of reiterating my hatred.

I murmured: 'If only I could send time back. If only I could go back to the time when I was in Paris. I could go home . . . instead of coming here . . .'

'You would have missed the greatest experience of your life.'

'The greatest degradation.'

Then I lost my indifference and shouted at him . . . my hatred and contempt.

He did not heed me. He just turned to me and showed me once more that I was his to command.

It was morning. I was awakened by the sound of footsteps and voices. I sat up in bed. My robe was lying on the floor where he had thrown it. Someone was coming into the room.

It was the Baron and with him . . . Bertrand.

I saw then that this was the final scene of a farce . . . comedy . . . tragedy . . . whatever he meant it to be. This was the climax towards which he had been working.

'Mademoiselle Collison is here,' he was saying. 'She has been here for three nights . . . with me. Well, Bertrand, there is no need for me to say more. I wish you a felicitous life together. I can assure you, Kate is a most desirable woman. Many will envy you. I myself for one. And another time, Bertrand, don't be a fool. Do as I tell you. You must not think because I have given you some independence you can flout me.'

That moment remains in my memory forever. There was a sudden stillness in the room. It was as though we were all inanimate outlines in a picture.

Bertrand stared at me first in amazement and then in growing understanding. Horror . . . disbelief . . . realization . . . disgust . . . I saw all those emotions in his face.

His lips formed my name: 'Kate . . .'

I raised myself holding the coverlet about me.

I cried out: 'I was brought here . . . drugged . . . forced . . .'

Bertrand continued to stare at me. Then he turned to the Baron who stood there smiling evilly . . . like the demon-gargoyle on Notre Dame.

He nodded slowly in affirmation. 'She fought like a wild cat,' he said. 'But I think we came to an . . . understanding.'

Bertrand's face was distorted. I thought he was going to weep. Then suddenly his expression changed. There was nothing but hatred. He sprang at the Baron but that wicked man was waiting for him. Bertrand was at his throat but the Baron picked him up and threw him from him. Bertrand went down and slid across the floor.

'Get up,' said the Baron. 'You are making a fool of yourself . . . and before Kate. Kate, your clothes will be brought up to you. Dress and take a little food.' He laid an envelope on the table. 'Here is the payment for the portrait as we arranged, and here also are the tickets you will need. You may leave in an hour's time. The carriage will take you to the station. All the connections have been checked. I presume you will want to go straight to England for a rest before you take up your next commission. Bertrand can conduct you as far as he wishes.'

With that he turned away and left us.

Bertrand had picked himself up. He was shaken by the fall but not so much as he had been by what he had seen and heard.

I was sorry for him. I could see that his humiliation was almost as deep as my own; and I knew in that moment that I could never marry him. I could never marry anyone after this.

He stood looking at me. 'Kate,' he said.

'He . . . is a monster,' I said. 'I want to go home.'

He nodded.

'I want to leave this place at the earliest possible moment.'

The woman came in with my clothes and hot water. Bertrand left us.

'I'll bring you some *petit déjeuner*,' said the woman, cosy as ever.

'No, thanks,' I said. 'I want nothing more here. I want to leave at once.'

She did not answer but set down the hot water. I washed

hastily and dressed. It seemed strange to be in my own clothes again. I even found the pins for my hair on the table with the mirror and I laughed a little hysterically to think how precisely everything had been taken care of.

Dressed, I felt myself again – a different person from the one in the furred robe and cloud of hair. Peering closely at my face I detected a difference there. What was it – a look of worldliness? Eve must have looked like that after having eaten the forbidden fruit.

I descended the short spiral staircase. The great iron-studded door was open.

I found my way out of the tower and down to the room where – it seemed so long ago – I had partaken of *pot au feu* and drugged wine.

Bertrand was outside with the carriage. There was no sign of the Baron. I supposed he had gone back to the castle. The little adventure which had ruined my life and brought him the satisfaction he had needed, was over.

I said: 'Let us go. Let us get away from this place.'

So we went together.

Bertrand said very little during the journey. I thought it would never end. We had left Rouen and were approaching the coast.

I said to him: 'There is no need for you to cross the Channel. I don't need an escort in my own country.'

He nodded again.

When we reached Calais, there was an hour to wait for the packet-boat.

I said: 'Don't stay, Bertrand.'

'I will see you safely on board,' he replied.

He sat looking over the sea. Then he did talk a little.

He said: 'I'll kill him.'

'It would change nothing.'

'It would be a blessing for mankind.'

'Bertrand, don't talk like that. It would be a double tragedy if you gave way to revenge.'

I was thinking: You would never do it. You could not. He would never allow it and he is the one who calls the tune.

Bertrand took my hand and pressed it. I tried not to show how I shrank from his touch.

Everything was changed. I believed I would never be able to shut out of my mind the images which crowded into it, and Rollo de Centeville dominated them all.

I did not think Bertrand wanted to marry me now. I had seen that look of revulsion in his eyes when he had looked at me in that bed. It was not that he did not believe I had been tricked and forced against my will . . . he believed all that without a doubt. He saw me as the victim I had been; but at the same time he could not forget that, as the Baron said, I had been his mistress.

I could never marry Bertrand. Everything between us had been over since that moment he came into the bedroom.

So for once Rollo would not have his way. The object had been to make Bertrand eat his words. He would marry one of the Baron's cast-off mistresses . . . so he had thought. He was fooled at last, for there would be no marriage.

I was glad to be alone.

His last words were: 'I will write. We will work out something . . .'

I smiled at him. I knew it was over.

I leaned over the rail looking at the swirling water and I was filled with an angry resentment. I thought of that Kate Collison who had crossed the Channel not long ago setting out on a dangerous adventure. And dangerous it had certainly been, for I had come within the orbit of that strange man, the barbarian who had changed my life.

Fury seized me. He had dared use me because he wished to show that he must be obeyed. Bertrand must obey him. It had nothing to do with his desire for me, which I had believed must have been great for him to go to such lengths to satisfy it.

That was the ultimate humiliation. That was what angered me deep down more than anything else that had happened to me.

Away in the distance I could see the white cliffs.

The sight had a healing effect on me. I was going home.

Nicole

It was a strange feeling travelling through the Kentish countryside. The orchards, the hop fields, the oast houses, the meadows and the little woods, they all seemed so fresh, even after the summer. They looked the same as I had seen them many times before. It was I who had changed.

People would surely notice. I could not be the same. I did not look quite the same. Would they ask questions? How should I answer them? One thing I knew and that was that I could never bear to talk of the shameful thing that had happened to me.

It seemed that every day my hatred for that man grew more intense. If he – barbarian that he was – had greatly desired me, although I could not have forgiven him, perhaps I might – beneath my resentment – have felt a little flattered. But it had not been like that. He had merely wanted his revenge on Bertrand and he had used me for that purpose, taken me as though I were some inanimate object to be picked up and thrown aside when he had finished with it. That was how he saw all people. It did not occur to him that they might have feelings . . . or did it? Perhaps he simply did not care that they had. Everything . . . everyone . . . was for his pleasure.

Well, he should not score this time. He had ruined my life . . . and Bertrand's too perhaps . . . but he was not going to get the result he was looking for. His plot was going to fail. He could say that I had been his mistress – albeit most unwillingly – but he could not make me marry Bertrand.

We could snap our fingers at him.

But I must stop thinking of him. He was over as far as I was concerned. I hoped never to see him again. I had to think of myself and what I was going to do. There was only one way to act and that was to carry on as though this had never happened.

Could I do that? I would soon be put to the test.

I took the station fly and very soon I was getting out at the familiar house.

There was a cry from within. 'She's here. It's Kate.'

And they were running out. I saw my father first and his face was shining with happiness.

'Kate!' he cried. 'Dear Kate.'

Then I was in his arms. He held me away from him and studied me. I felt myself flushing. Was it obvious? But he gave no sign of anything but the utmost joy . . . and pride – that more than anything.

'My dearest child,' he said. 'It was a great success . . . beyond my dreams.'

I thought: His eyes are not strong enough to notice the difference.

I saw Clare then. She was standing shyly in the background. Some of the servants were with her – Mrs Baines the cook and Jerry the handyman, and the maids. They were all grinning their pleasure.

Clare came forward and took my hand tentatively. I kissed her.

'You look well,' she said. 'We were all so happy to hear that the picture was such a success.'

Mrs Baines had cooked a steak pie. I had liked it as a child and had been eating it frequently ever since because it was said to be one of my favourite foods. Supper would be served early, she said. She reckoned that travelling whipped up the appetite.

Clare took me to my room.

'Oh Kate,' she said, 'I'm so glad you're back.'

I looked at her steadily and said: 'You know about my father now.'

'Yes, he told us all when he came back.'

'What is it going to do to him?'

She was thoughtful. 'Oddly enough,' she said, 'he doesn't seem as upset as you would think. It was due to all that success you had. He told us about it. How that Baron was it? had a special gathering and introduced you, and how you were going alone to do the miniature of the princess and how you had other commissions. He feels his talent is a precious gift and it has been passed safely into your hands.'

'You really think that's how he feels?'

'Oh, I do. He has talked to me about it.' She lowered her eyes almost apologetically. 'I think it's because of Evie . . . and my being a connection of hers. He feels he can talk to me.'

'It's for you yourself, Clare,' I assured her. 'Evie was a wonderful rock for us, but she wasn't particularly sympathetic about our painting. She said it was "very nice" but I think it was only acceptable because it was our livelihood. He feels you understand, Clare.'

'Oh, I do hope so.'

'One senses it,' I told her.

'You must have had a most exciting time. You look . . .' I waited apprehensively. 'Different,' she finished.

'Different?'

'Well . . . more worldly, I suppose. Naturally you would . . . travelling and being recognized. It has made a difference in you. You look . . . shall I say? . . . poised.' She laughed. 'Don't ask me to explain. I was never good at explanations. When you have washed and changed do go and talk to your father. He is so longing to have you to himself.'

I went to him as soon as I could. He was in his study. Hanging on the walls were two miniatures – one he had done of my mother and the other of me as a child. They were exquisite pieces of work – his best, I always thought. He would never part with them.

'Kate,' he cried. 'It is good to have you home. Now tell me everything.'

Everything? I should certainly not do that. I wondered fleetingly how my dear, good and rather innocent father would have reacted to the rape of his daughter.

'The Princesse's miniature . . .' he went on.

'It was approved.'

'Did the Baron come to see it?'

'No. I had to take it to him. He has paid for it.'

'My dear Kate, you will be rich. Was the Princesse an easy subject?'

'In a way, yes. She was just a young girl.'

'But a Princesse!'

'She was quite a normal girl really.'

'And the Baron . . .' There seemed to be a long pause. 'He really did like it, then. Was he as enthusiastic about it as he was about your portrait of him?'

'I don't know. I think he liked it though.'

'Wonderful. A man who would not be easy to please.'

I wanted to scream out: Please stop talking about him. The only peace of mind I can have is in forgetting him.

'What about you?' I asked. 'You have come to accept . . . the inevitable.'

'The fact that you have been recognized makes a lot of difference to me, Kate. I always knew you had a remarkable talent, but I did think it was going to be difficult to make the world realize it. And now thanks to the Baron . . .'

I said quickly: 'Has there been any change in your eyes?'

'I fancy I don't see as well as I did when we set out on our travels. It is like looking into a fog . . . a little way off . . . but the fog creeps nearer. That was a mad prank of ours, Kate, but the wonder of it was that it worked. If the Baron hadn't been a true connoisseur of art, it could never have happened.'

Could he not stop bringing the man into the conversation? He seemed obsessed by him.

'I have other commissions now,' I said quickly.

'Yes. That is wonderful.'

'I shall be going back to Paris to the house of the Duponts in three weeks' time. I have to paint the two daughters, you remember.'

'It's quite wonderful. And when I think what you owe to the Baron . . .'

I said: 'I think we should go to dinner now, Mrs Baines won't be pleased if we are late.'

So we dined – my father, Clare and I – and I tackled the steak pie to Mrs Baines's satisfaction and answered the questions which were fired at me.

Clare looked on with her big doe-like eyes, full of happiness because I was home and my father was coming to terms about his encroaching blindness.

It was amazing how many times my father mentioned the Baron. It was impossible to escape from the man and I felt as though he were sitting at our dining-room table with us.

And that night I dreamed of him. I was lying on that bed in the lodge and he was approaching me. I screamed and awakened, greatly relieved to find myself in my own homely bed.

I wondered then, was I ever going to banish that man from my life?

A few days later a letter came from Madame Dupont. She hoped I would come as soon as possible. Her sister-in-law wanted to talk business with me too. She also had a daughter and was eager to have a Collison miniature of her.

'Of course,' she wrote, 'I know you are committed to do the wife of Monsieur Villefranche first but please do not let him thrust someone else upon you before you do my sister-in-law's girl.'

I was indeed a success. And he had done that for me, but I could not be grateful to him. I could feel nothing but hatred and disgust.

I would go earlier than I intended. I felt I had to get away from all the interrogation which I had to endure concerning my stay in Paris and I could not bear my father's constant references to the Baron.

Moreover, life in Farringdon was not the same. I thought the vicarage family frankly boring and I had never been so very friendly with the Cambornes.

Clare was getting on very well in the village. She had fitted in like a native and was constantly at the vicarage, decorating the church and discussing means of raising money for the bells and involving herself generally in the affairs of the neighbourhood. They all liked her, but her particular friends were the Camborne twins. She talked to me about them. She was a little concerned because Hope had an admirer and she worried a little about poor Faith.

'What would she do,' she said, 'if her twin married. She can't join up with them, can she? I do think poor Faith is getting very apprehensive. How strange nature is . . . to make two people so close . . .'

I scarcely listened. The affairs of the village had become very dull to me.

I was glad when the time came for me to leave.

My father said: 'It looks as though you will have several commissions. There is this new one coming along with the sister-in-law. You must take advantage of it.'

'It could mean quite a long stay in Paris,' I pointed out.

'The longer the better . . . at this stage. You have to get known. Later you can be more selective. It would be a mistake to overload the market, but just at first you must get known.'

'I feel I can leave you in safe hands.'

'Clare is wonderful. Shall I whisper something? She's easier to get on with than Evie was.'

'That's exactly what I think. Evie was a marvel of efficiency but Clare is more . . . what shall I say? She's softer . . . more human . . .'

'You're right. You couldn't leave me in better hands. So . . . no need to worry about anything at home. Keep your mind on your work. You're going to be the best Collison of us all.'

I was rather relieved when the time came for me to set out for Paris.

In spite of everything, I couldn't help feeling exhilarated when I arrived in Paris. It was early evening when I stepped out of the train at the Gare du Nord and immediately caught that whiff of excitement which the city had previously aroused in me. I was caught up in the bustle and noticed immediately the noise. The French talked so much more loudly than we did in England and their hands were as expressive as their voices. I heard strains of music coming from somewhere; and I smelt the familiar smell of trains and perfume.

I thought then: The past is done with. I shall begin again from here.

But when the porter carried my bags and hailed a cab for me and I caught sight of the *cocher* with his blue coat and white hat, I could not stop the tremor of apprehension running through me. I would never entirely forget. Even as I stepped into the cab and was asked in a friendly voice where I wanted to go, I looked suspiciously into the smiling face and saw another there.

I pulled myself together and gave Madame Dupont's address. I felt deeply moved as we trotted down the familiar

Boulevard Haussmann. The Rue du Faubourg Saint-Honoré was not far off.

The Duponts' house was in the Boulevard Courcelles – nestling among a row of tall white houses which I came to recognize as typical of the town houses of those who had estates in the country.

I suspected the Duponts were of that genre, as they had been guests of the Baron. I was sure he would only know people who were rich or of noble lineage.

I was almost surprised when the cab drew up and the *cocher* courteously helped me with my bags.

The door was opened by a manservant in dark blue livery with touches of silver about it. He greeted me with deference. I was evidently expected.

'Madame has asked that you be taken to her as soon as you arrive,' he told me. 'Pray come this way.'

He signalled to a boy in the same dark blue livery but with less silver braid, which I presumed indicated that he was of inferior rank, to take my bags, while I followed him into a large room with dark blue walls and white draperies which were most effective. It was a sort of reception hall. The man knocked on a door and with a flourish opened it and announced that Mademoiselle Collison had arrived.

Madame Dupont swam towards me.

'Welcome, Mademoiselle Collison,' she cried. 'It is a great pleasure to have you with us. We are looking forward to what you are going to do for us. Now, we want you to be very comfortable while you stay with us . . . and I do hope you will be able to work for my sister-in-law. She is most anxious for you to make a pretty picture of her young daughter.' Madame Dupont put a finger to her lips as though to conceal a smile. 'I don't think you will find her such a rewarding subject as my girls. But you'll do something beautiful with her, I know. I think perhaps you would like to go to your room first and then . . . shall we say . . . meet the girls? I believe you have to talk to them . . . draw them out. That was what the Baron suggested, I think.'

'Thank you, Madame Dupont,' I said. 'You are very kind.'

'And it has been a trying journey I have no doubt.'

'Well, it is long and the crossing is always difficult.'

'Yes, of course. Now would you like some refreshment or will you wait for dinner? It is for you to say.'

I said I would wait for dinner and she replied that she would summon a maid without delay to take me to my room.

This she did and I was conducted to a charming room on the first floor with windows which reached from ceiling to floor. It had dark walls and white curtains – which seemed to be the motif of the house. It was very attractive.

My bed had a beautiful tapestry headpiece in what I recognized as the Fontainebleau pattern – near-white swirling flowers on a dark blue background. The coverlet was white broderie anglaise – charming and fresh. My dressing-table was curtained in dark blue velvet and it had a white-edged mirror with three sides.

My feelings rose in spite of everything.

It had been the best thing possible for me to come to Paris, I was sure, and after such brutal handling as I had suffered, after such bitter humiliation, it was comforting to be treated with respect. My spirits were rising. I was an artist to be recognized and appreciated. I must put that horrifying episode behind me and make a new start. I was lucky in the fact that I had been given a chance to do so.

I changed into a dress of green brocade. I was prepared to live in an elegant society, and although I had not brought many clothes those I had were all quite adequate. I had learned something of what the French called *chic* during my brief stay in their country and I had, I think, been born with something in common with them: I loved the way in which they mingled colours and that elegance which could make the most plain among women look interesting. The fact was I had taken a step away from the past. I was on my way to a new life and I believed that in time I would forget the Baron.

I was interested in the house and longing to see my new subjects. Already I was concerning myself with where I should work and how I should approach the portraits of the Demoiselles Dupont.

A certain feeling of elation continued throughout the evening. I dined with the family and Madame Dupont treated me as though I were a person of considerable importance. I was the great painter acclaimed by the Baron de Centeville. Monsieur Dupont was a mild gentleman who seemed intent on humouring his wife's wishes and deferring to her in every way. I discovered later that he kept a pretty mistress in a little house on the Left Bank and his great aim was to keep his wife content so that she did not interfere with this very happy arrangement of his. The two daughters, Emilie and Sophie, did not interest me greatly as people, and only because they were subjects did I force myself to be concerned with them. They were seventeen and sixteen respectively – on the verge of being brought out into society – hence the miniatures. They giggled a great deal and had a habit of whispering together, which I found irritating and rather bad manners. But that was no concern of mine. I thought I could make reasonable pictures of them. I would try to flatter them, for it was no use seeking hidden character in those vapid little faces.

I was an object of interest to the girls, who took covert looks at me throughout the meal and met each other's eyes across the table conveying secret messages. They were the sort of girls who made you wonder whether you had a smut on your cheek or some buttons undone.

Madame Dupont, however, doted on them, and I was sure she saw them through a rose-coloured haze. Her great aim, I soon discovered, was to find suitable husbands for them both, while Monsieur Dupont's was to keep his family occupied with each other while he retained his love-nest on the Left Bank intact.

Madame, during the meal, informed her husband that, in spite of my youth, I was an acclaimed painter. One of the Collisons and everyone . . . but *everyone* . . . knew of the Collison miniatures. They were said to be in the top grade of miniatures throughout the world. All the family had done them for hundreds of years. Wasn't that wonderful? I believe she thought she was very astute to secure me before my prices soared.

She knew I was a great artist because the Baron de Centeville had made that very clear to her, and everyone knew that the Baron was one of the most respected connoisseurs in the country. He even advised the Emperor and Eugénie. The miniature I had done of the Baron was quite superb . . . and so was that of the Princesse de Créspigny.

'I am sure those of our girls will be equally successful. The Baron will present his to the Princesse and she will give hers to him. Is that not a charming gesture for affianced people to exchange objects of beauty? A miniature set in jewels – the Baron's was set in diamonds and sapphires – more appealing than an exchange of rings, I think. Well, you girls will have your miniatures when the time comes . . .'

Madame Dupont was a great talker. I was glad of that. It made one's own contribution less demanding.

I was to paint Emilie first as she was the elder, and the next morning I was taken to an attic which was fairly light and gave me enchanting views of Paris. I sat Emilie with the light on her face. Like my other model, the Princesse, her nose was too large, but whereas there had been character in the Princesse's face, I could detect little of that nature in my new model.

She was happy though, and that gave something pleasant

to her face. The eyes – dark brown – were not bad at all. Her skin was on the olive side – not easy. But I wanted to get that sheen of freshness because I could see that Emilie's main attraction was that which is given to us all at some time: Youth.

She watched me mix my paints.

'I hope you'll make me prettier than I am,' she said.

'I shall try to make an attractive picture. I like your dress.'

It was pale mauve and suited her dark colouring.

'Maman chose it.'

Trust Maman! Whatever else she was, she understood how to dress herself and her daughters.

'It's perfect,' I said. 'Just talk to me . . . comfortably . . . easily . . . as though I were a friend.'

'What shall I talk about?'

'About what you like doing. About your clothes . . . your friends . . .'

She was tongue-tied. I imagined how she would giggle with her sister when telling her about this sitting.

Finally she forgot her shyness and told me how she was going to be taken to Court. Her cousin Françoise would be coming soon and she and Françoise would be taken together. Sophie had to wait another year. She was having new dresses made and she was looking forward to it. She would be presented to the Emperor and the Empress Eugénie. Then of course there would be balls and she would meet all sorts of people. It would all be very exciting and if she were a success she might be married very soon.

'And you would like that?'

'It would depend on . . .'

'On the bridegroom,' I said. 'Well, naturally. What sort of bridegroom do you hope for?'

'Handsome, brave, noble – and Maman will insist that he is rich.'

'That's a big bill to fit. Now if you could only go for one of those qualities, which would it be?'

She looked at me in bewilderment. I could see it was no use trying to introduce a light note into conversation with Mademoiselle Emilie.

She said: 'First of all there's the wedding. That will be a big occasion. Sophie will be allowed to attend the reception.'

'Oh, what wedding is this?'

'The Baron de Centeville and the Princesse de Créspigny.'

'Oh,' I said faintly.

'Next week . . . at Notre Dame. The streets will be crowded. Oh, it will be such fun.'

I had been promising myself to forget him and now it seemed he was back as vividly as ever. I could not go on painting. My hand had lost its steadiness.

I said: 'The light is not good enough. I'll have to stop.'

Emilie was nothing loath. She was the sort of sitter who would tire easily.

'How is it going?' she asked.

'Well, it is rather soon yet.'

'Can I see?'

'I should wait a day or so.'

'All right. Goodbye. Can you find your way to your own room?'

'Oh yes, thank you very much.'

She ran off to giggle with Sophie about the sitting and the curious ways of the artist, I supposed.

I went to my room and sat for a long time looking out of my window at the Paris street.

So next week . . . he would be married . . . What did that matter to me? I had cut him out of my life. Poor little Princesse! I wondered what Marie-Claude was thinking at this moment.

The miniature was progressing well. It was not difficult. Just a stroke of the brush to get the line of the jaw. She had a heart-shaped face which was rather appealing. I would accentuate that. The colour of the skin bothered me; but when she was excited there was a faint rosy tinge in her cheeks. I would try for that. It worked wonders and made her eyes look bigger.

Yes, I was making a pleasant picture of Mademoiselle Emilie. I should finish in good time and then start on young Sophie.

I thought: It is money easily earned. The Baron had fixed the price for me. He had said: 'People value you as you value yourself. If you charge too little they will consider you second-rate. Put your prices high and they will believe you are worth it . . . even if you're not. People always like to think they get what they pay for.'

Thanks to him, I could become a rich and fashionable artist with many commissions like this.

I had worked steadily, feeling there was no need for delay. I had probed the nature of the little sister – not that it was necessary to dig very deeply. So much the better. In a way it made the task easier if not so interesting. How different it had been working on the Baron. In him I discovered something new every day.

I could not get him out of my mind. I supposed it was because he was going to get married soon.

There would be no sitting on the wedding day.

It dawned bright and sunny. It was going to be hot as the day progressed. I thought of the frightened little Princesse awakening on this morning – her last day of freedom. How would she fare with that monster of iniquity? I shuddered to contemplate the union. He would take her back to the château, I supposed. I imagined her – little Marie-Claude – awaiting him in the nuptial chamber, all her fears upon her. For she was frightened of him. I had discovered that much – and no doubt she had good reason to be.

The house was quiet. The family had gone to the wedding. The servants would be out in the streets because it was something of an occasion, and I imagined crowds would be gathered around Notre Dame to see the bride and groom arrive separately and depart together.

And then there came the irresistible urge to go into the streets to mingle with the people, to see him once more. Just once, I told myself, and then never . . . never again.

I put on my cloak and went out into the street. I hailed a cab – still something of an uneasy adventure for me – and I asked the *cocher* to take me to the Sainte-Chappelle. I thought that would be near enough and I would walk the rest of the way.

He chatted to me. He recognized my accent at once as that of a foreigner, as they all did. It amused me to see the different reactions. Most were amused in a friendly way, eager to help; but there were some who were a little resentful and inclined to despise one for not being French. It was a common trick, I knew now, to pretend not to understand what I said. But this one was decidedly friendly.

Had I been to see the Louvre, the Panthéon? I should take a cab to Montmartre. I told him it was not my first visit to Paris and I had already seen a little of the city, which I found fascinating.

He was delighted and talked incessantly.

'It's a bit crowded down this way. There's this society wedding . . . That brings out the crowds. The Baron de Centeville is getting married. I think the Empress will be there. It's the Princesse de Créspigny he's marrying.'

'I had heard that,' I told him.

'I'd keep out of the way, if I were you. You'll see nothing but the crowd.'

I thanked him for his advice, paid him and alighted at the Sainte-Chapelle.

For once I forgot to marvel that this old building had stood there for six hundred years and made my way in the direction of Notre Dame.

The crowds were thick. I thought: I was a fool to have come. I shall see nothing – and in any case I don't want to.

But there I was mistaken. There was a sudden hush in the crowd and then a shout. I saw them in an open carriage. He looked magnificent. I had to admit that. He was wearing some uniform of blue with gold braid which made his hair look fairer than I remembered it, and on his head was a cocked hat which might have been an admiral's. I had known he was connected with the Navy. Probably an honorary post, I imagined. And there seated beside him was Marie-Claude looking very beautiful in a gown of white satin sewn with pearls and a head-dress of laces and lilies-of-the-valley.

The crowd gave a cheer. I stared at him. He didn't see me, of course; and if he had, what would it have mattered to him?

The carriage passed out of sight and the crowd was dispersing; and I felt a great desire to go inside the cathedral and be quiet for a while. I must stop myself thinking of them. It was no concern of mine. Poor little Marie-Claude. She had been forced into marrying him – but there was nothing more anyone could do about that.

It was strange how quickly the crowds had gone. I went to the porch and looked up at the face of the demon . . . the most wicked of them all. As I watched, the stone seemed to change and take on the shape of his features. It was like a replica of the drawing I had made.

I went inside and sat down. I tried to superimpose other images on that of them sitting together side by side in the carriage. – but I could not do this. The marriage of opposites, I thought, and I believed there would be little happiness for either of them. I was not concerned for him. He deserved nothing but revenge. But I was very sorry for the Princesse.

Stop thinking of them! There was one charming story I had heard of a hundred poor girls to whom Louis the Sixteenth had given a dowry on the occasion of their marriages, as a thanksgiving for the birth of his daughter, Marie Thérèse Charlotte. He had been present at the wedding of those girls here in Notre Dame and had sealed their marriage licences with his fleur-de-lis ornamented sword. A hundred young men advancing, each giving a hand to one of the waiting girls – it must have been an enchanting sight.

It was rare that the cathedral saw such charming events, and I immediately thought of a more recent one when, seventy years before, during the revolution, the cathedral had been turned into a Temple of Reason and a harlot seated on a litter had been carried in, while half naked women and men danced obscenely around her in the name of Liberty.

I had a sudden desire to look down on the city, every aspect of which was of great fascination to me, and I left the darkness of the exterior and found my way to the turret from which one can look down.

It was silent as I entered the dark turret and started to climb the stairs. There was a chill in the air. I counted the steps and when I was half way up I thought I heard someone labouring up behind me. I suppose that was natural. Why should I be the only one who thought it worthwhile making this long climb up to the summit to look down on Paris.

Fresh air at last! Oh, indeed the view was magnificent. I could look right down on Paris and on either side of me were the north and south banks. I could see the Marais behind the Tour Saint-Jacques to the north and in the south the Rue de Bièvre and the Boulevard St Michel with the district which lay between.

While I stood there I was aware of someone beside me. My heart started to hammer and for a moment I felt as though I was unable to move. Terror seized me, as it had when I had suddenly realized the man in the blue coat and white hat was no ordinary *cocher*.

Then a voice said: 'You remember me?'

I turned. I was looking into the face of Nicole St Giles.

'I think I startled you,' she went on.

'Yes. I . . . I thought I was alone up here.'

'People don't often trail up those steps. Do you know there are three hundred and ninety-seven of them?'

'It seemed like a thousand.'

She laughed. 'I was so pleased to see you in the crowd, but you didn't see me. I saw you start up the stairs and I guessed you were coming to look at the view. You're at the Duponts' in Courcelles, I believe?'

'Yes,' I said; and I thought: She would know, of course. She was at the château when it was arranged. How much more did she know?

'I couldn't resist coming to see the wedding,' she said.

'Couldn't you?' I looked at her searchingly. Did she care very much? She did not seem to.

'I hope it's a success,' she said, and I noticed she had not said that she hoped they would be happy.

I shrugged my shoulders.

'I hope, too, that you will come and see me while you are in Paris. I have a house on the Left Bank. Let me give you a card. It's not very far from the Sorbonne and near the Luxembourg Gardens. Quite pleasant.'

'You live there . . . all the time.'

'Yes, now. All the time.'

I thought: It is over for you then. You are just thrown aside.

But she seemed very happy.

'How are the portraits going?'

'Quite well. I have done the elder young lady. Now I have the younger and then there is a cousin. I think it better for me to do the three before I move on to the house of Monsieur Villefranche.

'So you will be in Paris for some time yet. I think the Villefranche house is in the Avenue de l'Alma just off the Champs-Elysées.'

'Yes, that is so.'

'You will be well acquainted with Paris by the time you have finished. What shall you do after the Villefranche picture?'

'Go back to England unless –'

'Unless there are other commissions? I should think there might well be. I hear your name mentioned a great deal.'

'Oh, do you?'

'Yes, with considerable awe. The fact that you are a woman seems to have added a piquancy. The Baron saw to that.'

I was silent.

'Do come and see me,' she said. 'I should love to show you my house.'

'Thank you.' I took the card and slipped it into the pocket of my coat.

'I shall expect you. I am really very pleased that we have met again.'

'Thank you. Do you think it is a little chilly up here?'

'Yes, let's go down. Will you go first or shall I?'

I followed her down. I thought how elegant she looked, how serene.

But what was she really feeling – this discarded woman?

I had finished Sophie's portrait and had begun that of Françoise when the fearful certainty came to me. I was going to have a child.

The horror of this crashed down on me. It had been a faint black cloud in the sky for some little while and then came the certainty. I should have realized that it was highly probable. I think I had felt that I could not contemplate anything worse than what I had already endured and had refused to look this possibility in the face.

A child. *His* child! I had promised myself that I would forget that humiliating incident but as this had happened, it would mean that that terrible interlude would be with me for the rest of my life.

It now seemed an inevitable consequence. We had been together for three nights . . . three nights of incessant rape, I called it. And now . . . a child . . . living evidence of what had happened to me.

Had he thought of this? I was sure he had. He had thought I was going to marry Bertrand and had no doubt considered that it would be rather amusing for me to bear a child to whom Bertrand could give his name.

There was, however, to be no marriage. I had not heard from Bertrand and I felt that I never would. I did not want to really.

But now . . . what was I going to do? I, an unmarried woman, was to bear a child.

I was amazed that I could work, but I did. I could throw myself wholeheartedly into work and forget everything while I was thus engaged. There was nothing for me but that young face which I had to produce for immortality. A hundred years from this moment people would look at my miniature of Francoise and know how she had looked at this time.

My work soothed me; in a way it revitalized me; it took strain from my mind; it gave me blessed forgetfulness of a future which must be fraught with difficulties.

But as soon as I had ceased to work the clouds settled round me.

Perhaps I had made a mistake. In my heart I knew it was no mistake. Something had warned me when I had seen him in the carriage with Marie-Claude that I had not seen the last of him.

I spent a lot of time in my room. Soon I should have to pass on to the house of Monsieur Villefranche. After that I would go home. I tried to imagine myself telling my father and Clare.

How could I do that? Well-brought-up young ladies did not suddenly announce that they were about to give birth to a bastard.

I heard myself telling my father: 'I was abducted, forced to submit to the wicked Baron. This is the result.'

It sounded feeble. Why had I said nothing about it until now? The inference would be that I had willingly dallied with the Baron knowing full well that he was betrothed to the Princesse.

'I hate him! I hate him!' I said aloud and then laughed at myself. What was the use of reviling him now?

But what was I going to do?

Here I was on the brink of a great career and this had happened to me. If it hadn't I could have forgotten in time. Perhaps I could have settled down to a normal life with someone else, although at the moment I felt that to be impossible. He had damaged me mentally as well as physically. I had heard this could happen. He had made me shrink from men because if ever one approached me I should see *his* face leering at me, looking like the demon-gargoyle of Notre Dame.

As I considered the implications of what had happened to me I began to get frightened. I had time to ponder, it was true. Moreover, I had another portrait to do before I returned to England so had not to go immediately. I kept wondering how I could tell my father. He would be kindly and understanding, I knew; but he would be very shocked and I did not see how I could stay at Collison House with all the village knowing about my child.

I walked a great deal during those days. I had plenty of time to myself, and if I worked all morning I did not take up my brush during the rest of the day. In the early afternoon I need relaxation and I never felt the light was good enough after four o'clock.

I had lost my eager interest in the city. I would walk

without even seeing the objects of beauty and antiquity. I was confronted all the time by my own seemingly insoluble problem.

One afternoon I sat down outside the Café Anglais where little tables had been set up under pink and white sunshades. It was getting a little chilly now, for we were well into September and there was a touch of autumn in the air. I wondered vaguely how much longer one would be able to sit in the streets and watch the people pass by as one drank a cup of coffee.

I was sitting there, deep in thought, when a voice called out: 'Why, hello. It's you again.' It was Nicole St Giles. 'May I sit with you?' she went on. 'I'd like a cup of coffee.' She called to the garçon to bring it to her; then she turned to me. 'You look worried. Isn't the picture going well?'

'Yes, the picture is going very well.'

'How fortunate you are to be so gifted! I suppose you feel that having this gift . . . well, it's a compensation for so many things, isn't it . . . almost everything?'

She was looking at me steadily and after a slight pause she said: 'Do tell me what's wrong. I'd like to help if I can.'

Perhaps it was the kindliness in her face. Perhaps it was the gentleness in her voice as she took my hand and pressed it. It might have been because I was so desperate. In any case, I clutched her hand and said: 'I am going to have a child.'

She looked at me intently and said: 'We can't talk here very well.'

I shook my head. 'I don't know why I told you.'

Her coffee had come and she stirred it absent-mindedly.

'You told me because you had to tell someone,' she said. 'I'm so glad I came along then. Come to my house. There we can talk in comfort. Don't worry. I am sure I can be of help. It's not such an unusual state of affairs you know. It has happened before . . . many times. The thing is to keep a cool head.'

Strangely enough I felt tremendously relieved, and when she had finished her coffee and the bill was paid she hired a cab and we sped away together.

The cab pulled up in one of the streets leading from the Boulevard St Michel. We were before a white house of some four stories.

'Here we are,' said Nicole, and led the way up three steps to a door guarded by lions. She opened the door and we were in a hall of quite large proportions with a moulded ceiling which was decidedly elegant. A door opened and a man – whom my knowledge of the city immediately told me was a concierge – appeared.

He said good day to Madame St Giles and eyed me curiously while we passed into a room with long windows looking out on a patio in which grew potted plants.

There was a grand piano in one corner, several settees, comfortable-looking chairs, and one or two tables; an ormolu clock chimed four on the mantelpiece over the fireplace and on either side of it were figurines, flimsy draperies covering their anatomy in those sections which it would have been considered, in polite society, immodest to reveal.

She certainly had a comfortable – even luxurious home.

'Do sit down,' she said, 'and tell me.'

I told her frankly what had happened. She nodded as I went along, and what was so comforting, did not question anything but believed all I said. Of course, she knew the Baron as well as anyone could.

She said at length: 'It's not an easy situation, but you can manage.'

'Manage!' I cried. 'I don't know what to do. I could go home, I suppose. Can you imagine what it would be like in a small confined English village.'

'Very much what it would be like in a small confined French one,' she said. 'But of course you won't go back there.'

'How how . . . where . . .'

She looked at me and smiled. I had always thought she had a sweet smile. 'Will you let me help . . . advise?'

'I am in such a state of anxiety that I would welcome any help and advice.'

'Don't panic,' she said. 'Remember it is not an unusual situation.'

'You mean . . . rape . . . and such consequences.'

'I really meant respectable young women finding themselves pregnant. You are fortunate. You have your work. That must be a great solace. Moreover, it is a means of livelihood . . . quite a good livelihood I imagine.'

'It is becoming so.'

'And it will go on getting better and better. You are on the road to fame and fortune. This . . . matter . . . must not interfere with that.'

'I don't see how.'

'I do. Because you are going to let me help.'

'I have no idea what I . . . or anyone . . . can do. Here I am a stranger in this city. I shall work while I can. Then I suppose I must go home. I know my father will help but it will be a great shock for him. He has had one shock. His eyes . . . you know.'

'Yes, I do know.' She leaned towards me and touched my hand briefly. 'Will you . . . let me be your friend?'

I looked at her in astonishment.

'It is difficult for me to say all I feel,' she went on. 'You probably regard me as little more than a stranger. I don't feel we are. You know a good deal about me. I know of you. And we both know the Baron . . . intimately.'

'Please, I don't want to talk about that wretched experience.'

'I understand. Listen. I am alone here. You are in this situation. Please let me help you?'

'How could you?'

'To begin with I could talk to you. It is always a good idea to discuss these matters, to consider what is the best way of tackling them. I know Paris very well. I would know where you could go to have your baby. I have this house. It is large. I don't use it all. I have thought of letting part of it. At night it seems so quiet here. Sometimes I give parties. I have many acquaintances . . . people I knew in the past . . . but very few real friends. I am putting a proposition to you. I know I can help you. Take some rooms in this house. Make one your studio. You need quarters in Paris. You want people to come to you to be painted. You don't want to go to their houses just when they call you. You have to set yourself up as a great artist . . . act like a great artist . . . live like one. Now this would be a good address for you. We are on the Left Bank . . . that is where the intellectual people are gathering . . . clerics, professors, students, artists are here . . . I am talking too much.'

'Of course you are not. Please go on. It is so kind of you. I could see no way out of my problem . . . I don't know why you take so much trouble about me.'

She was silent for a moment, then she said. 'In a way we are both . . . victims. No, I mustn't say that. It's not true.'

'You mean of the Baron de Centeville.'

'It is not fair to say that I am a victim. I'll explain all that to you some time, but now let us think of you. I realize this is all very sudden and you want time to think about it. But really, Kate . . . May I call you Kate? . . . I think we are going to be good friends. You have a great deal of planning to do and the sooner you begin the better.'

'You talk as though everything is so simple.'

'I wouldn't say that, but most things are not as difficult as one first thought if they are approached in a sensible and realistic way.'

'But I am going to have a *child*!'

'I always longed for children,' she said. 'I could envy you.'

'This child will be the result of something I want more than anything to forget. If only I could go back in time. If only I had gone straight home instead of making that journey . . .'

Again she touched my hand. 'Don't think back. Think forward.'

I contemplated her earnest face. I was a little unsure as I must be of anything connected with the Baron, and I reminded myself that she had been his mistress and probably his confidante. How could I be sure that this was not some fresh plot?

She understood the trend of my thoughts. 'You'll want to consider this very carefully,' she said. 'Go back now. The concierge will get a cab for you. You have my address. Think about everything. There is an attic right on the rooftops with plenty of glass. It was built for an artist. I will help you . . . having the child. I can put you in touch with the people you will need. You can make this your home, and let me tell you that in this part of Paris you are not expected to live the conventional life that you would be in the Faubourg Saint-Honoré. You could work here. Your patrons could come to be painted. It is a proposition. But I do understand that you will need time to decide.'

'It is very grand,' I said. 'Should I be able to afford it?'

'My dear Kate, you need to be grand to show how successful you are, and if you are successful you will be able to afford it. Come. You need to contemplate all this. Such decisions should not be made lightly.'

'I have a great deal of thinking to do, I know.'

She nodded in agreement. 'Go now,' she said. 'You have my address. You know where to find me.'

'But how can I thank you.'

She saw me into the cab.

'Remember,' she said. 'You are not alone . . . unless you

want to be. I will be your friend if you want me. It is for you to decide.'

That encounter changed everything. I could see before me an avenue of escape, however bizarre it seemed. I occupied myself during the next few days thinking about it. It was a mercy that while I worked I was able to shut out everything else but the portrait.

The more I thought of Nicole's suggestion, the more possible it appeared. It seemed the only possibility. I went to see Nicole again. She was delighted that I had come and I fancied that my predicament had given her a new interest in life which she badly needed at this time. True, I was a little suspicious. Surely anyone who had been treated as I had would be. This was chiefly because of her past connection with the Baron. Everyone who had been near to him could be polluted.

On my second visit, she said: 'I want you to come, Kate. I want to help you. I'm feeling very lonely . . . lately.'

'Because of . . . him?'

'I was with him for eight years. It's a long time. You don't speak. I can see that you do not understand.'

'I understand perfectly. We were both used by him. You happened to agree and I did not.'

'Yes, I suppose you could say that. But don't waste your sympathy on me. I knew this would happen eventually. He would marry and that would be the time for me to disappear. It was understood from the first.'

'Do you mean it was a sort of contract?'

'Not in the usual understanding of such a term. My mother was . . . well, not exactly a courtesan. Shall we say a demi-mondaine. She was the mistress of a great nobleman. He provided for her and looked after her when her services were no longer required. It was a life she was bred to. So was I. I was married when I was seventeen to Jacques St Giles.

He was a respectable young man who worked in one of our banks. We lived together for a year, but it was never meant to last. My mother wanted me to marry. I would then have a right to call myself Madame which, she always said, gentlemen preferred to Mademoiselle. A young girl could make demands which a married woman could not – so marriage made the situation so much more comfortable.'

'It all seems rather cynical.'

'Call it realistic. Then I was introduced to the Baron by my mother, who hoped that I would please him. I did. I had been well educated, brought up to appreciate art and to be what is called a cultivated woman. I was taught how to carry myself, how to dress, how to converse with grace. That was the theme of my education . . . to please. Well, it is what I did. And here I am. Thirty years of age, with my own house and a comfortable settlement. I need never work again as long as I live. You might say I was brought up in a rewarding profession, one which brings good returns and security. Better, I was always taught, than becoming a drudge and mother of many children. Do you understand?'

'I still think it very mercenary and, I must confess, immoral.'

'Oh, you will never understand. I don't suppose this sort of thing would happen in England. It's part of French life – the life of the demi-mondaine. I was born into it. I found a generous lover . . . and here I am. I see you are more than a little shocked. Please don't be – and don't be sorry for me. It was a very pleasant life.'

'With that man!'

'Let me tell you I became quite fond of him. I began to learn something about him.'

'And that made you fond of him?'

'It made me see why he was the man he was.'

'And you could really be fond of such a man?'

'Kate, what he did to you was unforgivable. Don't think I

don't realize that. If it had happened to me . . . and I had been like you . . . I should have felt the same.'

'It was monstrous,' I said fiercely. 'It is treating people about him as though they are of no importance beyond the use they can be to him. It is picking them up . . . exploiting them . . . and then throwing them aside.'

'I know. It was his upbringing. His father and his grandfather were like that. He was brought up to believe that that was the way men such as they were behaved.'

'It is time someone taught them differently.'

'No one will ever do that. You see how it is now. A word from the Baron and everyone acclaims you. He has power . . . even in these days he has it.'

'You mean money! Position!'

'Yes, but more than that. It is something in his personality. If you could understand you would realize why he is the way he is.'

'I don't care why. It is because he is that way that he maddens me. He should be punished, taken to law.'

'Would you be prepared to go to law, to accuse him of rape? Would you stand up in a court? Think of the questions they would ask. Why did you not complain at the time? That is what they would ask. You would hurt yourself more than you could hurt him. Be practical. Don't go on brooding on what has happened. Think of what you are going to do now.'

I said: 'I shall soon have finished Françoise's portrait. There is to be a ball. The miniatures will be shown there.'

'What the Baron does today the world does tomorrow. Madame Dupont is slavishly copying the style he sets. Never mind. It's all to the good. It may well bring in fresh business. From that ball I'll swear you get two more definite commissions at least – and perhaps many more.'

'After that I leave for the house of Monsieur Villefranche for his wife's picture.'

'And then?'

'I should go home and see my father.'

'And tell him?'

'I don't know whether I could do that. Perhaps when I come face to face with him I shall know whether or not I can tell him.'

'And if you could not?'

I turned to her. 'You have been so kind to me . . . so helpful.'

'I hope I shall be your friend.'

'I can tell you that since our meeting I have felt so much better. You have made me realize that I have to stop looking back. I have to plan. I am afraid I shall hate this child.'

She shook her head. 'Women like you never hate their children. As soon as this baby arrives you will love it and forget the way it came.'

'If it should look like him . . .'

'I will make a wager. You will love this child more because of the problems of its birth.'

'You are a very worldly woman, Nicole,' I said.

She smiled at me and said softly: 'It is the best way to survive.'

Madame Dupont gave her ball, which was to launch Emilie into society. There were many guests and I was treated with great respect. My work was admired and Nicole was right. Two people gave me definite invitations to visit their houses and paint portraits.

I was effusively complimented on the miniatures. Madame Dupont had had them set in frames embellished with diamonds and rubies. She could hardly copy the Baron so blatantly as to choose sapphires, but I felt sure she would have liked to.

However, it was very satisfactory and I could see that I was really being projected into a successful career.

How gratifying it would have been but for the part the

Baron had played in my life. If only I had never met him! But then all this would not have happened if I had not.

I was meeting Nicole regularly and getting to like her more and more. She was frank about herself. She told me she was lonely and wanted friendship. Perhaps she felt a little resentful about being cast off by the Baron (although she always insisted that he was not to blame and that the position had been understood from the first), perhaps she felt that we who had both known him would understand each other; however, the friendship between us flourished, and the more I thought of her proposition the more it seemed that it was the only road open to me.

I left the Duponts and went to the Villefranche house. Madame Villefranche was a pretty little woman with a happy temperament and very contented with her lot. She gave me little difficulty and I was able to produce a very beautiful picture of her.

I was feeling more calm now and no longer awoke in a cloud of horror. Nicole had convinced me that with a little careful planning, I could come through the ordeal which lay before me. Moreover, I was beginning to feel something for the child, and I realized that if I were to discover it were all a mistake after all, my feelings would be very mixed.

Nicole was right. I should love the child when it came, and the thought of its coming gave me a strange sense of fulfilment.

By the time I had finished the Villefranche portrait I had made up my mind that I would go to see my father immediately. I would stay at home for a week and then come back to carry out my next commission. During that time I would definitely decide what I was going to do.

Nicole said that was a wise procedure.

It was the beginning of October when I went back. I felt emotional as the train carried me across the Kentish country. I noticed that the hops had been gathered in. They would be storing them in the oast houses scattered across this part of the country; and now was the time for the fruit to be gathered in. Ladders were propped against the trees and rosy apples and russety pears were being packed into baskets.

Home! I thought. I shall miss it. But it is not so very far away. I can come back sometimes. Nicole will think of something.

So much would depend on what happened within the next week. If I could bring myself to tell my father, he might have some plan. Perhaps he and I could go away together. No, that would not do. Besides, how could we live? I knew he had saved enough to live on in a modest way, but that would not include travelling and how could he live away from Collison House, and how could I live there with my child? It would be in the minds of everyone in the village – even if they were kind as I knew my friends would be – that my child was a bastard.

A warm welcome was awaiting me. How comfortable it was! More homely than in Evie's day. A little untidy perhaps, but I could only repeat myself homely. That was Clare's influence.

She came out with my father when I arrived and they both hugged me tightly.

'It is wonderful to see you,' said my father, and Clare echoed: 'Wonderful, wonderful. Your room is all ready. I have made sure the bed has had a good airing.'

'Clare is always fussing about airing.' said my father fondly. 'She coddles us, in fact.'

Clare tried to look severe, which was impossible. 'It is something I insist on,' she said.

I felt more grateful to her than ever. Having someone like Clare to look after everything at Collison House made my decision so much easier.

My father wanted to know all that had happened. I told

him about the portraits I had done and the new commissions I had.

He was completely delighted. 'Splendid! Splendid!' he cried. 'It's like a miracle. Who would have thought on the day we received that letter from France all this would grow out of it.'

Who indeed? I thought. And if only he knew what had grown out of it!

'It's the most wonderful thing that could have happened to you, Kate,' he said. 'But for this you would have stayed here with me. Nobody would have given you credit for the work for years. It's changed you, Kate. You even look different.'

'How different?' I asked.

'Ready to face the world. Ready to take all it offers you.'

'Can you see a difference then?'

'I know you so well, my dear. You now look and talk like the assured artist you are . . I wish I could have seen those portraits.'

'I knew they were good,' I said.

'You have been doing fine work for a long time now.'

'And what of you, Father? What have you been doing?'

'I do a little painting. I have taken up landscapes and can manage quite well. One doesn't have to produce exactly what one sees. If you miss something you say, "That's art. This is not copying".'

'And you enjoy this landscape painting? I must see some of it.'

'Well, we have plenty of time for that.'

'I have only a week, you know. Then I must go back. I've promised.'

'Yes, yes, of course. You have to paint as many miniatures as you can while this fashion for you lasts.'

'Do you think it is just a fashion?'

'It may not be. In fact I think you're too good for that.

Let's say it began as a fashion because of the glowing comments of a man whose opinion is respected in art circles . . . and in society.'

'I have to make it more than that, Father.'

'You are doing so. As I said: Do as much as you can now. I am glad you found time to come and see me.'

Now was the time to tell him. He looked almost contented. He had come to terms with his disability; he was finding satisfaction in his landscapes. He would not be able to continue indefinitely with them, of course, but they were forming a pleasant bridge for him. He was not going to be catapulted into blindness without having time to prepare for it. And I knew that my success had been the greatest help of all in this sad matter. He could bear his own disability while he could think of my carrying on the family tradition.

I thought in that moment: 'No, I cannot tell him. I have to play it Nicole's way.

'There is something I want to talk to you about, Father,' I said. 'Do you remember Nicole St Giles?'

'Wasn't she a friend of the Baron?'

'Yes. He's married now. He married the Princesse. I saw something of the wedding. But I wanted to talk to you about Nicole. She is a very sophisticated woman and has a largish house on the Left Bank. I have become quite friendly with her.'

'A very pleasant woman, as I remember.'

'She *is* very pleasant. She has suggested that it would be better for my career if I took a place of my own in Paris . . . as that is where the work is. Her own house is too big for her and she has offered to let me part of it.'

He was silent for a few moments. I felt my heart beat uneasily. I thought: He doesn't like it. But the cloud passed. He said: 'You have to plan your career very carefully, Kate. You're handicapped by being a woman. I've always thought that was foolish . . . foolish and unworthy. A good painting is a good painting, whoever does it. You would live there on your own, Kate?'

'Well, Madame St Giles would be in the house . . . a sort of chaperone.'

'I see.'

'Sharing the house is her idea. There's an attic which could be turned into a studio and a magnificent room where I could entertain clients. Madame St Giles knows many people and it is her opinion that if I just carry out commissions that come in the way they have so far there will be a time when I shall run short of them. I should then return to England . . . and obscurity.'

He lapsed again into silence for a few seconds. Then he said slowly: 'I think she may be right. It's a bit of a venture. And, Kate, remember, if it doesn't work you can always come home.'

I put my arms round him and held him close to me. How I hated deceiving him! But I simply could not tell him that I was going to have a child. He was happier now than he had been since the fearful discovery. He was seeking so many compensations. Because he had lost his keen vision I was taking on the family mantle. I was being given my chance which he realized I might never have had. Evie had gone and at the time that had seemed a calamity but lo, here was Clare, to bring a warmer atmosphere into the house.

He was happy as things were and I had made my decision.

It was moving to see how pleased they all were to have me home and yet in a way it gave me an uneasy qualm to think of what I had to do. Mrs Baines had made the usual steak pudding, and as I knew the amount I ate would be reported, I did my best.

I had to hear what was going on in the village.

Clare knew a great deal about village life. She had thrown herself into it so wholeheartedly. Dear Clare, I sensed her delight in having become part of a family, part of a community. She must have been very lonely before coming to us.

Dick Meadows was fully qualified now and there was a new curate at the vicarage. Dick was doing a stint as curate somewhere in the Midlands and Frances was still keeping house for her father. 'Poor Frances,' said Clare with feeling, 'that will be her life.'

Her eyes filled with tears of compassion. She was, I knew, thinking of what Frances's life would be . . . looking after her father until she was middle-aged, and when he died it would be too late for her to have a life of her own. A fate which befell many daughters and could have been Clare's own.

'And what of the twins?' I asked.

There was silence. I looked from my father to Clare.

'There was a tragedy,' said my father. 'Poor Faith.'

'A tragedy!'

Clare shook her head and turned appealingly to my father. 'You tell her,' she begged.

'It upset Clare very much,' said my father. 'She was one of the last people to see her alive.'

'You mean Faith Camborne is dead?'

'It was an accident,' my father explained. 'You know Bracken's Leap.'

Indeed I knew Bracken's Leap. It was always forbidden to me when I was young. 'Don't go near the Leap!' I could hear those words now. They had been used so often, Bracken's Leap was that spot where the road wound upwards to a high headland. It rose stark up from the valley below. Someone had committed suicide there two hundred years before, and I had never known whether he had been named Bracken or whether it was so called because of the bracken which grew there.

'You mean Faith Camborne . . .'

'She fell,' said my father. 'We don't know exactly whether it was an accident . . . or suicide.'

'You mean someone may have . . .'

'Oh, no, no, no! Whether she did it herself or slipped and lost her balance . . .'

'But she would never kill herself. She was such a timid creature. Oh dear, what an awful thing. Poor Faith! It is terrible when something like that happens to someone you have known.'

I kept seeing Faith and I couldn't see Faith without Hope. They were always together. Faith clinging to her twin as though her life depended on that support. Poor, poor Faith.

Clare was clearly too overcome for speech. I remembered how friendly she had always been with the twins.

'It's dangerous up there,' my father went on. 'They've fenced it off now.'

'Rather like shutting the stable door when the horse has run away,' I commented. 'Oh poor Faith! What about Hope and the doctor and his wife?'

'Very cut up . . . all of them. It's a good thing that Hope is getting married and going away.'

'Do you think that Faith . . . Do you think it was because of Hope's engagement?'

'We don't know,' replied my father. 'The verdict was accidental death. It's better to leave it like that for everybody's sake.'

I nodded.

Clare was quietly crying.

I leaned over and touched her hands. She turned her swimming eyes to me. 'She was my special friend,' she said. 'They both were . . . but I think Faith specially . . . more than Hope. It was terrible.'

There was silence at the table. Then my father said: 'I wonder what she would have done when Hope married.'

'Poor Faith,' said Clare, 'she would have been lost without her sister.'

My father sought to change the subject which so clearly

upset Clare. He said: 'Kate has had a wonderful offer. Someone she met in Paris has offered to rent her an apartment in the heart of Paris. There is a studio and everything that is necessary for her work. She can take it for a while and see how things work out. Commissions at the moment are rolling in.'

Clare was smiling at me. 'Oh, Kate. I'm so happy for you. It is wonderful how everything is turning out for you. I love to hear about that party when that . . . what was he . . . Baron or someone . . . told them all what a great artist you are.'

'It's not more than she deserves,' said my father.

'How will you like living in a foreign city . . . away from everyone?' asked Clare.

'I shall miss you all,' I told her. 'But I shall come home when I can. And it seems to me the right . . . the only thing . . . to do.'

'Let's drink to Kate's success,' said Clare.

The tears for Faith were still in her eyes as she lifted her glass.

I often thought how much I owed to Nicole.

She was practical in the extreme and as soon as I returned to Paris to the house of the Régniers – my next commission – I went to see her..

'Well?' she said.

But I didn't have to tell her. She knew. She put her arms round me and held me close to her for a moment.

Then she said: 'Now we start to plan.'

After that I saw her almost every day. There was so much to talk about, so much to arrange. It was immediately decided that the attic should be my studio, and that I should have a room in which to receive people and discuss appointments and terms. We should share the salon and I should have a bedroom next to the attic.

'There is a suite of rooms up there,' she said, 'and you can have those when the baby arrives. They'll be suitable for the first few months anyway . . . until the child begins to walk.'

She had worked out everything. I must, of course, remain Kate Collison. But instead of being Mademoiselle I should become Madame. We could have a vague story in the background about a husband who had unfortunately died. 'The tragedy is fairly recent,' she explained, 'so we do not wish to discuss it. It is too painful. You retained the name of Collison because it means a great deal in the art world and you are carrying on the family tradition.' She paused and then went on: 'As soon as the present commissions are completed you will expect clients to come to the studio to be painted. In the meantime we will prepare it and make sure it is all that it should be to accommodate a fashionable and famous artist. You can go on painting right until the last month, I should think. In any case we can see about that when the time comes. I shall engage a midwife who I know is efficient in her job and does in fact attend the nobility. In the meantime we shall prepare for this infant. We shall have everything of the best for it. Leave that to me.'

'I want to be careful with money,' I insisted. 'I know I am highly paid now and I have saved quite a bit. But I have the future to think of.'

'The future is assured if you will let it be. You have to act like a great artist. That is of the utmost importance. Money affairs are mundane matters. They should not concern you overmuch. You are deeply interested only in art. I think we are getting everything arranged nicely. All we have to do now is to await the birth and in the meantime go on painting and piling up the shekels.'

'Nicole,' I said one day, 'why are you doing all this for me?'

She was silent for a moment. Then she said: 'Friendship.' And after another pause: 'I'm doing it for myself in a way. I was lonely. The days seemed so long. They don't any more. I always wanted children.'

'Do you mean . . . his . . . ?'

'Well,' she said, 'it wouldn't have been possible. He didn't want a wife then. He wanted a mistress.'

'And, of course, he thought only of himself, as always.'

'I never told him I wanted children.'

'He might have guessed that any woman would.'

'Not my sort of woman.'

'How can you talk of sorts of women! They are all individuals . . . no two alike.'

'No, perhaps not. But we can be roughly sorted into types. I mean, the women who choose the way of life I chose do not usually want children.'

'That way of life was chosen for you.'

'Well, most of us have something chosen for us. It is the bold ones who break away. No. I must be fair. I accepted that way of life because it was amusing and interesting. I had tried respectability, hadn't I, and I knew it wasn't for me.'

'Nicole, I fancy I'm growing up fast, through you.'

'I'm glad to be of help and what I wanted to say is that it is no use blaming anyone for what we are. It's in our hands.'

'"Not in our stars but in ourselves . . ."' I quoted. 'Oh yes, I see that.'

'And we should be lenient in our judgement of others.' She looked at me almost appealingly. 'The way in which we are brought up does affect our lives. You see, in my case, I was made to see a great deal that was desirable in pandering to the pleasure of someone who could give me a secure future. It's like many people's approach to marriage in a way. Think of all those fond Mammas parading their daughters for the highest bidder, one might say. It was the same with me. More honest in a way. I had to give more in return for what I received. I had to continue to please.' She laughed at me. 'It sounds immoral, doesn't it, to one who has been brought up carefully in a pleasant household. But you see, heredity and upbringing have made you a painter; the same thing has made me a courtesan.'

'They made you clever, understanding and kind, and I'm grateful to you, Nicole. In fact, I don't know what I should have done without you.'

'Well, it is not all for you. I was lonely. I wanted an interest. Oh Kate, I *am* looking forward to our baby.'

'Nicole, so am I. So am I!'

On another occasion she said: 'You don't feel so vehement about him now, do you?'

'The Baron?'

She nodded.

'I hate him as intensely as ever.'

'You mustn't.'

'I couldn't stop myself if I tried. I shall always hate him.'

'You shouldn't. It might be bad for the child. He is the father, remember.'

'I wish I could forget that.'

'Try to understand him.'

'Understand him! I understand him too well. He's a throw-back to the age of barbarism. He has no place in a civilized world.'

'He used to talk to me about his childhood sometimes.'

'I am sure he was the most horrible child who tortured little animals and tore the wings off flies.'

'No, he did not. He was fond of animals. He loves his dogs and horses.'

'Was it really possible for him to love anything besides himself?'

'Now you are working yourself up and as I told you that's bad for the child.'

'Anything connected with him is bad for everyone near him.'

'But he is the child's father.'

'For Heaven's sake, Nicole, don't keep reminding me of that.'

'I want you to see him in a new light. You must understand what sort of man his father was.'

'Just like him, I should imagine.'

'He was the only son. Everything was concentrated on him.'

'He liked that, I am sure.'

'No. It meant that he was always under observation . . . he was brought up in a way which made him what he is. He had to excel at everything. He was constantly made aware of his ancestry.'

'Those savage marauding Normans who raided the coasts of peaceful people, stole their goods and raped their women. I can well believe that.'

'A child is brought up like that . . . forced to excel in all manly sports, taught to be a stoic, taught the importance of power, brought up to see his family as the greatest in the world. He has even been named after one of them. Rollo apparently was the first leader who came to Normandy.'

'Yes, I know. He raided the coast and so harassed the French that to keep the invaders quiet they gave them a part of their country which was called Normandy. He was very anxious to tell me at the very beginning of our disastrous acquaintance that he was not French. He was Norman. I think he really believed he was back in those dark ages. He certainly behaved as though he were.'

'Yet in spite of this there was a certain sensitivity.'

'Sensitivity!'

'This love of art. I'll tell you something else: he wanted to be an artist. You can imagine the storm in the Centeville camp when that was discovered. There had never been an artist in the family. They were all hoary warriors. That was stamped on at once.'

'I am surprised he allowed that to be.'

'He didn't, did he? He became both . . . and because his efforts were divided he wasn't entirely successful at either.'

'What do you mean?'

'He is not a painter but I have heard it said that there is not a man in France who knows more about painting. He is ruthless, upholding his power and yet he has a sentimental streak which is quite alien to everything else about him.'

'Sentimental streak! Really, Nicole. You are romancing.'

'Didn't he proclaim your talent? Don't you owe the fact that you are on the way to him?'

'That was simply because he admired my work . . . recognized it for what it was, and he knew that I could paint a miniature as well as my father could.'

'But he did it, didn't he? He went to considerable pains to advance your career.'

'And then went to even greater pains to destroy it. No, I shall always hate him. I see him for what he is and that is . . . a monster.'

'Don't get excited,' said Nicole. 'It's bad for the child.'

I became more and more grateful to Nicole as the months passed. She carried off our masquerade with aplomb; everything she did was done in the true spirit of generosity which was to make me feel that the benefit was hers. She had been lonely, bored, and I had given her something to plan for. My desperate situation had relieved the monotony of her days. The only time she was impatient was when I tried to express my gratitude.

The arrangements in the house were perfect. The studio was large, airy and light. It was all a studio should be. She had one day a week when she received her friends. I was always with her on these occasions and this brought me many clients. I had worked right up to the time of my confinement so I was not going to be short of money and was able to pay Nicole a reasonable price for my rent, although I knew full well that she did not want to take it. However, I insisted on this.

She was introducing me to a new way of life. I had become Madame Collison, the famous artist; and Nicole, who certainly did not observe the rules of convention for herself, had decided that it might be advisable for me to give some regard to them. Therefore she hinted at a deceased husband and the posthumous child-to-be. It made a very interesting situation and surrounded me with a certain amount of mystery which made me an intriguing personality as well as a talented artist.

I enjoyed the evenings until I began to get too large and then I felt the need to rest. All sorts of people came to the salon. There was a great deal of music. Nicole played the piano with spirit and sometimes she engaged professional musicians. She liked, though, to choose people who were trying to get a hearing in that field. She was very sympathetic and whatever anyone thought about her past life, fundamentally good. I had reason to know that. Artists, writers, musicians came. It was an absorbing and exciting life; and I was beginning to be happy, for Nicole insisted that I should be. She would shake her finger at me and I would rush in with it before she had time to say it: 'For the sake of the child . . .'

During the last months I would lie on a sofa in the salon with a velvet cover to hide my body, and people came and sat beside me, and sometimes they knelt, which made me feel like a queen.

The midwife, chosen by Nicole, had moved in. My time was approaching.

Then came the all-important day and my child was born.

I came out of exhaustion to hear the cry . . . loud and lusty.

I heard the midwife say: 'This one will give a good account of himself.'

Then I knew I had a boy.

When he was laid in my arms, Nicole was there, smiling proudly. She told me that he weighed nine pounds, which was very big – and he was perfect in every way.

'He is going to be something . . . our boy,' she said.

She doted on him from the hour of his birth and we talked of nothing else but this marvellous boy.

'What shall you call him?' she asked, and for a moment I thought she was going to suggest Rollo and I felt anger welling up within me.

I said quickly: 'I am going to call him Kendal . . . after my father. There must be a K . . . just in case . . .'

She was laughing. 'But of course he must be Kendal,' she said. 'He must have the magical initials just in case he should turn out to be a great artist.'

She rocked him in her arms. She marvelled at him. I liked to see her happy.

Then she gave him to me and I held him close against me. I knew that anything that had gone before was worth it for his sake.

The Oriflamme Kite

I would not have believed I could be so happy. Two years had passed since the birth of my son and he grew in strength and beauty every day and in a manner at which both Nicole and I marvelled. The excitement of his first tooth, his first smile, the first word he uttered, the first time he stood alone on his two dimpled feet, was so intense, and the more so because it was shared.

He was at the centre of our lives. As soon as he was able to speak he said his own name, of which his version was Kendy. It occurred a great deal in his conversation. Intelligent as he was, he could not help but be aware of his importance, and sometimes I thought he believed the whole world was made for him.

Each morning, when I was in the studio, he would be Nicole's concern. I was getting more and more clients and there was hardly a day when I did not have work to do. It was very satisfactory and there was no doubt that my name was becoming more and more well known in Parisian circles. People came from the country too – which was very gratifying as it showed that my fame was spreading beyond Paris.

'Excellent, excellent,' Nicole would murmur, and she could never resist adding: 'Was I not right?'

She had been right in everything she had done. She had found a way out for me, and because I had the most adorable child in the world I could cast aside my regrets and be happy.

I wrote to my father about once a month reporting progress. He was delighted with the way things were going and quite understood that I could not spare the time to come home. As for him, his sight was fading and he did not feel quite able to undertake the journey to Paris. It was comforting therefore to receive my letters. He wanted to hear about my success and he thought that it had been the best thing that could have happened, particularly to a woman – to be acclaimed by someone like the Baron and then to have her own studio in Paris.

'I think of you all the time, dearest Kate,' he wrote. 'I am so proud of you. It is the one thing which could make it possible for me to accept my affliction with resignation.'

I thought a great deal about him. He was happy in Collison House and I grew more and more grateful to Clare for looking after him as she did. He mentioned her frequently in his letters. It was clear to me that the management of the house and the care of my father were in the best possible hands.

I had nothing to worry about. I tried not to think of the Baron and when I did to remind myself that although he had behaved so abominably to me, through him the commissions had come – and my child. It was strange to contemplate that my boy was partly his. I tried to dismiss that thought whenever it intruded, but I did notice, with a touch of apprehension, that Kendal was beginning to look a little like his father. He was going to be tall and broad with light blond hair and bluish-grey eyes. He will be brought up so differently though, I thought. He shall not resemble that man. I will teach him a better way of life. It may well be that he will become an artist.

He liked to sit in the studio and watch me work, although of course he was never there when the clients were. He insisted that I give him some paints, so I gave him some paints and he painted on a sheet of paper.

Such happy days they were, and as I watched his fair head bent over the paper in complete absorption I often thought: I would not have had it otherwise. He has made everything worthwhile.

One day when Nicole had taken Kendal out for his morning walk in the Luxembourg Gardens, I was painting in the studio. My subject was a young woman who wanted a miniature of herself to present to her husband on his birthday. I had met her at one of Nicole's soirées, as I did so many of my clients. She chattered on and on as I painted her, which suited me. I liked to catch the fleeting expressions as they talked. They were often very revealing.

She said suddenly: 'I saw Madame St Giles with your little son as I came in.'

'Oh yes,' I replied. 'They are just going for their morning walk.'

'What an enchanting little fellow!'

I was absurdly pleased when people said complimentary things about Kendal.

'I think so, but you know how these maternal feelings carry one away.'

'He is certainly a beautiful child. It is delightful to have children. I hope to . . . in time. Of course I am young yet. But then so are you, Madame Collison. You must have been very young when you married. And so sad . . . your husband never to see his son.'

I was silent.

She went on: 'I'm sorry. I shouldn't have spoken of it. It must be very painful . . . even now. Forgive me.'

I said: 'It's perfectly all right.'

'Time heals, they say, and you have your dear little boy. My husband was at Centeville last week. He stayed a night at the castle.'

I held my brush above the ivory. It was very necessary that my hand should be absolutely steady. Each stroke was so important.

'Oh yes . . .' I murmured.

'He said the Princesse was not very well. I understand she has not been . . . since the birth.'

'The birth?' I heard myself say.

'Oh, didn't you hear? It's quite some time ago. The child must be about the same age as your little boy. Did you say he was two? Yes, that would be about it . . . almost exactly, I should imagine.'

'No,' I said, 'I didn't know there was a child.'

'A little boy. It's a mercy that it was a boy. I hear the Princesse's health might prevent her from having other children.'

'I'm sorry to hear that. She's quite a young woman.'

'Oh yes . . . very young. But it was a difficult birth. Anyway, they have their boy.'

'Did you see him?'

'Only briefly. He looked rather sickly.'

'I'm surprised.'

'Well, you would have expected the Baron to have a child like himself, wouldn't you?'

'What have they called him?' I asked. 'Rollo, I expect.'

'Oh no . . . no. That's the Baron's name.'

'I had heard that it was and I would have expected the child to be named after him.'

'No. The child is William.'

'Ah, William the Conqueror.'

'He hardly looked like a conqueror, poor little mite. But children grow out of their weaknesses, I believe.'

'Yes, I believe they do.'

'You haven't to worry about your little one. He looks the picture of health.'

I could not get on after that. I could not shut out of my mind the thought of the Princesse in that castle. She had been afraid of it. And then to bear a child and suffer and become weakened by it. I thought the Baron would not be very pleased with that – now with a sickly child, boy though he was, son and heir and William the Conqueror.

Later that day when I was alone with Nicole I mentioned that conversation to her.

She nodded.

'You knew?' I said.

'I'd heard.'

'You didn't tell me.'

'You know how you felt every time his name was mentioned. You still do, a little, I think.'

'All the same, I would rather have heard from you.'

'I'll remember that if I get any more snippets of gossip.'

'Yes, do. I like to be informed.'

'Even about . . . certain people?'

'Yes, even about them. How did it go in the Gardens today?'

'Very well. Kendal is becoming interested in statues. He loved the one of Chopin and I had to tell him as much as I knew about the musician. I even had to sing some of his pieces, with disastrous results I'm afraid. Still, Kendal liked them.'

It was a few weeks later when I received a shock. Kendal had risen from his early afternoon nap and was as usual full of energy. We were finding it hard to keep up with him these days and Nicole often said it had been easier when he could only crawl. He had been out with Nicole all the morning, and after his nap I had promised to take him out. I had taken him to the shop where I bought my brushes and after we had made a few purchases we returned to the house.

As we entered I heard Nicole talking. Visitors, I thought, and was about to take Kendal up the stairs to our apartment when Nicole appeared. She looked rather flustered.

'Kate,' she said, 'Your father is here.'

I stood very still. I couldn't believe I had heard correctly, and just at that moment Clare appeared in the doorway.

'Kate!' She ran to me and embraced me. And there was my father. Kendal looked on at the visitors with curiosity. I had to make a hasty decision.

'Father,' I cried and we embraced.

'We have news for you. We had to tell you in person . . .' he said.

'What a dear little boy!' cried Clare.

I felt myself flushing scarlet. I was numb and could not think of what to say. Often I had pictured myself telling my father, for I knew that my son's existence could not be kept secret for ever. But I had certainly never imagined anything like this.

'There is a great deal to explain,' I said. 'Nicole, will you take him up. He can come down and see my father in a little while.'

'I want to see him now,' said Kendal.

'You've seen him, darling. I have to talk to him first.'

Nicole took him firmly by the hand and led him away.

I went into the salon with my father and Clare.

'First, tell me your news,' I said firmly, trying to find the words to explain Kendal.

'Clare and I are married,' blurted out my father.

'Married!'

'Three weeks ago. We didn't tell you because we knew you'd be too busy to come to the wedding and perhaps feel you ought and so make it difficult for you. We thought we'd surprise you on our honeymoon.'

'Oh, Father!' I said.

'You're not pleased,' said Clare quickly.

'Of course I'm pleased. I think it's wonderful. No one can care of him like you.'

'I want to care for him,' she said earnestly. 'Particularly now . . .'

My father was smiling in my direction and I realized that he could not see me very clearly.

I said slowly: 'As you have guessed, I have something to tell you.'

'Do you want to speak to your father alone?' asked Clare.

I shook my head. 'No, Clare. You're one of the family now. I'm afraid this will be a shock to you. The little boy is my son.'

There was a deep silence in the room.

'I couldn't tell you,' I rushed on. 'That's why I had to stay here. I couldn't come to see you . . .'

'You are married?' asked my father.

'No.'

'I . . . see.'

'No,' I said. 'I don't think you do.'

'What happened to Bertrand? You were going to marry him.'

'My child's father is not Bertrand.'

'Someone else?'

Clare said, 'My poor, poor Kate.'

'No,' I said fiercely. 'I am not poor. It happened . . . and now that I have my boy I wouldn't have had it otherwise.'

My father was looking bewildered. 'But you were to have married . . .'

'There was someone else,' I said.

'And you couldn't marry him?'

I shook my head. My father was struggling with his principles and his love for his daughter. It was a great shock to him that I should have an illegitimate child. I felt I owed him some explanation for I did not want him to think I had been blithely immoral with no thought to consequences.

I said quietly: 'It was forced on me.'

'Forced! My dear child!'

'Please . . . do you mind if we don't talk about it.'

'Of course we won't,' Clare said. 'Kendal dear, Kate is happy now . . . whatever happened. And she's successful with her work. That must be a great compensation for everything. And the little boy is such a darling.'

'Thank you, Clare,' I said. 'Perhaps I'll be able to tell you later. This has come so suddenly.'

'We should have told you we were on our way,' said Clare. 'We wanted it to be a surprise.'

'It's a wonderful surprise. I'm so happy to see you. It is just that . . .'

'We understand,' said Clare. 'You will tell us when you want to. In the meantime, it is not our business. You have this studio and all this success. It is what you dreamed of, isn't it?'

My father was looking in my direction as though he had been confronted by a stranger. I went to him and taking his hand kissed it.

'I'm sorry,' I said. 'It's been unfair to you. Perhaps I should have told you. I didn't want to make difficulties. Believe me, it was not my fault. It . . . happened to me.'

'You mean . . . ?'

'Please don't talk of it. Perhaps later. Not now. Oh, Father, I am so glad you are happy and that you have Clare.'

'Clare has been very good to me.'

I reached for her hand and we all stood close together.

'Please understand,' I said. 'I did not seek it. It . . . happened. I have a wonderful friend in Nicole who has smoothed the way for me. I believe that in spite of it . . . I have been lucky.'

My father clenched his hand and said softly: 'Was it that man . . . that Baron?'

'Father, please . . . it's over and done with.'

'He did a lot for you. So it was because –'

'No, no. That's quite wrong. Perhaps I can talk to you later . . . not now.'

'Kendal dear,' said Clare gently, 'don't distress Kate. Imagine all she has gone through . . . and then our coming so suddenly. She'll tell us when she's ready. Oh, Kate, it is wonderful to see you. Is the little boy interested in painting?'

'Yes, I really think he is going to be. He daubs a bit but I'm sure he has an eye for colour. I named him Kendal . . . just in case.'

My father smiled gently. He gripped my hand tightly. 'You should have come to me, Kate,' he said. 'It was my place to help you.'

'I almost did. I might have done if Nicole hadn't been there. Oh, Father, you have been so lucky to have Clare. I've been lucky with Nicole. It is a wonderful thing to have staunch friends.'

'I agree on that. I want to see the boy, Kate.'

'You shall.'

He murmured: 'Kendal Collison. He'll carry the torch perhaps.'

My father and Clare stayed with us for three days.

Once he had recovered from the shock, my father accepted my position in much the same way as he had accepted his oncoming blindness.

He did not ask any more intimate questions. Whether he presumed that I had actually been forced to submit to the Baron or whether he thought he had overpowered me with his persuasion, he did not ask and I did not tell him. He realized that talking of the matter distressed me and he wanted the visit to be a happy one. He wanted to stress the fact – which I already knew – that whatever happened to either of us our love for each other would remain as steady as a rock.

They talked of village matters. Hope had a little baby and was happy although for a long time she had been unable to get over her sister's death. Everything was the same at the vicarage. Frances Meadows was a wonderful worker and managed the household efficiently as well as countless village concerns.

'Life is very quiet for us compared with you in your wonderful salon,' said Clare. 'But it suits us very well.'

My father's sight had grown much worse. He did not wear glasses because they made no difference. I thought the time must come when he would be totally blind. I dreaded that day and I know he did.

Clare had long talks with me. 'He is adjusting himself gradually,' she said. 'I read to him. He loves that. Of course he can't paint at all now. It's heart-breaking to see him in the studio. He goes up there quite often still. I think your success means a great deal to him.'

'Clare,' I told her, 'I don't know how to be grateful enough to you.'

'It's I who should be grateful. Before I came to you, life was so empty. Now it is full of meaning. I think I was meant to look after people.'

'It's a very noble mission in life.'

'Your father is so kind . . . so good, I'm the lucky one. I am so sorry for people who haven't had my luck. I often grieve for poor Faith Camborne.'

'She was always so helpless,' I said.

'I know. I tried to befriend her. I did what I could . . .'

'You were always very helpful to her and I know she was very fond of you.'

'All we can do now is pray that Hope will stop grieving for her sister and enjoy what life has given her . . . a good husband and a lovely baby.'

'Dear Clare,' I murmured, kissing her.

Kendal was very excited to find he had a grandfather. He climbed all over him and peered into his face. He must have heard talk of his very imminent blindness because one day he climbed onto his knees and looking long into his face said: 'How are your poor eyes today?'

My father was so moved that he was almost in tears.

'I'll see for you,' Kendal said. 'I'll hold your hand all the time and won't let you fall over.'

And when I saw the expression on my father's face I could only rejoice once more in my boy and regret nothing – just nothing – that had given him to me.

They were going on to Italy. My father wanted Clare to see those works of art which had affected him so deeply when he had had eyes to see them. I believed he would see them again through Clare.

She was so gentle with him, so kind, not fussing too much but just enough to let him know how much she cared for him, letting him do what he could for himself and yet at the same time always being there if he should need help.

I felt glad that they had come. It was as though a great weight had been lifted from my shoulders. I no longer had a dark secret which must be withheld from them. I should be able to write to them freely in future.

'Please, Clare,' I said when they left, 'You must come and see me often. It is difficult for me to come to Farringdon, but do come again . . . soon.'

They promised that they would.

Two years had passed. Kendal was now approaching his fifth birthday. He could draw very well and there was nothing he liked better than to come to the studio in the afternoons when there were no clients there and sit at a bench and paint. He painted the statues he had seen in his favourite Luxembourg Gardens. Chopin particularly delighted him but he did some recognizable pictures of Watteau, Delacroix and Georges Sand. He had a skill which I thought was miraculous. I was writing to my father regularly for he was always wanting news of Kendal and was delighted to hear of his interest in painting; he wrote that at five years old I had begun to show such leanings.

'It is wonderful,' wrote my father, 'to know that the link is not broken.'

He and Clare came to Paris twice during that period.

He was almost blind now and his writing was becoming difficult to decipher. Clare often wrote in his place. She told me that the decline in his sight, though gradual, was definite. However, he had accepted it and was very happy to talk with her, and she was reading to him more and more. He was up to date with the news and always liked to learn what was happening in France.

'I don't read to him anything that I think might distress him,' she wrote. 'He did get a little uneasy about the situation over there. There seems to be a certain dissatisfaction with the Emperor and with the Empress. She is beautiful, I know, but we hear that she is extravagant and then of course she is Spanish and the French always did dislike foreigners. Look how they hated Marie Antoinette. I think your father is always a little anxious that what happened eighty years ago will start all over again.'

I didn't take much notice of that when I read it. Life in Paris was so pleasant. We had our soirées where beautiful and intelligent people congregated. We talked art more than politics, but I did notice that the latter were beginning to come more and more into the conversation.

Nicole was delighted with life, I think. She lived luxuriously and loved her soirées. I think now and then she took a lover, but there was no really serious relationship. I did not enquire and she did not tell me. I think in her heart she was always aware of what she called my Anglo-Saxon respectability, and she wanted nothing disturbed.

I was not without my admirers. I had never been beautiful but I had acquired something during my years with Nicole. A poise, I suppose. My work was highly successful and I was treated with great respect. It was considered a symbol of social rank to have a Collison miniature, and with the perversity of fashion, my sex, which had been a drawback, now became an asset.

I liked some of the men who made approaches to me, but I could never enter into an intimate relationship. As soon as they showed any signs of familiarity my whole being would shrink and I would see that face leering at me. It had become more and more like the demon-gargoyle of Notre Dame as the years passed.

We were all very happy. I engaged a nursery governess for Kendal. I could not expect Nicole to take him out every day although she liked to on occasions. Jeanne Colet was an excellent woman, kind yet firm. She was just what Kendal needed. He took to her immediately. He was a very lovable child. He was mischievous occasionally as most children are, but there was always an absence of malice in his mischief. He wanted to find out how things worked and that was why he destroyed them sometimes. It was never due to a desire to spoil.

I suppose I saw him as perfect; but it was a fact that others loved him on sight, and he was a favourite wherever he went. Even the grim concierge came out to see him as he passed in and out. He used to run in and tell me about the people he had met in the Gardens. He spoke a mixture of French and English which was enchanting and perhaps one of his attractions.

However, people noticed him and perhaps that was why when he came back and talked about the gentleman in the gardens I did not at first pay much attention.

There was a fashion at that time for kites. The children flew them in the Gardens every day. Kendal had a beautiful one with the oriflamme – the ancient banner of France – emblazoned across it. The gold flames on a scarlet background were most effective and it certainly looked very splendid flying up in the sky.

He used to take the kite into the Gardens every morning

and he would come back and tell me how high it had flown – far beyond the other kites. He had thought it was going to fly right to England to see his grandfather.

Then one day he came back without his kite. He was in tears.

He said: 'It flew away.'

'How did you let it do that?'

'The man was showing me how to fly it higher.'

'What man?'

'The man in the Gardens.'

I looked at Jeanne. 'Oh, it's a gentleman,' she said. 'He's sometimes there. He sits and watches the children play. He often has a word for Kendal.'

I said to Kendal: 'Never mind. We'll get you another kite.'

'It won't be my oriflamme.'

'I expect we can find another somewhere,' I assured him.

The next morning he went off kiteless and rather disconsolate.

'I expect it's with my grandfather by now,' he said, and that seemed to comfort him. Then he said anxiously: 'Will he be able to *see* it?'

His face puckered a little and he showed more than sorrow for the loss of his kite. He was thinking of how his poor grandfather would not be able to see that glorious emblem. It was that thoughtfulness, that feeling for others, which made Kendal so endearing.

'I'll find another oriflamme kite if I have to scour Paris,' I said to Nicole.

'I'll do the same,' she told me.

I had a sitting that morning but promised myself that I would go out to look in the afternoon. There was no need to. Kendal came back from the Gardens with a kite about twice the size of the lost one, and more glorious, more flamboyant was the red and gold emblem of ancient France.

He was so joyous I just knelt down and hugged him.

'Mind the kite,' he warned me. 'It's a very precious one.'

I looked at Jeanne questioningly. 'It was the gentleman in the Gardens,' she said. 'He was there this morning with the kite.'

'You mean . . . he's given it to Kendal?'

'He said it was partly his fault that the other one was lost. He and Kendal played with it all morning.'

I was a little uneasy. 'There was no need for him to replace it,' I said, 'and even so, to buy such an obviously expensive one.'

A few days passed and each morning Kendal went off with his kite. He had been flying, he told me, with the gentleman in the Gardens.

There came what I was waiting for – a cancellation from a sitter – and I seized the opportunity. I was going to see the gentleman in the Gardens for myself.

When I saw him I stood very still, trembling with a terrible fear. My impulse was to snatch up Kendal and run as fast as I could.

He was coming towards me. He bowed. Memories came flooding back. I wanted to shout at him: 'Go away. Get out of my life.'

But he stood there smiling.

'Mamma,' said Kendal and continued in his delightful combination of the two languages: '*Voilà* the monsieur of the *jardins*.'

'Kendal and I have become friends,' said the Baron.

'How . . . how long has this been going on?' I murmured.

'Long enough for us to have become good friends.'

I could not look at him. He terrified me. I knew his ruthlessness and I greatly feared what his next action would be.

'How did you . . . ?'

'I saw him. I was attracted by him . . . I discovered his name.'

Kendal was looking from one to the other of us.

'Are we going to fly the kite?' he asked.

'But of course,' replied the Baron. 'Is it not a fine kite?' he went on, looking at me.

'It's bigger than the one that went to England,' said Kendal.

'I hope your grandfather liked it.'

He knows so much! I thought. He has done this deliberately. Why?

He bowed to me. 'Will you forgive us? We must get the kite in the sky. It has to show these others how inferior their little efforts are.'

'Come on,' said Kendal.

I watched them move off together. I was dazed. What is he trying to do now? I asked myself. What does this mean? He has been coming to the Gardens to see the boy. Oh, why? When has he ever been interested in children?

So I had not escaped from him. The last few years when I had come to terms with life, when I had learned to accept what it offered me and be grateful for it . . . they were just the interim.

I was afraid of this man. I knew him to be without mercy.

What did he want with my son?

The appalling truth had to be faced. Kendal was his son too.

I watched the oriflamme rise in the sky. There it was, outshining all others. Everyone was pointing it out and Kendal's pride in it was immense.

What is he teaching the boy already? I asked myself. Already he is showing him that he must be superior to all others. He must fly a larger kite. He must put the others in the shade.

It was how the Baron had been brought up. He would try to turn my beautiful child into another such as himself.

I heard him say: 'Here you are. You hold it. Grip it firmly. Don't let go. Can you?'

'Of course,' said Kendal.

'Of course,' he repeated. 'I am now going to have a word with your Mamma.'

He sat beside me. Instinctively I moved away. He noticed and laughed.

'What a boy!' he said.

I did not answer.

'He looks just like my grandfather. I have a portrait of him at the boy's age. The likeness is amazing.'

I said slowly: 'This boy is my boy. He is never going to be like those Norse barons who rode roughshod over everyone who stood in their way.'

'There is a sweetness in him,' he went on, 'inherited from his maternal relations, I don't doubt. But he'll be a fighter.'

'I don't think there is any need to discuss him with you. If you will let me know the cost of the kite . . .'

'That was my gift to him.'

'I don't really care for him to take gifts from strangers.'

'Not from his own father!'

I turned to him sharply. 'What are you planning?'

'I merely made a comment. I am his father and I shall give him a kite if I want to . . . or anything else for that matter.'

'I am his mother. I have brought him into this world and cared for him ever since. It is not for you to come along now because you like the look of him and claim to be his father. How can you be sure that you are.'

He looked at me sardonically. 'You are a woman of impeccable morals, I am sure. Everything fits. One only has to look at him.'

'Lots of children look alike.'

'Not so like. Besides, I knew him at once as soon as I saw him. I said to myself: That is my son.'

'You have no claim on him.'

'Don't let him see that you are afraid of me. That might arouse his resentment against me. I have heard from him what a beautiful, clever mother he has. I have also heard talk of you. You justified my belief in you. The famous Kate Collison . . . beautiful . . . young . . . aloof . . . a little mysterious . . . living almost like a nun, they say.'

'Where did you get this information?'

'You live in the limelight, dear Kate. One cannot help but bear these things. I said to myself: There has been no one else in Kate's life. I was the one. I remain the one.'

'I see your opinion of yourself has not changed.'

'As a matter of fact, I'll tell you this, Kate. I am not a very happy man.'

'How is that? Surely you can juggle with circumstances and give yourself what you want?'

'It's not easy.'

'You have indeed changed. I thought you were omnipotent.'

'Not quite, alas.'

'Surely you are not content with being "not quite"?'

'Listen, Kate, don't let's waste time like this. I have thought of you often.'

'I suppose that is meant to be flattering.'

'It's the truth. That was a wonderful time for me.'

'It was hardly that for me.'

'It was, Kate. If you are truthful with yourself you will admit you loved it . . . every minute. Come, you know you did.'

'I hated it. I hated you. It ruined . . .'

'Your life? No. Look for yourself. Out of it came that beautiful boy. You wouldn't change that, would you?'

'I have my boy and I am going to keep him.'

'You wouldn't have him any different, would you . . . not in one little way?'

'Of course I wouldn't.'

'There you are. He had to be part mine to make him as he is. You might have married Bertrand. I saved you from that. I was surprised when he didn't go ahead. I told him to, but he defied me. He lost a great deal. He is a very poor man now. He married hoping his wife would bring him something. She did a little . . . not as much as he hoped though.'

'Did you have a hand in that?'

'He had to learn he could not defy me. Oh, you would have been so bored with him. Such a milk and water gentleman. It would have lasted with you, Kate. It would have ruined your career. Madame de Mortemer. No, I don't see you as that. Instead here you are, glorious Kate Collison, sought after but unattainable, the great artist, and the mother of the most delightful boy in France. Tell me, does he paint?'

'What is it to you?'

'A great deal.'

'I refuse to answer.'

'Oh Kate . . . the same Kate. It take me back so. I should never have let you go. You see I can make mistakes.'

'That's an extraordinary admission. Yes, you have indeed changed. It surprises me very much to hear you admit defeat.'

'I hope you will take pity on me.'

'I don't believe a word you say, you know. I never shall.'

'Oh, you admit we shall have other opportunities for disagreeing. That implies a continuation of our relationship which I very much desire.'

'I think I should be going.'

'You can't bring down the oriflamme yet . . . unless you would like me to take charge of the boy.'

'That I will never allow.'

'I thought not,' he said.

'Why have you come here?' I asked.

'To see the boy.'

'To ingratiate yourself with him.'

'I want his friendship.'

'It is not for you.'

'Shame, Kate. His own father!'

'I heard you have a son of your own . . . a legitimate one.'

His face hardened. 'I have no son,' he said.

'The Princesse has a son, I was told.'

'She has.'

'Then . . .'

'You knew, Kate. You were with her. I believe she confided in you. She did not come to me a virgin.'

I looked at him steadily, mockingly. He was very serious now.

'The child was born too soon,' he said. 'I knew it was not mine. She admitted that she had had a lover. Armand L'Estrange. So I give my name to a bastard. What do you think of that? It makes you laugh, doesn't it?'

'Yes,' I said, laughing. 'It makes me laugh.' Then I was sober suddenly. 'The poor little Princesse . . . I began.

'Oh, you are sorry for her, are you? That deceitful harlot.'

'I'd be sorry for anyone who had the ill fortune to marry you.'

'Well, you have the satisfaction of knowing that I have a share in that misfortune.'

'You are outraged, I am sure. Never mind. You have learned a valuable lesson. You can be deceived like anyone else. What is good for men is perhaps after all good for women. You should not feel so angry because you have been caught at your own game.'

'I had forgotten you are one of the advanced women, are you not? You are a woman and an artist. You stand side by side with men and compete with them.'

'I compete as an artist . . . if you call it competing. This is not a matter of sex.'

'I gave you your chance . . . remember that. Do you think you would have found it so easy if I had not?'

'No. But you claim to be a lover of art. You recognized my talent and for that reason only you pointed it out to others.'

'I was interested in *you*.'

'As an artist.'

'And as a woman. I think I proved that.'

'Oh, I thought that was a matter of sordid revenge.'

'It is always a good rule to combine business with pleasure.'

'Well, it is over now. You submitted me to the greatest humiliation one person can inflict on another. For that I shall never forgive you. You owe me something. Well, keep out of my way. Keep away from my son.'

'You ask too much.'

He took my hand and crushed it in his. 'I wouldn't harm either of you,' he said. 'I happen to be very fond of you both.'

'Who was it said, Fear the Greeks when they bring gifts? I have another comment and that is that when men like you play at being kindly they are at their most deadly.'

'Kate, you've changed. Understand that I have changed too.'

'I do not believe you will ever change for anything but the worse.'

'Won't you give me a chance?'

'No.'

'Cruel Kate.'

'There is only one way in which you can change my feelings towards you.'

'What is that?'

'Stay away from me . . . and mine. And do you want a word of advice?'

'From you, Kate, that would be golden, I am sure.'

'I had to face a frightening situation. When I discovered I was going to have a child I did not know which way to turn. I had a good friend and I came through; and now I have come to terms with life. You should do the same. You have a son.

You may have more children. You must not blame the Princesse because she did once what you have spent your life doing. At least in her case it was done by consenting parties.'

'Oh Kate,' he said, 'it does me so much good to be with you. Do you know, I feel more alive just to hear you talk. I really do enjoy being berated by you. Do you remember how you fought me? You really meant to fight, didn't you? Have pity on me. My marriage is a disaster, I hate my wife's sickly bastard, I despise my wife. She cannot have more children. Bearing the bastard did something to her. There's my sad story.'

'There's a moral in it.'

'What's that?'

'The wicked never prosper.'

He laughed and I stood up. He stood beside me. I had forgotten how big he was, how overpowering.

'I'd like to have a chance to put my case to you,' he said. 'May I?'

'No,' I answered. 'I am not interested in your case. I can only see you as a barbarian, a savage born out of your century. If you would please me . . . and God knows you owe me something . . . you will stay out of my life. Leave me with what I have suffered for and worked for. These things belong to me and you have no part in them.' I called: 'Kendal. Bring down the oriflamme. It's time to go home.'

The Baron went to the boy and helped him with the kite. Kendal was leaping round with excitement while the Baron handed him the kite.

'Thank you for it,' said Kendal. 'It's the best and biggest kite that was ever in the sky.'

I thought: Already he is making my son like him.

We made our way silently home. I was deeply apprehensive. I had not felt such fear for a long time.

Kendal walked soberly beside me, carefully carrying his oriflamme kite.

Paris under Siege

The peaceful days were over. I was now beset by anxiety because that man had come back into my life.

I talked it over with Nicole. She thought I was worrying unduly. 'Naturally he's interested in his own son,' she said. 'He just wants to see him and the best way of doing this, as you would not welcome him here, is in the Gardens. What harm is he doing?'

'I know that wherever he is there will be harm. What can I do?'

'Nothing,' replied Nicole calmly. 'You can't stop the boy going to the Gardens. He'll want to know why. He'll be resentful. Let him go. Let him play with the kite there. It'll be all right.'

'I'm terrified that he will try to take Kendal away from me.'

'He wouldn't do that. How could he? It would be kidnapping.'

'He is a law unto himself.'

'He wouldn't do that. Where would he take the child? To Centeville? No, of course not. He just wants to see him now and then.'

'Nicole . . . have you seen him?'

'Yes,' she answered.

'You didn't tell me.'

'It was only briefly and I thought it would upset you. As a matter of fact, he is concerned about the situation. Everybody is.'

'What situation?'

'We're on the brink of war. The Emperor is becoming very unpopular. After what happened to our country at the end of last century we are a sensitive people.'

She managed to subdue my fear for Kendal, but I found it very hard to work while he was out of the house. I arranged that he should go out in the afternoons when I could go with him. In the mornings he should be at his lessons. He was after all nearly five years old.

I knew that he had not seen the Baron for a week. Strangely enough he did not mention him. I had come to realize that children took almost everything for granted. The gentleman was there, he liked to talk to him, he had presented him with a kite . . . and then he was not there. That was life, to Kendal.

I was immensely relieved.

But when we had visitors there was continual talk of what they called the uneasy situation.

'How long is the Second Empire going to last?' one of my visitors asked me.

I wondered why he was so intense. I, of course, had not had grandparents who had lived through the Revolution.

'There are people,' I was told, 'who have felt they were sitting on the edge of a volcano ever since.'

'The Emperor has no right to meddle in Danish and Austro-Prussian wars,' said one.

'The French army is strong and the Emperor himself will lead it.'

'Don't you believe it,' said another. 'I don't trust these Prussians.'

I was too concerned with my own affairs to pay much attention.

June had been a hot month. It was now over and we were now in what was to prove for France the fatal July of 1870.

Nicole came in one day and breathlessly told me that war between France and Prussia had been declared.

I received a letter that day which completely put the thought of war out of my mind. It was from Clare and the news it contained shattered me.

My dear Kate [she wrote],

I don't know how to begin to tell you. This has been a dreadful shock. Your father is dead. It was so sudden. Of course he was nearing total blindness. Kate, he pretended to come to terms with it, but he never did. He used to go to the studio where you and he had been so happy together and sit there for hours. It was heart-breaking.

He was sleeping badly and I got the doctor to prescribe something for him to take at nights. I thought that was helping him. And then . . . one morning when I went in to waken him . . . I found him dead.

He looked so peaceful lying there. He looked young. As though he were very happy.

There was an inquest. They were very sympathetic. The coroner said what a tragedy it was that a great artist should be robbed of that which was most necessary to him. Others can lose their sight and accept their fate more easily. But not a man to whom his work had meant so much.

They called it suicide while the balance of his mind was disturbed. But his mind was as clear as ever. He just felt that he could not go on . . . without his eyes.

I don't know what I am going to do, Kate. I'm in a state of indecision at the moment. I shouldn't come here if I were you. It would only make you miserable. Everyone is very kind to me. Frances Meadows made me stay at the vicarage, which is where I am now, and Hope has asked me to go and stay with them, which I shall do at the end of this week. By the time you get this letter I shall probably be there.

There is nothing you can do. Perhaps I will come over and see you later on and we can talk about everything.

Your father spoke of you constantly. Only the day before he died he said how happy he was that you were so successful. He talked of the boy too. It was almost as though he felt he could die happily knowing that you would carry on the tradition.

Dear Kate, I know this is the most terrible shock for you. I shall try to make a new life for myself. I feel so desolate and unhappy, but I thank God for my good friends. I don't know what I shall do. Sell the house, I think, if you are agreeable to that.

He left me the house and what little he had – except the miniatures, of course. They are for you. Perhaps I'll bring them over to Paris sometime . . .

I'm afraid I've told you rather clumsily. I've written this letter three times. But there is no way of softening the blow, is there?

My love to you, Kate. We must meet soon. There is a good deal to decide.

Clare

The letter dropped from my hands.

Nicole came in. She said: 'The Emperor is going to lead the forces. He'll cross the Rhine and force the German States to become neutral. Why . . . what's the matter?'

I said: 'My father is dead. He has killed himself.'

She stared at me and I thrust the letter into her hands. 'Oh my God,' she whispered.

She had a wonderfully sympathetic nature and it always amazed me to see her change from the bright sophisticated worldly woman into the warm-hearted and understanding friend.

First of all she made a cup of strong coffee which she insisted that I drink. She talked to me, of my father, of his talent, of his life's work . . . and the sudden cessation of that work.

'It was too much for him to endure,' she said. 'He was robbed of his greatest treasure . . . his eyes. He could never have been happy without them. Perhaps he is happy now.'

I felt better talking to Nicole and once again I was grateful for her presence in my life.

I suppose it was really because of what had happened that I could only feel a lukewarm interest in the war about which everyone around me was getting so excited.

When the news came that the French had driven the German detachment out of Saarbrücken, the Parisians went wild with joy. There was dancing in the streets and the people were singing patriotic songs, shouting '*Vive la France*' and '*À Berlin*'. Even the little modistes' girls with their boxes hanging on their arms were talking excitedly about giving the Prussians a lesson they would never forget.

As for myself I could think of nothing but my father. When I had seen him he had seemed happy – content with his marriage to Clare, happy because I was successful and he thought Kendal was going to paint too. And all the time he had been keeping his thoughts to himself.

If only he had shared them!

There were times when I was on the point of making arrangements to return to England.

What was the use? said Nicole. What could I do? He was dead and buried. There was nothing I could do. Besides, how could I leave the boy?

How could I indeed. I thought of the Baron, prowling round. What would happen if I were not here?

'Moreover,' went on Nicole, 'it is not easy to travel in wartime. Stay where you are. Wait awhile. You will get over the shock of it. Let Clare come here. You can talk together and comfort each other.'

It seemed sound advice.

Then things began to change. The spirit of optimism had given way to one of apprehension. The war was not going as well as it had seemed to at first. Saarbrücken was nothing more than a skirmish at which the French had had their only success.

Gloom began to show itself in the streets of Paris. A mercurial people once applauding victory with enthusiasm were now sunk in gloom and asking each other, What next?

The Emperor was with the army; the Empress had taken up residence in Paris as Regent; and that first belief that it would soon be over and the Prussians taught a lesson began to fade. The French army was not what it had been thought to be. On the other hand the Prussians were disciplined, well ordered and determined on victory.

Everyone was talking about the war. It was a momentary setback, said some. It was not possible that a great country like France could be humiliated by little Prussia.

Even when sittings began to be cancelled and some of my clients were leaving Paris for the country, I went on thinking of my father and imagining what his thoughts must have been when he made his final and fateful decision. It was not until I heard that the Prussians were closing in on Metz and that the Emperor's army was in disorderly retreat blocking the roads and stopping the movement of supplies to the front, that I began to see that we were facing real disaster.

Then came the news of the dire calamity at Sedan and that the Emperor, with eighty thousand French troops, was a prisoner of war in the hands of the Prussians.

'What now?' asked Nicole.

'What can we do but wait and see?' I asked.

There was fury in the streets. Those who had been proclaiming the Emperor and crying *À Berlin* were now fuming against him.

The Empress had fled to England.

September had come. Who would have believed that there could be such changes in so short a time.

Those few days seemed endless.

'They'll make peace,' said Nicole. 'We shall have to agree to conditions. Then everything will settle down to normal.'

Two days after the fall of Sedan the Baron came to see us.

I was coming down to the salon when I heard voices. A visitor, I thought.

I opened the door and gasped with astonishment, for the Baron came swiftly towards me and taking my hand kissed it. I withdrew it quickly and looked reproachfully at Nicole. I had the impression that she had invited him here.

But this was not so and he dispelled that suspicion immediately.

'I came to warn you,' he said. 'You know what is happening.' He did not wait for a comment from us. 'It's . . . débâcle,' he went on. 'We have allowed a fool to govern France.'

'He did some good,' Nicole defended the Emperor. 'He is just not a soldier.'

'If he is not a soldier he should not go to war. He misled the country into thinking it had an army which could fight. It was unprepared . . . untrained . . . There was not a chance against the Germans. However, we waste time and God knows we have little of it to spare.'

'The Baron is suggesting that we leave Paris,' said Nicole.

'Leave Paris? To go where?'

'He is offering us the shelter of his château until we can make our plans.'

I said: 'I have no intention of going to Centeville.'

'Do you understand the situation?' he demanded.

'I have been following the news. I know there has been disaster at Sedan and the Emperor taken prisoner.'

'And that does not give you cause for alarm?'

I said: 'Nothing would make me come to your castle. I have been there before.'

'The situation is grim, Kate,' said Nicole.

'I know. But I shall stay here. It's my home now, and if it were impossible to live here I suppose I could go to England.'

'You will not find travelling easy in wartime.'

I looked at him steadily and I could not shut out the memory of him in that turret room with triumph in his eyes and the determination to enforce his will. 'I shall stay here,' I said firmly.

'You're being foolish. You don't understand what it means to have an occupying enemy in your country.'

'And what of you? You are in the same country.'

'The Prussians will not come to my château.'

'Why not?'

'I shall not allow it.'

'You . . . you're going to stand out against the Prussian armies?'

'We're wasting time,' he said. 'You should prepare to leave at once.'

I looked at Nicole and said: 'You go if you want to. I shall stay here.'

'Kate . . . it's not safe.'

'There is a choice of two evils. I choose this one.'

The Baron was regarding me with that quizzical look which I had seen before.

'Go, Nicole,' I said. 'You believe him. I don't.'

He raised his shoulders in a helpless gesture.

Nicole said: 'You know I won't leave you and Kendal.'

The Baron shrugged his shoulders. 'Then there is nothing more I can do. Adieu, ladies. And may you have better luck than you have good sense.'

With that he was gone.

Nicole sat down and stared in front of her.

'You should have gone with him,' I said.

She shook her head. 'No . . . I'll stay here. This is my home. You and the boy are my family.'

'But you think I'm wrong.'

She lifted her shoulders rather as he had done a few moments before. 'It remains to be seen,' she said.

Those September days were strangely unreal – hazy in the mornings and when the sun rose the city seemed to be touched with a golden light. There was tension on the streets as the people waited for news.

The whole of Paris was in revolt against the Emperor whom they declared had betrayed them. It seemed such a short while ago that they had cheered him and his beautiful Empress. Now they despised them. It had been the same with the kings, they said. The Bonapartes behaved as though they were kings and Paris had rejected those flamboyant rulers eighty years before.

I caught a glimpse during those days of what it must have been like in paris before the Revolution burst upon the city.

When France declared herself to be a Republic once more, there was excitement in the streets. No more kings. No more emperors. This was the people's land.

But this could not hold back the German advance, and as September neared its end came the final blow. Strasbourg, one of the last strongholds of the French, capitulated to the Germans, whose armies were now marching on Paris.

Then came the terrifying information. The King of Prussia was actually in the Palace of Versailles.

We had for some time begun to feel the strain. Food was fast disappearing from the shops. Nicole had said we must get together what we could. If we had plenty of flour we could at least make bread. And as long as we could we went on buying.

There came a day which I shall never forget. Nicole went

out to see what she could buy and while she was gone the bombardment started.

I heard the explosion and wondered what it was. I thought there must be fighting near the outskirts of the city. I was worried about Kendal. I thought then that I should have listened to the Baron. He was right. We should have left Paris.

There was just that one explosion.

Kendal was in the studio doing his lessons with Jeanne. He was using the studio now as I had had no clients for weeks.

I was thinking that Nicole seemed to have been away a long time when I heard the concierge calling me.

I ran down. A boy was there. 'Madame Collison,' he said, 'will you come at once to the Hôpital St Jacques. A lady there is asking for you.'

'A . . . lady?'

'Madame St Giles . . . She has been hurt. These cursed Germans . . .'

I felt sick with fear. The explosion! They were bombarding Paris and Nicole . . .

I had to go there as fast as I could, but I thought of Kendal.

I said: 'Give me a moment. I must tell them I am leaving.'

I called to Jeanne. 'Madame St Giles has been hurt,' I said briefly. 'I'm going to the hospital. Take care of Kendal while I'm away.'

Jeanne nodded. I could trust her.

Fortunately the hospital was only a few streets away and within a few minutes I was there.

Nicole – almost unrecognizable – was lying in a bed. She was wrapped in a white robe and there were bloodstains on it.

I threw myself on to my knees and gazed at her.

She recognized me, but I think only just.

'Kate,' she whispered.

'I'm here, Nicole. I came as soon as I could.'

'They're bombarding Paris. They're all round us . . . I was hurrying home to tell you . . .'

'Should you talk?'

'I must talk, Kate.'

'No,' I said. 'You shouldn't. Are you all right here? Is there anything I can do? Are you in pain?'

She shook her head. 'I can't . . . feel . . . much. Something's happened to me.'

'Oh Nicole!' I said and I was overcome with remorse and shame. She should never have been here. She would have gone away with the Baron but for me.

'Kate . . .'

'Yes?'

She gave me a crooked smile. There was no colour in her face. She looked dead . . . apart from her eyes.

'I . . . I want to tell you . . .'

'You shouldn't talk.'

'It's the end . . . for me. Strange . . . Shot in a Paris street. I often wondered what my end would be. Now I know.'

'You should try to sleep.'

She smiled. 'I want you to . . . understand . . .'

'I understand, my dear friend, that I could never have got through my troubles but for you.' I felt the tears welling into my eyes.

She blinked. I think she was trying to shake her head.

'Him . . . Kate.'

'Him?'

'The Baron?'

'He's safe in his Norman stronghold,' I said.

'Try Kate . . . Try to understand. He was the one. It was his house . . . He wanted to make sure that you were all right . . .'

What was she trying to tell me?

'Don't fret,' I said. 'Whatever it was doesn't matter now.'

'Yes . . . yes . . .' she murmured. 'Try to understand him, Kate. There's good in him . . .'

I smiled at her and a certain impatience showed itself in her slurred voice.

'He sent me . . . to find you, Kate. It wasn't by chance. He wanted to be sure that you were . . . looked after.'

'You mean that he knew all the time where I was?'

'It was his house. He looked after everything, Kate . . . paid for everything . . . arranged about the birth. He has looked after everything since. He sent the people who came for the portraits. You see . . . he cared, Kate.'

This was too much. It was one shock following on another. He had watched over me then. He had known where I was all the time. He must have guessed there would be a child. He had sent Nicole to look after me . . . to feign friendship . . . Oh no, not that. She had been my true friend. But in the beginning he had sent her. The elegant, comfortable house, with its convenient studio had been provided by him. Nicole had reported to him regularly and in time he had come to see his son in the Gardens.

It was a blinding revelation, but somehow it did not seem important with Nicole lying there . . . dying. Yes, I knew she was dying. She would never come back to us. That bohemian life of hers, living in elegant salons as mistress of one of the most powerful men in France had ended in a Paris street and here she was in a hospital for the poor.

'Oh Nicole,' I said. 'Dear Nicole, you must get well. You must come back with us.'

She smiled at me and her eyes were already becoming glazed.

'It's finished,' she said. 'It's all over. I've been too badly hurt. I know it is the end. I'm glad you came, Kate. I had to speak to you . . . before I went. Forgive him. There is good in him. You might find it.'

'Don't talk of him.'

'I must. I must make you see how it was. I loved him . . . in my way. He loved me . . . in his way . . . the light way. Not as he would love you. You could put the good in him, Kate. Please try.'

'You shouldn't be thinking of him, Nicole. Please rest. You're going to get well. How could we get on without you?'

'You forgive me . . .'

'What is there to forgive? It is you who should forgive me. I kept you here. I should have made you go with him. You knew that was right . . . and you wanted to. But I wouldn't go and because . . . Oh, Nicole, how can I thank you for all you did for me?'

'*He* did it.'

'No, Nicole, you . . . *you.*'

'Please, Kate.'

She was pleading with me and I knew she was dying.

I nodded my head and saw her expression change. I think then she was at peace.

She closed her eyes. She was breathing with difficulty. I sat on. I fancied my presence comforted her. It must have been half an hour before her breathing changed. She was making rasping noises, trying to get her breath.

I ran out to call someone. I found a nurse and took her to Nicole's bedside.

Nicole was silent now.

'She was badly hit,' said the nurse. 'She hadn't a chance.'

Then she closed Nicole's eyes and put the sheet over her face.

I stumbled out of the hospital. I could not take it in. Nicole dead! But that morning she had been alive and well . . . my dearest friend, the one on whom I relied. And now she was gone . . . and all in an hour or so. Life was harsh, I had reason to know, but that tragedy could come so swiftly had never occurred to me.

'May you have more luck than you have good sense.' I

could hear his voice now. He had come for us. He had cared for us . . . all the time. It had not been friendship which had prompted Nicole to help me in the first place. It had been done on his instructions.

And now Nicole was dead. How could I tell Kendal that he would never see Nicole again? How could I ever forget that but for me she would not have been in Paris. She would be alive at this moment.

The horror of it all burst on me. Shots such as those which had killed Nicole could take any of us at any time. Oh God, I thought. Kendal!

I ran as fast as I could.

The house was still there. I had half expected it to be destroyed.

War. We were at war. I had never thought of being involved in war. Now it had come with all its tragedy, its destruction, its maiming and killings . . . its breaking up of lives.

I ran into the house calling 'Jeanne! Kendal! Quick. Where are you?'

Jeanne came running to me. Her face was white. She was clearly distraught.

'Where is Kendal?' I asked.

She said: 'He's gone . . . gone to safety. The gentleman in the Gardens . . .'

The room seemed to be spinning round me. I felt sick with apprehension.

'He came just after you'd gone. He said Paris was no place for the boy. He was going to take him away to safety. I tried . . . but he just took him.'

'And Kendal . . .'

'He said he wouldn't go without his mother . . . but he was picked up . . . carried away . . .'

I covered my face with my hands. I said: 'This can't be true. He's taken him to Centeville. I must go after him. Oh Jeanne . . . Nicole is dead.'

She stared at me.

'I . . . I've been with her,' I stammered. 'And . . . while I was with her he came and took my son away. Jeanne, I must go after him. I know where. Come with me. You can't stay here. If you could have seen Nicole . . .'

'How can we get to this place?'

'I don't know. But we must go at once. Take all the money we can. There is not a moment to lose. We have to go after him.'

I ran to my room. I gathered together all the money that was in the house. I put on my cloak. Action, desperate action was the best way to live through a situation like this.

I went downstairs. Jeanne was already there.

I cried out: 'Come then.'

The door opened and he was standing there – the Baron himself, holding Kendal by the hand.

I gave a cry of relief and ran to my son, kneeling and embracing him, clinging to him. He looked bewildered but clearly shared my relief.

'There's not a moment to lose,' said the Baron. 'You are dressed. Where is Nicole? Go and tell her.'

I stared at him for a few seconds unable to speak.

'Hurry,' he shouted. 'This city will be under siege in a few hours . . . perhaps it is already. Get Nicole . . . quickly.'

I said: 'Nicole is dead. I have just left her.'

'Dead!'

'She is in the hospital. She was hit . . . by this . . . bombardment. I stayed with her until she died.'

He was stunned. I had never seen him moved by emotion before.

'Nicole . . . dead . . .' I heard him murmur. 'You . . . you're sure?'

'I have just left her. That's where I was. They sent for me . . .'

I turned away from him.

I heard him say: 'She was a good woman . . . the best . . .' And then he recovered himself. 'Come on. There's no time to lose.' He looked at Jeanne. 'You too. You can't stay here.'

We went into the streets. There was hardly anyone about. The bombardment had sent them all scurrying into their houses.

He said: 'I have horses nearby. We'll get away from here as fast as we can. Come now. Every minute is important.'

We were at the top of the street when I heard the second explosion of the day.

I think that was the worst moment of my life. A building beside us had been struck. Time appeared to slow down. I saw it stagger like a drunken man; then it started to crumble . . . slowly, and the façade seemed to slither to the ground. I saw . . . disaster. Kendal was staring up at it as though mesmerized. I heard the Baron shout at him. The boy turned but was too late to move before there was a violent rumbling and the air was full of blinding dust.

Kendal was sprawling on the ground. I knew that that pile of bricks and rubble was about to fall on him. I ran . . . but the Baron was ahead of me. It was too late to pick up the boy . . . so he threw himself on top of him for protection.

I screamed. I could see nothing for a second or so because of the blinding dust. 'Kendal,' I called desperately.

Then I was kneeling beside them tearing off the rubble.

There was blood on the Baron's leg. I kept calling Kendal.

Kendal crawled out and stood before me. I felt a crazy joy because he appeared to be unhurt.

But the Baron was lying there among the bricks and the dust . . . still and silent.

Jeanne, Kendal and I knelt down in the dust beside the Baron. His leg seemed to be twisted under him. He was unconscious and I thought that he was dead. Strange emotions swept over me. I had seen death once that morning. But it could not happen to the Baron. Never the Baron. He was indestructible.

'We must get help at once,' I said to Jeanne.

Jeanne stood up. People were now coming out of their houses to see what damage had been done. We called to them and soon there was a little group around us. I could not take my eyes from him – lying there, inert, blood on his clothes, his usually fresh coloured face deathly pale, his eyes closed. I was conscious of a terrible emptiness.

Nicole, my dear friend had gone for ever and that was a sadness which would haunt my life. But I could not imagine a life without the Baron, to remember, to revile, to hate.

Someone had brought out a ladder and they put him on it using it as a stretcher. They could take him to the hospital they said.

I replied on impulse: 'Bring him to my house. I can look after him there. And go and get a doctor . . . quickly . . . quickly . . .'

He was carried into the house. Kendal clung to my hand.

'Is he dead?' he asked.

'No,' I answered fiercely. 'No . . . he can't be dead. Not the Baron.'

That was the beginning of the siege of Paris, the most tragic and humiliating period of that great city's history.

I gave little thought to the war during the next day. My mind was solely on my patient. The doctor had come. Part of the bone in the Baron's right leg had been crushed. He might be able to walk again – perhaps with the aid of a stick. His vital organs were undamaged and strong and the loss of blood and the shock had not been too great for him; he would recover and be able to resume a restricted way of life.

I sat by his bed throughout that first night. He was unconscious then and we were at that time uncertain how much damage had been done. I was glad they had not taken him into the hospital. They had other victims of the bombardments there and were preparing for a rush of casualties so there was no pressure to send him. I said I could nurse him with the help of Jeanne and the doctor was only too glad that I should do so.

He showed me how to dress the leg. The wound appalled me. There was considerable pain, I knew, but the Baron bore that with the fortitude I would expect of him.

I had, with Jeanne's help, moved the beds down so that we were all on one floor and not too far from each other. I had a terrible fear that I might be separated from Kendal.

Every sound made us start for we feared that the bombardment would begin again, but it did not and the streets were quiet.

It was a strange night – that first one – sitting by his bed. I could not believe that only the night before I had slept in my bed with Nicole in her room and Kendal safe in his.

My great fear was for Kendal. I lived again and again that terrible moment when I had thought the building was going to collapse on him. And, if the Baron had not thrown himself upon him, if he had not protected him . . . my small child would surely have been crushed to death.

It was strange what I owed this man. All my humiliation, my subjection . . . and now . . . my son's life.

I kept hearing Nicole's voice. 'There is good in him. You can find it. Yes, I had found something good already. He had come to take us away . . . risking his life to do so, as it was now proved. He had saved my son's life.

I sat there through the darkness of the night. I did not light a candle. Nicole had said some days before that we must preserve the candles . . . we must preserve everything. There was certain to be a shortage.

So I sat there and watched the dawn come while I looked down on the contours of his sleeping face. A certain colour had returned to it and it no longer had that look of death on it. He was breathing more easily. I knew that he would live and I felt a great gladness in my heart.

I closed my eyes and I thought: Too much is happening in too short a time. Death is always close, I suppose, but at times like this it comes nearer. Nicole had always seemed so alive . . . and then suddenly, walking along a street, she is struck down . . . and that is the end. And the Baron! It could so easily have happened to him.

It was war. I had brushed it aside, shown little interest in it. Stupid wars which men fought to amuse themselves, for no one ever came well out of war. And people died . . . one's loved ones went into the street and that was the end.

I opened my eyes. He was looking at me.

'Kate,' he said.

I leaned over him. 'How do you feel?'

'Strange,' he said. 'Very strange . . .'

'It was the bombardment. A wall fell on you.'

'I remember.' Then quickly: 'The boy?'

'He's unharmed.'

'Thank God.'

'Thank you, too,' I said.

A smile touched his lips and he closed his eyes.

I felt the tears in my own. I thought: He will get well. Yes, he is indestructible.

I was glad he was with us. Even lying in a bed more dead than alive he brought a feeling of security.

Kendal had slipped into the room. I held out my hand and he ran to me.

'Is he asleep?'

I nodded.

'Is he very hurt?'

'I think he might be.'

'Do you think he would like to come to the Gardens and fly my oriflamme kite tomorrow?'

'Not tomorrow,' I said. 'But perhaps . . . one day.'

There was an unreality about the days which followed. My thoughts were entirely taken up with nursing the Baron, which was the main preoccupation of our days. It was a great relief when the bombardment stopped and the days were quiet, though ominously so. The Baron spent most of those first days in sleep. The doctor had given me something to make him do so and he had taught me how to dress the wound. He was an earnest young man, very concerned about the situation.

'We were expecting a rush of casualties,' he said, 'but I think the enemy realizes those sort of tactics don't work so well. They can batter the town but Paris is a big place and if the people see their city attacked they become stubborn. These Prussians know how to conduct a war and my view is that they will try to starve us into surrender.'

'A grim prospect.'

'For Paris . . . yes. Those Bonapartes have a great deal to answer for.'

He was a stern republican but I couldn't care about politics, and I was grateful for what he did for me.

Jeanne was a wonderful help. She went out every morning to see what she could buy and it was the excitement of the day to look through her shopping basket when she returned. We had a considerable amount of flour in the house so we were able to bake bread which would keep us going for some time if everything else failed.

I took Kendal for a walk in the afternoons while Jeanne remained at home in case the Baron wanted anything. I never went far from the house and I would not let Kendal out of my sight.

I explained to him what had happened to Nicole. He was an extremely intelligent child and once again I was amazed by the manner in which children adapt themselves to circumstances. He seemed to grasp the fact that there had been a war which the French had lost and because of this we were now living in a besieged city.

There was pitifully little to see in the shops. Quite a lot of the produce sold in Paris came from the surrounding villages. We had often heard them trundling in in the early hours of the morning on the way to Les Halles. They had come from all directions. Now no one came into Paris and no one went out.

The days had settled into a routine which seemed particularly quiet. It was an ominous monotony because nothing stays still for long in a siege.

The Baron was regaining his strength. His leg was still in a sorry state but his constitution was just about as strong as a man's could be and he was fast recovering from the shock and loss of blood.

Now he could sit up. I propped his leg up with pillows and I found a stick which he could use when he hobbled about. But even the shortest walk was such an effort at first that he would collapse exhausted after a few minutes.

It was strange to see him stripped of that strength which had been so much a part of him.

'You're like Samson,' I told him, 'shorn of his locks.'

'Remember,' he said, 'his hair grew again.'

'Yes. And you will regain your strength.'

'And be a cripple?'

'You're fortunate. It could have been worse.'

'It might have been better too,' he added ironically.

'You are thinking that if I had not stubbornly refused to leave Paris when you first asked, this would not have happened to you. Nicole would be here . . .' My voice broke and he said: 'We all make mistakes . . . sometimes.'

'Even you,' I said, with a flash of the old enmity.

'Yes,' he said, 'alas, even I.'

Our relationship had changed. That was inevitable. He was the patient; I was the nurse; and we were living in a situation charged with danger. We did not know from one moment to the next when death would come to claim us.

My great hope was that I should not be left and that if death came it would take me and not Kendal or the Baron. I used to lie awake and think: If I were taken he would look after Kendal. He cares for him. He saved his life. I should hate to think of my son's being brought up to be such another as he is, but he would save him and he loves him. So please God, don't take them and leave me.

There were no servants now. They had left before Nicole died. Some of them had had the wisdom to get out of the city. They were country girls who had homes to go to. So there were just myself, Kendal, the Baron and Jeanne. The concierge and his wife were in their apartments, but they kept very much to themselves.

I spent a great deal of time with the Baron. When I came into the room where he lay I noticed the pleasure which showed in his eyes. Sometimes he said: 'You've been a long time.'

Then I would reply: 'You don't need constant care now. You're getting better. I have other things to do, you know.'

I spoke to him like that, with a touch of asperity just as I used to. I don't think he wanted it to change and nor did I.

'Sit down there,' he would say. 'Talk to me. Tell me what the madmen are doing now.'

Then I would tell him what I had learned of the war, that the Prussians were surrounding Paris and even penetrating the north of the country.

'They'll take the towns,' he said. 'They won't bother about places like Centeville.'

Then I told him goods had almost disappeared from the shops and it was going to be difficult to feed ourselves if it went on like this.

'And you have saddled yourself with another mouth to feed.'

'I owe you that,' I said, 'and I like to pay my debts.'

'So the balance has changed. *You* are on the debit side now.'

'No,' I replied. 'But you saved my son's life and for that I will look after you until you are well enough to stand on your own feet.'

He tried to take my hand but I withdrew it.

'And that other little misdemeanour?' he asked.

'That act of savagery? No, that is still outstanding.'

'I will try to earn a remission of my sins,' he said humbly.

That was how our conversation was – much as it had always been, although now and then a light and bantering note would break in.

He was getting better. The leg was healing and he could spend longer walking about the house without exhausting himself. But in the afternoons I used to insist on his resting while I took Kendal out for a walk, leaving Jeanne in charge.

He was always watching the door for my return.

'I wish you wouldn't take those afternoon rambles,' he said.

'We have to go out sometimes. I never go far from the house.'

'I am in a state of anxiety until you return and that is not good for me. Every nurse worthy of the name knows that patients should not be subjected to anxiety. It impedes recovery.'

'I'm sorry you don't think I'm worthy to be a nurse.'

'Kate,' he said, 'come and sit down. I think you are worthy to be anything you want to be. I'm going to tell you something extraordinary. Do you know . . . here I am incapacitated, probably about to be crippled for life, in a besieged city, lying in a room with death looking in at the window, now knowing from one moment to the next what dire tragedy will descend on me . . . and I'm happy. I think I am happier than I have ever been in my life.'

'Then yours must have been a very wretched existence.'

'Not wretched . . . worthless. That's it.'

'And you think this is worthwhile . . . lying here . . . recuperating . . . doing nothing but eating when we can get something to eat . . . and talking to me.'

'That's just the point. It's talking to you . . . having you near . . . watching over me like a guardian angel . . . not allowing me to stay up too long . . . bringing my gruel . . . this is the strangest thing that has ever happened to me.'

'Such situations have not been frequent in my life either.'

'Kate, it means something.'

'Oh?'

'That I'm happy . . . happier than I've ever been . . . being here with you.'

'If you were well enough,' I reminded him, 'you would get yourself a horse and be out of the city in an hour.'

'It would take a little longer than that. And there won't be any horses left soon. They'll be eating them.'

I shivered.

'They have to eat something,' he went on. 'But what were we saying? I'd be out of this city with you and the boy . . . and we should take Jeanne, of course. But these days . . . there has been something very precious about them for me.'

'Well, you have realized that you'll be able to walk again one day.'

'Dragging one foot behind me, perhaps.'

'Better that than not walking at all.'

'I know all this and yet it's the happiest time of my life. How can you explain that?'

'I don't think it needs an explanation because it's not true. The happiest times of your life were when you were triumphing over your enemies.'

'My enemy now is the pain in this accursed leg.'

'And you are triumphing over that,' I said.

'Then why am I so contented with life?'

'Because you believe you are the great man and that no harm can possibly come to you. The gods of your Norse ancestors are seeing to that. If anyone attempted to harm you, old Thor would flash his thunder at them or throw his hammer and if that couldn't save you Odin, the All-Father, would say, "Here comes one of our chosen heroes. Let's warm up Valhalla for him."'

'Do you know, Kate, you are so often right that I cease to marvel every time you display your understanding.'

'Good. Shall I dress your leg?'

'No, not yet. Sit down and talk.'

I sat down and looked at him.

'How strange,' he said, 'when you think of our being together in that tower bedroom. Oh, what a time that was. What an exhilarating adventure.'

'It was something less than that for me.'

'I have never forgotten it.'

'Nor,' I said pointedly, 'have I.'

'Kate.'

'Yes?'

'When I was lying here in the beginning, I watched you. I pretended to be unaware . . .'

'I would expect such subterfuge from you.'

'You seemed to watch over me . . . tenderly.'

'You were hurt.'

'Yes, but I thought I detected a special caring . . . a special involvement. Did I?'

'I remembered that you saved my son's life.'

'*Our* son, Kate.'

I was silent for a while and he went on: 'I'm in love with you.'

'You . . . in love! That's not possible – unless it is with yourself, of course, but that is a love-affair of such long standing that it calls for no special mention. In fact it is superfluous to comment on it.'

'I love to be with you, Kate. I love the way you slap me down all the time. I enjoy it. It stimulates me. You are different from anyone I have ever known. Kate, the great artist who is so eager that I should know she pretends to despise me. *Pretends* . . . that is the whole point. In your heart, you know you like me . . . quite a lot.'

'I am grateful that you saved Kendal, as I have told you many times. I appreciate the fact that you came to take him out of the city.'

'To take you too. I shouldn't have gone without you. I could have got clear of the city . . . if I had not waited for you.'

'You came for the boy.'

'I came for you both. You don't think I would have taken him and left you. I just want you to know that I could not have done that.'

I was silent.

'You worry a great deal about that boy, don't you?'

I nodded.

'He's a natural survivor. He's my son. He'll come through . . . as we all shall.'

'I fear that something will happen to me. Yes, I fear that terribly. What would become of him then? It is my main worry. What is happening to the children of those who have been killed . . . or die of starvation?'

'There is no need to worry about Kendal. I have made arrangements.'

'What arrangements?'

'I have made provision for him.'

'When did you do that?'

'When I saw him, when I assured myself that he was my son, I arranged that he should be well provided for whatever happened.'

'What of this country? What will happen to it? What happens when countries are overrun by their enemies? Will what you have done be worth anything if France is a beaten nation?'

'I have made arrangements both in Paris and in London. After all, he is half English.'

'You have really done this!'

'You look at me as though you regard me as some sort of magician. I may be in your eyes, Kate, but these arrangements are commonplace. They can be made by any man of business. I have seen the way things were going here. I had made plans to leave for a while, but I wanted to take you and the boy with me. However, that failed. But at least . . . if the boy were left without either of us, there would be people in London who would find him and he would be looked after.'

I could not speak. Even lying there he exuded power. I had the feeling that while he was there all would be well with us.

'You are pleased with me,' he said.

'It was good of you . . . kind of you.'

'Oh, come, Kate, my own son! I always wanted a boy like that. He satisfies me . . . completely, as you do.'

'I am glad you have some regard for him.'

'One day he may be a great artist. He will get that from you. From me he will get his handsome looks . . .' He paused waiting for comment, but I gave none. I was too moved to speak. 'His handsome looks,' he went on, 'and his determination to get what he needs . . . his force, his strength of purpose.'

'None of which qualities could come from anywhere else,' I said with a mockery tinged with gentleness. He had lifted a great burden from my shoulders.

He said: 'Had you been here when I came I would have got you out of Paris. I had planned to take us all . . . you, the boy, Nicole . . . and of course the governess. Poor Nicole . . .'

I said: 'You loved her.'

'She was a good woman . . . a good friend to me. We

understood each other. It is hard to believe that she is dead.'

'You have known her a long time.'

'Since she was eighteen. My father did not want me to marry young. He chose a mistress for me. He wanted to make sure that I made the right marriage. He put great store in the calibre of the offspring.'

'Like breeding horses?'

'You could say that. All the same, the principle applies.'

'Nicole, I presume, had not the necessary points?'

'Nicole was a beautiful and clever woman. She had been married to a bank clerk. My parents arranged the meeting with her mother. We liked each other and it turned out to be a very satisfactory relationship.'

'Satisfactory for you and your calculating family, perhaps. What of Nicole?'

'She never gave any sign that she was not satisfied with the arrangement. It is the way things are managed in France in families like ours. The necessity of a mistress was understood and one was provided. It was marriage which was the serious question.'

'So that is how to make a perfect marriage. It didn't work in your case, did it?'

'It's something you learn as you get older. You can make plans but you forget that when you are dealing with people you can go wrong.'

'So you have learned that at last.'

'Yes, at last I have learned it.'

'You thought the blood of princes would enhance the family strain.' I laughed. 'It's a matter of opinion, of course. And you are clearly not satisfied with your marriage . . . royal blood though there is.'

'I am completely dissatisfied with my marriage. I think often of how I can end it. Lying here, I have been thinking a great deal about that. If ever I get out of this place, I shall do something. I shall not spend the rest of my life . . . shackled.

Don't you agree that I should be a fool to let things stay as they are?'

'I can't see how you can do anything else. You planned and your plans went wrong. You thought your Princesse was a puppet to be picked up and put in a certain place at your will. Her duty was to supply a little blue blood to the great Centeville stream . . . though I should have thought – in your opinion at least – no royal blood could compare in worth with that of barbarian Norsemen. However, you picked her and put her where you wanted her – and lo, you have discovered that she is not a puppet. She is a warm, living human being who, having no wish to make the donation of royal blood her mission in life, turned to someone else who pleased her better than the barbarian Baron. There is only one thing to be done now. As we say in England: You have made your bed. Now you must lie on it.'

'That is not my way. You should know that well enough by now.'

'If things don't please you the way they are, you set about changing them. That is it, is it?'

'Yes, Kate.'

'Well then, what will you do? There would have to be a dispensation, wouldn't there, to annul the marriage?'

'On the grounds of her adultery it should be easy.'

I burst out laughing.

'I am glad I amuse you,' he said.

'Oh, you do. *Her* adultery. You must admit that is very funny. Besides, is it adultery? She had her lover before her marriage. She did – though in a more human, civilized manner – what you have done many times, I am sure. And you talk about divorcing *her* for adultery. You see why you make me laugh.'

He was silent for a while. Then he said: 'Kate . . . if we could go back to that time when we were together . . . do you know what I would do? I would marry you.'

I laughed, but I was inwardly pleased, though I would not let him know it if I could help it.

'How?' I said. 'You can't exactly force a woman to take marriage vows. It isn't as easy as rape, you know. That's just a matter of physical strength.'

'You would have agreed.'

'I should never have agreed.'

'I sometimes think of it. In fact, lying here, I've thought of it a great deal. Married to Kate! That boy acknowledged as my son! We'd have others too, Kate. I see what I ought to have done.'

'They would not have had the blue blood which you were after.'

'They would have been part of you . . . and part of me. That's what I dream of. That's what I want more than anything in the world.' I stood up and he went on: 'What do you say? Where are you going?'

I said: 'It is time to dress your leg and I am going to get the dressing.'

He looked at me with his head on one side. He was laughing at me, but somehow I knew that he had meant what he had said.

I felt suddenly very happy.

The winter was on us and it seemed particularly severe. We had plenty of wood to make a fire but we watched it carefully, rationing ourselves every day. The cold was more bearable than the lack of food. We were able to wrap ourselves in fur rugs and bed coverings and we all huddled together in that room in which the Baron lay. He needed to rest his leg a good deal. It was impossible to get medical attention. I did not see the doctor now. He had ceased to come and I wondered what had happened to him.

There was rioting occasionally in the streets and I did not go out. The Baron begged me not to and I did not want to leave Kendal nor take him with me. I was terrified of what might happen to him.

He was a wonderfully intelligent child and he understood that we were besieged and what that meant. The Baron had explained to him. The boy would sit on the bed and listen not only to an explanation of the present situation but to tales of the past glories of marauding Norsemen. He loved such stories and would eagerly ask questions, and when some of the stories were repeated – for he often asked for them again and again – if there was a divergence from the first version, he would immediately point it out. They were very happy together, those two.

Later when I heard what was happening in the city I realized how fortunate we were. Jeanne was a wonderful asset to the household. She would go out occasionally and sometimes come back with a little food . . . some potatoes or other vegetables . . . some wine . . . We still had some flour left. How I had reason to bless Nicole's careful housekeeping! She had been interested in the kitchen, for she had loved entertaining and had always seen that there was a good supply in the larders of the sort of food which could be kept. Thus, although we scarcely had a haven of plenty, we did have something to eat during those first three months.

There was no way out of the city and no way in. The frontiers were guarded, and the only communication with the rest of the country was done by means of carrier pigeons, Jeanne told me.

She was brave, and I think she undertook her forages into the city in an adventuous spirit.

So we passed through those months.

December came and as far as we knew there was no sign of the breaking of the siege. The winter lay before us. The days were dark. Through the windows we saw the snow falling and there was hushed silence everywhere.

Jeanne came back one day with a piece of salted pork.

'In the Ananas Inn,' she told us. I remembered the place with the pineapple sign outside. It was only a few streets from the house.

The innkeeper had been a friend of hers, she explained. Occasionally at a high cost he let her have something. The Baron had plently of money but the irony of it was that people did not want money nowadays. What they wanted was food.

We would have the pork on Christmas Day, I said. We should have a real feast. After living on bread and wine for several weeks that would indeed be a treat.

That Christmas will stand out forever in my mind. A cold dark day. Jeanne lighted the fire early as a special treat and we gathered in the Baron's room.

I am sure food had never – or ever has since – tasted so good to me as that hard salt pork. It is indeed true that hunger seasons all dishes.

We talked and Kendal recalled last Christmas Eve when we had had a party with a lot of guests. He had got out of bed and watched. The ladies all had pretty dresses and they had all laughed and danced and there was music.

'Well,' said the Baron. 'Paris was not under siege then.'

'How long will it be?' asked Kendal.

'Ah, that is a question I cannot answer. It can't last, though. Soon we shall all be rejoicing. There'll be bonfires in the streets.'

We looked at the poor little wood fire struggling in the grate.

'Last year we gave presents to each other,' said Kendal.

'We'll give presents to each other this year,' the Baron replied.

'Can we?' cried Kendal excitedly.

'Well, just see them . . . in your mind's eyes. How would that do?'

'Oh yes, let's,' cried Kendal. 'What will you give me, Baron?'

'Guess.'

He tried to think and the Baron said: 'All right. I'll tell. It's a pony . . . a pony of your own. A white pony.'

'Where shall I ride him?'

'In the fields.'

'There aren't any fields here.'

'Then we'll go where there are fields.'

'Shall I just sit on it?'

'Just at first you'll have to have a leading rein.'

'What's that?'

The Baron told him.

'What's his name?' asked Kendal. 'Ponies have to have names, don't they?'

'You will choose his name.'

Kendal thought for a while. Then he leaned towards the Baron and putting his arms round his neck whispered in his ear. 'Would that do?' he asked.

'I think it might do very well.'

'After all,' said Kendal, 'you gave it to me and that's your real name, isn't it?'

'It is, and now it is the pony's. Ha, Rollo! The best and most beautiful pony in France.'

Kendal smiled blissfully. I knew he could see himself galloping through fields.

He stopped suddenly and said: 'You haven't given the others anything.'

'No. We were so taken up with your pony. Well . . . Jeanne . . . what shall I give her?'

Kendal whispered to him.

'Yes, that will do very well. Come here, Jeanne. I shall pin it on your bodice.'

'It's a beautiful brooch,' cried Kendal.

'Of course it is,' said the Baron. 'It's made of diamonds

and emeralds. That will suit Jeanne very well.'

'Thank you. Thank you,' said Jeanne, playing the game to perfection. 'I never thought to have such a brooch in all my days.'

'And now Maman,' said Kendal. 'What have you got for her? It should be something very nice.'

'Oh, it is,' said the Baron. He took my hand and went through the motions of putting a ring on my finger. 'There!' he said. 'Isn't that magnificent. That's a family heirloom.'

'Is it real gold?' asked Kendal.

'As real as can be. And the blue stone . . . that is a sapphire. The finest sapphire in the world. The others are diamonds. The ring has been in my family for generations. It is handed down through the years.'

'Do they give it to the brides?' asked Kendal.

'That's right,' cried the Baron as though in wonder. 'How did you know?'

'I just did,' said Kendal, looking wise. 'Does that make my Maman . . .'

He was looking at the Baron eagerly. No one spoke for a few seconds.

Kendal went on: 'Then,' he said rather shyly, 'you'd be my father. I'm glad. I never had a father. Other boys seem to. I would like having a father.'

I wanted to get up and go out of the room. I was overcome by my emotions.

I forced myself to say: 'It's my turn to give the presents.'

We played guessing games after that – chiefly the old one of thinking of something and making the rest of the party guess what it was . . . a never-failing favourite with Kendal.

Then as a special treat we had a little more of the salt pork though prudence told me it would have been wiser to have saved it for another day.

But this was Christmas Day . . . the strangest I had ever spent, and yet in spite of everything I was not unhappy.

There was a change after Christmas Day, and two days later the bombardment started again. It seemed that the enemy was concentrating on the forts rather than the centre of the city and a great deal of damage was done to those of Vanves and Issy.

There was no more salt pork or any luxuries. The Baron confessed to me that the innkeeper at the Ananas had held the food for him which he had stocked there just in case something like this should happen.

'I thought I should get you away in time,' he said 'but in case I did not – as it turned out – I made a little preparation. I gave the innkeeper permission to take half of the food himself. It would have been too much of a temptation to have it there in the midst of his starving family. I was surprised that he did not take the lot. Even in these circumstances he was afraid of Monsieur le Baron.'

He had reported the last with a certain pride and I thought: He has not really changed. He only seems to have mellowed because of these strange days through which we are living. If ever his life becomes normal again, he will be just the same as he ever was.

But I did not entirely believe this. I had seen him with Kendal and I knew that there was a steady affection between them. Kendal thought him wonderful. That pleased me while it gave rise to a certain apprehension.

I was glad of their relationship now but I often wondered what would happen if ever we moved out of this strange nightmare into which we had been drawn.

We had passed into January. Jeanne reported that people were dying of starvation. They were too weak to riot and were ready to do anything for deliverance.

We had very little to eat now. The Baron said that he had

such reserves of strength that he needed little to keep him alive. I discovered that he often gave his share to Kendal. That moved me as much as anything he had done, and I felt then that I almost loved him.

There was a slight change in the weather. The cold wind had dropped and the sun came out. I felt an irresistible urge to step outside. I would not go far and tell no one that I had gone, for they would protest and try to stop me. But the bombardment had stopped now and streets were safe. The Prussians must have realized that the most effective way to make Paris surrender was through starvation.

I wished I had not taken that walk. I would never forget the sight of the child, He was lying against some palings and for a moment I could have thought it was Kendal lying there. The child's fair hair escaped from a woollen hat and I thought he had fallen. I went forward to help him.

I touched him and he fell backwards so that he was lying there, pale and cold. He was just bones in a red coat and hat. He must have been dead some time . . . dead . . . of starvation. There was nothing I could do for him now. If I had had food to give him, it would have been too late.

I turned and ran back to the house. Kendal came towards me.

'Have you been out, Maman?'

'Yes . . . yes . . . Just a little way.'

'The sun's shining,' he said.

It shone on his face, showing up the pallor, the lack-lustre in those eyes which had once been so bright . . . the pale thin little face.

I turned away because I could not bear to look at him.

'Oh God,' I prayed. 'End this nightmare. Don't let that happen . . . not to Kendal.'

The Baron was standing nearby. He limped towards me and taking my hand drew me into his room.

'What happened?' he asked when we were alone.

I fell against him. I was half sobbing.

He said gently: 'Tell me, Kate.'

'It was a child . . . out there . . . a dead child . . . a boy . . . like Kendal.'

He stroked my hair. 'He'll be all right. This can't go on. They'll have to call a halt. It's coming soon. It must. We'll survive.'

I stood there clinging to him. He held me very tightly and went on: 'Don't give way. That wouldn't be like you. It won't be long now.'

He comforted me as no one else could have done at that time. I believed him. He would take care of us and he could never fail. What had happened to him would have killed most people. But not the Baron.

Such was the way in which he had built himself up for me. We must be all right while he was there. He had found a means to get us some food. He gave the food which he wanted himself to Kendal. He loved the boy who was his son.

I just stood there leaning against him and he put his lips to my hair. That scene from the turret room flashed before my eyes and I thought how different this was. I was glad to be held thus and that he was the one who held me.

'Kate,' he said after a while, 'I want to talk to you. I've had it in my mind for a few days now. This really is going to be over soon. There'll be an armistice and then I shall want to get us out of Paris as soon as it is possible.'

'I can't leave Paris,' I said. 'My work is here. When things are normal . . .'

'How long do you think it is going to be before things are normal! Who is going to want portraits painted? These people want to eat. They want to recover. And even when the food starts coming into Paris, how long do you think it will take to get enough provisions here? Paris is going to be a sad city for some time to come. We are going to get away just as soon as the frontiers are open.'

'Where to?'

'To Centeville for a start.'

'To the castle . . . no, no.'

'You must come. You've got to be nursed back to health. So have I. So will anyone who has lived through this siege . . . and particularly the boy.'

'I am so frightened for him.'

'No need to be . . . if you are sensible. Now I know how you feel about the castle. I have a proposition. There is a little place known as *La Loge du Château.* It is just inside the moat and was used by servants at one time. I shall take you there and you can live there with the boy and Jeanne until Paris is fit for you to return.'

I was silent.

'You will have to sink your pride if you are going to consider the boy,' he said.

'When have I ever let anything interfere with his well-being?' I demanded.

'The answer to that is Never, so you will be sensible now. The child is ill-nourished and has been for three months or more. Thank God he is strong enough to stand it. But he needs good food . . . fresh air . . . country life. He needs to be built up. He's going to have all that, Kate, if I have to kidnap him to give it to him. He needs that more than anything at the moment, and I repeat, he is going to have it.'

I met his eyes steadily. 'I accept your offer,' I told him.

He smiled slowly. 'I knew you would, Kate. It'll come soon. I know it. This simply cannot continue.'

'How will you get out of Paris?' I asked. 'What means of transport?'

'I'll find a way.'

'I can't see how.'

'But you know I will, eh?'

'Yes,' I agreed. 'I know you will.'

Then he leaned towards me and kissed me swiftly on the forehead.

'You will not be far away from me, Kate,' he said softly. 'We have grown close, haven't we . . . in these months?'

I said: 'You have been good to us in many ways.'

'Do you expect me not to be . . . to my own?'

I broke away from him. I went into the salon. Grim. Cold. Deserted. What a travesty of other days. I sat down and covered my face with my hands. I couldn't help thinking of the little dead boy.

But the Baron had comforted me. I knew he would take care of us and that because of him we were going to come safely through.

The armistice was signed on the twenty-seventh of January. There would have been rejoicing in the streets if the people had not been too weak for it. The next day the city capitulated. The siege of Paris was over.

The Baron seemed to have taken on new strength. He now walked at normal speed, although he dragged his right leg a little, it was true; but it did not seem to inconvenience him very much.

He was gone all day and I began to be worried. I prayed desperately for his safe return; and in the late afternoon he came home.

He was pleased with himself.

'We leave tomorrow,' he said. 'I'm getting horses.'

He took both my hands in his and kissed them; then he drew me to him and held me close, laughing.

'We're almost there,' he said.

'How did you do it? There are no horses!'

'Coercion. Bribery. It happens, you know, even in the most disciplined armies.'

I caught my breath. 'You mean . . . the Germans?'

'I'm paying a good price. Money, it seems, is still the key

to most things in the world. What a mercy I have a certain amount of that useful commodity.' Then he shouted: 'Kendal. Where are you? Come here. We're going away. We're going to the country. We leave at the crack of dawn tomorrow. Jeanne! Jeanne, where are you? Be ready. The horses will be here tomorrow morning. I want to get going as soon as it is light. Kate, you and Jeanne will ride together. I'll take the boy.'

How excited we were! There was a little bread dipped in wine which was all we had for supper. We didn't care. It was over. Tomorrow we should be on our way. The Baron had said so; and we believed that he could do anything however impossible it might seem.

The Loge

How happy I was to leave that beleaguered city behind me. That we escaped as we did was something of a miracle and I realized afterwards that only the power and sheer effrontery of Rollo de Centeville could have achieved it.

The people in the streets were like so many pale skeletons. They were quite different from the lively, voluble people I had known. They had emerged from the ordeal angry and bewildered and were clearly prepared for further evils to befall them. The Baron had not only hired horses but a guide, who must have been one of the hangers-on of the occupying army, to get us through the city. I did not ask questions. I thought it better not.

We took the quickest route going southwards, for it was of the utmost importance to leave Paris behind us as soon as possible.

As we passed the Luxembourg Gardens memories flooded back. I could almost see the oriflamme kite flying in the sky. I glanced at Kendal to see if he remembered and again I was struck by his pallor. His arms were like sticks whereas once they had been rounded and plump. He was intent now, sitting there, no doubt thinking of that imaginary white steed which the Baron had "given" him for Christmas. There was a light of excitement in his eyes. I thought: It's true. We shall soon nurse him back to health.

The Baron kept glancing towards me, to make sure that I was still there. He smiled at me encouragingly. I knew he was prepared for setbacks, but I saw the same love of adventure in his face as I saw in Kendal's. I thought: They are astonishingly alike. And I knew we were going to get through.

And we did.

When we left the city behind us, the Baron paid off the guide and we were on our own. It was wonderful to breathe the fresh country air. We came to an inn and stopped there and had some refreshment. There was not a great deal to be had but we were no longer in famished Paris. The Baron ordered a little soup. 'Not too much at first,' he said. 'We will eat little and frequently.'

The soup tasted delicious. We had hot bread with it and I thought there could not be anything more appetizing in the whole world. I knew the others were of the same opinion.

'We'll get along,' said the Baron. 'The sooner we reach Centeville the better.'

It was a hazardous journey for there were soldiers everywhere. They did not take much notice of us – a man who was crippled, two women and a child. They were not very curious.

'Even so,' said the Baron, 'we will avoid camps, if we can.'

We stopped again and took a little bread and cheese. The Baron was able to buy some cheese and bread, which we took with us. There was not a great deal of food to be had, but as he said, after such privation as we had suffered, we had to eat sparingly for a while, so it suited us.

The Baron had plenty of money which he scattered freely and which gave us what we needed. We stayed at an inn one night and spent another in a derelict hut close to a farm.

It was an exciting journey and with each hour the fact that we had escaped gave us courage and the necessary strength to carry on.

I was amazed that in the condition we were in, we could ride as we did.

'People do what they have to,' said the Baron.

And at length we came to the castle.

He had been right. It was untouched. I knew what a proud moment it was for him when he rode under the portcullis.

The effect was amazing.

I heard voices shouting. 'It's the Baron. The Baron is here.'

People seemed to be running in all directions.

'The Baron is back. The Baron is safe.'

We were exhausted . . . even he was. We had needed all our strength to get here and now we had arrived we realized how great the strain had been.

'What has happened in my absence?' asked the Baron. 'Have the soldiers been here?'

He was told no. They had been in Rouen. They had occupied the towns, but had left most of the smaller places alone.

'We need rest and food,' said the Baron.

I had never seen such activity. Kendal's eyes were round with wonder. This was the castle about which the Baron had told him. His eyes were like brilliant lamps in his pale little face. The stories to which he had listened with such enchantment were becoming reality.

I found myself in a room with him. A fire burned in the grate. Food was brought to us. Soup again – hot and savoury.

'I like castles,' said Kendal.

Then we lay on the bed together and slept far into the next day. I remember opening my eyes and suddenly realizing where I was. The siege was over. I was safe in the Baron's castle . . . safe in his care.

Kendal was sleeping beside me. How pathetically his bones stood out! But there was a smile on his lips.

For a moment I made myself forget everything . . . Nicole's death, the terrible moment when I had thought I had lost my son, the face of the little dead boy . . . I pushed it all away. I was here . . . safe in the castle and the Baron had brought us to safety. He would take care of us.

I just lay still and slept again; and when I awoke it was late afternoon.

A servant was standing by the bed.

She said: 'Are you awake, Madame? We had orders to let you sleep until you awoke.'

'I have slept for a long time, I think.'

'You were exhausted. The other lady is still sleeping. And the little boy.'

I nodded and said: 'And the Baron?'

'He was up this morning. He sent me to see if you needed anything. A meal will be served in half an hour if you would like to take it.

Kendal, hearing voices, had awakened. He sat up and I saw the slow smile spread across his face as he looked round the room.

I said: 'I should like to wash if that is possible.'

'But of course, Madame. Hot water shall be brought.'

'Thank you.'

Kendal watched her, wide-eyed, as she went out.

'Are we going to stay here . . . *always*? This is the Baron's castle. I want to see it . . . all of it.

'I dare say you will,' I told him. 'We'll wash and then we'll go down and see what happens next.'

When we were washed we still looked somewhat bedraggled, for we had only the clothes we had travelled in and naturally had been unable to bring anything with us.

I took Kendal's hand and we went down together.

'You know the way,' he whispered in awe, looking round at the thick stone walls with their tapestries of battle scenes.

I gripped his hand tightly, feeling that we were walking into the unknown.

We came down into the great hall where the Baron was waiting . . . with a woman. I recognized her at once, although she had changed a great deal from that young girl whom I had painted in the Rue du Fauborg Saint-Honoré.

'Kate,' said the Baron coming towards me, 'you are rested? And you, Kendal?'

I said we were, and Kendal just gazed at the Baron, his eyes round with wonder and admiration.

'You have, of course, met the Princesse.'

I stepped forward and Marie-Claude held out her hand. I took it.

'Mademoiselle Collison,' she said, 'it seems a long time since we knew each other. And you have been through a terrible ordeal. The Baron has been telling me of it.'

I said: 'We are fortunate to have come through it alive.'

'And this is your son?' She was looking at Kendal and I could not guess what she was thinking.

'Yes, my son Kendal,' I said.

Kendal came forward and took her hand. He kissed it in the French manner.

'Charming,' she said, then she turned to me: 'The siege must have been terrifying.'

'We will go into the dining-room,' said the Baron.

She hesitated. 'The boy . . . should he eat with William?'

'Not today,' said the Baron. 'We will see later.'

'There is another woman . . .' began the Princesse.

'I gather she is still sleeping. Something can be sent to her room when she wakes.' He spoke authoritatively, and his voice was distinctly cool when he addressed her. Knowing him now, I thought, quite well, and also knowing a little of her, I tried to picture what their life together was like. I imagined that normally they saw very little of each other.

Kendal had gone to the Baron and was smiling at him, and I noticed how the Baron's face softened as he looked at him.

'I like your castle,' said Kendal. 'I want to see all of it.'

'You shall,' the Baron promised.

'When?'

'Some time.'

The Princesse led the way into the small dining-room

where I had eaten before, so it was familiar to me. The Baron sat at one end of the table, the Princesse at the other. Kendal and I were opposite each other, and as it was a large table we seemed very far apart.

There was soup first. It seemed easier to eat and the most satisfactory food, for after almost four months of deprivation one had to adjust oneself to eating normally. There was an impulse to overeat at the sight of so much delicious food and we all knew – even Kendal – that we had to restrain that impulse.

The Princesse said: 'You must tell me all about your terrible ordeal. We knew that the Baron was in Paris, of course, and we thought we might never see him again.'

'It must have been a shock when I turned up,' said the Baron coldly.

The corners of her mouth lifted nervously and she smiled as though he was joking. She said: 'We waited every day for news. We did not know what would become of us all. These fearful Germans . . .'

'The French will admit defeat,' said the Baron. 'There'll be treaties, unpleasant consequences for us, and then I suppose the French will begin rebuilding.'

'The Baron does not consider himself to be French,' said the Princesse to me. 'He dissociates himself from their defeat.'

'It was mistaken tactics from the first. Folly which resulted in the only possible outcome.'

Kendal said: 'Are there dungeons?'

'Yes,' the Baron told him. 'I will show them to you.'

'Is anybody in them?' asked Kendal in a low voice.

'I don't think so. We'll have a look tomorrow.'

I said: 'It's very good of you, Princesse, to be so hospitable.'

'We are honoured, *Mademoiselle* Collison.' She stressed the Mademoiselle . . . 'The great artist to stay under our roof!

Remember "Men can make kings but only God can make an artist." Mademoiselle told me that on our first meeting. Do you remember, Mademoiselle?'

There was something defiant about her, I detected. She was frightened of him. She hadn't changed very much from the girl who had come to my bedroom on that very first night and pretended to be a maid.

'I remember very well,' I said, 'and I repeat, it is very good of you to have me and my son here.'

She spread her hands. 'It is natural that you should come here. You have been with my husband . . . suffered with him . . . acted as nurse to him, I hear . . . and now you have escaped with him. You must try this fish. It was caught only this afternoon and is very lightly cooked without sauces as after your ordeal you will have to eat very carefully at first, it has been explained to me.'

'Thank you. You are indeed very good. You understand that the Baron has very kindly offered us the Loge until I can get back to Paris.

'I know. It has to be made ready as it has not been used for a long time. For a few days you must stay here. I hear your studio in Paris was a great success . . . before the siege.'

'I had many clients.'

'It is a long time since we last met. Six years . . . or more. My little William must be about the same age as your boy.'

'Yes, I dare say.'

The Baron had said little. He was watching us intently.

He talked mostly to Kendal, who wanted to know if they would defend the castle if the Germans came here.

'To the last man,' the Baron told him.

'Are there battlements?'

'There are indeed.'

'Shall we pour boiling oil down on the invaders when they use their battering rams?'

'Boiling oil and tar,' said the Baron solemnly.

The Princesse smiled at me and lifted her shoulders.

'War, war . . .' she said. 'Talk of war. I'm tired of war. Mademoiselle Collison, after we have finished I will come to your room and talk to you. You need clothes. You must need many things.'

'We did leave in a great hurry,' I explained, 'and so brought nothing with us.'

'I am sure we can help.'

'Perhaps,' I suggested, 'there is some seamstress who could make something for us. I hope soon to be working again. I do have money. Money was not the problem in Paris.'

'I am sure we can arrange something,' she said.

There was a little chicken after the fish. The menu had been carefully chosen. It was the first real meal I had had for months and I felt revitalized. There was a faint colour in Kendal's cheeks. I could see he was thoroughly enjoying this adventure.

The Baron took him off after the meal and the Princesse came to my room with me.

When the door of my room shut on us, she seemed to change. She dropped the pose of châtelaine, and became the young girl I had known.

'Life is odd,' she said. 'Fancy seeing you again. I've thought of you every time I've looked at the miniatures, and of course I heard about your salon in Paris. You really became well known, didn't you? It seems such a long time ago.'

'It is.'

'Kate,' she said. 'I called you Kate, didn't I? I liked you . . . from the start I liked you. You had an air of independence about you. "Take it or leave it. If you don't like me, employ another artist." You have a child now. Bertrand de Mortemer's, I suppose. Yet you didn't marry him . . . even though there was a child.'

'No,' I said, 'I didn't marry him.'

'And you had a child . . . and you were not married!'

'That's right.'

'You were brave.'

'I didn't want to marry. We . . . er . . . didn't want to marry each other.'

'So you had the child. How did you manage?'

'I was befriended, and then I had the salon and people came, and in that world it didn't seem to matter so much as it would in a more conventional one . . . If you understand.'

'I do. I wish I had been in a less conventional world. Your boy is beautiful. He needs a good deal of feeding up.'

'He has been four months in a siege. We were near starvation when we came out.'

'And the Baron brought you out. My noble husband! What was he doing in Paris?'

'You must ask him.'

'He never tells me anything.' She hesitated, and I think she was on the verge of a confidence, but she seemed suddenly to realize that she might be somewhat indiscreet. 'I'll bring some clothes for you to try,' she said.

'And the seamstress?'

'That's for later. At first let me give you something. You are taller than I and so thin . . . That might help . . . your being thin. You won't take up so much. I'll send one of the maids in with some things.' She looked at me wistfully. 'When I used to hear about you in that Paris salon, I envied you. I missed Paris. I hate it here . . . this gloomy old castle. I feel like a prisoner sometimes. I get so tired. I have to rest a lot. It is since William's birth.'

She turned away and went to the door.

I sat down. The food was having its effect and made me feel sleepy. I lay on the bed for a while but did not sleep. Now that my mind was freed from the preoccupation with food, I began to see the situation in which I found myself more clearly.

I could not go on here. It was only a temporary respite. Even if I stayed in the Loge I should be living on the Baron's bounty and I could not endure that for long. I must get back to Paris. But how could I get back to Paris? It would be months – perhaps a year – before there would be a hope for me to work there.

I kept thinking of his words: 'You have to consider the boy.'

Yes, I had to consider Kendal. He must be my first responsibility. No matter what personal humiliation I suffered, as long as Kendal profited that was all I must think of. After all, the Baron was his father. It was not like taking from a stranger.

The maid came in with three dresses, and some petticoats and undergarments.

'The Princesse asked if you would try these, Madame,' she said.

I thanked her and tried on the dresses. They were not a good fit, but they would suffice until I could get something made.

I had to admit to myself that it was a great relief to get out of the clothes which I had worn for so long.

As I changed into a green velvet dress, I thought: There is nothing I can do but accept what fate has thrust upon me. I need rest as well as food; my mind needs adjusting. One does not go through the ordeal of losing a great friend, one's father, and four months of starvation with death threatening at every turn without needing some adjustment.

Until this was made I must shelve other problems.

Kendal and I remained for a week in the castle while the Loge was prepared for us. The Baron had decreed that after our ordeal we needed to rest there for a while.

His word was law in the castle and no one questioned anything he commanded. That he should arrive with two women and a child from the siege of Paris was treated as though it were a part of the natural course of events – because that was how he wished it to be accepted.

When I thought about it, I could see that a perfectly logical explanation could be put on what had happened. He had found himself in Paris; he had seen a child about to be crushed to death and had thrown himself on the child and borne the brunt of the collapse of bricks and mortar. He had discovered the child to be the son of an artist whom he had once employed and because of the disorder in the Paris streets and the inability to get medical attention, she had taken him in – injured as he was – and he had stayed in her house to be nursed by her. It was all perfectly logical – except one thing. He could not hide his affection for Kendal; and when it was considered how he behaved towards William – who was generally accepted as his son – this was very strange. Moreover, William was small and dark with his mother's Valois nose. He seemed to be a nervous child but I quickly deduced that this was due to the treatment he had received. The man he believed to be his father ignored him and his mother seemed indifferent towards him too. Poor child, he had been made to feel that his presence in this life was rather unnecessary.

So of course they were wondering about us. Then there was the fact that the Princesse constantly referred to me as Mademoiselle Collison – and indeed I had been so called when I visited the castle all those years ago, and many of them remembered me. Moreover, the resemblance between Kendal and the Baron was becoming more obvious every day.

Oh yes, understandably there were speculations.

They were strange days. I think that if I had been my previous self I should never have stayed at the castle. But I had been more weakened by that sojourn in Paris than I realized. I was still suffering from the shock of Nicole's death, which had been temporarily muted by other momentous events, but now that I had left Paris behind me, I thought of Nicole a great deal. Then again there was the death of my father. The days of my childhood were constantly in my mind when my father had been closer to me than any other person. I was only now realizing that I should never see him again. So I mourned the two of them. I longed to hear what was happening to Clare. So my thoughts were dominated by my father and Nicole. I mourned them both afresh. The knowledge that it was the Baron who had sent Nicole to care for me made no difference to my feelings for her. She would always be remembered in my heart as my good friend-in-need, and it was only now that I fully realized what a big gap her death – following on that of my father – had made in my life.

As for the Baron, I did not want to think of him. Not that I could stop myself. I had to accept the fact that my feelings towards him had changed. I remembered so much about him – his lying on that bed suffering pain and refusing to admit it; the tenderness I sometimes saw in his face, the relief when I came into the room; his love for Kendal – for love it was, although strongly tinged with the pride of possession. 'This is my son!' That was what he thought every time he looked at Kendal; and the fact that he so resembled him made the boy doubly endearing to him.

Somewhere at the back of my mind was the thought that he would never let Kendal go. And what would that mean to me?

It seemed that I was in a hopeless situation, and I saw it more clearly since I had come to the castle.

The Baron wanted his son. I believed that if he were free he would attempt to make me marry him. I should, of course, refuse; but he would attempt to bring it about. He always got what he wanted and now he wanted Kendal.

Two doctors came to the castle to look at the Baron's leg.

While they were there he insisted that all of us – Kendal, Jeanne and myself – should be examined to make sure that the months of famine had not impaired our health. We were assured that we had come through without harm but that we needed good nourishing food to make us really healthy again.

That was true, I knew; and it was a great joy to see the change in Kendal every day.

I walked often during those days – a little at first and gradually increasing the distance. I used to wander down to the edge of the moat and sit there remembering the day when he had come behind me and seen what I was sketching.

Now he found me there, and we sat in silence, looking at the water. Then he said: 'We came through, Kate. There were times when I thought we should never get out of that house.'

'I thought you always believed we would.'

'It was just the occasional doubt. The boy is recovering fast . . . faster than any of us.'

'He's young.'

'He's a de Centeville.'

'Also a Collison.'

'Divine combination.'

'We can't stay here,' I said.

'You're going to the Loge. Have you seen it yet? I'll take you over it.'

'Now?'

'In a little while. Let's sit here and talk first. Kate, what are we going to do, you and I?'

'I am going to the Loge and I shall return to Paris as soon as everything is normal.'

He laughed. 'How long is Paris going to take to recover, do you think? There is rioting in the streets now. They are setting fire to some of the buildings there, I hear. How long do you think it is going to take France to recover?'

'Perhaps I should go back to England. I might set up a studio in London.'

'I want you to stay here.'

'Here! In the castle!'

'No . . . somewhere not too far away. I'll find a place. I shall be with you . . . most of the time.'

'You mean I should become your mistress?'

'You could call it that.'

'Isn't that what it would be called? The answer is no.'

'Why not? I want to keep the boy. I thought of legitimizing him . . . making him my heir.'

'But you have an heir. You have William.'

'You know that he is not mine.'

'He is in the eyes of the law.'

'I don't accept that sort of law.'

'Unfortunately for you, the rest of the world does.'

'You know how it is with this marriage of mine.'

'You should try to understand the Princesse. You could grow fond of her if you made an effort to do so. I know her. I worked on her portrait. It is surprising how one gets to know people whose portraits one paints.'

'I know this: I don't want to be with her . . . to see her . . . She has foisted that bastard on me. It is the worst thing she could have done to me.'

'See it her way. You understand these sudden impulses. Why should it be accepted that a man may indulge his and it is so dreadful when a woman does?'

'Because of the results when a woman does.'

'There may well be results, which should concern the men.'

'I did concern myself.'

'I know. You sent Nicole to discover what was happening to me and when you knew I was to have a child you set up that elaborate establishment.'

'You see, I cared. I made sure that you had the clients you would need. I satisfied myself that you were in good hands. I did everything I could.'

'Except that which you should never have done in the first place.'

'Are you going to hold that against me all our lives?'

'Yes,' I said.

'Well, you will have to be with me to show me your resentment.'

'I have no help for it at the moment. I know it sounds ungrateful, but in view of everything, you must understand. I would not be here if it were not for the boy.'

'I know. Every time it is the boy.'

'And would you want me here if you did not have to have me to get Kendal?'

'That's where you are wrong. If there were no child, I should want you just as much. Kate, be sensible. You know I want you . . . you only. More than I want the boy, I want you. We could get more boys like Kendal. You did something to me.'

'I am glad there was some retaliation.'

'I feel vital when I am with you.'

'I thought you felt magnificent all the time . . . as the greatest man the world has ever known.'

'Well, that's just a natural feeling. There is something special in it when I am with you. I want you *and* the boy. I would to God my wife would go to sleep one afternoon and never wake up. Then we would be married, Kate. I would convince you then.'

'Don't dare say such things . . . in my hearing,' I cried. 'Other people have their lives, you know. We are not all on Earth to serve your needs. You used me for revenge . . . the pettiest revenge. You married the Princesse that your children might have that French royal blood which seemed so important to you . . . once. Now, you no longer feel that it is necessary. France is a republic now. *A bas la noblesse.* Therefore let us remove the Princesse.'

'I did not say I would remove her. I said I do not love her. I have never loved her. She irritates me and I loathe being near her. I wish she would die in her sleep. She is always complaining about her ill health. She does not seem to take much pleasure in life so perhaps she would not care greatly if she left it and ceased to be an inconvenience. At least I am truthful. I doubt whether I am the first husband with an unwanted wife who has felt the wish – even if he has not expressed it – that she will pass gently out of his life. And as I married her, and she is a Catholic and royal, she would need a dispensation to annul her marriage, and I am sure she would never agree to that. It is only human nature that I should wish her gently to pass away. There. I am honest.'

I turned to him. 'You alarm me when you talk like that.'

He took my hand and kissed it.

I went on: 'You seem to get what you want . . . always.'

'Yes, Kate, so I do. And one of these days I'll have you and the boy . . . and all the others we shall have. We were meant for each other. Your spirit . . . your independence . . . your lovely dark-red hair . . . I think of them all the time. I shall have no peace until we are together as once we were for three nights . . . remember. One day we shall be together again. Don't tempt me too far, Kate.'

I said: 'I see I must leave the castle.'

'You will be in the Loge close by.'

'You make it very difficult for me. I don't see where I can turn. I know I ought to go away though . . . right away.'

'And take the boy? Submit him to . . . what? He needs care. He needs peace of mind. The sort of life he had to lead in Paris has its effect on a child's mind. I won't have him taken away from here.'

'You couldn't stop me if I wanted to take him. You have no claim.'

'As his father . . .'

'Your part in his conception was minimal. The sort of chance encounter. There are many such. I can never understand why it is thought that a father should have a claim to compare with that of a mother. That child has grown in me . . . he has been my life from the moment I was aware of his existence. Don't talk to me about claims.'

'Fiery Kate. Beloved Kate. Every moment you convince me that I cannot live without you.'

'What has the doctor said about your leg?' I asked.

'Nothing can be done. It needed attention at the time. I've lost some of the bone. I shall limp for the rest of my days.'

'And the pain?'

He shrugged his shoulders. 'Sometimes it's there. Not as it was. Now it's merely an irritating nagging. It is worse when I'm angry and when the weather is cold.'

'You can't change one,' I said, 'but you can the other. So . . . don't get angry.'

'Take care of me then . . . as you did in that house . . . only differently. Let's be lovers as we were before . . . only differently again. Let us be the tender passionate lovers which we could be, you know.'

'Let us go and look at the Loge,' I said.

He rose obediently and we walked round the moat.

The Loge was there nestling under the shadow of the castle . . . growing out from its walls, as it were.

'It was added on several hundred years after the castle was built,' he said. 'Some time in the eighteenth century, I believe. One of my ancestors built it for his mistress. Afterwards it was used by some of the servants. I don't think it has been inhabited for some years now.'

He led me in. There was a big room with a great fireplace and a flagged stone floor. There were some pieces of furniture in the hall – an oak settle, a long table and some chairs.

'You could make it cosy,' he said. 'There is a fairly large

kitchen and several bedrooms. Remember it is just a port in a storm.

I turned to him. 'It's really good of you,' I said. 'I'm afraid you think I'm rather churlish at times. I know I owe you a great deal . . .'

'But nothing will ever settle the score, will it? Perhaps in twenty years' time, when you and I are no longer young and I have shown you a lifetime of devotion – and that with you and the boy, and the other children we shall have, I can be quite different from that savage you once knew – when you recognize in me the only husband you could possibly love, then we shall call it quits. Do you think so?'

I turned away from him, but he was beside me. 'Do you, Kate?' he insisted.

'You speak of the impossible.'

'It might not always be impossible,' he replied.

I was to remember that . . . later.

I was growing more apprehensive. The more I returned to what I called normal, the more I realized the difficulties of the situation into which I had fallen. There was one great recompense and that was Kendal. In less than a week he had started to put on flesh; he had regained his normal vitality; he was a healthy, happy boy. That he loved the castle and this new life was undeniable. He was growing more and more fond of the Baron . . . I was beginning to call him Rollo to myself now. Kendal was not in the least in awe of him and I don't think Rollo had ever had that sort of regard before. He spent a lot of time with the boy.

It was only the third day after our return when he told Kendal that he wanted to show him something rather special in the stables; and when they had gone down there together a white pony, such as he had described on Christmas Day, was waiting.

Kendal came in to tell me about it, cheeks scarlet and eyes glowing.

'There it was, Maman . . . There it was . . . just like the Baron said . . . and it's mine.'

After that he had to learn to ride. Sometimes Rollo took him out and they would ride round the greensward by the moat. Sometimes one of the grooms took him.

The next day Jeanne came to me, her eyes glowing with wonder. 'Look what the Baron has given me,' she said. 'Do you remember the Christmas presents we talked of? Well, here is the brooch . . . just as he described it. He said I had been so good, looking after you all . . .' She turned away, her eyes filling with tears. She was delighted with the brooch. She had never had anything approaching its value before. Being a practical Frenchwoman she would see it as a nest-egg, but it would have a sentimental value for her as well.

Kendal was overjoyed when he saw it. He kept talking about it and when I went down to the moat I saw him on his leading rein with Rollo beside him.

He shouted to me: 'Watch, Maman. Watch me. Baron, please . . . don't hold the reins.'

He was allowed to trot on his own.

'He's going to be a fine horseman,' said Rollo.

I stood there looking at my son, his eyes sparkling, his cheeks flushed with health, laughing proudly, watching us to make sure we were admiring him.

He came back to us.

'Jeanne has a brooch,' he said. 'It's her Christmas present come true.'

Then he laughed suddenly and took my hand. He was looking for the sapphire ring which Rollo had described.

He was disappointed. I said: 'Well, aren't you going to trot again?'

But Rollo would not let it pass. 'You are looking for the ring,' he said.

'Maman is the only one who has not got her present.'

'Hers is not ready yet,' said Rollo.

'When will it be ready?' demanded Kendal. 'She *ought* to have it, oughtn't she?'

'Yes,' said Rollo, 'she ought to have it.'

'But when . . . ?'

Rollo looked steadily at me. 'When?' he repeated.

'We can't all have presents,' I said. 'You are lucky to have this lovely pony, and Jeanne is lucky too.'

'*You* ought to be lucky, Maman.'

'I'll tell you something,' said Rollo to Kendal. 'She will have that ring one day.'

He was looking at me steadily with that burning gaze which reminded me of that long-ago bedroom . . . I felt excitement rising within me.

My feelings for this man were beginning to be beyond my comprehension.

Marie-Claude was showing a great interest in me. She wondered, naturally, how I should have come to be with her husband in Paris. She could not quite accept the account of the chance meeting during the bombardment when he had saved Kendal's life.

She had changed in some ways from that young girl who had blithely gone off with her lover at the *fête champêtre* and conducted an intrigue with him. Then she had been reckless and impuslive. Now she had become a nervous and apprehensive woman.

She was far from displeased that I had come to the château and had no wish for me to leave and go to the Loge. I think, strangely enough, I offered some comfort to her.

Then there was William. Poor little William! My heart went out to him from the moment I met him. Poor child, he must have been unwanted before he actually made his appearance. I wondered what Marie-Claude's feelings must have been when she knew that she was pregnant and she would not be able to hide the fact that the child was not his from the husband who terrified her.

I believed that she had resented being forced into marriage and that in a spirit of rebellion she had taken a lover. She was a sad shadow of the defiant girl she had been. The birth of William had nearly killed her, I discovered.

As for William, he was a small frightened child. I felt indignant both with Rollo and Marie-Claude when I considered the child. Whatever his disillusion and her defiance, they had no right to let the child suffer for it.

Ignored by his parents, he was constantly trying to assert himself. I understood why he did this, but those about him seemed to have made up their minds that he was simply an unpleasant little boy. He was, of course, greatly interested in Kendal. My son had been wrapped about with love ever since his birth. I must have conveyed to him that he was the most important part of my life; Nicole had loved him; Jeanne, though firm and never failing to correct his faults, was devoted to him. And now Rollo showed him a very special attention. He was built up in security. It had been just the opposite with William. His parents had not wanted to be bothered with him; whenever he saw his mother she seemed preoccupied with something else and he was told that he must not stay with her too long because of the effect he had on her nerves. He told me this when I had gained his confidence. As for his father, he did not seem to be aware of him.

William confided in me that he believed there had been wicked fairies at his christening who had decreed that whenever his father was there a cloak should be thrown round William to make him invisible. Then they made him do something to worry his mother's nerves. He did not know what nerves were; all he was aware of was that he possessed some mysterious power to disturb them.

'I don't know what I do,' he said. 'If I did I wouldn't do it. Oh, it is these wicked fairies.'

I talked about him with Jeanne. She was teaching Kendal and she said she would take on William with him; and as they were only too glad to be rid of William in his own nursery, the two boys took lessons with Jeanne.

We were pleased to discover that William was by no means dull. 'In fact,' said Jeanne, 'I think with the right teaching he might turn out to be quite clever. We have to break down these barriers first, though. He is on the defensive all the time.'

At first Kendal did not like him and demanded to know if he *had* to be with him. 'He can't run as fast as I can,' he said contemptuously.

'All the more reason why you should be his friend,' we told him.

'He's rather silly really.'

'That's what you think. He might think you are.'

That astonished Kendal and he was very thoughtful. After that I caught him observing William very closely. I knew he was wondering in what way William could possibly think he was silly.

Then when William found the answer to a sum before Kendal did, so Jeanne told me, it seemed to mark a difference in their relationship. Kendal had had proof that William was better at some things than he was. It was a good lesson for him.

Jeanne had a way with children. She laid down rules which had to be obeyed and they seemed to like that. William was always in the schoolroom in time and Jeanne and I noticed that the two boys often went off together. Kendal was undoubtedly the leader of the games and decided what they should play, but in the classroom William would often answer first.

'I allow a little subterfuge now and then,' said Jeanne. 'It is more important for them to be friends. So I pretend not to see it, when William passes an answer to Kendal. I want Kendal to realize that he is not superior because he can ride and run better and is an inch or so taller.'

I was given the room in which I had first worked on the Baron's miniature in order that I might paint if I wanted to. The boys used to come up there and Kendal loved to draw and paint.

I gave William some paints and let him try his hand. It was clear that he was not going to be an artist.

'See if you can draw a face,' I said, 'and then paint it. But draw it first.'

William did something which was meant to be a portrait. I could not tell who it was meant to be.

'It's my father,' he said. See . . . he's big and strong. He's the strongest man in the world.'

'That's not like him,' said Kendal, and proceeded to do a sketch which undoubtedly bore more than a slight resemblance to the Baron.

William was overcome with awe. He looked at me sadly. 'I wish I could draw my father,' he said.

I let my hand rest lightly on his shoulder and replied: 'Never mind. It was a good try. Always remember that if you can't do one thing, there are always others you can do. Mademoiselle Jeanne tells me you are quick with your sums.'

'I like sums,' he said, smiling.

'Well then . . .' I leaned towards him and whispered: 'I think you beat Kendal at them . . . and he can draw a little better than you can. He's my son and I'm an artist. His grandfather was an artist and his great . . . great . . . as many greats as you can think of . . . were. It's in the family.'

'He's like them. I'll be like my father when I'm grown up.'

It all came back to one thing. He idolized the father who ignored him. I felt my anger rising against Rollo once more.

Rollo was always seeking an opportunity to be alone with me. It was time I left the castle. When I was in the Loge it must be easier, I told myself. Then it occurred to me that it might be worse. I should not go there. I should leave without delay. But where could I go to? And what of Kendal? He must not get thin and ill-nourished again.

I remonstrated with Rollo. 'You are cruel to William' I told him. 'Why do you have to behave as though the boy is not there?'

'It's the easiest way to tolerate him.'

'You vent your petty spite on a child. I think that is despicable.'

'Dear Kate, I can't pretend to like the boy. Every time I see him, I remember who he is. L'Estrange's bastard. You couldn't expect me to treat him as though he were my own child.'

'You could pretend.'

'I'm not good at pretence.'

'I thought you were supposed to be good at anything you put your mind to.'

'Not that. I never want to see the boy.'

'And now Kendal is here, it is worse. I saw William watching you the other day when you were with Kendal. He came running to you and you went on talking to Kendal as though William were not there. Can't you see what you are doing to the child?'

'I don't see him at all.'

'It's cruel, and for some incomprehensible reason, the boy seems to idolize you.'

'It's obviously the right way to treat him then.'

'A little notice from you would make him completely happy.'

'You are sentimental Kate. Turn your sentiments to a more worthy cause.'

'You wonder why I don't care for you. If you would take a

good look at yourself, you would see why nobody could.'

'You are illogical, Kate. A moment ago you were telling me the boy idolized me. But why, when we are together, do we waste our time talking about him?'

'I happen to be interested in him.' I shrugged my shoulders and turned away.

He was beside me, taking my hand.

'It's hard going on like this,' he said. 'Every night . . . you're in the castle . . . and not with me.'

'I shall be going to the Loge tomorrow.'

'And I shall be thinking of you there in just the same way.'

'I wonder if I ought to try to get to England. They'll be worried about me. Good heavens, they will be thinking I am still in Paris. They'll know the news, of course.'

'I should think the whole world knows of the humiliation of Paris.'

'Is it possible to get a letter to England?'

'It might be. I don't know what's happening at the ports. The situation is rather vague. I gather that the Communists of Paris are now fighting against the new Republic. They don't want a peaceful solution. It seems they want revolution again. There is no law and order in the city. Thank God we got away when we did, heaven knows what would have happened to us among that mad rabble. They are rioting still and destroying buildings. It seems it is just for the sake of destruction. You would think Paris had suffered enough.'

'It seems as if I shall never get back.'

'It will be a long time.'

'I am sure my stepmother will be anxious. I haven't heard from her since the death of my father. That was just before the siege started. She wrote a heartbreaking letter to me. Poor Clare! She is very gentle woman . . . unable to take care of herself very well. I should like her to know that I am safe.'

'I'll tell you what I'll do. Write your letter to her and I'll send a man to the coast with it to see what the position is. I don't know whether the packet boats are going back and forth across the Channel. It may well be that they are. Write your letter and he will take it. If he can send it, all well and good. If not . . . well, we'll try again later.'

'Thank you. That's good of you.'

'Oh, Kate, you would find out how very good I can be if only . . .'

'It's a forbidden subject.'

'Tell me one thing. If I were free . . .'

'You are not free. Please don't talk in this way. You cannot be free, and there is an end to it. If I could leave for England, I could stay with my stepmother for a while until I decided what I could do.'

'Then perhaps I had better not send that letter.' He laughed at me. 'No, Kate, you take me too seriously sometimes. Of course, I'll get that letter across if it is possible. I'm not the man to be frightened of a stepmother.'

'Thank you,' I said.

The next day Kendal, Jeanne and I moved into the Loge.

Jeanne and I found it more comfortable living in the Loge. There was a cosiness about it which the castle lacked. We could get the place warm because it was so small, and nestling below the castle meant that it was protected from the cold winds which buffeted the great edifice above us.

It had been arranged that Jeanne and Kendal should go to the castle for lessons because William would join them there. Jeanne and I flattered each other and ourselves that there was a perceptible change in William since we had come; he had lost a little of his nervousness and the fact that he had his moments of triumph in the schoolroom gave him confidence. Kendal had taken up an almost protective attitude towards him since Jeanne and I had told him that he must not be too rough with him; and instead of resenting this attitude, William seemed to appreciate it.

As for myself, I was very restive. I did not like to be so reliant on Rollo's hospitality. Had I been alone, I should have attempted to get to England, but because of Kendal I was very uncertain. Having seen him so wan and ill-nourished, I was afraid to subject him to anything like that again. I often wondered if the ordeal had weakened him a little – although he showed no signs of it. In any case, because I was determined not to subject him to anything like that again, if I could help it, I must submerge my pride and accept this position for that reason.

I was not blind to the fact that it was an explosive situation. There were schemes in Rollo's mind, and I had reason to know to what lengths he would be capable of going in order to carry them out. His passion for me seemed to increase and he was getting impatient. He made no attempt to disguise his pride in Kendal, and I found it disturbing to live under the same roof – for one might say that, even though I was the Loge – as himself and his wife.

I must get away. I told myself that a hundred times a day. But how? That was the question.

I was eager for news of what was happening in the country. Paris was in turmoil. There was news of a National Assembly to be held at Bordeaux. There were meetings at Versailles. The country was in disorder, and we were fortunate to be in our little oasis, the like of which there could only be a few in remote country places throughout the whole of France.

So I must be careful. I must not be rash. I must swallow my pride and accept this extraordinary situation until I could see a way out of it.

If I were honest with myself I would admit that I did not want to go away. It was going to take me – no less than the others – some time to recover from the fearful ordeal through which I had passed in the Paris siege. There was only one thing to do . . . wait. And I was relieved in a way that circumstances forced me to accept this.

On my first morning at the Loge, Rollo called. Jeanne and Kendal had gone up to the castle for lessons so I was alone.

He was clearly delighted by this and, I expected, had arranged to come at this time.

'Well,' he said, 'how do you feel about this place?'

'It is very comfortable.'

'And we are not far apart. In a way this is probably more convenient.'

'Convenient?' I asked.

'There is more . . . solitude.' He was looking at me earnestly. 'What are we going to do, Kate?'

'Do? We? Kendal and I will have to stay here until I can work something out.'

'I can think of a pleasant way of working it out.'

'I must get back to Paris or go to England. I think perhaps the latter would be best for, as you say, it will take a long time for Paris to get back to normal.'

'What would you do in England?'

'Paint.'

'You are not known in England.'

'My father was.'

'You are not your father. I set you up in Paris. It was my recommendations which brought those sitters.'

'I know that now, but I must try. Merit will win through in the end.'

'Meanwhile, in the tradition of artists, you will starve in your garret. Artists can only be successful if they are fashionable. People are like sheep. They are told: "This is good" and they say: "This is good". If they are not told they do not know . . . and obscurity for them means incompetence.'

'I know that it is true, but I think that eventually hard work wins through.'

'When you're dead, perhaps. But that is not going to keep

you and the boy in luxury . . . not even the necessities of life. Be sensible Kate. You and I will be together. You shall have a studio. I swear I'll never interfere with your work. I'll have the boy legitimized.'

'How can that be?'

'It's possible. It won't be the first time it has been done. We'll have a home together. We'll choose the place. *You* shall choose it. We belong together. I know that to be true . . . more than I have ever known anything.'

'You are a man of wide experience,' I said, 'and you make your plans and decide what is to be done not only by yourself but by everyone else. There is one thing you have not learned yet and that is that where two people are concerned there are two opinions . . . two wills. You may have been able to bend people your way in the past, but it does not work like that with everyone.'

'I know, Kate. I'm learning.'

'You are becoming quite humble . . . for you.'

'It's all part of what you are teaching me, and you are teaching me a great deal, Kate. I never thought I could become as obsessed by a woman as I am by you.'

'Might that be because you cannot have me?'

'Cannot is a word I don't accept.'

'It is a word we all have to accept at times . . . even you.'

He took me in his arms suddenly and kissed me violently. I was taken off my guard and for a few seconds did not fight back. The thought flashed into my mind: We are alone in this house. I am at his mercy. And although I tried to suppress the wild excitement which possessed me, I could not.

I was desperately afraid that he would sense my feelings. He must never know how he could take me off my guard, stir my emotions, make me feel that I wanted him to use violence against me. I dreamed sometimes that I was in that bedroom in the tower, and when I awoke it was not with a sense of fear and revulsion, but of longing to be there in fact.

At the back of my mind this change in my feelings towards him was one of the reasons why I knew I ought to get away before it overwhelmed me.

I withdrew myself with a show of indignation.

'I think,' I said slowly, 'that I ought to go away . . . now . . . without delay.'

He took my hands and kissed them.

'No,' he said passionately. 'No, Kate, never leave me.'

I tried to work up a fury against him. 'You know the position I'm in here. I have nowhere to go. I have a child who has to be cared for. I have to stay here . . . against my will I have to stay. But I have no intention of setting up as your mistress . . . like . . . Nicole . . .'

My voice shook and I felt the tears rush to my eyes.

The mention of Nicole's name sobered us both. He had been more deeply affected by her death than he had betrayed. I was wondering now what her advice would be if she were alive to give it.

I walked away from him and went to the window.

I said: 'I want to earn something while I am here. I don't want to live on your bounty. I should like to paint again. I was going to ask if I might do a miniature of William.'

'William! Why would anyone want a miniature of William?'

'If he had good parents that would seem a superfluous question. Alas, poor boy, he is sadly neglected. I want to do something. I want you to ask me to paint a miniature of William.'

'All right,' he said. 'Do it.'

'I shall have to come to the castle. The light wouldn't be good enough here.'

'Kate, you may come to the castle whenever you wish to do so.'

'Thank you, and I shall tell William that you want this portrait of him.'

'I?'

'Yes, you. That will please him so much. And perhaps when it is being done, you will come to the studio and display a little interest in what is going on.'

'I'm always interested in your work.'

'Please show a little interest in William.'

'For you . . . anything,' he said.

William was delighted when I told him I was to paint his portrait.

'Will it be a little one?' he asked. 'And will Kendal have one too?'

'Perhaps. Kendal has many. I used to paint him when we were in Paris.'

'Show me.'

'I can't. When we left Paris we had to leave everything behind. Now we shall have to see if we can find the necessary paints to make your portrait.'

Rollo was helpful. He knew of an artist who lived a few miles away and he thought it was possible that he might be able to supply the paints we needed, although it was doubtful that he would have the ivory I should need for the support. I sighed to think of all we had left behind in Paris.

Rollo went to see the artist and brought back paints and vellum as there was no ivory available.

'I can use vellum,' I said. 'After all, it was used in the sixteenth century and was the foundation of many miniature masterpieces.'

The boys were with me in that room in the castle where I had first painted Rollo. They watched me stretch the vellum over a stiff white card glueing it where it overlapped and then pressing it between sheets of paper.

William was particularly excited. It was wonderful to see that look of haunted defiance leaving his face.

I thought: I will make an interesting portrait of him. I will show him and everyone else how he can look if he is happy.

I felt alive again. It was wonderful to be working. I could shut out all my problems as I did in the old days. I would sit chatting to William, and Kendal was there too. He was sketching William and, sitting there, with all attention focused on him, William seemed to grow in stature. It was the first time in his life that he had felt he was important to someone.

I would work slowly on the portrait, I decided. After all, I was not only making a picture, I was helping to adjust the mind of a little boy who had been very unfairly treated.

The boys took lessons in the afternoons as I liked to paint in the mornings, and while they were with Jeanne, I took the opportunity to walk or ride. I liked best to ride. When walking, it was difficult to get out of sight of the castle. One had to go a very long way to lose it, for it seemed to dominate the landscape.

There were plenty of horses at the castle and I had the pick of several mounts, but there was a little bay mare of which I was particularly fond. She was a little frisky but responded to firm treatment, and I think she liked me to ride her.

One afternoon I went to the stables and Marie-Claude was there. A horse was being saddled for her – one which, I knew, had a reputation for being quiet and docile.

'Good afternoon,' she said. 'Are you going to ride?'

I said that I was.

'Then we shall go together?'

I said that would be very pleasant and we rode out under the portcullis and down the slope, chatting as we went.

'I didn't realize that you were a horsewoman, Mademoiselle Collison,' she said.

'I ride in England.'

'Of course there wasn't the opportunity in Paris. How glad you must be to have escaped from all that.'

'It was a great experience to have lived through, but one never wants to have to do it again.'

'There must be lots of people in Paris who feel like that. But . . . how I miss Paris! The old Paris, that is. I think I shall never be happy away from it.'

'Alas, you would find it sadly changed.'

'I know. Those stupid people and their wars!'

We rode in silence for a while. She took the lead and I followed.

'I never ride far,' she called over her shoulder. 'I get so tired. I like to go to my favourite spot and look at the view.'

'Are we going there now?'

'Yes. I thought we'd tie up the horses and . . . talk. It's impossible to hold a reasonable conversation on horseback.'

I agreed and we fell once more into silence.

I looked back. I could not now see the castle. She noticed me and guessed what I was thinking. 'That's one of the reasons why it is my favourite spot. From it, it is impossible to see the castle.'

We skirted some woods. The countryside had become more hilly now. I caught a glimpse of the river running below us; it glinted silver in the sunlight.

'It's pretty here,' she said. 'I like to sit right on the crest of the hill. There are bushes up there and some of them grow quite high . . . high enough to give a little shelter from the wind when it blows. I sit up there and look out. You can see for miles.'

We reached the top of the hill.

'We'll tie our horses there. Isn't it strange that we should have come together again.'

We tethered the horses and walked a little way.

'Sit here,' she said and we sat down in the protection of the bushes. 'I never thought I should see you again,' she went on, 'unless it was at some gathering. That was when I thought you were going to marry Bertrand de Mortemer. Then it would have been quite reasonable for us to meet.'

'Strange things happen in life,' I commented.

'Very strange.' She turned to look at me. 'I'll confess to being very curious about you, Kate. I may call you Kate? I did before, didn't I? Will you call me Marie-Claude?'

'If you wish.'

'I do,' she replied with a touch of the imperious manner I remembered from the past.

She went on: 'I admire you very much. I wish that I had had your courage. You have a child but you did not marry its father. How wise you were! If I had not been married how much happier I should have been! But I suppose it was easier for you than it would have been for me.'

'Yes,' I said.

'I didn't really love Armand L'Estrange. Perhaps if I had I should have defied everyone and married him. I was always terrified of Rollo . . . in fact I could never be anything else. He is a ruthless man, Kate. Only those who have lived near him know how ruthless.'

'I think I have gathered that.'

'The marriage was arranged, as you know, and I was angry. I didn't want to marry him. You know that. You were there before I did. You wouldn't want to marry someone who terrified you, would you?'

'Indeed not,' I said.

'And then there was Armand. He was so charming . . . so different. He was gallant and made me feel that there was something very special about me. I just wanted to be loved. You know about us. You were at the *fête châmpetre* and then there were the notes you took. Do you remember the time Rollo tried to get hold of the notes which you collected for me at the modiste's? That matter of the taxi . . .'

'I remember it well.'

'He must have suspected then, I was so frightened. If that had happened before . . . I don't think I should have started with Armand.'

I sat staring ahead thinking of that terrifying ride across Paris in the cab.

'You see he suspected me . . . even then.'

I hesitated, but I could not tell her that it was for a different reason that I had been nearly abducted.

'And yet,' she went on, 'he pretended to be surprised. I shall never forget my wedding day . . . I mean the horror of it. I suppose nobody ever forgets a wedding day . . . but other people's would be remembered differently. I don't know how I lived through it. And he knew, of course. I don't think he minded so much about that. It was when the child was to be born too soon that he was mad with rage. I tried to get rid of it. It didn't work. Who would have thought to look at William that he could have been so obstinate! Rollo had a way of finding out things, then he made me tell him . . . everything. He was to have a child which was not his! You can understand how furious he was.'

'Yes, I can,' I said.

'You think he had reason to be. But I didn't want to marry him in the first place. If I had seen your example then I might have stood out against him. I might have been free . . . as you were. Why didn't you marry Bertrand? You were betrothed. You were in love. And there was to be a child and yet . . . you didn't marry him. That seems very strange.'

'I did what I felt was best.'

'It was brave of you. And you set up that studio in Paris and you didn't care . . . And nobody seemed to mind.'

'I lived in a bohemian society, and as I told you, conventions are not considered to be of such importance there as they are in Court circles.'

'I wish I had lived in such a society. Nothing was right for me. I was married to a man I was afraid of . . . I was going to have a child which was not his. Sometimes I wished I could just die and leave it to other people to sort out.'

'You must never feel like that.'

'But I do . . . now and then. You see, the fact that I tried to get rid of William did something to me. It didn't stop his coming but . . . there was some damage. I can't have any more children. That's another reason why Rollo hates me.'

'He can't hate you.'

'Now you are talking as so many people talk. Why can't he hate me, pray? Of course he hates anyone who stands in the way of what he wants. He would like to get rid of me and marry someone who could give him children . . . sons just like himself.'

'We all have to adjust ourselves to life. Even he has to do that.'

'Sometimes it doesn't seem worth the effort. Imagine how it was. I was going to have the child who was going to appear too soon. I was sick and wretched . . . desperately frightened of childbirth and even more frightened of him. I used to come up here and sit down and think. I'd look over there. That's where Paris is . . . In that direction . . . if only there wasn't so much in between. I longed to be back there. Sometimes I thought of climbing a little higher to the Peak. That's a spot where the land stops suddenly and there is a big drop down. Someone fell over not long ago. It was in the mist. It was a farmer who had lost his way and couldn't find his bearings. He stepped out . . . into nothing. I'll show you before we leave. It's just up there. I used to think how easy it would be to take that step. That would end it. No one could blame me for anything then. And how pleased Rollo would be. He could wipe me out of his life and start again.'

'How unhappy you must have been!'

'More frightened than anything else. Believe me, at one time I thought it would be easier to do that than to go on.'

'Poor Marie-Claude, how you must have suffered!'

'Even now . . . sometimes I think, is it worth while going on?'

'You have your little boy.'

'William! He's the cause of all the trouble. But for him I should probably have had more children. I might have grown less scared of Rollo. Who knows, I might have been able to give him what he wanted.'

I was feeling vaguely apprehensive. I guessed that later she might regret having told me so much. She turned to me impulsively. 'Mine is such a wretched story. Don't let's talk of it any more. How different it must have been for you. Tell me about it.'

'You know a great deal of it. I had my child and I set up in a salon and painted. Clients came to me, and it was all going very well until the war came.'

'The war!' She mused. 'It seemed rather remote to us here in the château. Isn't it strange that Rollo should be able to keep himself aloof from it? It is almost as though he had magical powers. Sometimes I think he is more than a man . . . a demon perhaps. Someone who has come on earth from some other place. Do you understand what I mean?'

'Yes,' I admitted.

'I thought you did. He's always been against this war. He said it was folly and the Emperor was a fool. He thinks of himself after all these centuries as a Norman. He's powerful . . . more powerful than any one man should be. He owns a great deal of property . . . not only here but in England and Italy. It is because he is so rich and powerful that my family wanted the marriage, and it was because of my descent from the Royal Houses of France and Austria that he wanted me. How can people expect a good marriage to be based on such reasons? You are very fortunate, Kate.'

'I know I am fortunate in some ways.'

'Your little boy is beautiful.'

'I think so. And so is yours.'

She shrugged her shoulders. 'Rollo seems to like your son.' She looked sideways at me and I felt the colour begin to rise from my neck to my forehead.

'He is generally popular,' I said, trying to speak lightly.

'He was pale and thin when he arrived with you and Rollo and Jeanne.'

'Who wouldn't have been after that ordeal.'

'Yes, you were all showing signs of what you had been through. But you have recovered wonderfully now.'

'That's something I'm thankful for.'

'Rollo has never taken the least interest in any child before. It is remarkable how much attention he bestows on yours. I never quite understood how Rollo came to be there at the precise moment when all that masonry was about to fall on your child.'

'You would have had to be in Paris to understand how things happen.'

'I know people died. What I meant was that it was an odd coincidence that he happened to be there at the precise moment.'

I shrugged my shoulders. 'He saved the boy's life,' I said. 'There is no doubt of that.'

'Do you think that could be the reason why he is so fond of him?'

'I think one would be rather fond of someone whose life one had saved. It's getting chilly,' I went on. 'Do you think we ought to sit here?'

I helped her up.

'It was such an interesting talk,' she said, 'that I forgot I was cold. Before you go I want to show you my spot. The Peak, remember.'

'Oh yes. It's not far from here, you say.'

'Just over there. Come on.' She took my arm. She seemed a little breathless.

We walked across the grass and there it was before us – a

wonderful panorama of little hills and woods far away to the horizon.

She pointed. 'Over there would be Paris . . . if it were near enough for you to see.'

I looked down at the river below. I could see rocks and boulders protruding from the water and yellow coltsfoot growing on the bank.

'Are you scared of heights, Kate?' she asked.

'No.'

'Then why do you hang back?' She had released my arm and stepped nearer to the brink. 'Come on,' she commanded, and I approached the edge. 'Look down,' she said.

I did so. My first thought was that if she had thrown herself over as she had contemplated doing, she would have had little chance of survival.

She was close to me . . . standing behind me now. She whispered: 'Imagine falling . . . falling . . . You wouldn't know much about it, just that quick gasp . . . a sort of wild thrill and then down . . . down . . . You'd be dead in a matter of seconds.'

I was seized with sudden fear. Why had she brought me here? Why had she talked or she had? What was she implying?

She knows that Kendal is Rollo's son, I thought. She must believe that we were lovers in Paris and perhaps still are.

She hated him. But would that prevent her resenting the fact that he might love me? That he made it so clear that he loved my child?

I had always known that the Princesse Marie-Claude was impulsive, inclined to be hysterical. I was sure that the ordeal of marriage to Rollo when she was to bear another man's child had been too much for her. Had it unbalanced her mind?

In those next seconds I was sure that she had brought me here for a purpose and that purpose might well be revenge.

Revenge on me? More likely on him. If she thought he loved me, how could she hurt him more than by destroying me.

It would be so easy. An accident, they would say. The ground crumbled. She slipped. She went too near the edge.

I felt sure that she was about to push me over the edge . . . into oblivion.

I turned sharply and stepped away from the edge.

She was looking at me enigmatically, almost resignedly, I thought.

'You were standing very near the edge,' she said, as though admonishing me. She gave a little laugh. 'For a few moments you frightened me. I had a vision of your falling over. Let's get back to the horses. I'm shivering . . . with the cold. This is not the time of year to sit about chattering.'

The Way Out

I felt very shaken after that experience. I did convince myself that I had imagined I was in danger, but I tried to remember in detail everything we had said and what had actually happened while we had stood there on the edge of the Peak. She had asked pertinent questions about Kendal; but then I supposed others were asking similar questions. It was true that Rollo did show great interest in Kendal, while at the same time he did not attempt to hide his indifference to the boy who was supposed to be his own.

I felt I was moving towards a climax, and one part of me warned urgently that I ought to get away while another posed the continual question of How and Where?

The miniature of William was progressing. Rollo used to come to the studio as I had asked him to, and it was touching to see William's delight in having him there showing such an interest in the portrait.

He would look at William intently and then comment on the miniature.

'You've caught the expression in his face,' he would say. Or: 'The colour of his skin is not easy to get, I should imagine.'

William sat basking in the unusual interest he was arousing and while I worked I was able to dismiss all my fears and be happy. It was wonderful. Kendal insisted on being there. He was doing a portrait of William too.

'I like a big picture,' he said; and indeed, in spite of his immaturity, he was producing something which had a look of William.

So there were the four of us together, and as I painted a serenity crept over me and I wished that we need never break away from those magical moments. Even the children felt it, the deep contentment in that room. Rollo seemed to have forgotten his desire and was ready to settle down in what I can only call an atmosphere of peace.

It could not last, of course. Soon the miniature would be finished. But it had done what I had wanted it to. It had given something to William which he might never have had. The boy had changed perceptibly. Between us, I thought, Jeanne and I have given him confidence – with a little help from Kendal.

The news was bad. There were dissenting factions all over France. The government was republican but there were strong partisans of monarchy in it. Fighting continued in strife-torn Paris and the rioting of those who were more concerned with making trouble than setting the country right was bringing complete disorder to the capital.

What could I do? Where could I go? I thought again of trying to get to England. I could go to Collison House and live there with Clare. I had had no reply to my letter so I wondered if it had reached her. I was sure that she would give me a warm welcome.

When I suggested to Kendal that we might leave the castle he was overcome with horror. He loved the castle. He had been extremely happy ever since he had come.

'Don't let's go, Maman,' he said. 'Let's stay here. What would the Baron do if we went?'

I did not answer. The question in my mind for a long time had been: What will the Baron do if we stay?

The picture of William was finished and the Princesse admired it. 'Your work is so good,' she said. 'I often look at those you did of the Baron and me. The one of him is particularly interesting.'

'Do you think so?' I asked.

'Oh yes. You seem to have seen something in him when we didn't . . . until you pointed it out.'

'I'm glad you think so.'

'There is an expression in his eyes which is almost benign.'

'We all have many sides to our characters,' I reminded her.

'And it takes certain people to bring them out,' she agreed. 'Why, you have made William look quite an attractive child.'

'He is an attractive child.'

'He is better since you came. Sometimes, Kate, I think you have an effect on us all. You are not a witch or something, are you?'

'No indeed. Only a painter.'

'A very good painter. You must agree to that?'

'If I didn't think so, how could I convince other people that I was?'

'You are very wise, Kate. I am sure Rollo thinks so.'

I turned away. I was always uncomfortable when she talked of him. I remembered that mischievous streak from the past which I had discovered when she came to my room dressed as a maid. That spirit of mischief still lingered. Was she trying to tell me that she knew her husband had been my lover – still was – and that this child who was beginning to look too like him for the resemblance to be coincidental was his?

They were uneasy days.

I must go. I *must*. And the answer was always the same: Where? How? And Kendal must not be put at risk.

Because he understood my feelings so well Rollo found work for me to do. He had been searching through the castle library, he told me, and he had found some old manuscripts which were in need of restoration.

He would show them to me if I could come to the castle the

following afternoon while the boys were at their lessons.

I did wonder whether there were, in fact, any manuscripts or whether he just wanted to talk to me. I found him in the library. It was an impressive room lined with bookshelves, as I had imagined it would be, of course, but the books were on various subjects and most of them beautifully bound.

'This is my sanctum,' he said. 'Do you like it?'

I said it was delightful and impressive at the same time.

He took my hand and pressed it to his lips.

'We go on in the same old way, Kate,' he said. 'Don't you want to change it?'

'Yes. I want to go from here really because that is what I feel I should do.'

'We want to change it for the better,' he said tersely, 'not for the worse.'

'Have you brought me here to show me old manuscripts, or to talk of impossibilities?'

'To talk possibilities and to look at manuscripts. But first let us talk. How long will it be before you realize that we can't go on like this?'

'We can,' I contradicted, 'until I can get away. If it were not for Kendal, I would risk trying to get to England. I am beginning to think that that is what I must do. I have talked about it to Kendal.'

'What does he say?'

'He doesn't want to leave, of course.'

A slow smile spread across his face. 'He is such a wise boy,' he said.

'You have charmed him with your attentions.'

'Naturally my own son likes me.'

'You have not made yourself so charming to poor little William.'

'I said my own son. I can't account for bastards.'

'You are a cruel, hard man.'

'Not to you, Kate . . . never to you.'

'Once . . .' I began.

'That was necessary and it was the beginning of love, wasn't it?'

'No, pure lust for revenge.'

'Oh, that . . .'

'Which failed.'

'It was highly successful because it showed me that there was one woman in the world who could satisfy me.'

'*You!* Everything comes back to you. Please show me the manuscripts.'

'In due course. First we talk. I'm tired of this . . . subterfuge.'

'There is no subterfuge on my part.'

'When you pretend that my son is not my son!'

'How could I do otherwise! I have an idea that your wife already suspects.'

'What does she suspect?'

'That Kendal is your son.'

'Then she is correct in that.'

'That I am your . . .'

'Mistress?' he said. 'Well, let us hope that she will soon be correct in that too.'

'Please do not talk in that way.'

'But if the first of her suspicions is true, then the second must be.'

'I don't agree.'

'Oh, Kate, let us make it so. It is a pity to cheat people of their assumptions.'

'You haven't changed, have you? I believe that the Princesse . . . resents my being here.'

'She has said she is delighted that you are here. The picture of her son gives her a great deal of pleasure. She says the boy is better since you have been here. He likes playing with our boy and he is losing that hang-dog look of his. When he was having his portrait painted I almost liked him.'

I said: 'Even if it were possible, a woman would have to think very hard before throwing in her lot with a man like you.'

'Now, Kate, be honest. Do you think I don't know your feelings towards me? Your lips tell lies when they speak, but sometimes they are more honest. Could you let them speak the truth regarding me . . . for once?'

'I hope I always speak the truth.'

'Not on one all-important matter, and that is your feelings for me.'

'I prefer not to discuss the subject. I have in any case told you many times how I feel about your actions and it is not really very complimentary.'

'That's why I say your lips lie. Think back, Kate, to everything that has happened to us. You know that you love me. You can't leave me. You're trying all the time to get back to that room in the tower. It's not very far from here, you know. It's undisturbed by the war. We could go there. We could recapture that night.'

I faced him angrily. I thought: It is lust, pure lust that he feels for me. He wants me because I don't want him. He hasn't changed since that night and is as capable of rape now as he was then. Even his affection for Kendal is nothing more than pride . . . pride of possession.

My instincts were warning me. I should be wary of him, wary of my own feelings for him. What it was I felt for him I was not sure, but it was not love.

When I had seen him crippled because of what he had done for Kendal, I think I had come near to loving him. I had nursed him with care and tenderness, and perhaps because of the terrible dangers through which we had lived, my feelings towards him had changed. Now he was in his own domain; he had come through the siege of Paris, though not entirely unscathed; he suffered certain pain from his leg, I knew; he would never walk as he had before; but all that did not stop him from doing everything that he wanted to. Here, in the background of his Norman castle, he was the barbarian again, the strong ruthless man who, when he felt a wish, let nothing stand in the way of its gratification.

I said to him: 'Please understand that I came to see the manuscripts. If you are not going to show them to me, I shall go.'

'My dear vehement Kate, of course I am going to show you the manuscripts. Then you won't have to answer my questions truthfully, will you? You should never be afraid to face the truth, you know.'

'It is you who will not face the truth.'

'But I do. I agree with your opinion of me. But you won't face what it really is. Do you think I don't know that if I took you now . . . as I did that night . . . you would not inwardly rejoice? But I want it to be different now. I want you to come to me willingly. That's what I've set my heart on. I've become sentimental. What I want most of all is to marry you.'

'It is easy to make such a proposal,' I reminded him, 'when you know it is impossible to carry it out.'

'It won't always be impossible.'

'Why don't *you* face the truth? You are married. Yours is no ordinary marriage because your wife is a Princesse. You married her for her royal blood, remember? But the children did not come and the blue blood can't be used. That's not a good enough excuse for annulling a marriage, and she would never agree to it. Therefore how can your proposal to another woman be of any substance at all?'

I saw that cold look in his eyes which made them look like ice. 'You're wrong, Kate. You accept defeat too easily. I'll tell you this: one day it will come to pass.'

I was afraid then . . . afraid of him, as not long ago I had been afraid of his wife.

'Shall I see the manuscripts?' I said as coolly as I could.

'But certainly,' he replied.

We pored over them together. They were fascinating. They had been in the castle for centuries, and he believed they had been presented to the family by a monk who had given up his calling and come out into the world. He had worked at the castle and made the manuscripts while he was there.

'Fifteenth century, would you say?' asked Rollo.

'I think they might even be a little earlier. Oh, it would be a wonderful job. My father used to love this kind of work . . .' I heard my voice tremble a little as I mentioned my father, for I was thinking of how he had found this life so unendurable without his sight that he had decided to leave it. Then my thoughts switched to Marie-Claude who had at one time had the same idea. How cruel life could be sometimes!

Rollo was watching me intently. 'You have such an expressive face,' he said. 'So many emotions flit across it. You are sad now, thinking of your father. My dear Kate, it is your mouth rather than your eyes which betrays you to me. That is why I know that beneath that façade of resentment which you show me, you love me . . . you really do.'

I looked down at the manuscripts.

'It would be difficult to get the paints I should need to restore them.'

'We can try.'

'It is always difficult at any time. These people mixed their own colours and no artist used the same.'

'We can try together. We can go and visit the artist about whom I told you. He has lived near here since he was a young man. He is a good artist. I found him and brought him here to work for me. He may well have some of the paints you require. You will be occupied and if you are working you will be content and push aside this ridiculous notion that you ought to be somewhere else.'

Then he drew me to him and kissed me gently. I knew that

he was right. In spite of everything he was dominating my thoughts. If that was falling in love, then that was what I was doing.

The weeks were slipping past. I was absorbed by the work on the manuscripts, so I was at the castle every morning. While I was working Kendal was taking lessons with William and every day seemed very like another. Spring had come. There was still trouble in Paris, and I was no nearer returning there than I had been when I first arrived here.

It was easier to move about the country now, though, and with the coming of May what was known as the Treaty of Frankfurt was signed. There was peace at last. The French grumbled about the terms which had been imposed on them, for they had to hand over Alsace and a great part of Lorraine to the Germans as well as paying a huge money indemnity.

Soon, I thought, I shall have to go to Paris.

I wondered what had happened to the house in which we had lived so long.

At the end of May, Rollo did go to Paris to see what it was like there now. Most eagerly did I await his return.

I had had several conversations with Marie-Claude over the weeks, and she really did seem glad that we were there. I think we enlivened the days to a certain extent. She watched me, I knew; and I think it probably gave her an interest to speculate on the relationship between her husband and myself.

Sometimes I caught a certain satisfaction in her face, as though it was amusing that I should be there and that there should be this frustration between Rollo and me.

I was sure that she thought we had been lovers at some time – even though she might be a little uncertain as to our relationship now; in any case she was intrigued, and her nature was such that she enjoyed that.

She spent a great deal of time in what she called 'resting'.

She liked to think of herself as a semi-invalid. I believed that weakness added an interest to her life. I wondered, too, whether she used it to keep Rollo away. Like so many men of outstandingly good physical health, he would have little sympathy with illness. He had been impatient of his own weakness, and although he had at one time suffered great pain, he had always been reluctant to admit it.

His attitude towards Marie-Claude was one of dislike and contempt, and being the man he was, he took no great pains to hide it.

He came back from Paris with the depressing news that the city was not yet settling down, although it would do so in time. The house had been destroyed with everything in it. Rioters must have set fire to it.

'All part of the whole stupid business,' he said angrily.

So I would have nowhere to go in Paris. Perhaps I should go back to England for a while. I could stay with Clare. I presumed that my letter had not reached her as I still had had no reply.

It was late afternoon of a lovely May day. The boys were playing somewhere in the castle precincts. I had been working all the morning and some of the afternoon on the manuscripts, as it was such a good light. I was in a peaceful frame of mind as I often was after a day's work, feeling pleasantly tired and immensely satisfied with the work I had done. I had, that afternoon, thought of a new way to get the Venetian red and cobalt blue which I needed. I was looking forward to the next day when I should be able to test my new method.

I had gone outside the Loge for it was a lovely balmy day and I was sitting on the grass near the moat deep in thought when I heard one of the maids calling my name.

I jumped up and went to her.

'Oh Madame Collison, there is a lady come to the castle. She is asking for you.'

I turned. Another maid was coming towards me and with her a woman. I could not believe my eyes.

'Kate!' she cried.

I ran to her and we were in each other's arms.

'Is it really you, Clare?'

She nodded. 'No doubt of it. I had to see you. It's been so difficult to get news. But your letter came . . . at last. it was a long time getting to me, I could see from the date . . . But it told me where to come, so I didn't trust another letter. I came.'

We clung together again, laughing, almost crying.

The two maids watched us.

I said: 'It's all right. This is my stepmother.'

The one who had brought her set down her travelling bag inside her and they slipped away together.

'I got a lift from the station in a sort of fly,' said Clare. 'It was hard making myself understood.'

'Has it been a difficult journey?'

We were gazing at each other, talking trivialities because we were too moved for anything else.

'Come into the Loge,' I said. 'This is where we live . . . temporarily.'

'My dear Kate! Whatever has it been like? I was so worried. I kept telling myself that it was a good thing your father had gone. He would have been half crazy with anxiety.'

'It has been a very difficult time, Clare.' I took her bag in my hand and opened the door of the Loge.

'You see,' I said, 'it is separate from the castle, but part of it . . .'

'And how long have you been here?'

'We came directly after the siege of Paris. We were lucky to get out . . .'

'Thank God you are safe.'

'Oh yes, we were fortunate. My poor friend Nicole St Giles

– you met her – was killed during the bombardment.'

'How dreadful! And . . . Kendal?'

'Kendal is all right. We suffered a great deal during the siege, as you can imagine. We almost died of starvation.'

'I thought of you constantly. I tried to get in touch, but there was no way of getting communications across the Channel.'

'I know. It was to be expected with France at war. But never mind that now. You're here, Clare, and I am so glad to see you. Are you hungry? Can I get you some coffee. The boys are playing together somewhere.'

'The boys?'

'Oh yes . . . the son of the Baron and the Princesse . . . William. He and Kendal are good friends.'

'Is it all right for me to be here?'

'But, of course. You can stay at the Loge. There is plenty of room.'

'Are you working here?'

'Yes. I am restoring some manuscripts and I have painted a miniature of William . . . the boy I was telling you about.'

'The Baron's son, you say. And he and Kendal get along well together?'

'Oh yes.'

'Did you come straight her from Paris? This château is the first place you came to when you first arrived in France . . . you and your father?'

'Oh yes, we came here. After the siege the Baron brought us back here.'

'What was he doing in Paris?'

'He was there on business. He saved Kendal's life. You've no idea what it was like. You see, the Prussians were bombarding Paris and Kendal would have been crushed to death if the Baron had not been there just at the right moment to protect him from the falling masonry. The Baron was injured and I looked after him . . . and then as soon as the siege was over we got out. There was nowhere else for us to go but here. It is difficult to explain . . .'

'And you met him just by chance in Paris . . . just at the moment when Kendal was in danger. How wonderful and how exciting that he should happen to have been there.'

'It was a blessing that he was. We might never have go out of Paris if he hadn't helped us and brought us here. The city got worse after we left. There was fighting and rioting and setting fire to buildings. The house where we were was destroyed by fire.'

'My poor Kate! I've thought of you so much. It's been so lonely. I promised myself that as soon as it was possible I would get to you. I realized it was no use just writing, and I can't tell you how wonderful it was to get your letter . . . although I did receive it long after you had written in.'

'Let me make that coffee,' I said, 'and then we can talk.'

We did. I found it difficult to explain what had happened and quite clearly she continued to think that it was the oddest coincidence that the Baron should have happened to be on the spot when Kendal was in danger. I guessed how her mind was working. My father had suspected that the Baron was Kendal's father and it may have been that he had discussed this possibility with Clare. After all, she had been his wife.

I could see that she really believed the Baron had been with me in Paris and that she was carefully wording her questions to avoid embarrassment.

Then I wanted to hear what she had to tell me.

'A very different story from yours, Kate,' she said. 'I have been so lonely since your father . . . went. It was like the end of everything. We were so fond of each other, right from the first.'

'I know. You were wonderful to him. He told me so. I am so glad you found each other. You were a great comfort to him.'

'Not enough,' she answered. Her lips trembled and there were tears in her eyes. 'I often wonder if I did right. You see, I ought to have made it so that he could be happy . . . even though he was getting blinder every day. But he couldn't face it, Kate. His eyes had meant so much to him, even more than they do to most other people. He had always loved looking at things and he saw them so much more clearly than most people. You know what I mean because you are the same. He just could not face the future, Kate.'

'No. There was nothing you could have done more than you did. I understand how he felt. His work had been his life. I shall never forget his misery when he first told me. Then after a while I thought that even though he couldn't do the close work he'd been doing all his life, he would be able to paint . . . at least for a while.'

'But he was losing his sight completely, Kate. In a few months he would have been totally blind. Oh, I do hope I did the right thing by him. I think of it often. I torment myself. Was there something else I could have done . . . or left undone?'

'You mustn't distress yourself, Clare. You did everything for him. You made him happier than he could possibly have been without you.'

'I like to think so. I wake up in the night and tell myself that.'

'Dear Clare, you mustn't brood on it. Remember the happy times you shared with him. It must have come over him suddenly . . . like a dark cloud. Oh, I can imagine it. He couldn't sleep towards the end, could he? That meant he was worried. Then I imagine in a fit of depression he just took the overdose . . .'

'That was how it happened.'

'You have to forget, Clare.'

She brightened. 'I try to. I want to. Now I must tell you what has happened. He left everything to me, Kate, except the miniatures. Even the house he left to me. He said: "Kate's all right. She'll be able to look after herself. She won't want to come back to England." But the miniatures are yours, Kate. I have had them put into the bank for safety. I thought they should be valued too. They are worth a small fortune . . . even more than your father believed them to be worth. He talked a great deal to me. He said: "If ever she should happen to fall on lean times, she'll have the miniatures. She could sell them singly, if necessary, and live for two or three years on the price she would get for one of them." He was a very practical man in some ways, when he was planning for those he loved, for instance. You don't mind his leaving the house to me, I hope?'

'My dear Clare, I'm glad he did.'

'There wasn't a lot else. He had saved a little, and you will know that he kept the family going on what his work brought in. He left that little bit to me with the house. It is enough for me to live on, simply, of course.'

'Then you are quite comfortable?'

She nodded. 'I can manage. But what I want to say is that Collison House is your home, Kate. I don't look on it as my house. It was in your family for years. It's yours, Kate, as well as mine, and if at any time you wanted to come there . . . Well, in short, it'll always be your home as well as mine.'

So we talked, and in time Kendal came running in. He was very interested to see that we had a caller. I explained who Clare was, for he had been too young to remember when she came to Paris.

I was proud because I could see that she thought him a very fine boy.

Jeanne returned. She remembered Clare and I explained that she had come to stay with us for a while. Jeanne was pleased to see her and Clare was very happy to get such a warm welcome from everyone.

Jeanne cooked a meal for us and we all sat round the table

talking – Kendal being allowed to stay up as it was a special occasion.

There was an extra bedroom in the Loge, so accommodating Clare was an easy matter. Jeanne made up the bed and when I took Clare to her room I kissed her tenderly and told her how pleased I was that she had come.

I said goodnight and left her, but I lay awake a long time that night. Clare's coming had made me think of my father and as I mourned him afresh I kept thinking of what state of mind he must have been in when he had decided to take his life.

Then a thought struck me suddenly.

Clare's coming had brought my solution. I could leave France with her. I could go back to Collison House and make my life there. And if I could not attract rich sitters, I had a small fortune waiting for me in the miniatures. I knew the value of them now. Some of the sixteenth-century ones must, individually, be worth a great deal of money.'

Suppose I sold one . . . or even two . . . to give me enough money to set up a studio in London. I did not want to sell any of them, of course, but if it were necessary I must do so.

It was a way out.

Until now I had believed the situation was insoluble. It was no longer so. I no longer had the excuse to stay here for the sake of Kendal because we had nowhere else to go.

We had. Clare's coming had opened up a way out.

Clare's arrival caused quite a flurry of excitement at the castle.

When I went over the following morning to work on the manuscripts, a message from the Princesse awaited me. Would I go to her room? She wished to speak to me.

She was lying in bed – she never rose very early – and was propped up with pillows. A cup of chocolate was by her bed.

'I hear you have a visitor from England,' she said.

'Yes, my stepmother.'

'I did not know you had a stepmother. You didn't tell me when you came to paint me.'

I was surprised that she should remember so much about me. 'I did not have one at the time,' I explained. 'She married my father afterwards.'

'She is . . . not an old woman?'

'No, quite young. A few years older than I . . .'

'She sought you here?'

'Yes, I wrote to her from here soon after I came. I knew she would be anxious about what was happening to me in Paris. My letter took a long time to reach her but she finally received it and instead of writing she decided to come and see me.'

'She sounds . . . adventurous.'

'Well, I'd hardly say that. But she would go to a great deal of trouble for people she cared about.'

'So she cares much for you?'

'I think so.'

'There is a tradition that stepmothers never like children of the first marriage.'

I laughed. 'Clare is not in the least like the traditional stepmother. She is more like a sister. She has been a friend of mine from the moment I met her, which was before I came to France.'

'You must allow me to meet her.'

'I will bring her to see you, if I may.'

'This afternoon. I am eager to meet your stepmother.'

'What time would you like me to come?'

'Four o'clock. After I have had my rest.'

'I am sure she will be delighted to meet you.'

'Is she going to stay long?'

'I don't know. She arrived only yesterday. We had so much to talk about. We hardly stopped all last evening.'

'What of your father? Did he not come with her?'

'My father is dead.'

'Dead? Oh yes, I remember I did hear something of it. He was going blind. Such cruel things happen to people . . .' She looked melancholy for a moment; then she brightened. 'Yes, bring her to me this afternoon. I want very much to meet her.'

The meeting between the Princesse and Clare was an immediate success. Clare's luminous brown eyes were full of compassion and in a very short time the Princesse was telling her of her invalidism, which was a subject very dear to her heart.

She explained to Clare that this was not one of her good days. I had heard this many times before and although I had expressed sorrow at her indisposition, I had never been able to imply very great sympathy, for I had always felt that she made a fetish of her illnesses and if only she would not concentrate so wholeheartedly on them, she would be much better.

Clare, however, had always had immediate sympathy for lame ducks. She was truly compassionate towards them, and they, sensing her sympathy to be genuine, were drawn towards her.

Thus it was with Clare and the Princesse, and after a very short time Clare was receiving detailed accounts of the Princesse's afflictions.

Clare admitted that she too had the occasional headache or had done until she had found a miraculous cure. It was a herb concoction which she made herself. She never travelled without it. Perhaps she could persuade the Princesse to try a dose. The Princesse declared that she would be delighted.

'I could hand it in at the castle tomorrow,' said Clare.

'Oh, but you must bring it to me yourself,' was the Princesse's reply.

Clare said it would give her the greatest pleasure.

'I hope that you will plan to stay here a little while,' said the Princesse, 'and do not intend to rush away quickly.'

'How kind and hospitable everyone is!' cried Clare. 'I had to come to see how Kate was. I could not bear the suspense any longer. It is so kind of you to let her stay here . . . and now to be so welcoming to me.'

'My husband, the Baron, arranged for the occupation of the Loge.' There was a sharp note in her voice which I believed Clare had noticed.

'Yes. Kate told me how it was . . . how they came from Paris.'

'They were in a sad state when they arrived here.'

'But completely recovered now,' said Clare, smiling at me.

'They have such good health,' the Princesse sighed. I thought: She is working round to her favourite topic again. 'It would have killed me,' she added.

'Good health is one of the best gifts fate can bestow,' said Clare.

It was small wonder that we all liked Clare. She had the gift of being whatever her companions wished her to be at the time. With my father she had talked art and learned a little about it; with me she discussed my predicament and the best way out of it; and with the Princesse it would have appeared that illness and its remedies were of greater interest to her than anything else.

'You have been a great success with the lady,' I said as we came out of the castle and made our way to the Loge.

'Poor Princesse,' she said. 'She's a very unhappy woman. That is why she concerns herself so wholeheartedly with her ailments.'

'One would have thought you had given a life time's study to them this afternoon.'

'Well, she wanted to talk about them. I understand that. She wanted to pour out her troubles. Of course, that's not the real trouble, is it? There's something deeper than that. I don't think she is very happy . . . with her Baron.'

'You are a student of human nature, Clare.'

'Perhaps. You see, I like people. I care about them. I like to know why they act as they do. If I can, I like to do something for them.'

'Well, you did something for her this afternoon. I have rarely seen her so animated. She really took to you.'

'I shall visit her if she wants me to, and if she will talk to me and there is anything I can do to help her . . . I'll be glad.'

Yes, I thought, Clare loves people. She makes their troubles her own. That must be why we all like her so much.

I was glad she had come and her coming had brought me the solution which I had been looking for. It was true that at times I wanted to reject it. Clare's coming had made me realize how very much I wanted to stay here and the reason for that was that I was exhilarated, stimulated and roused – often to anger – but always excitingly by the Baron. Her coming and the possibility of returning to England with her, of saying goodbye to him forever, had made me face the truth. I should find life desolate without him.

A few days later Rollo came into the room where I was working on the manuscript.

He shut the door and stood leaning against it, smiling at me. I could not stop my heart beating a little faster as it was apt to do when he appeared suddenly.

'I have come to see how the manuscripts are progressing,' he said.

'Quite well in the circumstances. I am leaving this one. I shall never get that shade of red which was used at the time. I do need it.'

He came and leaned over me, kissing the back of my neck. I turned sharply and, standing, faced him. He took me by the shoulders and held me against him.

'Oh, Kate,' he said, 'this is the most absurd situation.

You're here. I'm here . . . and we have to keep up this ridiculous pretence.'

'Pretence of what?'

'That we don't want to be with each other . . . that we don't realize we were meant for each other and no one else is of the slightest interest to us.'

'What a lot of nonsense. I find other people of interest to me.'

'I mean in this particular way.'

'Well, I am coming to a decision. I have been making plans. Ever since Clare came I have been thinking of going away.'

'No!'

'Yes, I shall go soon.'

'I shall not allow it.'

'How will you try to stop it? Put me in a turret and keep me there as your prisoner?'

'Don't tempt me,' he said.

'You did that once, but you could not do it again.'

'I shall not let you go,' he said firmly. 'You can be sure of that.'

'Let us be sensible. Your life is here. Mine is not.'

'You have been happy . . . comfortable since we came from Paris.'

'You and the Princesse have been kind and most hospitable.'

'You belong here, Kate. You belong to me.'

'I have no intention of belonging to anyone but myself.'

'I believe that you have given yourself to me. That's what I meant.'

'Given myself! It was you who took me . . . against my will.'

'Will you always hold that lapse against me? It is different now.'

'You humiliated me doubly. First by forcing me to submit

to your lust and secondly because it was not desire for me that prompted you, but revenge.'

'Ah, I understand so much. It was the second part that angers you. It wouldn't be like that next time. It would be you . . . and you only that I was thinking of.'

'Oh, please stop this talk. You make me realize that I should go without delay, as I have been planning.'

'What is that?'

'Go back to England.'

'How would you live? Where would you live?'

'There is an answer to that now. I should go back with Clare to the house where I was born. It is hers now but she has said that it shall be my home for as long as I want it.'

'And what clients would you have there?'

'I could restore manuscripts like this. I could paint miniatures. I am my father's daughter and many people would want me for that reason.'

'Is Clare rich enough to support you and the boy?'

'No.'

'Then would you not be taking a risk?'

'No. My father had a collection of miniatures. They represent a small fortune and they are mine. They are worth enough to keep me going for years . . . if I sold them.'

'And you would sell the family heirlooms?'

'Yes, if I needed the money to live. I could sell them one by one until I could earn enough money. If I became rich, who knows? in time I might buy them back again.'

He was really shaken. He had always stressed the fact that I must stay here because I had to keep myself and Kendal. Now he saw that there was a way out and he did not like it at all.

'You have told me something about the village. What will they say if you, an unmarried woman, turn up there with a child?'

'Clare has told them that I married and kept my name

Collison for professional reasons. Clare thinks of everything.'

'I am beginning to wish she had never come here. Kate, you wouldn't go. You wouldn't leave me. You couldn't. I'd come to England after you. I assure you, I am not going to rest until you and I are lovers again.'

'Again!' I cried. 'We never were.'

'Why don't we go away from here? Why don't we have our own house?'

'Like you and Nicole?'

'No, different from that. Nicole and I did not set up house together.'

'You just blatantly announced that she was your *maîtresse en titre*, is that so?'

He did not answer. Then he said: 'I love you, Kate. If I were free . . .'

'You are not free,' I said quickly. 'You went into this marriage willingly after you had forced yourself on me and given me the child. Don't think I regret having him. He makes everything I went through worthwhile. But *you* didn't care. Now you are married to the Princesse and I want a good life for Kendal. I don't think he would have that as son of the Baron's mistress . . . the illegitimate son of the Baron. Your place is here with the Princesse. She is your wife. Don't forget you are married. As for myself, I shall go back to England.'

'If I could offer you marriage,' he said quietly, 'what then? To be together . . . to claim the boy as my own . . . Oh, Kate, I never wanted anything in my life as much as that.'

'I think you have learned something,' I told him. 'You were always under the impression that you only had to take what you wanted. You forgot there were other people in the world . . . You forgot that they too might have feelings . . . desires . . . Their lives meant nothing to you. They were just there to be used as best suited you. Now you know that other people want to live their lives the way they choose . . . not the way you choose for them. I want a settled life for my son. He is *my* son. you resigned all claim to him when you married the Princesse and didn't mind what happened to him.'

'That's not true. I cared very much what happened to him . . . and to you.'

'You sent your mistress to look after us.'

'Wasn't that caring?'

'You didn't come yourself. You delegated another. It was only when you saw the boy and took a fancy to him that you came back into our lives. Do you think I don't understand you? You are selfish and arrogant. You suffer acutely from a disease called megalomania. Now you will have to realize that there are other people in the world whose lives mean as much so them as yours does to you.'

'You are trembling,' he said. 'I believe you love me very much.'

'You are ridiculous.'

He took me into his arms then and kissed – and went on kissing me. He was right, of course. Whatever this was I felt for him, I did not want to resist. I wanted it to be as it had been all those years ago in the turret bedroom.

Oh, what a betrayal it is when the feelings of one who prides herself on her good sense demand that she act in opposition to everything that she knows is right.

For a few moments I let him hold me I let his fingers caress my neck.

I thought: It is natural, I suppose, for a woman to be aroused by a man like this, one who emanates power, domination . . . which is I believe in many cases the ultimate in physical attraction.

His lips were on my right ear. 'You're not going to leave me, Kate. I won't allow it.'

I drew myself away from him. I knew that I was flushed and that my eyes were shining. He was aware of it, too, and what it meant. I felt angry with him because he was able to understand the truth.

Smiling at me sardonically, he said: 'There is the boy, for one thing.'

'What of the boy?'

'Do you think he would go away . . . willingly?'

'He would have to if I went.'

'You would break his heart.'

'Hearts don't break. It's a physical impossibility.'

'Metaphorically speaking.'

'Children get over these things very quickly.'

'I don't think he would. He knows that I am his father.'

'How could he know such a thing?'

'He asked me.'

'What? Why should he do that?'

'He had overheard the servants talking.'

'I can't believe it.'

'That servants talk? They do, you know. All the time. Do you think for one moment that they don't know how things are between us? Do you think they can't see the affinity between Kendal and myself?'

'What did you say to him?'

'I couldn't lie, could I? To my own son.'

'Oh! How could you!'

'Believe me, he is delighted. He climbed up on me. I was sitting at the time and do you know, he put his arms round my neck and hugged me. He kept shouting: "I knew it was true. I knew it." I asked him if he was pleased with his father, and he said he wouldn't ever want another father. I was the one. He had chosen me from the moment he saw me. There! What do you think of that?'

'Oh, you shouldn't have told him.'

'Should I have lied? Why should he not know the truth? He's happy. He said: "Then if you are my father, this castle is really my home." Oh, he's one of us. No doubt of that.'

'One of the glorious Norman conquerors, you mean?'

'Exactly. And now you see, Kate, why it is impossible for you to take him away.'

'I don't see that at all. I think that if the servants are talking there is all the more reason why I should go away. I want Kendal to go to school in England.'

'He can do that from here when the time comes. We'll take him over to his school. We'll go and get him when school holidays come round. There is nothing in our way.'

'As I see it, there is everything. You have made up my mind for me. I shall tell Clare that we must get ready to go at once. We can't stay here any longer.'

'What of your work here?'

'You know you have only given it to me so that I shall have something to do. If I don't finish the manuscripts, someone else will. Yes, I see it clearly now. We must go. Now that you have told Kendal you are his father, I see it is impossible for us to remain.'

I wanted to get away, to think. He had shocked me deeply. I knew that Kendal would now be asking all sorts of questions. I must have the right answers ready.

He had done it purposely. He had deliberately told the boy.

I tried to brush past him, but he caught me by the shoulders. 'Kate,' he said, 'what are you going to do?'

'Get away . . . to think . . . to make plans.'

'Wait a while. Give me time.'

'Time . . . time for what?'

'I will think of something. Something is going to happen . . . I promise you. Don't do anything rash. Give me a little more time.'

Then he had me in his arms again. He held me to him. I wanted to stay there . . . just like that. The thought of going away was unbearable.

And as we stood there, I heard a movement. The door was opening.

We broke away guiltily as Clare came into the room.

'Oh!' She gave a little exclamation. I noticed the uneasy look in her large brown eyes. 'I thought you were alone here, Kate . . .'

The Baron bowed.

She acknowledged his greeting and went on: 'I only wanted to say, would you mind if we ate a little earlier today as the boys want to get out into the woods. It's some new game, I think. One goes off ahead of the other and leaves a trail . . .'

We were not concentrating on what she was saying. Nor was she. She must have seen our embrace and it had upset her. She hated conflict of any sort and I knew she would be deeply disturbed at the thought of my conducting a love-affair with the Baron while his wife was on her invalid's couch in another part of the castle.

She did not mention what she had seen and I said nothing to her immediately about my decision to go back with her. She was visiting the castle every day and her friendship with the Princesse was growing fast. If she did not go to the castle a message would come to the Loge asking if she was well and if so would she come at once.

I knew what it was – that special brand of sympathy. As I have said, the Princesse, who revelled in self-pity, would find the ideal listener in Clare. It had always been like that. I remembered poor little Faith Camborne who had been so devoted to Clare. I was not surprised that the Princesse found in her the ideal companion. I suppose there are few people in the world who want to listen to other people's troubles all the time. But Clare was one who could do this admirably. She scarcely ever mentioned herself and had always had the gift of making other people's troubles hers.

I remembered how my father had written of her, telling me how much she had done for him. Clare was indeed a rare person.

It was afternoon – three or four days after she had surprised Rollo and me together. I had said nothing to her yet, but I was making plans in my own mind. I must admit I kept postponing them, making excuses to myself why I could not put them into action immediately. I wanted to work everything out very thoroughly, I told myself. I wanted to imagine going back to Collison House . . . living there . . . finding a niche in that country life where one's neighbours knew most of one's business. It seemed that they did here too; but that somehow was different. The Baron was here to protect me. I suppressed that thought as soon as it came. Could I do it? I had money which I had earned in Paris. I had enough to get me to England and to last me for about a year while I put out feelers. And at the back of my mind was the thought of the security that collection of miniatures had brought me.

I need not worry financially and that had been the main cause of my anxiety.

Jeanne had gone into the nearby village to shop and taken the dog-cart with her. It belonged to the castle, of course, but we had been given permission to use it.

The fact that both she and the boys were out gave me an opportunity to talk to Clare.

I knew that she wanted to say something to me and did not quite know how to begin.

I said: 'Are you seeing the Princesse this afternoon?'

'Yes. She expects me.'

'You and she have become great friends in a very short time.'

'I am sorry for her. She is really a very unhappy woman.'

'Oh, Clare, it is your mission in life to look after people, I know. But I do think if she tried to rouse herself . . .'

'Yes, but her inability to do so is part of her illness. She can't rouse herself. If she could . . .'

'She could if she tried. She does ride now and then. I have ridden with her.'

'Yes,' said Clare. 'She has taken me to that favourite spot of hers. There again, her fancy for that is morbid. She told me that once she contemplated throwing herself over the Peak.'

'I know. She told me, too. How much has she told you, Clare?'

'She talks all the time . . . of the past mostly. Of the wonderful time she had in Paris. I know that she had a lover and that poor little William is not the Baron's child.'

'She has told you her whole life story, it seems.'

'I'm sorry for her. I do what I can to help. But there is so little one can do, but sit and listen and show sympathy.'

'Can't you make her interested in something?'

'She is interested only in herself. Oh, Kate, I am worried. I'm worried mainly about you and your involvement in all this.'

I was silent and she went on: 'We have to talk. It's no use pretending things are not what they are. Kendal is the Baron's son, isn't he?'

I nodded.

'He must have been born about the same time as William was.'

'There is little difference in their ages.'

'Even when the Baron was about to be married, you . . . and he . . .'

I just could not bear the reproach in her eyes.

'Of course,' she went on, 'I suppose he would be considered a very attractive man . . . to some people. All that power . . . all that masculinity . . .'

I interrupted her. 'Clare, it was not as you think. I was going to marry a distant cousin of his and the Baron had a mistress. He was fond of her and wanted her settled. He wanted my fiancé to marry her. My fiancé said he would not marry the Baron's mistress. So the Baron . . . oh, I know this sounds crazy to you, coming from home where everything is so different. But these things do happen, and they happened here. He abducted me, kept me a prisoner, and forced me to submit to him.'

Clare gave a cry of horror. 'Oh no!' she said.

'Oh yes. The result was Kendal.'

'Oh, Kate. And you could love a man like that!'

'Love him?' I said. 'We are not talking of love.'

'But you do love him . . . now . . . don't you?'

I was silent.

'Oh dear,' she went on. 'I am so sorry. I just did not understand.'

I told her how he had sent Nicole to look after me, how he had saved Kendal's life and brought us out of Paris.

She said: 'He is a strong man.' She lifted her shoulders. 'I begin to understand . . . a little. But he is married to the Princesse. She hates him, Kate. He wants to marry you, doesn't he?'

I remained silent.

Then she went on: 'But he can't because of the Princesse. Kate, you must not become his mistress. That would be wrong . . . very wrong.'

'I am thinking of going home,' I said. 'I have been wanting to talk to you about that for some time.'

'The Princesse told me that he had demanded that she divorce him.'

'When?'

'A few days ago. She won't, Kate. She is adamant about that. I haven't seen her so alive . . . ever before. At last she has a chance to take her revenge . . . and she is going to take it. She knows that you and he have been lovers. She knows that Kendal is his son. He makes that clear enough. He dotes on the boy. And then, the way he ignores poor William. It's all very obvious . . . and very sad. He is a cruel man in some ways.'

'You see, I must go back to England with you. I wanted to talk to you about that.'

'We will go whenever you say.'

'It will be so strange to be back at Collison House.'

'It was your home for a long time.'

'Kendal will hate it. He loves the castle. He loves the Baron.'

'Children get over these things quickly.'

'I wonder if Kendall will.'

'It's the best way, Kate. In fact it is the only way.'

'You are so understanding, Clare.'

'Well, my life has been very quiet really. I looked after my mother until she died and then I came to you . . . Nothing much had happened to me until I married your father. Who would ever have thought I should marry! I was very happy. It was terrible what happened.'

'You did everything for him. You made him so happy.'

'Yes. It seems to me that I have always lived other people's lives. I looked after him. His life was mine. And now there is you, Kate. You are his daughter and it is what he would want me to do. I want to take you out of this situation which is becoming more and more intolerable. I feel it is going to blow up into a big storm and I'm afraid for you.'

'Oh Clare, I'm so glad you came. You have offered me the way out.'

'But you don't want to take it, Kate.'

'I have to take it. I see with you that it is the only way.'

We sat for some time without speaking. Then she went off to pay the promised visit to the Princesse.

To Die for Love

My thoughts were in a turmoil. I knew that I had to get away. Having talked to Clare, I realized it with greater understanding.

I listened to Kendal, talking of his new stalking game which he and William played in the woods. It was the favourite of the moment and the woods and surrounding country were an ideal setting for it.

'There's a man, you see,' Kendal explained, 'and he was a prisoner in the dungeons. He starts out from the dungeons. The Baron said we could. We draw lots for prisoner and hunter. Then if I'm the prisoner, I go to the dungeons. I break out and have to hide myself. Then if I'm the hunter, William goes to the dungeons. We have to leave clues and then the hunt starts.

'It sounds very exciting,' I said. 'Kendal . . . you know we can't stay here always.'

His thoughts were far away in the woods working out the clues which he would leave for William to follow. He did not at first seem to grasp what I had said and then suddenly it struck him.

'Why not?' he said sharply. 'It's our home.'

'No, it's not.'

'But it is now . . .'

'Wouldn't you like to go to the house where I was born?'

'Where is it?'

'In England. It's called Collison House after our family.'

'I might . . . one day.'

'I mean soon.'

'I like it here. There's so much to explore . . . and the castle is so big and there's so much to do.'

I said: 'We might have to go home.'

'Oh no, we wouldn't have to. This is our home. The Baron wouldn't want us to go, and it's his castle.'

How difficult it was. In a cowardly manner I shelved the subject. I should have to return to it later. I did not want to spoil the afternoon's game in the woods.

He ran off to the dungeons, planning his clues. I wanted to get right away in order to think. I went to the stables.

My mare wasn't there. One of the grooms came over to me. 'The mare you like to ride has been taken to the blacksmith's,' he told me. 'But if you are wanting a horse, there is old Fidèle.'

'Isn't that the horse the Princesse rides?'

'Yes, Madame, but she has not ridden him for several days. He needs a bit of exercise and you'll find him a steady old thing. He's very reliable. A bit lazy though. You understand?'

'All right,' I said. 'Let me take Fidèle.'

'I'll get him ready. Why, just take a look at him. He's getting excited. He knows he is going for a ride. He's pleased about that, aren't you, old fellow?'

So I rode out on Fidèle and I was amazed how he took charge of our direction. I realized he was taking me to the spot where he must have taken the Princesse many times.

Yes. I was right. There we were. The weather was mild and it was beautiful up here. Summer would soon be with us. It did not surprise me that Marie-Claude came up here very often. There was a peace about the place. One felt remote from everything.

I decided to find the spot where we had once sat together.

I tethered the horse where we had left ours when I came up here with her, and then I found the sheltered spot by the bushes where we had sat.

I leaned against them and let my thoughts wander back to my talk with Kendal, and I asked myself why I had not been firmer with him.

He was going to hate leaving so much. He was no longer a small boy who could be picked up and taken anywhere without protest. He loved the castle . . . passionately. He loved the Baron too. I was well aware of that. He was going through that phase of babyhood into boyhood and he saw himself as a man. Since I had been there I had detected in him certain similarities to his father, and I was beginning to think that Rollo must have been very like Kendal when he was his age.

But I had to tell him we must leave. Whatever his reluctance, we had to get away.

I heard the sound of a horse's hoofs in the distance. I supposed in a spot like this one could hear from a long way off. No. They were coming nearer. Now they had stopped suddenly.

My thoughts went back to how I was going to comfort Kendal. In comforting him perhaps I could comfort myself. It was foolish not to admit that to leave the castle would be as great an unhappiness for me as for my son – and perhaps it would take longer for me to recover.

I was aware that someone was close to me. Footsteps came slowly up the incline from behind the bushes which not only sheltered but hid me. It must have been the rider whom I had heard.

I sat still . . . waiting and then a sudden fear took possession of me. I realized how lonely it was up here and I remembered that occasion when I had been here with Marie-Claude and we had stood on the brink of the ravine looking down, and I had had a strange uncanny feeling that I was in danger.

Whoever it was was very close now. I heard the snap of bracken . . . and then footsteps . . . slow and deliberate.

I stood up suddenly. I was trembling.

Rollo was coming towards me.

'Kate!' he cried in astonishment.

I stammered: 'Oh . . . it is you, then.'

'I didn't expect to find *you* here. Why are you riding that horse?'

'Oh . . . of course . . . I've got Fidèle.'

'I passed him . . . and I thought . . .'

'You thought the Princesse was here.'

'It's the horse she usually rides.'

'My bay mare is at the blacksmith's. They suggested I take Fidèle.'

He was laughing now, recovered from his surprise. 'What good luck to find you here!'

'I was very startled when I heard your stealthy approach.'

'What did you think I was? A robber?'

'I didn't know what to think.' I looked round me. 'It's very lonely up here.'

'I like it,' he said, looking at me intently. 'Were you sitting there?'

'Yes, sitting there . . . thinking.'

'Sadly?'

I paused. 'Of leaving,' I said. 'I have to go. I've made up my mind.'

'Please, not yet, Kate. You promised . . . not yet.'

'Soon. It must be soon.'

'Why? You're happy here. There's work for you. I could find more manuscripts.'

'I think we should leave in about a week's time. I've talked to Clare.'

'I wish that woman had never come here.'

'Don't say that. She is a wonderful woman. The Princesse is devoted to her already.' I went on slowly: 'You have spoken to her . . . The Princesse . . . haven't you?'

'I've tried to cajole; I've demanded; I've threatened. She is having her revenge on me at last, but I shall find a way. Never fear. I am going to marry you, Kate. I'm going to legitimize the boy, and we are going to live here happily for the rest of our days. Tell me what you would say if I could do that?'

I did not answer and he gathered me into his arms and held me fast.

I thought: Soon this will be over and I shall never see him again. I felt that was unbearable.

'You love me, Kate. Say it.'

'I don't know.'

'You can't endure the thought of going away . . . right out of my life. Answer truthfully.'

'No,' I said, 'I can't.'

'That's the answer to the first question. We are two strong people, Kate. We are not going to let anything stand in our way, are we?'

'Some things must.'

'But you love me and I love you. It is no ordinary love, is it? It's strong. We know so much about each other. We've lived each other's lives. Those weeks in Paris . . . they bound us together. I wanted you from the moment I saw you. I liked everything about you, Kate . . . the way you looked, the way you worked . . . the way you tried to deceive me about your father's blindness. I wanted you then. I was determined to have you. That business of Mortemer was an excuse.'

'You could have suggested marriage then when you were free to do so.'

'Would you have had me?'

'Not then.'

'But now you would. Oh yes, you would now. Don't you see, we had to be ready. We had to know. We had to go through all we went through to learn that this thing we have for each other is not passing . . . not ephemeral . . . as so many loves are. This is different. This is for a lifetime . . . and it is worth everything we have.'

'You're so vehement.'

'I have said that about you. It is what we like about each other. I know what I want and I know how to get it.'

'Not always.'

'Yes,' he said firmly. 'Always. Kate, you must not go yet. If you do, I shall come after you.'

I said nothing. We sat there side by side and I lay against him while he held me tightly.

I felt comforted by his presence. For the first time I was facing the truth. Of course I loved him. When I had hated him, my feeling for him had overwhelmed everything else. From hatred I had slipped into love and as my hatred had been strong and fierce, so was my love.

But I was going to England. I knew I had to go. Clare had made me see that.

I roused myself. 'I must get back. Clare will be coming from the castle. They will be expecting me and wondering where I am.'

'Promise me one thing.'

'What is that?'

'That you will not attempt to leave without first telling me.'

'I promise that,' I said.

'Then we stood for a while and he kissed me in a different way from that in which he had previously, gently, tenderly.

I was so filled with emotion that I could not speak.

Then he helped me to mount Fidèle and we rode back to the castle.

'Kendal,' I said, 'we are going to England.'

He stared at me and I saw his mouth harden. He looked remarkably like his father in that moment.

I went on: 'I know you hate leaving the castle, but we have to go. You see, this is not our home.'

'It *is* our home,' he said angrily.

'No . . . no . . . We are here because there was nowhere else for us to go after we left Paris. But you can't stay in other people's houses for ever.'

'It's my father's house. He wants us here.'

'Kendal,' I said, 'you are not grown up yet. You must listen to what I say and know that it is for the best . . . for you and for all of us.'

'It's not the best. It's not.'

He was looking at me as he never had before in the whole of his life. There had always been a strong bond of affection between us and I could not bear to see that look in his eyes. It was almost as though he hated me.

Could Rollo mean so much to him? He really did love the castle, I knew. True, it was a storehouse of wonderment to an imaginative child; but it was more than that. He had made up his mind that he belonged here and Rollo had done his best to make him feel that.

He robbed me of my virtue, I thought. He turned my life upside down; and now he would rob me of my child.

I felt angry suddenly. I said: 'I see it is no use talking to you.'

'No, it isn't,' said Kendal. 'I don't want to go to England. I want to stay at home.' Then I saw that stubborn look in his face again, which reminded me so much of his father. I thought: He is going to be just like him when he grows up, and my fear for him was mingled with my pride.

I said: 'We will talk of it later.'

I did not feel I could bear to say any more.

It was late that afternoon. Jeanne was cooking – which she liked to do – and Clare had just come in. She had been to the castle.

'Madame la Baronne is in a defiant mood today,' she said. 'I don't like the way things are going up there.' She looked at me anxiously.

'This time next week we shall be setting out for home,' I reminded her.

'It's best,' she said compassionately. I thought it was wonderful, the way she understood. 'Where is Kendal?' she went on.

'He went off with William playing that hunting game they are so fond of, I believe. I saw them go off. He was carrying something. It looked like a bag of some sort.'

'Laying his clues, I suppose. I am so pleased that he and William have become friends. It is such a good thing for that poor little boy. I'm afraid he didn't have much of a life before.'

'No. I wonder what he will do when we have gone.'

Clare knitted her brows. 'Poor little thing! He will revert to what he was before.'

'He has changed a good deal since we came.'

'I can't bear to think of him. Has Kendal told him we are going?'

'No. Kendal won't accept that we are. He became so angry . . . so unlike himself . . . when I talked of it.'

'He'll be all right. Children adjust very quickly.'

'He seems to have become obsessed by the place . . . and the Baron.'

'A pity. It'll all come right in the end.'

'You believe in happy endings, Clare.'

'I believe that we can do a great deal towards bringing them about,' she said quietly. 'I've always thought that.'

'You're a great comfort.'

'Sometimes I think I ought not to have come here.'

'Why ever should you think that?'

'When I came, I offered you a way out. Sometimes I think that is the last thing you wanted.'

I was silent, thinking: I believe she notices everything.

'I *needed* a way out, Clare,' I said. 'You showed me a way. So please don't say it would have been better if you hadn't come.'

We were both silent for some time. I was thinking about Clare and what her life must have been like when she was looking after her mother until she died . . . and then coming to look after my father. Now it seemed she was looking after me. It was true that she was the sort of person who spent her life looking after other people and had no real life of her own.

It must have been about half an hour later when she reminded me that Kendal had not come home.

'He is late,' I agreed.

Jeanne came in then and asked where Kendal was.

We all agreed that he was late, but we were not really concerned until about an hour later when he was still not home.

'Wherever can he have got to?' asked Jeanne. 'He should have been back long ago.'

'He must have got caught up in the game.'

'I wonder if he is at the castle,' suggested Jeanne.

Clare said she would go and look, and put on her cloak and went out.

I was beginning to feel uneasy.

Clare came back soon looking very disturbed. Kendal was not at the castle. William was not there either.

'They must still be playing,' said Jeanne.

But two hours later when they had still not returned I was seriously alarmed. I went up to the castle. I was met by one of the maids who looked at me with that speculation to which I was becoming accustomed.

I cried out: 'Has William come home yet?'

'I don't know, Madame. I will go and enquire.'

It soon transpired that William was not at home. Now I knew something was wrong.

Rollo came into the hall.

'Kate!' he cried, the delight obvious in his voice at the sight of me.

I cried out: 'It's Kendal. He's out somewhere. We expected him back hours ago. William is with him. They went out this afternoon to play in the woods as they often do.'

'Not back yet! Why, it will be dark soon.'

'We must find him,' I said.

'I'll make up several search parties. You and I will go together, Kate. Let's go to the stables. I'll bring a lantern and alert the others. There's no moon tonight.'

In a short time he had formed search parties and sent them off in different directions. He and I rode off together.

'To the woods,' he said. 'I'm always afraid of the Peak. If they got too near the edge . . . there might be an accident.'

We rode in silence. I was getting really frightened now. It was dark in the woods and all sorts of fearful pictures kept flashing into my mind. What could have happened to them? Some accident? Robbers? What would they have that was worth stealing? Gypsies! I had heard of them carrying off children.

I felt sick with anxiety and at the same time relieved because Rollo was with me.

We went to that spot which Marie-Claude had first shown me and where I had met Rollo later. I peered into the eerie darkness. We rode right to the drop. Rollo dismounted and gave me his horse to hold while he went to the edge of the ravine and looked over.

'Nothing down there. The ground hasn't been disturbed. I don't think they came to this spot.'

'I have a feeling they are in the woods,' I said. 'They came to the woods to play their game. They couldn't have played it in the open country.'

Rollo shouted: 'Kendal, where are you?'

His own voice echoed back.

Then he did a shrill whistle. It was ear-splitting.

'I taught him how to do that,' he said. 'We practised it together.'

'Kendal, Kendal!' he called. 'Where are you?' And then he whistled again.

There was no response.

We rode on and came to a disused quarry.

'We'll ride down here,' said Rollo, 'and I'll shout again. It's amazing how one's voice echoes from here. I used to call to my playmates when I was a boy. You get the echo back. I showed this to Kendal too.'

I wondered briefly how often they had been together. When Kendal went off into the woods, was the Baron there too? Did he join in the game of hunter and hunted?

We rode up to the top of the quarry and shouted again.

There was silence for a few seconds and then . . . unmistakably . . . the sound of a whistle.

'Listen,' said Rollo.

He whistled again and the whistle was returned.

'Thank God,' he said. 'We've found them.'

'Where?'

'We'll find out.' He whistled again and again it came back.

'This way,' he said.

I followed him and we made our way through the trees.

The whistle was close now.

'Kendal,' called Rollo.

'Baron!' came the answer; and I don't think I ever felt so happy in my life as I did at that moment.

We found them in a hollow – William white and scared, Kendal defiant. They had contrived to build a tent of some sort with a sheet spread out over the bracken.

'What's this!' cried Rollo. 'You've led us a pretty dance.'

'We're camping,' said Kendal.

'You might have mentioned the fact. Your mother has

been frantically wondering where you were. She thought you were lost.'

'I don't get lost,' said Kendal, not looking at me.

Rollo had dismounted and pulled back the sheet.

'What's this? A feast or something?'

'We took it from the kitchens in the castle. There was a lot of food there.'

'I see,' said Rollo. 'Well, now you'd better come back quickly because there are a lot of people searching the countryside for you.'

'Are you angry?' asked Kendal.

'Very,' said the Baron. He seized Kendal and put him on his horse.

'Am I going to ride back with you?' asked Kendal.

'You don't deserve to. I ought to make you walk.'

'I'm not going to leave the castle,' announced Kendal.

'What?' cried Rollo.

'I'm going to stay with you. This is my home and you are my father. You said you were.'

Rollo had turned to me and I was aware of his triumph. The boy was his. I knew that he was very happy in that moment.

William was standing up looking expectantly about him. Rollo lifted him up and set him on my horse in front of me.

'Now we'll get these scamps home,' said Rollo.

As we approached the castle several of the servants saw us approaching and a shout of joy went up because the boys were safe.

I dismounted and helped William down.

'It wasn't William's fault,' said Kendal sullenly, as he was put on the ground. '*I* made him come.'

'We know that,' said Rollo, sternly proud.

Jeanne and Clare came running up.

'Oh . . . you've found them!' panted Jeanne.

'Thank God!' cried Clare. 'Are they all right?'

'There's nothing wrong with them,' I told her.

'Have you some hot food for them?' asked Rollo. 'Though they don't deserve it.'

'I'm hungry,' said Kendal.

'So am I,' added William.

'Come along into the Loge,' said Jeanne. 'You shall have something in next to no time. Whatever did you do this for?'

Kendal looked steadily at Rollo. 'We were going to camp in the woods until my mother had gone,' he said. '*You* won't let them send me away, will you?'

There was a short silence and then Kendal ran to Rollo and seized him round the legs.

'This is where I live!' he cried.

Rollo picked him up. 'Don't fret,' he said. 'I'm not going to leave you.'

'Then that's all right,' replied Kendal.

He wriggled to be let down and Rollo put him on the ground. Rollo was looking at me and I was aware of the triumphant gleam in his eyes.

Both the children had a bowl of soup and when they had eaten William went back to the castle with Rollo.

He did not reprove William at all. His reproaches had been levelled at Kendal, but they were not really reproaches. Kendal had made everything very clear. He had run away and prevailed on William to go with him to show us that he was not going to leave the castle willingly.

Just for a moment I wondered whether Rollo had suggested the whole thing. Kendal had answered so promptly to the whistle. They might have planned it between them.

Oh no, surely not. Kendal was too young to take part in such schemes. But with Rollo one could never be sure how far he would go.

Kendal was tired out and after he was in bed I sat talking with Clare.

'What a determined child he is!' she said. 'To run away

just like that to show you that he resents being taken away from here. What use did he think that would be?'

'His intention was to camp in the woods until we had gone, and then to emerge and go back to the castle.'

'Good heavens! What a scheme!'

'He is very young.'

'That man has woven a spell about him,' said Clare quietly.

'It is because he has admitted to him that he is his father. Kendal has always wanted a father.'

'Children do,' said Clare, and lapsed into silence.

That day will stand out forever in my memory.

It began ordinarily enough. I went to the castle to work on the manuscripts; Kendal had already gone with Jeanne for his lessons. In the afternoon I busied myself with getting a few things together with my imminent departure in mind.

I was thinking of Kendal. He had said nothing more about our leaving, but I knew by the set of his mouth and his attitude towards me that there would be more trouble to come.

Perhaps, I thought, we should stay. Perhaps I could make some excuse to Clare. I could tell her that I wanted to finish the manuscripts and we would follow her later. I knew that If I did that I should capitulate, for I could not hold out much longer against Rollo.

I remembered the way he had looked when he had said: 'Kendal, don't fret. I am not going to leave you.'

He had meant that. He must have plans. In my heart I wanted those plans to succeed. I wanted him to carry me off somewhere . . . as he had on that other occasion and to say: 'You are staying with me forever.'

And yet I went on, as though in a dream, making preparations to leave.

The afternoon wore on. Jeanne was in the kitchen preparing to cook. Kendal had come in and was in the kitchen with Jeanne. Clare was in her room, probably resting, for she had been out all the afternoon.

We sat down at table at the usual time and while we were eating we had a caller. It was the housekeeper from the castle.

There was mingling anxiety and excitement in her face.

'Oh, Madame,' she cried. 'I wondered if Madame Collison had seen Madame la Baronne.' She was looking at Clare as she spoke.

'Seen her?' I said, puzzled.

'She is not at the castle. It is unusual for her to stay out without saying. I wondered if she were here . . . or if you had any idea where she had gone and when she would return.'

'No,' said Clare. 'I saw her yesterday. She did not tell me she was going anywhere special today.'

'She may be back now. I am sorry to have troubled you. It is just that it is so rare . . . and I thought either you, Madame, or Madame Collison might have had some idea.'

'I expect she has taken a ride,' I said.

'Yes, Madame, but it is rather long since she went.'

'She will probably have returned by the time you get back.'

'Yes, Madame, and I am sorry to have troubled you. But . . .'

'It was good of you to be so concerned,' said Clare softly.

She left us. Clare looked a little worried, but neither of us said anything because Kendal was present. When the meal was over I went up to Clare's room.

'Are you worried about the Princesse?' I asked.

She was thoughtful for a moment. 'I'm not sure . . . She has been a little strange lately. It was since the Baron asked her for a divorce.'

'How was she different?'

'I don't know. Defiant, perhaps. I fancied she was hiding

something. She has never been very good at keeping things to herself. Perhaps it was upsetting for her to be asked for a divorce. That would be all against her principles. He must have known that she would never give him a divorce. There would have to be a dispensation, in view of everything . . .'

'I do hope she is all right,' I said uneasily.

'So do I. I think it is a very good thing that we are leaving. It will take you right away from all this. You'll settle in England, Kate. We shall be together. I'll do everything I can to help.'

'What of Kendal?'

'He'll be all right. He's lived through some very strange times. It's bound to have had an effect on him. He'll settle though. A year from now we'll all be happy together. This will be like a forgotten dream . . . I promised your father that I would look after you.'

'Dear Clare, I'm so thankful for you.' I went to the window. 'I wish we could hear that Marie-Claude was safely back. She might have had an accident. I don't think she is a very good horsewoman.'

'Oh, she'll be all right on old Fidèle. He'd never bestir himself to anything violent.'

As I stood there looking out, I heard noises. Voices . . . shouting . . . and the sounds of activity.

'Something's happening at the castle,' I said. 'I'm going to find out what.'

'I'll come with you,' said Clare.

There was consternation in the castle. The Baron was shouting orders. I gathered that the Princesse was missing and that Fidèle had returned to the stables alone. He had been found patiently waiting there for how long no one knew.

One of the grooms said that he had saddled the horse for the Princesse in the mid-afternoon and she had gone off on him.

That must have been several hours before.

The Baron said there must have been an accident, and, as he had done when Kendal was lost so recently, he was arranging for search parties to go off in various directions.

He was in perfect command of the situation as he had been a few nights earlier.

I raised my horror-stricken eyes to his and said: 'Can I be of any help?'

He returned my gaze steadily, and I could not guess what was in his eyes. Then he said: 'You go back to the Loge. When there is news I shall see that you get it without delay.'

He glanced at Clare. 'Take her back,' he said; and added: 'And stay with her.'

Clare nodded and slipped her arm through mine. We went back to the Loge.

Time seemed as though it would never pass. A terrible fear had come to me. Rollo's face kept flashing in and out of my mind. I remembered words he had said: Something would be done. He was not going to lose us . . . myself or Kendal.

And Marie-Claude stood in his way.

I am imagining impossibilities, I told myself. But he always says that nothing is impossible. He is ruthless . . . determined to get his own way. I kept seeing him as he had been in the turret room. Implacable. Bent on domination. What happened to those who impeded him? He swept them aside.

Oh Marie-Claude, I thought. Where are you? You must be alive and well, you *must*. And I must leave this place. I must forget my dreams. I have to get away and make a different life for myself. I have to forget the past . . . forget the excitement, the sort of love I had glimpsed lately. I must settle down to a humdrum life . . . but one of peace. Peace? But would there ever be peace again?

Kendal went to bed. I was glad he had not noticed that

anything was wrong. He was so obsessed by his own problem that he was not aware of anything else.

Jeanne came and sat with us. We talked in whispers and waited . . . and waited.

It was nearly midnight when there was a knock on the door. It was the housekeeper from the castle.

'They've found her,' she said. She looked at us with wide eyes, the expression of which was half horror, half excitement.

'Where?' whispered Clare.

The housekeeper bit her lips. I noticed that she avoided looking at me. 'They searched the woods. They thought the horse had thrown her. They couldn't see down the ravine. It was too dark. They had to go down . . . And that's where they found her. She had been dead some hours.'

I felt dizzy. Clare came to me and put her arm round me.

'Poor soul,' she murmured. 'Poor, poor lady.'

'I was sent to tell you,' said the housekeeper.

'Thank you,' answered Clare.

When she went out, Jeanne looked from me to Clare. 'It's terrible,' she began.

Clare nodded. 'It's a great shock. She must have done it . . . deliberately. She had talked of doing it . . . and now she has.'

I noticed that Jeanne did not now look at either of us. I could guess what thoughts were in her mind.

Clare said briskly: 'There is nothing we can do. We should really try and get some rest. This is a terrible shock. I'll make a little drink for us. We need it. Go to your rooms. I'll bring it up to you.'

We were all glad to be alone, I think. I wanted to try to work out how it could have happened. I could not shut out of my mind the thought of her standing on that spot with the steep drop before her. And in my thoughts there was someone else standing close to her.

And then I remembered that occasion when I had gone there with Fidèle and he had come up and been surprised to find me there. He had been expecting to come upon *her*.

'No, no,' I whispered. 'Not that. I couldn't bear that. Not murder.'

I know he was capable of drastic action. I knew that he took bold steps. But not murder. That would stand between us far more strongly than ever Marie-Claude could have done.

The father of my son . . . a murderer!

I could not accept that. I would not listen to the voices in my mind . . . the voices of reason and logical deduction. If I believed them, it was over . . . over forever, and that was something I could not bear.

This night had brought no new solution for me. Unless it had shown me the only possible path I could take.

Clare came in stirring something.

'It will make you sleep,' she said.

She sat down on the bed and looked at me.

'This changes everything,' she said.

'I don't know. It's too soon yet. I can't think clearly.'

'You're shocked.'

'Clare, do you think that he . . .'

'No,' she said emphatically. 'How could you suggest such a thing? It's obvious that she killed herself . . . unless it was an accident. She was a hypochondriac. She had often talked of killing herself. The more you think of it, the more simple the answer seems.'

'I wish I could be sure.'

'Do you really think that *he* murdered his wife?'

I was silent.

'My dear, dear Kate, he wouldn't do it. I know he wouldn't. To murder for gain . . . that's the coward's way. It means you can't fight for what you want by any other means . . . and that another person is too strong for you. No, that's not the Baron's way. I've been thinking that we ought to go away . . . for a while. Then all this will blow over. We could live quietly at Collison House and in a few months . . . or after a suitable time has elapsed . . . he can come over for you and you can be married.'

'Oh Clare, you work everything out so very precisely.'

'It's because I am of a practical nature. The poor Princesse has gone. Poor woman. I was so sorry for her. She hadn't much to live for, had she? I think it was the best way. It may be that she saw this, and realized it would make it easier for everyone. You see it was just her unhappiness against you, him, Kendal . . . and her own child too. How do you think young William would have felt if you and Kendal had gone away? You've done wonders for him between you – you, Jeanne and Kendal. He would be a wretchedly lonely little boy again. Perhaps she knew this. Perhaps she weighed it up and saw the best solution . . . the noble way out.'

'I don't think the Princesse would have thought like that.'

'My dear Kate, how can you ever know what is going on in other people's minds? Now try and sleep. When you are rested you will be able to take a clearer view of all this. Then we'll talk again.'

'If I could believe . . .'

'You can believe. I tell you, you can. I know. I can see it so clear. I really knew her better than anyone else here. She was open with me. She confided in me. I knew something of what was in her mind. She has taken her life because she thought it was the best thing for herself . . . and for others. I see it clearly.'

'I wish I could.'

'You will . . . and when this has all blown over . . . you are going to be happy. I promise you.'

'You are wonderful, Clare, You comfort me . . . as you comforted my father.'

I took her draught. It did enable me to get a few hours'

sleep, but I was awake early and I trembled to contemplate what the day would bring forth.

There was much coming and going at the castle all during the morning. I did not go out. I could not bear to. Jeanne took Kendal out walking in the woods.

Rollo come that morning. He looked very serious but I could not guess what he was thinking.

Clare, who had been in her room, came down dressed for going out.

She left us together.

I said: 'Rollo, this is terrible. How could it have happened?'

'She killed herself. She took the leap. You know how unstable she was. Why are you looking at me like that?'

He came towards me, but I shrank back.

'You are thinking . . .' he began.

I did not speak.

He went on slowly: 'I know. It is what some people will think. It's not true, Kate. I did not see her at all during yesterday. She went out alone. I was here all day.'

'You . . . you wanted her out of the way,' I heard myself say.

'Of course I wanted her out of the way. She was stopping us . . . I knew you would never really want to come while she lived. And now . . . she is gone.' He paused for a few moments, then he went on: 'She killed herself. It was suicide.'

'But why? How?'

'Why? She was always sorry for herself, saying she had nothing to live for. She has talked of doing it many times . . . and now she has.'

'I wish . . .'

'What do you wish? Are you telling me that you don't believe me? Say it, Kate. Say you think I did it. You think she went to that spot . . . as she generally did. You think I followed her there.'

'Did you . . . once before . . . and find me?' I asked.

'Yes,' he admitted. 'I wanted to get away from the castle and talk to her quietly. I always knew we were overheard. I wanted to meet her there . . . alone . . . to talk to her . . . to reason with her . . .'

'And yesterday?'

'I have told you I did not see her yesterday. Why are you looking at me like that?'

He had taken me by the shoulders. 'Tell me what's in your mind,' he said.

'I . . . I think it would be best . . . for all of us . . . if I went away.'

'Go away . . . now that we are free!' There was a look in his face which frightened me. I thought then: He killed her. He has to have his own way.

'It will be difficult,' I heard myself stammering. 'There will be questions . . . enquiries . . . So much is known about us. Whispers . . . scandals . . . I should never have stayed here with Kendal. What will it be like for him here? Whatever happens there will be talk. There will be this shadow hanging over him. I must get away. That seems very clear to me now.'

'No, you shall not go. Now now.'

'You have always taken everything you wanted,' I told him. 'But there comes a point when you cannot go on. People cannot be brushed aside just because they have become an impediment.'

'You're condemning me as a murderer, Kate.'

I turned away. I could not bear to look at him. He was angry now. He had my shoulders again and he shook them.

'Is that what you think of me?'

'I know you are ruthless.'

'I love you and the boy, and I want you with me for the rest of my life.'

'And she was in the way.'

'She was . . .'

'She will always be there. Don't you see that? I shall never be able to forget her lying in that ravine . . . sent to her death.'

'Sent! It was her own wish.'

I shook my head sadly. 'There will be accusations.'

'People are always ready to accuse. Even you, Kate.'

'Please swear to me that you did not kill her.'

'I swear it.'

For a moment I allowed myself to slip into his embrace and to feel his kisses on my lips.

But I did not believe him. Everything he had done had shown me that he would always attempt to get his own way. Now he wanted me and Kendal and she had stood in the way. So she was now dead.

Whatever I said, whatever I did, she would always be there.

I said: 'There could be a trial.'

'A trial of whom? Of me? My dearest Kate, this is a case of suicide. Nobody would dare officially to accuse me of murder. What, here . . . in my own domain . . . and the country in turmoil, still struggling to set itself to rights! There is no fear of that.'

'What do you fear, then?'

'Only that you will leave me. I have nothing else to fear. She no longer wanted to live so she took her own life . . . and in doing so she has left me free. I had to see you, but I think it would be better if you didn't come to the castle just yet. One of the maids can bring William here for his lessons. This unpleasant business will soon blow over. I shall come here to see you, Kate. Tell me that you love me.'

'Yes,' I said, 'I'm afraid I do.'

'Afraid? What are you afraid of?'

'Of so much.'

'In time, we'll build something, you and I. I'll have what I have always wanted . . . one whom I could truly and wholeheartedly love . . . and the children we shall have together.'

'I wish it could be so.'

'It shall be. It can be now. I promise you.'

I wanted to believe him. I tried to force myself to believe him. I said to myself: We will live through the difficult days and ahead of us there will be the happiness which we both want.

But the terrible misgivings stayed with me and I knew that forever she would be there between us, the shadowy third whose death had been the key to our own desires.

Clare came to sit by my bed that night. She said: 'I heard you tossing and turning and I made another little draught for you. You mustn't get into the habit of wanting them, though.'

'Thank you, Clare.'

'What did he say today?'

'That he didn't do it.'

'Of course he didn't. She did it herself.'

'That was what he said. But even if it were true, he drove her to it . . . he and I together.'

'No. She drove herself. I've told you so many times how well I knew her, how she confided in me. She saw that it was the best way. She would never have been happy. She had decided against making a try to be so a long time ago. Invalidism appealed to her. She had a child but she neglected him. Some women could have found happiness in him. I think she saw all that at the end. She thought hers was rather a worthless life and that others could gain so much from her departure from it.'

'I knew her too, Clare, and I don't think she would have reasoned that way. If she would have done, why should she deny Rollo the divorce he wanted? No, I think she was looking for revenge on him. Why should she have taken her life to make it easier for him? A divorce would have been enough to give him his freedom.'

'Well, divorce is not considered a true break-up of marriage in some quarters. The Baron wanted there to be no suggestion that his sons were not recognized as legitimate . . . everywhere.'

'But his son *is* illegitimate.'

'When you are married he'll get him made legitimate. That can be done.'

'William is recognized as his son.'

'And isn't.'

'Oh, it's all so involved . . . so tragically involved. I don't think I could ever be truly happy. I should always see her lying there. I should never be able to forget her, and in my heart I would always suspect that my happiness had come through . . . murder.'

'I believe you have convinced yourself that he killed her.'

'Not convinced . . . but – and I would tell no one else but you – I should always wonder. Others would too. It would be a shadow to haunt our lives. We should never be free from her. It would affect our love for each other. We should be haunted . . . haunted, Clare, forever. I think I ought to get right away. I want to take Kendal with me.'

'He will never be happy away from here.'

'He will learn in time. I shall have to deceive him just at first. I think I shall tell him that we are going back for a holiday . . . let him think that we are coming back here.'

'And you will come back?'

'No, I shall try to start afresh. I shall find somewhere in London. Rollo must never know where. I can't go back to

Collison House with you. I shall have to have somewhere where Rollo cannot find me.'

'If he did, he would persuade you that what you are doing is wrong.'

'Do you think it is wrong, Clare?'

'Yes, I do. You have a right to happiness. You can be happy. You love him. I know what he did to you. I know the sort of man he is . . . but he is the man you love. Kendal adores him and he is his father. He'll never be happy away from him. He is too old to get over it now. He will always remember and yearn for him.'

'He must forget . . . in time.'

'I tell you he will never forget his own father.'

'He didn't know he had one for a long time.'

'You are contemplating doing the wrong thing. You should take what happiness is offered you. There will be a difficult time to follow, perhaps, but that will be forgotten and then you will come into your own. I long to see you as Madame la Baronne . . . and Kendal happy . . . and little William . . . he'll be overjoyed. You should be happy, Kate. We're put into this world to be happy. I promised your father that if ever it was in my power to make you happy. I would do everything possible.'

'You have, Clare.'

'Yes, I have. And now you are talking of throwing away this chance. I want to see you happy before I go.'

'Dear Clare, you are so good. You care so much for others . . . and make their problems yours. But I know myself, and I think I know best about this. I am never going to be happy with this shadow between us.'

'Because in your heart you believed that he killed her?'

'I can't stop myself. The doubt will always be there. I can't live with it. I have made up my mind. I am going to start afresh.'

'He will never permit it.'

'He won't know how to stop it. I want you to help me. I am going to slip away . . . quietly. And then I shall lose myself in England. Somewhere where he will never be able to find me.'

'You will let me know where you are?'

'When I have found a place I will write to you at Collison House, but you will have to promise to keep my secret. Will you?'

'I will do anything for you, you know.'

'Then you will help me now?'

'With all my heart,' she said solemnly.

When I awoke in the morning I was certain I had come to the right decision, though I had never felt so unhappy in the whole of my life. I realized only now how deep my feelings for this man had gone. There would never be another in my life. I would dedicate everything to my child, but I knew that he would never forget and perhaps continue to blame me for taking him from the father he had grown to love and admire more than anyone in the world. And when he no longer saw the Baron, I knew that the picture he retained of him would grow more and more splendid.

I saw the weary years stretching ahead, bereft of joy. I must start a new life. The plan was beginning to evolve. I must make my way to London, find lodgings there until I could find a studio in which to work. All I had to recommend me was my father's name. That counted for something. But would the success I had had in Paris have been heard of?

That was what I had to discover. So I must slip away from here secretly. I wondered how I was going to get Kendal to come with me. He was no longer a small child – in fact he was old for his years, and already I could see Rollo in him. But I had to find some way of getting him to leave quietly. Clare would help me.

One thing was certain. Rollo must not know, for if he did

he would do everything he could to prevent me. But I must go. Of that I was certain.

I walked round the moat and looked at the castle. I would remember it always in the years to come. There would be a perpetual ache in my heart and a longing for something that never could be.

Marie-Claude dead had driven as big a rift between us as she ever had alive.

My thoughts were in turmoil when I returned to the Loge. It seemed quiet and empty. Kendal and Jeanne were not there. Nor, it seemed, was Clare.

I went up to my room to take off my cloak and there lying on my bed was an envelope addressed to me. It was in Clare's handwriting.

Puzzled, I took it up and slit the envelope. There were several sheets of paper inside.

I read the opening words. They danced before my eyes. I could hardly believe I was not dreaming. I seemed to be plunging deeper and deeper into nightmare.

> My dearest Kate [she had written], I have been up all night trying to work out how to do what I must do. I realized when we talked last night what I had to do. It seemed that there was only one way.
>
> Marie-Claude did not commit suicide. She was murdered and I know who killed her.'
>
> Let me explain to you. I have always been the sort of person who had little life of her own. I always seemed to be on the edge of things looking in. I loved hearing of people's lives . . . I loved sharing them. I was grateful to be taken in and allowed to. I grew so fond of them. I have been deeply fond of many people . . . none like you and your father though, because you brought me right into your family . . . you made me one of you . . . and gave me more of a life of my own than I had ever had.

I do want you to understand me. I know you think you do, but you don't really know the essential part of me and you have to if you are going to understand how everything happened. We all have hidden places. Perhaps I haven't any more than anyone else.

When I was young I had no life of my own . . . There was only my mother's. I was with her all the time . . . reading to her . . . talking to her . . . towards the end doing everything for her. She was very ill and suffered a lot of pain. I loved her dearly. It was hard watching her. She wanted to die but she couldn't. She just had to go on lying there suffering, waiting for the end. It is unbearable watching someone you love suffer, Kate. I thought constantly of how I could alleviate her pain. One night, I gave her an extra dose of the pain-killing medicine the doctor had given her. She died peacefully then. I didn't regret it. I knew I had done the right thing. I was happy because I had done that and saved her from the terrible nights of pain.

Then I came to you and you were all so warm-hearted and you accepted me in Evie's place and you seemed to be so fond of me. I loved the life. It was so different from what it had been. I was fond of everyone in the village. Such nice good kind people . . . particularly the twins. I was drawn to them . . . mainly because of Faith. Poor Faith, she wasn't happy, was she? She was always afraid. I suppose we all have a certain amount of fear in us, but Faith had a double share because she had her sister's as well. I knew she was very unhappy and tried to hide it because she didn't want to spoil everything for her sister. Did you know at one time Hope almost decided not to marry because she knew it would break that close tie between herself and her twin? She was desperately worried about how Faith would get on without her. They were like one person. Well,

Faith wasn't happy. Hope wasn't happy . . . but when Faith wasn't there, Hope could be. They used to confide in me, both of them . . . so I saw the picture from both sides.

There was that spot, you remember. Rather like the one here. That dangerous drop. What was it called? Brackens Leap? Well, I talked with Faith. We walked together and we talked and we talked . . . and there we were looking down. I didn't plan it. It just came to me that it was the right thing to do. And it was. Hope is very happy now. Those lovely children she's got, they are charming. It's such a happy family. And they visit the grandparents, and all the tragedy is forgotten now . . . because joy came out of it. Faith is forgotten now . . . as you would have forgotten the Baronne.

Then there was your father. He pretended to come to terms with his blindness, but he never did really. I knew him so well and I knew how sad he was. Once he broke down and told me what the loss of his sight meant to him. 'I am an artist,' he said, 'and I am going into a dark, dark world. I shan't see anything . . . the sky . . . the trees . . . the flowers and you and Kate and the boy . . .' I knew his heart was broken. I knew that to take his eyes away from an artist was about the most cruel thing life could do. One day he said to me, 'Clare, I'd be better off dead.' Then I knew what I had to do. I remembered how easy it had been with my mother.

And that brings me to the Baronne. She wasn't happy. She never would have been. She looked inward all the time . . . to herself. She didn't see anyone but herself very much. That poor little William . . . he was so neglected and unhappy . . . until you came with Jeanne and Kendal. What would he have grown up like? But he will have a chance now with you there. And there is Kendal. He would never have been happy away from his father. He's a strong, wayward boy. He needed a father. And there's the Baron – he needs you, Kate. He needs you to show him how to live. He didn't know how to . . . until he met you. If you left him he would go back to what he was . . . blustering through life . . . wasting it, really. No, he needs you more than anyone. And then, my dear, dear Kate, there is you. I look upon you as my daughter. I know I am not much older than you but I married your father. I married into a family . . . and I look upon it as mine. I am deeply fond of you, Kate. I think more than anything now I want you to be happy with your family . . . with your work . . . Oh, life can be so good for you.

You belong together . . . you and the Baron. You must be together now, otherwise it will all have been in vain. That is what I want. It is the very reason why I did what I did.

I walked out there to meet her. We talked. We looked at the view. It was easy. I just had to touch her and she was gone.

That brings me to my last murder and when you read this it will be done.

Perhaps I should not have interfered. We are not supposed to take life, are we? But whatever I did, I did it for love. I did it to make a better life for people. That must be rather an unusual motive: Love so deep and sincere that it leads to murder.

Be happy with your Baron. Teach him how to live. Kendal, I know, will grow up into a fine strong boy now. And you will do everything you can to make a happy life for little William.

Remember, Kate, all I did was done for love.

I dropped the letter and sat staring into space.

Clare had done this! I could not believe it . . . and yet

looking back everything slipped into place.

My poor Clare, who had always seemed so quietly sane, was sick. Her mind was unbalanced. It must be if she believed that she had the right to take life. And she *had* believed that. 'It was for their good and the good of others,' she would say. And I could see how she convinced herself of this. It was true that she had cared deeply for others, and she had killed those whom she had loved. How tragic it was! She, Clare, had assumed the Divine power to act – and even if she believed it was a benevolent power, she was still a murderess. I wished that she had talked to me. I wished that I could have helped her, made her understand that there are no circumstances when murder must be committed. But it was too late now.

I made my way to the castle.

He was there and I threw myself into his arms.

I said: 'I know now. I have it here. I know what happened . . . exactly. I want you to read this now . . . to tell me that I am not dreaming.'

He took the letter and I watched the amazement spread across his face as he read.

Then he looked at me, long and steadily, and I wondered how I could ever have thought of leaving him.

We rode out to the ravine together. Clare was lying there with a sweet seraphic smile on her face.